stolen from her mother

BOOKS BY RACHEL WESSON

RACHEL WESSON

stolen from her mother

bookouture

Published by Bookouture in 2022

An imprint of Storyfire Ltd.
Carmelite House
50 Victoria Embankment
London EC4Y 0DZ

www.bookouture.com

ISBN: 978-1-80314-091-9
eBook ISBN: 978-1-80314-090-2

For Mam—You showed me by example how to love, listen, and care. You proved what resilience and courage meant. You led by example, everyone was treated the same regardless of race, color, creed, or background. I'm so proud to be your daughter. I miss you every day.

ONE

ASHEVILLE, NORTH CAROLINA

September, 1941

Carol Andersen opened her eyes, wincing at the bright light. She glanced up at the petite nurse, barely five foot tall, in an unblemished white uniform dress, matched by a hat starched to perfection sitting atop a mass of auburn curls, smiling back at her.

"Hello there, I'm Diana, your nurse. I'm just going to check your bandages." Despite her youthful looks, the nurse acted confidently and with purpose.

Carol wrinkled her nose at the antiseptic smell before flinching as Diana's cold hands inspected her wound. She attempted to distract herself by looking around the room, at the gray-green colored walls, a small closet for her clothes, a half-open door opening into a private bathroom, the beautiful arrangement of pink and yellow roses on the windowsill, and the jug of water on the little table next to her bed.

"About time you woke up, we were worried. Haven't you beautiful blonde hair, look like a film star, you do, with those piercing blue eyes." The nurse pushed the hair back from Carol's brow before placing a cool flannel in its place. "Don't move just yet. The doctor wants to examine your head wound." Carol ignored the nurse, her hands moving automatically to her stomach. She couldn't feel her baby move. Nothing. Panicking, she looked at the nurse, but she wouldn't meet her eyes.

"Nurse, my baby. Where's my baby?" She pushed back the covers, trying to get out of bed, but her legs refused to move. Her swirling stomach made her feel nauseous.

"Please, Mrs. Andersen, lie down. Matron and the doctor will be here in a moment. They won't like to see you agitated."

Agitated. That wasn't the word she'd use to describe her deepening fear. There was no baby. She knew it. An empty feeling overwhelmed her as she sank back further into the bed. The door opened as the medical team arrived.

"Mrs. Andersen, you are back with us. You gave us all quite a fright. How do you feel?" The doctor barely glanced at her, his white coat billowing outward, showing the crisp white shirt and charcoal suit he wore underneath. Was he on his way to a charity dinner or some other worthy occasion?

"Doctor..."

"Shush now, don't speak. You need to conserve your strength. Your head wound will heal in a few weeks, and you won't be left with a scar. Nothing to mar your pretty face."

She didn't care about her looks. "My baby. I remember the sedan, the lights coming toward me, I couldn't move, I tried..." She brushed away the tears before whispering, "And then everything went black."

He took her hand, his cold one patting hers as if she were a child who'd lost her candy. "Now, don't excite yourself. I'll give you something to help you sleep."

She tried to shake her head, but he ignored her, taking a syringe from the nurse and inserting the contents into the vein in her arm. A tiny scrape, a quick pinch and then she felt herself losing consciousness. He still hadn't answered.

· · ·

When she woke up next, glorious sunshine flooded her room. Vase after vase of beautiful flowers covered every available space. The scent of lilies dominated the others, reminding Carol of her mother-in-law, Priscilla Andersen, related to the Cecils of the Biltmore Estate. Or so she told everyone. Her father-in-law, his face a grave mask, sat beside her bed, watching her.

"Carol, how are you feeling? Silly question. We've been worried sick since the accident. You are lucky to be alive. Josh will be pleased."

"Josh?"

"He sends you his love. He couldn't get away from Washington but he will be down as soon as he can get leave. That vase of flowers is from him."

She closed her eyes. What else did she expect? With Josh the military came first, second, and last. She'd known that from the day she married him. There was little point in complaining now.

"Dean?" she replied.

"Yes?"

"The baby? They won't tell me."

Josh's father stood up, walking around the bed before returning to his seat. "Priscilla will be here shortly. She'll talk to you. Just try to rest."

"My baby." A single tear escaped quickly, followed by another one. Her father-in-law's face paled. He hurried to the door, calling for the nurse. "She's getting herself in a state. Crying and everything. Can you..."

The nurse arrived, frowning at Dean before turning a gentle smile toward Carol. "Now, dear, tears are normal given the circumstances. Cry as much as you want to."

"Doctor Meynard said he'd left instructions to keep her sedated," said Dean.

"The doctor's needed for an emergency. Mrs. Andersen will be fine. Please, sir, come back in the morning. Your daughter-in-law is exhausted—she needs to rest."

Why wouldn't anyone tell her what happened?

Dean opened his mouth as if to argue, but he closed it again. Without looking at Carol, he left the room, his shoulders weighed down with disappointment.

Carol hiccupped, the tears choking her. Her father-in-law had been so excited about the baby, told Carol that she was the best thing Josh had ever done for the family, yet now he couldn't bear to look at her. The nurse fussed around her.

"Mrs. Andersen, you let the tears out. Forget about keeping up appearances. Here you are free to behave as you like." She handed Carol some more tissues, her expression matching the soft tone of her voice.

"Nurse, tell me, please," she begged. "What happened to my baby?"

Bile filled her mouth as the sound of tires skidding, metal screeching combined with her screams, flooded her memory. A terror-stricken look on the strange man's face seconds prior to the lights of his car blinding her as his vehicle slammed into hers. She swallowed hard, covering her stomach with her hands, seeing the bruised skin for the first time, the faint indentation of the steering wheel. She'd thought she'd protected her baby...

"You lost a lot of blood in the accident. The surgeons operated but they couldn't save your son."

The nurse hesitated, her eyes flitting away from Carol, her face increasing Carol's sense of panic. There was more to the story, she was sure of it. But what could be worse than losing her baby? As the nurse fixed the pillows behind her head, Carol used every ounce of strength she possessed to grab the woman's hand.

The nurse glanced behind her and then leaned in, whispering, "The doctor doesn't believe you are strong enough to know the full story. But you deserve to know. You had to have a hysterectomy. I'm so sorry."

Carol's heartbeat slowed, the pounding in her head growing louder. Her baby boy dead. And no chance of any other children.

"It took me years to get pregnant. Everyone said he was a miracle. He can't just die." Carol turned beseeching eyes on the nurse, begging her to say it was a mistake. "I failed. I should have protected him."

The nurse put her arms around Carol's shoulders, careful not to hurt her.

"Mrs. Andersen... Carol, you couldn't have done anything. The accident wasn't your fault, and you were lucky to live. Thank God for that miracle."

Carol closed her eyes, not wanting to see the pity in the nurse's expression.

She turned to face the wall. She loved Josh but she'd always wanted to be a mother. His dream was to be a father. Josh could remarry and have the family he deserved. Without her son, there wasn't any reason for her to live.

She must have fallen asleep as the next time she woke her husband's hand was on her forehead. He was usually a picture of health, a poster boy for the Air Force with his tanned good looks, short blond hair and perfect white teeth. But now his face was drawn, the loss in his eyes dissolving her to tears again. She couldn't bear her own pain, but his...

"Darling, thank God you're awake. I thought you'd never open your eyes. I'm sorry I couldn't get here earlier. How are you?" He took her hand, caressing it.

She tried to push herself up in the bed but failed. She stuttered, "Josh, the baby... I—"

He bent over and kissed the tears from her face. "Don't, sweetheart. They told me. You were very lucky. If not for Doctor Meynard's skill, I could have lost you as well." He held her hands tighter, his gaze holding hers. She saw her tears mirrored in his eyes, his jaw clenched as he struggled to control his emotions. Her husband, a trained serviceman, crying.

"Is there anything I can get for you?" he whispered.

"Hold me. Please."

He did as she asked, holding her awkwardly, as she couldn't sit forward or get out of bed. "Josh, I'm sorry. You wanted a son."

He pushed her back gently, staring into her eyes. "As long as I have you, I don't care about anything else."

"But your mother—"

He kissed her, cutting off her words.

"She can mind her own business. I love you. You're my wife. Together we will face our new future." He leaned in, his face right next to hers. "Losing you is something I couldn't live with, Carol. Now I understand what you feel every time I go away. Don't give up on me, on us. Please, darling, get better and come home. I need you."

Together they let the tears flow for their son. He was holding her hand when she fell asleep. He was still there when she woke later in the evening. But the next morning he'd gone.

TWO

Sunday, December 7, 1941

My darling Carol,

How I wish I could be with you, but duty keeps me here in Washington. I hope you are resting and following doctor's orders. I've been assured the private nurse Dr. Meynard recommended is of the highest standard.

Do what she says, my darling. I know it's only been eight weeks and I hate to put you under pressure, but I need you by my side. You make me whole.

Carol sniffed, closing her eyes and imagining her husband by her side. She missed him too. Buddy jumped up on the sofa beside her, climbing onto her lap and pushing the letter out of his way. The dog whined, licking her face. "It's okay, little fella," she reassured the puppy before picking up the letter again although she knew it word for word.

I know you don't feel like celebrating but I've declined as many invitations as I dare. There are only a couple of parties I must go

*to and I'd love you there with me... I'm sorry I didn't get home for
Thanksgiving but hope to be there by Christmas. I know the cele-
brations are a chore but as Mother says, they are useful for my
future career.*

*I hope you liked the gift. Mom said the nurse wasn't pleased as
dogs aren't suitable for patients. But I thought the little guy would
keep you company while I am stuck here in Washington.*

See you soon, my darling.

Love,

Josh

Buddy gave her one last lick before jumping down to find his
ball. He kept pawing at the couch.

"Have you lost it again? You'll get me in trouble with Nurse
Skinner. She already thinks you should live outside in a kennel."

Carol got up from the couch, getting down on her hands and
knees to retrieve the ball. She rolled it across the thick white pile
carpet, giggling as the puppy raced after it. She rested back on her
knees, slightly breathless at the exertion, her stomach aching.
Putting one hand on the edge of the strong wooden coffee table,
she pushed herself to her feet. Smoothing down the couch, she
fluffed up the cushions.

Someone shouted from outside the window. "Turn on the
radio. Pearl Harbor's been bombed."

Heart racing, fear making her mouth dry, she heard horns
honking in the street. She moved to the radio on the cabinet opposite the couch, turning the dial until the news filled her room. The
mirror on the opposite wall captured her horror as the implication
of his words sank in.

*"This is KGU in Honolulu, Hawaii. I am speaking from the roof
of the Advertizer Publishing Company Building. We have
witnessed this morning from a distance, a view of a brief full*

*battle of Pearl Harbor and the severe bombing of Pearl Harbor by
enemy planes, undoubtedly Japanese... We cannot estimate just
how much damage has been done, but it has been a very severe
attack."*

She turned the dial, eager to stop the news filtering in. Josh. If
it did mean war, he'd be the first overseas. Finding energy she
never thought she'd have again, she raced out of the living room
door, and up the stairs calling for her maid, Myrtle, on the way. In
her bedroom, she pulled open the door of the closet, taking out the
suitcase from the top shelf. She ignored the dart of pain caused by
her actions, throwing the suitcase on the bed. Opening it, she
started chucking clothes into it. She had to get to Washington to
see Josh before he shipped out.

The young maid rushed in the door, coming to a halt as she
took in the view of the case amid the garments. Her eyes as wide as
her open mouth, Myrtle seemed frozen, apart from her fingers
picking at her white apron. She looked even more like a child
wearing the ridiculous black dress and white apron that Carol's
mother-in-law insisted the servants wore.

"Myrtle, can you help me, please?"

The girl brushed her face with her arm. "Miss Carol, you hear
the news? Do you think it be true? My cousins, they over in Pearl
Harbor."

Her words brought Carol to a halt. "What did you say?"

Myrtle gulped, misunderstanding Carol's concern for censure.

"Miss Carol, you sit down and rest. I'll pack your things. Are
you going to Washington to see Mr. Josh? Will he be sent
overseas?"

Carol put her hand over her stomach. This poor girl had family
already in danger and here she was worrying about packing her
case.

"Never mind about that. What did you say about your family?"

"My cousins, they're both mess attendants on the *Arizona* in
Pearl Harbor. Do you think they are alive or dead? They'd be safe

on a big ship, wouldn't they?" Myrtle didn't manage to hide her sob, her eyes pleading with Carol to reassure her.

Carol put her hands on the younger girl's shoulders.

"Go home to your mother and stay with her until she finds out. The poor woman thinks the world of her nephews."

"I know, Miss Carol. Mammy raised those boys since they were little babies but I got to work and you can't do this yourself. You're making a big mess. Those clothes will look like you slept in them, Miss Carol. Mr. Josh expects you to look nice and Miss Priscilla, she won't like it at all. No, she won't. She will be all worked up like an old rooster kept away from his hens."

Carol ignored Myrtle's chatter. The girl didn't seem to take a breath, the words flowing out of her mouth from sunup to sundown, every day except for at church on Sunday. There she didn't talk, she sang.

"Put the case in the car, please, Myrtle. I'll drive up to see Josh."

Myrtle stopped mid-stride; her fingers flew to her open mouth as her eyes rounded. "You? But you haven't driven since..."

"It's about time I started. It's the quickest way to get to Washington."

A knock on the front door interrupted them. Ice flowed through Carol's veins. She grabbed Myrtle's hand for comfort even though her rational mind told her Josh was safe, he hadn't been anywhere near Pearl Harbor.

Together they listened as old Isiah shuffled across the wooden hallway floor to open the door. She then heard her father-in-law greeting the old manservant.

She forced herself to walk down the stairs despite the impulse to run. It wouldn't do to let her father-in-law see her lack of control.

"Dean, come in." She kissed his craggy cheek in greeting. "The news is horrendous, isn't it? You almost missed me. I'm on my way to see Josh."

His raised eyebrows gave away his shock but that was the only sign. Instead of commenting on her driving, he said, "Glad I caught you in time. He called me at the office. He's been given a forty-eight-hour leave and should be here day after tomorrow."

She slipped into the chair behind her, his words chilling her to her core.

Getting leave so fast meant he was shipping out, but to where?

Dean walked to the drinks trolley and poured a small brandy, handing her the glass before pouring a straight whiskey for himself and downing it in one. Her father-in-law wasn't a drinker. She sipped on her brandy, allowing its heat to warm her insides.

Dean poured a second drink, taking a seat before saying, "Priscilla is planning a welcome home dinner. We thought—"

No, the last thing she wanted was to share her husband with his parents—at least not on the first night he was home in two months. She took another sip for courage before putting the drink back on the side table. She held her father-in-law's gaze, giving him a warm smile.

"Thank you for the offer, Dean, but I hope you understand that I'd like to have Josh to myself for a little while. I can't remember the last time we had dinner alone." She lied; she could remember. It was before the accident, they'd been so happy about the baby... Quickly, she closed down those thoughts. "I know you and Priscilla will be dying to see him too and, of course, we'll come over to see you both. What about lunch the next day?"

Dean looked like he was about to argue, but changed his mind, closing his open mouth and nodding instead. "That's just fine. I'll handle Priscilla. Any news from your family, Myrtle?"

The girl was struck dumb for once.

"Myrtle told me her cousins were..." Carol hesitated, seeing the terror on her maid's face. She corrected her tense. "They are both serving in Pearl Harbor, on the *Arizona*. I said she should go home, but she insists on staying."

"My driver will drop you at home, Myrtle. I insist. I'm sure Carol can unpack her own case."

"I can. Thank you, Dean." She leaned in and kissed him on the cheek, relieved to see him smile in response. He was such a nice man, especially when his wife wasn't around.

Myrtle protested, but it was obvious she wanted to be with her family. Carol rang for the butler.

"Isiah, Mr. Andersen is going to drive Myrtle home."

Was she mistaken or were the old man's eyes filled with tears? He didn't have family, at least none she knew of. But, of course, he wanted to be with his own people at a time like this. Yet having served the Andersen family since before Josh had been born, he'd never ask. "Will you please go with Myrtle? Her family and your community have more need of you at the moment."

Dean gave her a nod of approval but the look of gratitude on the old servant's face meant even more.

"Yes, ma'am, thank you, Miss Carol. This is a dark day for all of us. Come, Myrtle child, let's get you home to your mammy."

Once they had left, Carol turned on the radio and listened in horror to the repeated broadcasts. She was all alone with just Buddy for company. She couldn't bring herself to leave the couch but stayed listening until well into the early hours.

———

After a sleepless night, she got up and unpacked her case. Isiah and Myrtle had yet to return. She went downstairs, let Buddy out into the garden and made a coffee. Then she turned on the radio. She picked up her drink before putting it back down as the radio announced the President's address. Sitting, hands clasped together, Carol imagined she heard grief, mixed with a little anticipation, in Roosevelt's voice. It was well known he believed they should have been helping the Allies before now.

"Yesterday, December 7th, 1941—a date which will live in infamy —the United States of America was suddenly and deliberately attacked by naval and air forces of the Empire of Japan...

"The attack yesterday on the Hawaiian Islands has caused

severe damage to American naval and military forces. I regret to tell you that very many American lives have been lost. In addition, American ships have been reported torpedoed on the high seas between San Francisco and Honolulu."

Rising, Carol switched the radio off. She didn't need to hear the President announce they were now at war. She clasped her hands together in prayer, not just for Josh and herself, but also for Myrtle's family. She prayed the girl's cousins would come out of Pearl Harbor alive.

THREE

GALWAY, IRELAND

December, 1941

Kate Ryan flicked her long red plait out of the way before she patted the cow on the rump, picked up the bucket of milk and headed back out into the darkness to return to the house. The ground crackled underfoot, making her thankful for her warm boots. Shivering in the cold, her teeth chattering, she was looking forward to the heat of the kitchen fire. She'd had to remove ice from her bedroom window this morning. She glanced at the sky, the lack of clouds allowing the stars to shine despite the early morning hour. Would they have a white Christmas after all? The children around the village would be delighted at the chance to make snowmen, but she was long past seeing snow as something fun. It made farm work more difficult, especially for Da, who had to hunt down the sheep if the snowfall was heavy. Still, the snow might take the children's minds off the war. The conflict, so far away, was on everyone's minds, due in part to the Germans torpedoing merchant ships on which their family members served.

Kate wondered how De Valera, Dev as they called their

Taoiseach, slept at night—his job as leader of the country wasn't an easy one. Despite the decision to declare Ireland as a neutral country, the Germans had bombed them at least eight times, killing countless innocents. Was this the reason that a number of the local men had deserted from the Irish army, heading to England to fight for the Allies? She hoped Dev knew what he was doing keeping Ireland neutral; her da believed he was but her mam... Her mother believed Ireland should ally itself with the Nazis.

Something made her hesitate, a noise in the distance. She was sure that she heard the sound of crying carried on the wind. It sounded like it was coming from the neighbors' farm, two fields away. She put the milk on the shelf in the larder and went back out into the yard. Before she could question the wisdom of what she was doing, she headed across the quarter acre, the frost-covered grass leaving a track of footprints, toward the Cumiskey farm. As she got nearer the cowshed, she recognized the person making the wailing noise. Shane, one of the young orphans the Cumiskeys fostered from the orphanage. She picked up her skirt, breaking into a run. Shane was a brave little fellow; he must be hurt bad to cry like that.

"It's me, Kate Ryan," she hissed. "Shush now before you have the whole village out on top of us. Come on out. 'Tis a miracle nobody has heard ya."

The five-year-old's pale face peeked out from behind the shed door, his tears glistening on his cheeks. She held her arms out, encouraging him to come close, and he glanced around before he moved toward her.

"What have you done?"

"I tried to milk the cow, but she kicked me."

Kate pulled the child closer and ran her eyes over his body, her breath catching as she spotted the unnatural angle of his arm.

"We need to get you to the doctor, Shane."

"No!" The boy pulled away, shrieking. "Mrs. Cumiskey will kill me. She'll whip me."

The terrified child paled before he fell forward in a dead faint.

Kate caught him before he hit the ground, and with barely a glance at the Cumiskey household, she picked him up and carried him back in the direction of her house. Da would help her.

Her small thatched home seemed farther away on her return journey. She moved carefully, taking care not to slip on the grass and let her precious bundle fall. Despite his emaciated frame, Shane was heavy. Her breathing grew labored as his weight increased. Leaning against the frame of the blue back door, she heaved Shane up in her arms before pushing the wooden door open. It creaked, announcing her entry, the welcome heat from the room a sharp contrast to the brisk morning air.

She faltered, seeing her mam bending over the fire baking bread on the skillet. She glanced toward the back bedroom but the door was open. Da must have been out in the shed. Kate hesitated. Should she turn and head outside to her da before her mam noticed? Too late.

"Kate Ryan, where did you get to?" said her mother, before adding more turf to the fire, sending a cloud of smoke into the small room. "I found the bucket of milk just in time before that blasted cat got into it. You haven't collected the..." Her mam turned to look at her, her mouth twisting as her narrowed eyes focused on Kate's arms. "What do you have there?"

"Shane, Mam." Kate carried the young boy to the bench by the table. She edged her body onto the seat, holding him tight in case he fell. Despite her best efforts, he whimpered but his eyes remained closed.

"He's hurt bad, Mam. He wouldn't let me get Mrs. Cumiskey, thought she would whip him. Look at the size of him and they had him out milking that cranky old cow of theirs. I thought Da might be able to help him, but I think we may need the doctor."

Kate rubbed Shane's good hand and his face, trying to wake him. He opened his eyes, glancing around. They widened when they landed on her mam before quickly flickering back to her. She smiled in encouragement before moving him off her knee so he could sit on the bench.

Her mam's tone would have given her frostbite. "We've no money for the doctor. He gets enough as it is. What did you have to bring him here for? Mrs. Cumiskey is paid to look after those illegitimate brats she fosters."

Kate took a deep breath, trying to soften her tone. She couldn't risk upsetting her mother despite wanting to remind her of their Christian duty to help those less fortunate. Wasn't that the message the priest had lectured them on just yesterday?

"Mam, please. He's only five years old. The pain must be unbearable. Look at his little face, see how pale he is. He's skin and bone too."

Mam rolled her eyes, her lips pinched together before spitting the words out. "Times are hard, Kate. For everyone. The Cumiskeys have enough of their own children to feed without having to worry about those little tykes they take off the nuns. Can't understand them taking them on. Bringing those ba— brats into a decent community."

To Kate's relief her da walked through the door, whipping the cap from his dirty-blond hair. She caught his eyes widening with pity at the sight of Shane.

"Kate, who do you have there?" he asked, softening his tone, his head tilted to the side.

"Shane, Da. The little orphan boy I told you about. He lives on the Cumiskeys' farm, with the other children they foster."

Her mother banged a pot on the table, making them all jump. "All children of sin. Take him back where you found him, Kate."

Kate heard her da's slow intake of breath, saw him shake his head before snapping at his wife.

"Whist, woman, and show some charity to the child. Kate, fetch me a bowl of hot water and some of your grandmother's herbs. Let's have a look at this fine young fella. Haven't you a grand set of hair and beautiful eyes, son. Bet you have the women staring everywhere you go."

Shane tried to laugh but his eyes kept darting to his arm. Kate watched as her father expertly examined the child, doing his best not to inflict more pain. "It's broken all right. Going to have to strap it. Kate, can you wash it while I find a suitable piece of wood to make a splint? The doctor is away up to Galway with old man Brown. He thinks he might have the cancer, God bless him." Her da crossed himself, while her mam muttered a prayer. Kate was more concerned about Shane than a crotchety old man who had been born in the reign of Queen Victoria.

She watched as her father mixed a salve his mother had made for them when they were younger, adamant the vile-smelling concoction helped with bone healing, even though the doctor said there was no evidence it did.

"Kate, hold Shane steady. Boy, this will hurt so you scream and rant as much as you want to. I'll be as gentle as I can."

The boy turned his large blue eyes on her da and nodded. Kate held him tight as her father administered the salve, using a sharp tug to snap the bone into the correct position before splinting it. Shane turned rigid with the pain but apart from the tears rolling down his cheeks, the brave little boy didn't make a sound.

Once finished, Kate's father patted him on the head. "I've seen grown men cry out for their mothers with less serious fractures. Well done, young man."

Shane swallowed, brushing his tears away with his good hand. Curiosity lit up his eyes.

He hiccupped before asking, "Where did you learn to do that?"

"My old mam, God rest her, made up the salve but the medical tricks, I learnt them in the war, son. Helped if we learned a thing or two about patching each other up. The medics being busy most of the time."

Kate watched her da's facial expression darken as it always did when thinking of those horrible years. Not that he spoke much about them.

Her da started coughing, holding up his hanky to hide the blood but not in time to stop Kate from seeing it. "Da, sit by the fire and rest. I'll get you a mug of tea."

She set Shane on a chair at the table.

"Can I give Shane some breakfast?" she asked. Her mother glared at her in response, causing Kate to add quickly, "He can have mine. I'm still full after that fine dinner you prepared last night, Mam."

Her attempts at flattery, while obvious, worked a little as her mam seemed to soften. "I guess it's been a while since the child tasted a decent breakfast."

Kate hid her triumph. Her mam was so concerned about what the neighbors might say that she'd never let it be known she turned away anyone hungry from her table. She watched as the older woman put a boiled egg, a bacon rasher, a sausage and a piece of black pudding on the plate. She added two slices of tomato before placing it in front of Shane.

The boy's eyes bulged out of his head at the plate with food heaped onto it. "This is all for me? Just me?"

Kate exchanged a look with her da before nodding. "You dig in. Have you ever tried some of my mam's freshly made bread? You don't know what you are missing."

She carved off a hunk of bread and smothered it with some of their own homemade butter, followed by blackberry jam made from the fruit she and her mam had collected the previous September.

"Go on, eat up, young fella. Need to put some fat on those bones," Da commented before coughing, the wheezing from his lungs worrying Kate.

The child clearly wanted to eat but he glanced out the window at the lightening sky, the slightly red tinge to the newly arrived clouds suggesting rain was on its way.

"I'd best get back or they'll think I've run away..." Shane's breathing accelerated. "Then they'll phone the Gardai or the priest. He'll beat me worse than old Missus Cumiskey."

Kate waited for her father to intervene.

"You leave the Cumiskeys to me, son. They shouldn't be left in charge of a pack of rats never mind young children like yourself."

Shane paled even more if that was possible. "No, sir, please. They'll send me back to the nuns and I don't want that to happen. I'll speak to Mrs. Cumiskey, make her understand it was an accident. In fact, I'd best get back before I'm missed. Thank you for your help. I'll try to repay you one day." Shane stood but staggered as the pain hit him. Kate reached for him as her mother spoke.

"He's right, you stay out of this. Father Devine himself placed the children with the Cumiskeys. He obviously thinks hard work and plain food is suitable penance for their sins."

Kate put her arm on Shane's good shoulder and pulled him close, wanting to cover his ears. Her mam couldn't blame the child for his parents, or lack of them, could she?

Her da's eyes narrowed as he turned on his wife. "What sin? The child is barely old enough to spell his own name. Not that he has much chance of attending school despite the Irish Free State's new constitution protecting the right of education back in 1922. What happened to you? You used to believe in giving children the best start in life." He turned away from his wife but not before Kate saw the sadness in his eyes. "Child, sit down and eat up,' he said, smiling at Shane. "We don't waste food in this house."

Her mam's face hardened, her features twisting. "These children belong to unmarried mothers. There's no place for those women or their spawn of the devil in this part of the world. They should be kept locked up, away from decent people."

Da's expression darkened and for a second Kate was afraid, but then the back door opened, admitting Joseph, her older brother. Relief flooded through Kate as her mam never said no to Joe. Mam believed the sun, moon and stars shone on her son. If Kate hadn't loved her brother so much, she would envy him her mother's favor.

Joe ran a hand through his too-long hair, pushing it back from his face to show his wary expression.

"What are you shouting about, Mam? I could hear you down the lane. Oh, hello, young fella." Joe smiled warmly at Shane. "To what do we owe the pleasure of your company?"

Shane sat taller, his admiration for Joe evident by his widening pupils and slightly flushed face.

Joe's smile dropped as he noticed Shane's arm. "What happened to you? If those Cumiskeys have been mistreating you, lad—"

Mam cut off his words by snapping at him. "About time you came home, Joseph Ryan. What time do you call this? Father Devine will have words for you if he gets wind of you being out all night up in Galway."

Joe's knuckles turned white. "Father Devine doesn't need to poke his nose in my business, Mam. It's my life and I'll live it my way." Joe breathed through his nose before turning on the smile once more. "Now, lad, eat up that breakfast before I eat it for you. My throat is as dry as a bale of hay. Mam, feed your favorite son, there's a good woman."

Kate turned her face so her mother wouldn't see her grin. Joe could do and say anything and get away with it. Their mam made some noise but if anyone else, including Father Devine, were to criticize her favorite son, heaven help them. Mam muttered as she returned to the stove.

"Shane was hurt trying to milk the Cumiskeys' cow," said Kate.

Joe's eyebrows raised. "They should have sent that animal to the slaughterhouse long ago. It has the temperament of the devil himself. How come a little fella like you was doing a job like that?"

Da took a fit of coughing as the silence lingered. Kate handed him a glass of water as Joe clapped him on the back, exchanging a look of concern with his sister. They all looked to the child, waiting for an answer. He seemed to diminish in front of them. He whispered, "Mrs. Cumiskey told Michael to do it, but he said I'd to do it or he'd kick my hide."

Joe's jaw clenched for a second before he reached out and ruffled Shane's hair. "You eat your breakfast, and we'll go back together to the Cumiskey farm. I'll sort out the milking. Da, will you get away back to bed? They can hear that cough of yours up in Dublin. Go on. I can handle the chores this morning."

Kate expected her father to argue but he didn't. When he stood up, he seemed more stooped than ever. "Thanks, Joe. You're a fine man."

Joe colored at the praise but he didn't meet his da's eyes. Kate knew her brother worried about their father, just as she did. Their father was deteriorating fast. The coughing fits were getting worse and he was little more than a bag of bones. But Joe was torn; he didn't want to live on the farm, saying it wasn't any life trying to drag a living out of such a small holding full of stones and bogland, rather than decent grazing ground. This was the reason all of the Ryan boys had left as soon as they were able.

Joe had tried to get their older siblings to come home but they'd said it was too expensive to travel back to Galway from London and New York. She barely remembered her older brothers who had left for America when she was still a baby. Patrick should have inherited the farm being the eldest son but he'd headed for the bright lights of New York on his sixteenth birthday. Matthew, John and David had followed him so their da had written a will giving the farm to Joe. She vaguely remembered their emigration parties or wakes as the locals called them. They couldn't come back now, not even if they wanted to, thanks to America's entry into the war two weeks ago.

She had some memories of her sisters, Gretta, Louise and Orla. They'd gone nursing in London and had come home every couple of summers at first. But then they'd got married and started their own families. Money was tight in the 1930s during the Depression. Now with the war, travel was difficult. Their husbands were away fighting and nobody expected them to make the journey from London when they had to deal with bombings and evacuations.

The boy ate quickly, one eye on the sky outside as if by looking he could stop the passing of time. Joe exchanged a look of understanding with his sister.

"Come on, Shane, let's get you home. Mam, can you fetch my old jumper? It'll be far too big for him but at least it might keep him warm. Who'd let a child out at this time of year dressed like that? Kate, will you come along with me?"

"I need your sister here," replied their mother, her eyebrows knitted.

"Mam, we'll be back shortly. Kate will benefit from the walk and the child will feel more comfortable with her."

Mam relented as she always did for Joe, but Kate knew she'd pay for her freedom later. Still, she didn't care. Whatever her mother had in store for her was nothing compared to the punishments inflicted on Shane and the other foster children living at the Cumiskeys'.

As they walked down the lane, Shane kicked at the stones for a few seconds. Despite Joe's jumper, Shane shivered in his light clothing, the bare branches of the trees and bushes overgrowing the land not providing any cover from the biting wind. They could see the smoke from the Cumiskey chimney curl up into the sky, the sweet smell of burning turf tickling their nostrils. As Shane walked slightly ahead of them, Kate turned to her brother.

"Joe, what made Mam say those horrible things about children like Shane? He can't help who his parents are?"

"People judge the girl when it takes two to get into trouble. But blaming the child is unforgivable. Didn't the Bible itself tell us to love the children? Someone should make Father Devine eat his words."

They both fell silent, remembering the priest's latest target. Young Sarah Shandon, herself barely more than a child, was called out front of the whole Mass and chastised for being pregnant. Everyone, including their mother, knew that the child had been assaulted by her uncle, but nobody said a word to him, a police sergeant up in Galway. Sarah, humiliated and shunned by her community, had been sent off to Tuam, to the Sisters of the Bon Secours Mother and Baby Home. Kate didn't think she'd ever forget the girl's face as she screamed for her mother. Mrs. Shandon had kneeled in the pew, rosary beads wrapped around her fingers while her mouth moved in constant prayer. Shuddering, Kate pushed the horrible scene from her mind, contemplating her brother instead. His mouth was twisted like he'd swallowed turned milk.

"You're not thinking of doing anything, are you, Joe? You can't get into trouble with the priest. He'll call the Gardai and make things difficult." The local police had a fearsome reputation for acting with a heavy hand towards youths of Joe's age, especially those from poorer families.

"He's a big woman hiding behind those skirts of his. He has a streak of cruelty running through him as wide as a forest. The things I've heard about him, if even half of them are true, well, it's enough to turn my hair gray. You're to keep out of his way, Kate, you hear me?"

"Yes, Joe." Kate shivered at the cold look in her brother's eyes.

The house was just ahead as Shane came to stand by Kate.

"Right, let me handle this," Joe said as they arrived. "You just watch over Shane."

Kate nodded, holding the little boy close to her side as they approached the door of the Cumiskey farm. Joe had barely touched the door when Mrs. Cumiskey threw it open, nostrils flaring as she bared her teeth, her gaze focused solely on Shane.

"What on earth do you mean by running off this morning?" said Mrs. Cumiskey to Shane. "The milk was all over the barn by the time I found the bucket. What— Kate and Joe Ryan, 'tis a bit early for visiting." The woman ran a hand through her hair, the other patting her dress. Joe was a handsome man even if he was twenty years younger.

"Kate heard Shane's cry for help when that bad-tempered old cow of yours kicked him. Da splinted his arm but says you should get the doctor to have a look as it's a bad break. Mam fed Shane some breakfast as the lad was hungry. I came to check what help you may need seeing as food is rather scarce."

Mrs. Cumiskey flushed from the neck up as Joe's insinuations hit home.

"Thank you for your concern, Joseph Ryan, but my husband is

an excellent provider. Our family want for nothing," the woman replied, struggling to remain neighborly.

Joe ignored the frosty tone. "So why is the child starving? He's little but skin and bones."

"He's a fussy eater. I can't force-feed him, can I?"

Joe stood, his arms folded across his chest, holding the woman's gaze. "I'll call over to check on him in a few days and have a look at his arm."

Kate asked, "Does he not sleep in the house? It must be sub-zero temperatures in the barn."

"We don't have room," replied the woman. "The foster kids sleep in the barn, but it's been fixed up nice for them. Nicer than they were used to. Father Devine says I deserve a medal."

"He would," muttered Joe under his breath. "Shane, lad, you know where we are. Don't be a stranger."

Shane raised his good hand in a wave, but with a terrified glance in Mrs. Cumiskey's direction fled inside the closest barn.

Later that evening, when the chores were done and Mam had gone to bed, Kate got a chance to speak to her brother. He was sitting staring into the fire, a cup of tea going cold on the table beside him. She pushed the clothes rail to one side so she could take the seat her mam had recently vacated.

"What will happen to Shane? Do you think the Cumiskeys will keep him? He should be going to school every day, not doing a man's job."

Kate knew that orphans from the homes came to school. They always arrived ten minutes later than everyone else, walking in a single file, their tattered clothes and empty eyes a sign, if anyone needed one, of the neglect they were subjected to. The farm children weren't allowed to mix with the orphans, who also left ten minutes earlier than everyone else. It was as if the powers in charge felt being an orphan was contagious.

"Children like Shane have few options. They can't join the

priesthood or become a member of the Gardai. It's wrong but that's the rules. Nobody cares what happens to them. Maybe he'll be sent back to the convent or more likely the Christian brothers. They have industrial schools for boys like Shane."

Kate clutched her brother's arm. They'd all heard stories about the cruelty and abuse taking place in industrial schools, but people were too fearful of the Church to protest. "But Shane didn't do anything wrong. He's a sweet, caring boy. You should see him around the baby animals. The lambs all love him, and the dogs go crazy for him."

"Animals always tell the good from the bad," Joe replied, lighting a cigarette, watching the smoke curl.

"Can't we do anything for Shane? You could ask Mam to take him in. He could live here instead."

Joe released a sigh. "Mam wouldn't do that, Kate. Not even for me. Having a child like Shane under the same roof as you will ruin your reputation. You know Mam has the future all mapped out for ya. She has her heart set on you becoming a Bon Secours Sister over at Tuam. Maybe when you're a nun you can help children like Shane."

Kate rubbed the back of her neck. How many times did she have to tell them she wasn't going to join a convent? She crossed her hands across her chest, before speaking through her teeth. "I'm not going to be a nun, Joe. Mam can't force me. I don't have the calling. I want to go to Dublin, or even London, and make something of my life. I love children and want to be a mother one day, but first I want to see a bit of the world. Well, a bit further than Galway City anyway."

Her brother eyed her sadly.

"Don't underestimate Mam, Kate. You know she had the same plan for Gretta, Louise and Orla. They all got away. It's only made her more determined to make sure you don't."

"You'll help me, won't you?"

The silence lingered, her heart growing cold. "Joe?"

Joe exhaled before grounding the cigarette out in the dish.

"You know I'd do anything for you, but I won't be here," he replied, making Kate's stomach sink. "I'm off to follow my own dreams soon. I told you I want to see the world. I'm heading over the sea to England and from there, the world is my oyster. There's more out there than Galway City. Who knows, maybe Mam will change her mind... Go on now, off to bed with ya. There's a pint with my name on it down in the village."

He didn't rub her hair or touch her shoulder as he always did. Instead, he wouldn't even look at her—and that made her fear grow even stronger. He was leaving, and soon.

FOUR

ASHEVILLE, NORTH CAROLINA

March, 1942

The sun shone in the window, the rays glinting on the mirror on the opposite wall, highlighting the tastefully decorated room. Carol Andersen threw the newspaper to one side, getting up from her seat on the sofa. She was sick of reading about the Japanese and their victories over the Americans in the war. Buddy sniffed at the ball she rolled over to him but even the puppy was out of sorts.

Pacing back and forth across the deep pile carpet, she wondered what Josh was doing over in London when he was off duty. He'd written about the devastation caused by the Blitz bombing, the numbers of men, women and children killed. He and his crew were flying bombing raids over Germany in retaliation.

She picked up the framed photograph of her husband from its position of pride on the piano. He looked so handsome in uniform, proudly representing the 8th Air Force. She wished the mail would hurry up; maybe she'd have another letter from him.

The doorbell intruded on her thoughts.

"I'll get it," she called out to Myrtle as she strode to the front door. The poor girl had lost both her cousins at Pearl Harbor.

"Dean? To what do I..." She trailed off as she registered the look of complete devastation on her father-in-law's face. "Not Josh, please God, not him as well." Her legs turned to jelly as she slumped forward.

Dean grabbed her arm and pulled her into the house, shutting the front door with a kick behind him. Calling for Myrtle, he half carried Carol to the lounge and helped her to the sofa.

"Is he dead?" Carol managed to get the words through her clenched lips.

"He's missing. I was at the base when the news came in. That's why I headed over here. Didn't want you to read it in a telegram."

"Why, because it will say missing believed dead?" Carol retorted.

Myrtle stood with her hands over her mouth, tears streaming down her face. "Is Mr. Josh dead?"

"He's missing, darn it, not dead. Get some brandy, girl, and give it to her."

"Yes, Mr. Dean." Myrtle's hand shook as she poured, splashing brandy onto the new carpet, but nobody said a word.

"Tell me," Carol demanded, waving away the drink.

"The news is a bit sketchy but there was a raid over Germany. Josh's plane was hit. They saw it go down."

"Parachutes?" she whispered, locking her eyes on his, willing him to be truthful with her.

He shook his head. She sensed he couldn't bring himself to say the words out loud. Instead, he grabbed her glass of brandy and drank it in one gulp.

"It was a mess out there, lots of flak. Josh could have bailed out. We'll know more in a couple of days."

Carol forced her head to move, the rest of her body slowly freezing inside. Feeling as if she was somehow detached from her own body, Carol pushed her feet to the floor and stood up. Buddy yelped as she stood on his paw; she picked the puppy up, soothing him and herself.

"Thank you for coming, Dean, but I'm sure Priscilla needs you now. You should be together. You know how much Josh means to her and how she worries so much about him."

To her ears, she sounded cold and unemotional. She loved Josh so much but if she let herself feel even a fraction of the devastation she knew was coming, she'd crumble in front of this kind man who'd been like a father to her. "I must get changed. One of the other boys on Josh's crew is married, his wife lives quite near. She's eight months pregnant. I should go to her."

Dean's eyes widened with disbelief. "But, Carol... do you think that's wise? You know, after..." Dean didn't finish. He didn't have to. She needed no reminding of what she had lost six months ago. Her baby, Josh's son. And now Josh too.

"Don't worry about me, Dean. Josh would expect me to go and help if I can. He always said the pilot had a duty to his crew. Go on now, stop worrying about me." She leaned in and kissed him on the cheek, touching her hand to his for a brief second. "Go home to your wife. Myrtle is here with me."

She knew she'd done the right thing as Dean muttered, "I don't know how Priscilla will take this news. You know how much she loved Josh."

Carol noticed the past tense even if Dean didn't seem to. She walked him to the door, holding herself together. Once he left, she told Myrtle to go home too. She wanted to be alone.

She sat in the sitting room, holding her husband's photo in her hands, unaware of the light changing in the room as the sun went down. Buddy stayed by her side as if he realized her heart was broken. Only when it became too dark to see Josh's face clearly did she realize the time. She'd lost everything that meant anything to her. First her parents, then her baby, and now... Josh, the love of her life, was gone too. There was nothing left for her. She walked upstairs still holding the photograph in one hand; in the other she carried a bottle of his favorite whiskey. Going into the bathroom, she took a bottle of the pills the doctor had given her to help her sleep in the days after her hysterectomy.

She closed her bedroom door, and went to his closet and found his favorite jumper. She put it on and sat on the bed. She poured a glass of whiskey; she didn't like the taste but the smell reminded her of Josh. She opened the pill bottle and shook a few into her shaking hand, some falling to the floor. She took two, washing them down with a glass of water. Buddy growled before barking. Then she heard the doorbell. Who would be calling this late?

"Ma'am. She's upstairs."

Carol jumped to her feet in her haste, knocking the bottle of whiskey to the floor. She watched the liquid pooling around the white tablets, hearing the noise of footsteps on the stairs, her mother-in-law calling her name. What was she doing here? Carol wished she could disappear, Priscilla Andersen was the last person she wanted to see.

"Carol, Isiah telephoned me." Priscilla's shrill tones made the hair stand up on Carol's arms. "Can I come in...?" The question was rather redundant as she pushed the door open, followed by her husband, Dean. Carol's gaze met his. She watched his eyes widen in horror as he took in the whiskey and the pill bottle.

"My dear girl, thank God Isiah called us." The look in his eyes changed to pity. "This isn't the answer. Josh may come back and how would he live with himself?"

"Never mind *my dear girl.*" Priscilla gave her a slap across the face. "Wake up, Carol. Have you any idea of the damage you could have done? The scandal. The newspapers." Priscilla pushed each word past her scarlet-red, thinning lips. "Dean, get her into the bathroom. We must make her vomit. Get whatever she's taken back up."

"Priscilla, be nice. You promised..."

She could see Dean's mouth moving, but his words came from a distance. She put a hand out to reach for him before the blackness came.

"Quick, Isiah, help Mr. Dean take her to the bathroom. We

don't know how many tablets she's taken. She smells like she washed in the whiskey."

Carol tried to protest, but her brain didn't seem to connect with her mouth. She mumbled something, but it was no use.

The sound of screaming woke her up. Her nose wrinkled. This wasn't her room or her bed. Her muscles ached. She tried to move her arms but couldn't. She was restrained. Panicking, she opened her eyes. Shadows cast the room in a low light, the window screened off with shutters. In the dimness, she could make out a muscular man sitting on a chair in the room staring at her. His expression was inscrutable.

Her stomach churned with fear. "Release me at once. Why have you tied me to the bed?"

There was no response. Carol gripped the side of the bed, trying to sit up but it was useless. Her legs were secured as well.

"What am I doing here?" Carol demanded. But despite trying to sound confident, her voice trembled. No reaction. She tried again. "Where am I?"

"Calm down, Mrs. Andersen. The doctor will be along shortly."

"Doctor? I don't need a doctor. I have to get home. There might be news of my husband."

The man simply stared. Carol tried to wiggle free, but it was useless. They'd trapped her. The clock ticked down the seconds. She could hear it high on the wall behind her but couldn't see it. What time was it? The lack of daylight didn't mean it was night-time because of the shuttered window. She tried to breathe deeply to relax, but it was pointless. She closed her eyes, remembering the whiskey, the pills, but she had taken none. Her mouth felt furry, and her head thumped. Had she? A key scraped in a lock before the door opened, pushing forward into the room. She held her breath. Who was coming in? A grizzly gray-haired man with glasses and a white coat walked in.

"Mrs. Andersen, good to see you awake. We had to sedate you for your own safety."

She channeled her mother-in-law, desperate to take control back.

"And the restraints?"

The doctor didn't even blanch at her tone. "Also for your own safety."

"That's ridiculous. I'm not a criminal. I demand to be released. I want to go home." At his lack of reaction, her tone changed to begging. "I need to go home, there might be news."

"All in good time, Mrs. Andersen. Your mother-in-law signed the admittance papers. You are a risk to yourself."

Priscilla! What had the cold old witch done? "Where am I?"

"You are in Highfield Hospital."

Carol closed her eyes, her knuckles whitening as her nails bit into her palms. Highfield, the Asheville asylum? This was where Zelda Fitzgerald was a patient. What was she doing in a mental institution? She had to get out of here. She forced her voice to stay calm despite the quivering inside. "My in-laws are mistaken. They posted my husband as missing yesterday. I went to bed with his photograph and his jumper. I just wanted to be closer to him."

"And the whiskey?"

"The smell reminds me of him. I don't drink liquor. I hate the taste." Even as she said the words, she realized how lame they sounded.

"I see."

She could see he didn't believe her.

"I swear I didn't drink anything."

He ignored her. "Mrs. Andersen, your mother-in-law wishes us to be discreet. She is a true philanthropist, such a kind-hearted woman."

Carol wanted to contradict him, but he didn't give her a chance.

"Given your family's position in society and the criminal nature of a suicide attempt..."

She jerked upright, forgetting about the restraints, wincing as they stopped her movement. "I didn't try to kill myself. My doctor gave me the pills for sleeping. I took two to help me sleep. I let some fall on the floor and then I knocked over the bottle of whiskey when the doorbell startled me. You must believe me," Carol screamed. "Believe me. I—"

"You're hysterical." The doctor put the injection into her arm almost before she realized what happened. "We'll speak again tomorrow, Mrs. Andersen."

Darkness descended as the door closed behind the doctor.

FIVE

GALWAY, IRELAND

April, 1942

Ignoring her weary legs and tired arms, Kate forced a joyful note into her voice as she repeated the Irish legend again, around the small campfire with the sound of the waves crashing against the shore in the background. The children, just as tired as she was, lay or sat on the surrounding sand, after a hard day's work foraging edible seaweed and shellfish to supplement their diet. The newspapers were full of talk about rationing introduced by the war, but it made little difference to the residents of their town. They were even poorer now, as the food parcels and money from relatives living abroad had ceased when war broke out.

"Before Deirdre was born, a wise man said she would be a great beauty, so King Conor ordered she be taken from her family and sent to live with a wise old woman. The woman would bring her up in a suitable manner befitting that of a queen."

Kate shifted on the sandy grass as she spoke, while Shane moved slightly to sit closer to her feet. He acted like her shadow on the rare occasions he escaped from the watchful eye of his foster mother. Kate had promised Mrs. Cumiskey a share of fresh seaweed and some shellfish in return for Shane's help at the seaside.

"What does 'befitting' mean?" little Cathy Kelly asked, her long black hair splayed around her face, her brown eyes lit with intelligence.

Her twin sister, Ellen, gave her a thump. "Shush up, Cathy. Let Kate tell the story. Go on, Kate."

"It means so she could act all queen-like when she was a grown-up. Deirdre did grow into a beautiful woman with long red hair but she was also kind and gracious. The old woman grew to love her like her own child but Deirdre was lonely and keen to meet people of her own age. The old woman introduced her to a man called Naoise. He was so handsome, tall with dark hair, pale skin and bright blue eyes." Kate wondered if all the Irish men with that complexion had died out along with Naoise. The locals were covered in freckles and had mousy brown hair, their skin rough from years working on the shore eking out a living catching fish and doing odd jobs.

Ellen Kelly elbowed her. "Why do have you a mushy look on your face, Kate?"

Kate blushed, her daydreams interrupted. "I don't, now whist will you, I'm trying to tell you a story."

"Will you fall in love?" Ellen sighed as if it was something she wished for. "When you go away for the summer?"

Kate's cheeks burned. She turned back to the children around her feet. "Do you want me to go home or tell you the rest of the story?"

Cathy rolled her eyes at her twin, before saying, "The story."

"Deirdre and Naoise fell in love and wanted to get married, but the old woman knew the king would be very angry. She tried to persuade Naoise to leave but he wouldn't go without Deirdre, so they ran away. Naoise's two brothers went with them to protect them. They lived happily for years and had two children, a boy and a girl."

Tommy Flanagan kicked the sand with his bare foot. "That's boring. Nobody fought or anything. You should be telling them stories of the Easter Rising in 1916 or what we did to get the British out of Ireland."

"Whist, Tommy. You're ruining the story." Ellen Kelly glared at the boy, before turning back to Kate, urging her to continue. "King Conor was angry and he sent his men to get Deirdre to come home, back to Ireland. So what happened next, Kate?"

Tommy interrupted. "Where was she?"

Ellen rolled her eyes. "She'd gone to England."

"He was right in fetching her back home. An Irishwoman has no place going to that heathen land."

"Tommy! Shut up." Ellen had her hands on her hips, eyes flashing. "The English didn't bomb Dublin and try to kill our president."

Tommy, equally determined to be right, retorted, "The Germans said it was an accident. They thought they were bombing Britain."

Ellen stamped her foot, sending sand flying everywhere. "Those Germans knew what they was doing. Killing all those people and they only out shopping. My mam says she'll never forgive those German bas—" Ellen yelped as her older sister whacked her across the legs.

"Don't you be cursing or Mammy will get the wooden spoon after ya."

"Ouch, you're a big bully, Sheila."

Little Alice O'Hara spoke up. "Kate, ignore them. Did the men catch Deirdre?"

"Not at first. Naoise and his brothers were brave men, fierce fighters and they kept her safe. But then King Conor tricked them. He said they were welcome to come home, and all would be well."

Ellen sat back down, her hands pressed together as if this was news to her. "Oh no, they shouldn't have come back. He killed her, didn't he?"

Kate glanced at the sky. The sun looked like it was sitting on the water at the edge of the world. Mam would be heading home soon. A quick look over at the older women showed her mam in deep conversation with the twins' mam, Maire Kelly.

"No, Ellen. But he killed Naoise and his brothers, so Deirdre had to marry him after all. She died of a broken heart."

Ellen sighed loudly before Cathy poked her in the side. "That's sad. What happened to their children?"

Before Kate could answer, she heard her mother calling. "Kate Ryan, will you stop gassing with those children and get back home. It's bad enough you are going off gallivanting to your uncle's for the summer but I can't do all the packing myself."

Kate bit back her retort. Everyone knew she was going to work for her uncle as he sent money home to help the Ryan family. Still, it wouldn't do for her to remind her mam of that fact, not in front of the neighbors.

"Coming, Mammy." Kate jumped to her feet.

Alice O'Hara, the youngest of her audience, grabbed her legs. "Kate, you'll come back, won't you? I'll miss your stories. You tell the best ones."

"Of course, Alice, where else would I go? Mammy needs me at home to help with the farm what with my da being sick."

The child walked along the street holding Kate's hand. "Will there be men like Naoise where you are going?"

Tommy kicked a stone. "You're an *amadan*, Alice O'Hara, a right fool. The only men over there in the Curragh are our enemies —the English and Germans locked up because of the war. Kate might find a decent Irish soldier who has the job of minding them."

Before she could react, her mother intervened. "Tommy Flanagan, you go home to your mother. She'll wash your mouth out with soap for you. Catherine is joining a convent, as well you know. She doesn't have time for boys."

"Yes, Mrs. Ryan. Sorry, Mrs. Ryan." Tommy ran before Kate's mammy could clout him around the head.

"Ah, Emer, will you leave your daughter be. She's a natural mother, if anyone was ever meant for love and a family she was."

Mrs. Kelly smiled warmly. "Did I hear your Joe was above in Dublin?"

"You mind your own business, Maire Kelly." And with that her mother marched up the road.

Giving Mrs. Kelly a look of apology, Kate quickened her pace. Shane followed until they got to the turn for the Cumiskey farm. "Give that to Mrs. Cumiskey and tell her you worked very hard." Kate handed him the lion's share of her basket, hoping he would eat well that night.

Shane hugged her in return. "I'll miss you, Kate. I miss Joe too." He hurried away before she could reply.

Joe had been in Dublin, she'd seen the postmark on the letter he'd sent to their mother, but it would be a long time before her brother would be home in Galway. He'd told Kate he was off to see the world and that there had to be more to life than catching fish and attending Mass. Now Kate's mother refused to mention her youngest son. She'd been convinced he'd join the priesthood and took it as a personal insult that he hadn't.

Kate's father agreed with him going—not that he'd tell his wife —Joe had told his sister on his last morning at home, when he'd woken her early to walk with him on the road to Galway City.

"I wish I could take you with me, Kate," her brother had said as they walked together. "Da isn't strong enough to stand up to Mammy and she's getting worse as time goes on. She should just move into the convent and be done with it. The amount of time she spends with those nuns."

Despite being alone on the road, Kate looked around before whispering, "Don't be saying things like that, Joe. Bad things will happen to you."

He'd picked her up and twirled her around, making her giggle. "Nothing will happen to me. Wasn't I born lucky?" Then his smile had dropped. "Take care of yourself, Kate, and keep on her good side. You hear?"

"Yes, Joe." She'd pushed the words past the lump in her throat. Her brother was everything to her. She loved him more than anyone and not just because he protected her from the worst of her mam's temper. He was her big brother—what would she do without him?

"Be careful, Joe, and write to me, won't ya?" she'd replied, biting back her tears.

"You bet. I'll write to Uncle Pat too and ask him to invite you to his place for the summer. He's a grand man."

Joe had kissed her cheek, and then he was gone.

Kate picked up the last of her clothes, folding the dress before putting it into her suitcase. Hearing footsteps on the stairs, she forced the case closed and slid it off the bed to stand near the bedroom door. There was a knock, and then her da entered, puffing heavily.

"Da, you should have called me. I'd have come down and saved you the stairs."

"Don't fuss, *Alannah*." The Gaelic term for "loved one" nearly broke her resolve not to cry; the lump in her throat grew bigger. "Just let me catch my breath." He sat on the chair by the wash-stand and, breathing hard, sucked air into his lungs.

Kate felt awful about leaving—her da needed her here to help with the farm.

"Kate my darling girl, stop looking so glum. I want you to go to Pat with a smile on your face and a spring in your step. Take this chance of freedom away from the farm and... well, the rest."

Her father nodded his head to the door, telling her he meant her mam but without putting it into words. She brushed away a tear from her eye, as her father handed her a brown paper package.

"'Tis not new but it's in good condition. I asked old woman Flaherty to keep an eye out for me for a good book for you to read on the bus. She said this was the one the girls wanted."

Kate kissed her da on the cheek, feeling his bone almost piercing his skin, before gently opening the present. She restrained the urge to rip the paper but it was scarce enough given the war. "*Little Women*. I love that story. Sister Augustine used to read it to us sometimes. Well, the bits she thought were appropriate. Thank you, Da, I'll treasure it."

"You're a fine young woman, Kate, and never forget it. I wish I could go with you to the Curragh to see my brother. I..." His voice faltered. He coughed and pulled himself up. "I miss him. Now I'd best get back downstairs to your mam. Not a word of this." He indicated the book and winked at his daughter.

Early the next morning, Kate stood in the rain waiting for the bus. The service from Galway had been reduced due to the war impacting fuel supplies. The war was responsible for lots of things, including a lack of material, food and even tea. Her mother had always been frugal but now the leaves were used so often the tea resembled dishwater. Kate suspected her da collected his ration of cigarettes and swapped it for chocolate as he always had a little bit to give to children in need, like Shane.

Her mother scowled beside her as the bus failed to show up on time, wanting to get to the shop to exchange the eggs for cash. The money she earned from that went towards little extras to make life easier, like the new shoes pinching Kate's feet. But with shoes on ration, she couldn't complain. Not that her mam would have listened.

"Maybe you should have taken the train, they run on turf now, so have no excuse for being late. Did you pack your ration book?" her mother said.

Kate gritted her teeth. Her mam had asked that question about ten times now.

"Mammy, be away home. There's no need for you to get drowned."

"Catherine Mary Ryan, I can decide for myself whether I stay or go. I am not in my dotage yet. Now you behave yourself. Your uncle Pat, a saint of a man in many ways, is not as strict as he should be with that girl of his. Remember your position and keep your knees together."

Kate didn't understand what her mother was talking about, but she let her ramble. A rumble in the distance announced the arrival of the bus.

"Think of your mortal soul, Catherine Mary Ryan, or heaven help ye."

"Yes, Mammy. Tell Da I'll write to him."

Her mother stood ramrod straight as Kate leaned in to give her a kiss on her cheek. She wouldn't see her for the next six months, but her mam acted like she would be back that afternoon.

As the bus pulled up, Kate didn't recognize the driver.

"Fine morning, if you were a duck. Where are you off to, love?" His Dublin accent was out of place on the quiet streets of the Galway village. He stepped down from the driver's seat, holding a cigarette between his lips as he spoke. Taking the case from Kate, he stashed it into the hold.

"Catherine is going to stay with Patrick Ryan of the Curragh, not gallivanting off somewhere," replied Mam.

"Grand man, Pat Ryan," the driver replied. "Serves a mean pint."

Kate thought her mother would have an apoplectic fit. She kissed her cheek again and moved toward the bus. Her mother, rendered speechless, simply watched.

The bus driver winked at Kate but was careful not to let her mother see him. Kate hid her face as the blood rushed to her cheeks. Scrambling aboard the bus, she quickly found a seat. She took out *Little Women*, her hands running over the cover, already missing her da. Her eyes filled at the thought of him sitting in a chair by the fire, old before his years. He'd fought in the last war and paid the price in more ways than one. Injured at the front, he was a hero and should have been treated accordingly. Instead, he was insulted and given cold quarter from his neighbors for taking the King's shilling. They would have had to leave Galway a long time ago if her mammy wasn't a well-respected Murphy. Mammy's brothers had died in the last war too, but they had died in 1916 fighting for a United Ireland and were feted as heroes. Their sacrifice was the reason the Ryans were tolerated, as her mother so often reminded her da. Kate couldn't help wondering why her da stayed married to a harridan and shunned by his countrymen. But Da insisted he'd fought for freedom and that meant he should be able to choose where he lived.

Despite everything, Kate loved Galway, especially the wild Atlantic Ocean. She spent hours trailing the beach, gathering seaweed for her mother and shiny black stones, pretty seashells and other treasures for herself. She'd looked across the raging water towards America. So many had left Ireland for the distant shores of the United States, never to return again. What would it be like to go and live there?

SIX

KILDARE, IRELAND

Five hours later with a scheduled stop in Limerick and another stop caused by a run-in with one of the numerous potholes along the way, she spotted Uncle Pat's pub. The bus braked hard, flinging Kate into the seat in front of her as a crowd of men cycled past cheering as they went. "Bloody Germans," the driver swore under his breath, blushing when he glanced in his rear-view mirror and saw Kate staring at him.

"Germans?" Kate queried, not sure she had heard him correctly.

"They're krauts all right, despite the lack of uniform. Under the terms of their internment, the servicemen from either side aren't allowed to wear their uniforms. Still, you can recognize one as easy as a rat in a barn. They wear their hair cut tighter and sit like they have a pole stuck up..." The driver's voice trailed off. He shrugged another apology in Kate's direction.

Kate's eyes followed the group of cyclists as they headed over the enormous green, heading for the wide-open space of the Curragh. They just looked like any other group of young men enjoying a carefree ride in the sunshine. You could see for miles, with not a tree or house ruining your view. She could spot some golfers out on the course in the distance.

Turning her head away from the enormous green area on the opposite side of the road, Kate grinned at the sight of the beautiful flowers, a mix of heather, petunias and geraniums, adorning the windowsills of the old pub that had stood in the same spot for one hundred years. The roof had been recently re-thatched, the stones re-painted, along with the wooden window frames and front door. She spotted the small wooden hall built onto the stone building— her cousin Mary had written about the dance hall they had added. Uncle Pat's business must be thriving.

Kate rubbed her eyes and ran her hands over her face, afraid she'd been dribbling in her sleep. Mary must have heard the bus as she came running out of the pub and over to greet her cousin.

"You're a sight for sore eyes, Kate Ryan," said Mary, hugging her once she had stepped off the bus and collected her bag. "Pretty as a picture and look how tall you've got. Da will have to fight the men off with sticks. Good job he keeps his old hunting rifle behind the bar."

Kate giggled as her cousin teased her. Despite the war, Mary was dressed in the latest fashion, no homemade outfits for her. Her hair was cut short as well, curling under just behind her ears. In the past, she'd taken regular trips to Dublin and bought her clothes in Clerys or Arnotts stores. Since the bombings back in 1941 when the Nazis had bombed the center, Uncle Pat had forbidden visits to the city.

"I wasn't sure your mam would let you come," Mary carried on. "Da said he might have to go and collect you himself, only it's been that busy in the bar. To think, you could have traveled in style on the back of the horse and cart." Mary's eyes danced as she teased her.

Kate pinched the inside of her wrist. This was real, she wasn't dreaming. "Your da sends money to Mam, it was only fair I came to help out. Mam's pride wouldn't have it any other way."

"Joe was right then. I heard him say as much to Da before he left. I've a bunch of letters inside for you from your brother. Wish

Frank would write to me as often as Joe writes to you. He's useless, is my brother."

Despite her words, Kate knew Mary adored her only sibling. "How is Joe? Mam tears his letters up. She doesn't even open them."

Mary's face contorted at the mention of her aunt. "Joe's great. Da has almost forgiven them both. Can you believe the nerve of them? Heading into the Gardai station and telling the Gardai they needed the papers to find work in England. As soon as they got to Liverpool, they both joined the British navy. He said he'll try to get home if he can."

Kate stilled. "Joe's in the British navy?" Stupidly she heard herself ask, "He went to war? Why did the police get involved? Is he in trouble?"

"Take that worried look off your face. Nobody can leave Ireland and travel to England without permission from the authorities. As for being in trouble, the war is no joke but Frank will keep an eye on him and they'll be home before you know it. Sure, can't they swim like fish. The navy will be the making of them, might cure them of the wanderlust. My brother needs to get rid of that before he takes over the bar."

Kate pictured her cousin Frank with his jet-black hair and big smile. He fancied going to Hollywood to work in the films. Nobody paid him a bit of attention; big dreams were always his thing. If anyone could make them come true, Frank could. He was born holding a four-leaved clover, or so he told Kate the last time she'd seen him.

The driver coughed as if to remind them he was still standing there.

"You must be starved. Come on inside. I made an apple tart, plenty for you and all, Seamus," Mary said to the bus driver. "Been saving a bit of the flour ration. Da gets extra what with having the bar. He told the inspector he had to serve something and with a lack of alcohol, a bit of home baking kept the men happy."

The driver whipped the cap off his head and bowed, making them both laugh.

"Will you marry me, Mary Ryan?"

"Go away with ye, you silly man. I'm an engaged woman to my Ciaran and you're already married to your Sarah, the mother of your five children."

"Sarah is a fine woman but she doesn't live in a pub and have the gift of baking you have."

Mary and Kate laughed as they linked arms and headed into the main part of the house. Decent women didn't drink in the bar, and even if they wanted to, Uncle Pat wouldn't serve them. It was a male domain. A place for a man to have a drink and a chat in peace. Seamus headed for the bar where a whiskey and pint would be waiting for him. He had an hour before he had to make his way on to Dublin.

Kate loved the old kitchen with the huge blackened stove on one side and the big wooden family table on the other. Mary insisted Kate sit while she served up a large plate of steaming lamb stew with potatoes, peas and carrots on the side. Mary was a fabulous cook and her meals always tasted better than Mam's, but then her cousin benefited from a thriving farm with a large vegetable garden, and Uncle Pat slaughtered his own animals for meat. No wonder he'd opened a small room at the side of the pub to cater for travelers who wanted to stop and eat a hearty meal.

After Kate could eat no more, she sat chatting with Mary over a pot of tea stronger than Kate had tasted in a long time. Every so often Uncle Pat would call for a hand, but Mary wouldn't hear of Kate working.

"Plenty of time for you to start tomorrow. For now, you rest. It's a long time on that bus and knowing your mother, she's had you working hard for weeks."

Kate didn't answer. Still, the next time Uncle Pat called his daughter, Kate set about cleaning up the kitchen. She put the dishes in the large sink, adding a few flakes of soap before pouring the hot water from the kettle that boiled away on the top of the stove. She washed and dried the dishes, looking out the kitchen window into the large yard. Unlike the yard at home, the weeds were conspicuous by their absence, the mud neatly raked over where her uncle's chickens roamed, pecking at the dirt. She had the dishes put away, wiped the table down and refreshed the pot of tea with boiling water, when the door opened from the bar.

"Kate, what are you doing?" said Uncle Pat, entering the room. "Mary told you to rest while you could. The hard work starts tomorrow. Come here and give your uncle a big hug."

She hugged him close, the scent of beer wafting up her nose. Unlike most publicans her uncle wasn't a big drinker, but he had a couple of pints every so often.

He held her at arm's length. "Taller and prettier you are, Kate. Your da must be that proud of you. How is he?"

"Same as before, Uncle Pat," Kate replied, looking away from the hope in his eyes. "Says he isn't in much pain, but we know he's lying. I wish the doctors could do more for him."

"So do I. I offered to bring him up to Dublin to see a specialist but your mam wouldn't hear of it. If I thought it would do any good, I wouldn't let her stop me."

"Da likes to keep the peace. You look well. Is Mrs. Mooney still chasing you?"

Her uncle laughed, his belly jiggling with the sound. "Your mam would give you a clip around the ear if she heard you talking like that. Maureen Mooney is a fine woman, she knows how to look after a man. We're friends and that's all we'll ever be. The only woman for me is lying above in the graveyard with our boy."

Kate swallowed, kicking herself for saying anything. Her aunt had died in childbirth ten years back and her uncle had taken the deaths badly. He still laughed and joked with everyone but his eyes often wandered in the direction of the graveyard, an expression of loss so keen it would break your heart.

"Sorry, Uncle Pat. I loved Aunt Kathy too. I was only teasing."

"I know you were, love. Now did I smell a fresh cup of tea? My old throat is like sand."

Kate took the hint and dished up a large slice of apple tart with cream on the side. She poured the tea into Pat's mug.

"Did Mary tell you there are a few letters waiting for you from Joe?"

"Yes, I can't believe he went into the navy. Can you?"

"No doubt it was my Frank's idea. Kathy used to joke the fairies took our son and left Frank as neither one of us had any interest in leaving Kildare, never mind Ireland. But as soon as Frank was old enough to learn about the world, he was talking about traveling to Africa or America or even Australia. It's the old songs about all the men and women leaving Ireland. I think he believes there would be an Irish welcome no matter where he went."

Kate grinned. "For Frank there would be a warm welcome, Irish or not. He could charm the honey from the bees."

"You're right, he could."

The door to the bar opened, letting in a cloud of smoke and the chatter from the pub. "Da, can you come in? It's getting busy," said Mary from the doorway.

"That's my nice rest over. I'll see you later, Kate, you make yourself at home."

"Can I come in and help ye?" asked Kate. "I can collect some glasses?"

Her uncle's eyebrows furrowed. "Are you not too tired?"

"No," she lied. "You sound rushed off your feet."

"We are and we could do with the help, although Mary might kill me." Mary glanced at them but didn't protest. "Thanks, Kate. I'm thrilled you are here."

She beamed at the praise and together they walked into the pub.

The place was busier than Kate had seen it before. The old bar shone under a layer of waxed polish; the bottles of different drinks glimmered on the shelves behind. The mirror behind the bottles was spotless, reflecting the light coming in from the windows on the wall opposite. Each small table was occupied with a few people reading newspapers or playing cards. She didn't recognize many of the men who all bore similar cropped hairstyles. The usual culprits stood at the bar, a pint of the black stuff in one hand, a cigarette in the other. A few punters looked up and waved a hand in greeting.

Dirty glasses were piled up on the end of the bar, and she hurried over, starting to wash them before Mary and Uncle Pat ran out. The cigarette smoke, the chink of glasses and the buzz of conversation made her smile. She was a million miles away from her beloved seaside, but this was her second home.

After a while, the pile of glasses grew manageable. Mary and Uncle Pat served quickly and efficiently, and the bar ran like clockwork.

"Where did all the extra customers come from?"

"They're from the prisoner of war camp up the road. K-Lines it's called. The Germans and the Allies come in for a drink and a chat on alternate days. It's the Allies' turn tonight." Mary chucked her under the chin. "Take that worried look off your face. Da and the other regulars keep things under control. War doesn't break out in this pub, at least not between the Nazis and the Allies." Mary winked before turning back to pour more drinks.

Two hours flew by with a regular stream of customers, even if they didn't have quite as many drinks as they would have in the prewar days.

Mary took the last of the clean glasses from Kate. "Thanks for helping but you can go away up to bed now. I left Joe's letters on your bed."

The tiredness had hit about an hour earlier with her back cramping and legs complaining. But the sound of raised voices made her turn, recognizing Paddy, a regular at the bar since before Kate was born and another man she wasn't familiar with.

She held her breath; he looked like a vision of Naoise straight out of her book on Irish legends but for his hair, which was blond not dark. It was cut tight into his neck just above his shirt collar, his eyes were as blue as the sea on a stormy day and his cheekbones would send most girls to confession to confess the sin of envy.

Although dressed in civilian clothes that didn't quite fit him, he was very attractive.

"You're not a prisoner of war, son, you are a guest of the land," Paddy said to the other man, before slurping his pint.

"I am a prisoner. I can't walk out and go home, can I?" He had a funny accent, not local and not English.

"Sure, why would you want to go and do that? Ireland is the finest place in the whole world to live. Here you can have a drink, meet a pretty girl or two, play your football and sleep in a dry, clean bed. What would you want to go back to a war where you could lose your life?"

Kate watched the young man's facial expressions, anger and disbelief fighting for dominance as Paddy continued talking.

"Go on, have a pint of the black stuff and a small whiskey chaser. You're here now and you might as well enjoy it."

"There are Nazis marching up and down your street despite being dressed in civilian clothes, drinking in your bars, and walking out with your women, and you want me to have a drink?"

"I didn't say you had to drink with the Germans, did I?" Paddy scratched his head before continuing. "Us Irish aren't stupid, you know. You can't mix the drink with politics, sure any eejit knows that. Anyway, they aren't Nazis but the Luftwaffel, or something like that. Airmen just like yourself. If there wasn't a war, sure you'd have a lot in common, like."

Kate and Mary exchanged a grin as Paddy stumbled over the German word but he did well enough seeing as he was on his fifth or sixth pint.

The man strutted forward. "Did you just compare me to a Nazi?" He held his hands balled in fists by his side, his eyes wide with anger.

Even in his drunken state, Paddy seemed to sense the danger as he moved nearer the bar. "I wasn't meaning any offense. I just meant you both fly them airplanes. Never saw one of them up close myself."

Uncle Pat intervened. "Now, son, take a seat and I'll get Kate to drop over your drinks. Don't be paying any attention to this eejit. Paddy barely knows his own name after the amount he's had to drink. Go on now, lad. Off you go. You don't want to be put on a charge, do ye?"

The airman threw Paddy a filthy look before taking Uncle Pat's advice, moving towards his friends in the corner of the bar. Kate ducked behind the counter and picked up the tray her uncle had laden with pints for them.

"It's unbelievable. They've gone mad. How can anyone expect us to sit out the war in this..." The man colored as she approached with the drinks. "Pardon me, miss."

Kate held her breath. Up close he was even more gorgeous. The white shirt brought out his baby blue eyes, and his skin was clear and bronzed from the sunshine. Was it the sun that gave him such blond hair as well? He coughed. She was staring. Flustered, the tray rattled in her hands, almost sending the drinks crashing to the floor.

"Leave the girl alone and sit down, Tony."

Startled, Kate stared at the stranger who spoke just like the presenters on the BBC radio. The man winked at Kate before continuing. "Things are different here. It's pointless trying to escape. Some Canadian bloke did that a few months back. He got to Dublin, took a train to Belfast and reported to an RAF base in Northern Ireland and was promptly ordered back here."

"They sent him back? But we were told it was our duty to escape and head home. That's why I learnt French, remember?"

"That's different. This isn't enemy territory. Old Winston might not like the Irish staying neutral but he doesn't want to upset them either. It suits us for them not to side with the Germans. Can you imagine what would happen if Hitler's lot got control of all the ports in this land?" The airman stood and took the drinks from Kate's tray. "So, take the weight off and enjoy the view. Irish women are natural beauties, isn't that right?" He patted her arm but she shrugged it off. He had that sneering look some men used when talking to women. If he was an ice cream, he'd eat himself.

But Tony...

Tony caught her glancing in his direction and smiled. Blushing, she walked quickly back to the bar, feeling his eyes on her back the whole time.

"Despite the rationing, they still get through a lot of drink, don't they?" Kate said to her cousin.

Mary leaned in closer. "Some of them are drinking the poitín but we pretend not to notice. With nothing but bad news in the papers and the effects of rationing and shortages, Da said to turn a blind eye. Mind, we have to be careful if the Gardai or the MPs call in."

Kate knew her uncle would get into a lot of trouble if either the police or the military police found poitín on his premises, the brewing of bootleg alcohol from potatoes being illegal. The strength of the stuff could fell a grown man. Her mam had warned all the children that a sip of the evil liquid would make them blind. Kate's nose wrinkled with distaste.

"What? You smell something bad?"

"No, I was just remembering Granny Ryan giving me Guinness mixed with milk to build me up. Something about the level of iron in it helping me. No matter how long it's been, I can still taste it."

Mary giggled. "Granny Ryan was a *divil* for the drink. She used to put whiskey in the babies' bottles, said it helped them sleep at night. Mammy was always checking on our cots just in case Granny had tried to be helpful! She was a great woman, wasn't she? Wonder what she would have thought of this lot being here." Mary looked around the bar.

"She must be spinning in her grave," Kate sighed, yawning.

"Go on to bed, Kate. Read your letters. I left a writing pad by your bed. I'll call you in the morning so enjoy your lie-in. It will be the last you'll have before you go back to Galway."

Kate smiled at her cousin, kissed her cheek and headed out the back through the kitchen and up the back stairs to the bedroom. Kate pushed open the heavy wooden door, her eyes immediately focusing on the large double bed with its embroidered white bedspread, her case sitting at the end. Opposite the bed was a large window, although the view out on the countryside was cut off by the heavy drapes. Shivering, she glanced at the picture of the Sacred Heart of Jesus; the eyes seemed to follow her no matter where she stood in the room. She'd mentioned that to Mary once, but her cousin just laughed and told her off for having a vivid imagination.

Undressing quickly, she put on her nightgown, unpacked her bag and placed the case on top of the wardrobe. This was her home for the next six months and she was going to enjoy every minute. She kneeled by the bed to say a few rushed prayers before climbing in and opening the letters, settling down to take in her brother's words. After reading them all, she picked up the first one again.

Dear Kate,

I wrote to you at Uncle Pat's because you didn't reply to my last letters. I don't know if you are really annoyed with me or Mam didn't give them to you. I hope it's the latter.

I hope you aren't angry I didn't tell you I planned on joining up. I knew Mam would stop me if I asked. She's intent on me joining the priesthood but that's not the life for me. That's why I had to run away. Frank came with me, so don't worry I won't get into trouble. We joined the navy as we didn't want to land in the trenches like Da did in his war. I can't tell you the name of the ship as the censors won't let the letter through but it's a real beauty. The crew are nice too, which is a bit surprising, especially after everything Mam said about the English. But they are just the same as us, missing their family. A couple of them saw your picture and thought you were my girl. You should have seen their faces when I said you were my sister. They all wanted your address. Not that I gave it to them. You know what they say about sailors, a girl in every port.

We've already been on one trip and made it back in one piece.

I got to see places I only dreamed of, Kate. I know I shouldn't say this, with the war and everything, but it's a great way to see the world. Will you write back to me care of the above address? I hope to find your letters waiting when I get into port next time.

Your loving brother,

Joe

Grinning from sheer relief at finally hearing from her brother, Kate picked up the paper and pencil by her bed and began scribbling. She had so much to tell him, she couldn't get the words out fast enough.

Dear Joe,

I could never be angry but Mam is. She won't open any of your letters but puts them straight in the stove. I tried asking her to let Da have them but got a belt for my troubles.

Thank you for asking Uncle Pat to invite me to stay. Mam is worse since you left. I swear Da is a saint for all he puts up with. If she isn't going on about the English and how they want to dominate the whole world, she talks about how much she admires Hitler. Da won't listen to her when she starts on the Nazis. He told her so too, first time in a long time I saw her fall silent from shock. She still talks about the Germans but only when Da is away off working in the fields. I've asked the locals to help him as much as they can, what's left of them around. Most of the lads have either joined the Irish army or headed across the water to work in the factories or down the mines in England. Of course lots have joined up like you did.

It's very odd here in Kildare. I haven't seen it yet but Mary says there is a big prisoner of war camp up where the IRA guys are imprisoned. Did you know the government rounded the IRA supporters up and put them behind bars in case they fell in with the Nazis? Well, next door to their camp is another one for the Nazis and Allies that land here. Yes, you read that right. There is one camp, divided down the middle by some barbed wire with the enemies on either side. The Irish army is in charge. Paddy, you remember the aul man from the bar, he says that the men aren't prisoners of war but guests of the state, but the men in the bar tonight don't seem to agree with him. They want to get back to fighting the war. What is it with men and killing?

What's it like in the navy? Do they treat you right or do they gang up on you 'cause you're Irish? You tell them we are all the same and fighting for the same thing, the end of the war and your return home.

God bless and tell Frank I said hello and to mind himself. Keep an eye on him, you know how clumsy he can be. I don't want him falling overboard or being left behind when you leave the next country you stop in.

Oh, Joe, I miss you. Please take care. I pray for you every night and am so relieved to finally read your letters. Keep writing. I will write to Da with your news.

All my love,

Kate

After she was finished, Kate got back out of bed and kneeled to say more prayers, slowly and with more intent this time. She prayed for all the people suffering through the war, but most of all for her brother Joe, cousin Frank and with a smile she added Tony to the list.

SEVEN

The next day, the sun rose bright and early, flooding her bedroom with light. Kate jumped out of bed, opened the curtains fully and gave herself time to enjoy the view. There was field after field of green, a carpet of colorful wildflowers breaking up the grass here and there.

She dressed quickly before racing downstairs to help Mary with the chores. Without being asked, she headed outside where she did the milking. Her uncle kept a small herd of cows and paid two of the local children, the Donnelly twins, to round them up and bring them into the milking shed.

"Mornin', Kate, did you bring us any seashells?" Con Donnelly asked as he expertly steered Tilly and Polly into their respective stalls. Kate reached into her pocket and took out two almost perfect long razor shells.

"Wow." Con took them from her hand before passing one over to his shyer twin, John Joseph. "You could cut someone's throat with these."

"Not likely, Con Donnelly, now put those away until we have this milking done. Uncle Pat will be after me for keeping ye from your work."

"Pat Ryan is a saint of a man," Con said as he gazed at the shell.

"He gave Mam and my sister a job in the dairy churning the butter." He stopped chatting, his eyes taking on a faraway look. She knew he was thinking of his da.

"I smell bacon so why don't we hurry up and get back inside for a bite to eat and a cup of fresh milk?" Kate said, anything to take the boy's mind off their father, lost at sea after his merchant ship had been torpedoed. God bless Uncle Pat for giving the whole family work, allowing them to keep their pride rather than go looking for charity.

Con rubbed his belly, smiling at her over the shell.

The cows seemed to sense her good mood, giving up their milk easily and without kicking out or swishing their tails in her face.

"Give me that, you shouldn't be carrying an urn that size on your own," the twins' eldest brother, Mark, said to her, taking her by surprise and making her jump.

"Sorry, Mark, didn't see you there. You've grown a lot since I saw you last. Thank you."

The boy blushed from the roots of his ginger hair to the tips of his ears. He was big for his thirteen years.

"Will you come in for breakfast after or will I ask the twins to bring you it out to the shed?"

"The shed, please. There's a lot to be done today and I need to get on."

Kate watched as he carried the urn into the side shed, where his sister and mother waited to separate the milk for general use from that which would be left to cool. Tomorrow they would skim off the cream into the earthenware pail and when there was sufficient, would start to churn it into butter. Kate's arms ached just thinking about that chore but everyone who lived on a farm took a turn. There was an art to making butter, one all Irish farm children learned as soon as they were strong enough to hold the paddle. How lucky the Donnelly family was that Pat was able to employ them all.

Kate hurried through the rest of the chores, before washing her hands under the pump in the garden and heading into the kitchen, where the scent of fried bacon and mushrooms made her mouth water.

"'Tis a saint you are, Mary Ryan." Con blessed himself before taking a seat at the table, where he dove into his plate of bacon, egg, fried potatoes and swede fried in bacon fat. To finish, he took a piece of bread and rubbed it around the plate leaving it so clean, you'd have thought it was washed. Only then did he speak. "That was a grand feed, so it was." He pushed his chair back, grabbed his brother by the arm and headed out the door.

Mary and Kate exchanged a glance as the door banged shut behind the boys. "Does he ever stop talking, that one?"

Mary shook her head. "Thank God he's still much the same as he was before Siobhan got the telegram about their father. I still can't believe he's gone. Such a fine, strapping big man and now he's lost at the bottom of the sea."

Kate didn't want to think about ships being torpedoed as Joe's face flickered into her head. "You and Uncle Pat are very good to feed them, as well as giving them work."

"That's how we pay them. Da doesn't have much spare cash so he barters food in return for labor. Helps Siobhan out as growing boys have hollow legs. I just hope we can keep it up."

"Why?" Kate didn't like the troubled look on her cousin's face.

"This bloomin' war, that's why. We're grand now, we slaughtered a couple of pigs and a few steer, but that isn't going to last forever. Da says not to worry but how will we keep the herd in feed if we don't get the hay in on time? The locals don't have much money to spare for drinking and, even if they did, Da is finding it harder to keep the stock in. I swear if I got my hands on that bowser, Hitler, I'd... I'd... well, I don't know what I'd do to him."

Kate hugged Mary. "We'll be grand, you'll see. Uncle Pat has brains to burn and you are too talented in housekeeping for anyone to go hungry. Look at the way those boys ate up your swede. There's only one place that stuff belongs and that's as animal feed."

Mary flicked the tea towel at her as they both laughed.

"Can you take some parcels to the post office for me this morning, Kate?" asked Mary. "I've knitted the boys some socks, two hats and a couple of scarves. Frank says he is always cold. They must be on the North Atlantic run, do you think?"

"I don't know, every time Joe mentioned where he was, the censor blacked it out."

"Do you mind going out for me?"

"Not at all. I've got a letter for Joe and one for Mam." She brushed aside the feelings of guilt at what she hadn't included. Her mother would have a fit if she knew she was working in the bar and talking to men of all ages. Uncle Pat warned her not to mention it and let her mam think she was only working on the farm and doing housework.

She walked down the street, greeting people as she went, wishing she'd brought a coat. The bright sunshine of the morning had disappeared behind some heavy dark clouds.

The other houses in the village weren't in as good a state of repair as the pub, with flaking paint and roofs in need of re-thatching. As she walked past one house, Captain—a horse who'd been a part of the village for as long as she could remember—ambled over to the wall to greet her. She patted his head, wishing she had an apple or something to give him. "Next time, Captain, I promise."

The road was full of potholes as usual; some things never changed. Up ahead she saw a group of men cycling in the direction of the golf club. Wasn't it a weird war where the prisoners in the camp got to play golf, while Joe and Frank risked their lives every day out in the Atlantic?

Outside the post office, there was the same airman, Tony, this time dressed in a short-sleeved shirt and trousers, a large grin lighting up his face. She almost walked straight into him.

"Top of the morning to you,' he said in his unfamiliar accent, making her burst out laughing. His expression turned from friendly to confused. "What did I say?"

"We don't talk like that around here."

"Yes, you do. You say funny things, like calling people names and cursing at them. You don't even seem to know you're doing it."

She must have looked perplexed as he quickly clarified. "Your uncle called that man an eejit. It's not polite where I come from to call someone a fool."

"Don't worry about defending Paddy. He and my uncle are thick as thieves. Sure, didn't they grow up together." She hesitated as the smile on his face widened. "What did I say wrong now?"

"Nothing. You don't talk, you sing."

"Go on away outta that. I do not." Kate walked past him, heading into the post office. She wasn't sure if she was happy or sad when he followed her.

The ageing shopkeeper looked up from her paper at the ring of the door. "Morning, Kate, isn't it a beautiful day?"

"It is indeed, Mrs. Scanlan. How are you and the family keeping?"

"Sure, there is no point complaining. Nobody will listen to the likes of me. Fergal will be pleased to see you. Have you seen the ?" The welcoming smile slid off the woman's face, surprising Kate. "What can I do for you?" she directed coldly to the airman.

Tony seemed impervious to the frosty tone. "I'll wait, ma'am, until you finish. Then I'd like to buy a stamp."

Mrs. Scanlan's smile returned. "You're American?"

"Yes, ma'am."

"Here was me thinking you were English."

Tony rolled his eyes at Kate but she hid her grin. It was pointless trying to explain to a Yank that Mr. Scanlan had lain in the cemetery the past twenty years thanks to two bullets from the Black and Tans. Uncle Pat said Mrs. Scanlan had taken to inviting some of the German prisoners to her home for dinner. "She'll be laying out the swastika next," was his caustic comment.

"Why's a nice American boy like you fighting for the British?"

"Fighting for freedom, ma'am. I don't fancy life under Hitler and his cronies. Do you?"

Kate put a hand to her mouth to cover her smile. Mrs. Scanlan looked fit to be tied. She turned away in a huff. "Kate, a letter to your dear mother, is it? Next time you write to her, would you tell her I've a mind to write a piece for the local newspaper about her brothers and their sacrifice for our beloved Ireland on the next anniversary."

Kate nodded, not trusting herself to speak. She handed over the money for the stamp, licked it and stuck it to the envelope before handing it back to Mrs. Scanlan.

"I've to hurry back, Mrs. Scanlan. Mary needs help with the baking this morning."

"You're a good girl, despite what your father did. Go on then." Her warm smile disappeared. "Is it one stamp you want, soldier?"

"Sorry, ma'am, but I just remembered I have some back at camp. Excuse me."

Kate heard the comment and wasn't surprised to find him at her side seconds later.

He pursed his lips, his head tilted to one side as he looked at her.

"What?" she prompted when he remained silent.

"Why do I feel I just escaped enemy territory?"

"Don't mind her, she'd give you the coat off her back if you needed it. She just has strong political opinions."

"That's rather charitable given her remark about your father. What did he do? Murder someone?"

"He did what you did. Went to England and joined up. In the last war. Got injured and was sent home, but some in Ireland see him as a traitor."

"Why?"

"Ireland was governed by England at that time and by going to fight, some, like Mrs. Scanlan, say Da supported English rule. The Irish were fighting for freedom, well, some of them were. Some thought it would be better to fight for England and then get freedom when the war was over." He looked confused and she didn't blame him. How could she explain the issues caused by eight hundred years of occupation in a few simple sentences? "When the war was over, the First World War, I mean, the English sent over a ragtag army to keep the Irish in their so-called place.

They didn't have proper uniforms, only bits and pieces, so they got the nickname the Black and Tans. These men, most of them veterans of the last war, were violent and murdered a lot of innocent men and women."

"And Mrs. Scanlan? Her family was killed?"

She shook her head in answer, trying to think of the right words to explain the widow's reaction.

"The Black and Tans killed other people in incidents all over Ireland. Mrs. Scanlan believes her husband was one of the innocents."

"And you don't?"

Kate shrugged. "I tend to stay out of politics. Mr. Scanlan fought to free our country—does that make him a terrorist or a freedom fighter? Either way, he deserved a trial, not to be gunned down in his own home in front of his family. But you don't need to know all about this. You just asked about my da. Mrs. Scanlan feels he betrayed Ireland because instead of staying out of the last war, he took the King's shilling and fought the Germans."

"Anyone who fought in that war deserves better. My father told me about the trenches and whatnot. He was a medic in France. I guess I better find another place to buy stamps then."

"Or you could just send your letters through the normal channels." She smiled as he blushed realizing she knew that, as he was in the air force, he should use the camp postal service.

"You caught me. What else was I supposed to do? Where I come from you can't just walk up to a beautiful girl and ask her out. Especially as you didn't seem too pleased with Alistair."

The look in his eyes made her legs feel like they would crumble under her.

"Alistair?" she asked, as she started walking in the direction of the pub.

"The airman who told me off for arguing with Paddy, the guy with the mustache. He's usually a hit with the ladies."

Not this lady. For one horrible second, she thought she had spoken out loud.

"Are you in a hurry? Could you spare an hour to show me around?"

She hesitated, worried about getting back to the bar.

"Please?"

She stopped walking. "There isn't much to see?"

"What about the church?"

She glanced at him, wondering if he was serious. What would the priest say if she arrived with a man?

He looked at her, his blue eyes wide in his face as he tried to adopt a look of innocence.

"I just want to spend a little time to get to know you. Away from the bar."

She wavered, buying time by smoothing her skirt even though it was perfect, torn between wanting to spend time with him and leaving Mary to cope alone. Guilt won. Reluctantly she said, "I have to get back to help my cousin."

"At least let me walk you home?"

She giggled at his earnest expression, deciding to tease him as she tried to take her mind off the butterflies in her stomach. "All the way to Galway?" At his confused expression, she clarified. "I don't live here. My home is in Galway, but I'm staying with my uncle for a while. To help, at least that's what he tells my mother. He knows life at home can be difficult. He gives me a chance to get away for a while and sends her some money, without hurting her pride. He's a lovely, thoughtful man..." She gasped, realizing she had just told this complete stranger the truth about her mother. "Sorry," she spluttered. "I could talk the hind legs off an old goat."

"Would you spare an hour or so if I give you my legs?"

Kate laughed. He was easy enough to talk to. Who was she kidding? Her butterflies were flapping harder every time he glanced her way, which was often.

"We could sit over there in the field and just talk. It's perfectly respectable as everyone can see us from the road; it's not like there's a tree to hide behind."

He indicated a large pasture of flat land with views as far as the eye could see. She hesitated only momentarily and then nodded. Mary wouldn't mind. They took a seat on the grass as Tony told her more about living in the camp.

"I couldn't believe it when I first arrived. When the plane crashed, we thought we'd landed in France and one of the lads tried speaking French to this man. He told him to shut up with that foreign gibberish and speak English. I was so relieved; I can't describe it to you. I thought we would be patched up and sent back to England in no time at all." He hesitated, looking at her beaming back at him. "Why are you laughing? I swear from the air, France and Ireland look very similar. At least in places, both have green fields and—" He stopped as she giggled even more.

"Isn't grass green everywhere?" she asked.

"Actually, not where I come from. Back home, in Colorado, the prairie grass doesn't stay green too long in the heat. Anyway, instead of treating us like friends, the man who found us treated us like we had just walked dirt all over their new suit or crashed their Ford or something. He took us to a police station, and they brought us here. Your police, that is, they have a funny name."

"The Gardai. That's what we call them, it's Gaelic, Irish, as you would call it. What did they do?" She loved listening to him talk, his accent and the different words he used.

"They made it quite clear we weren't going back to Britain. I would swear some of them looked pleased to be locking us up. Drove us down here to a prisoner camp, what they called the K-Lines, but that's not the proper name. I couldn't believe what I was seeing. There's barbed wire separating us from the Germans. Although we have to wear civilian clothes when we leave the camp," he said, looking down at the trousers and shirt he was wearing, "they change back into their Nazi uniforms and march around singing songs about victory or spouting their ridiculous claims about being the master race. It's just not right, you know. We're fighting to keep places like Ireland free from scum like that and you lot lock us up with them."

She held up her hand, stopping his tirade. "I don't understand any more than you do why they don't send you back. My da would say it's because Ireland is supposed to be neutral. If they sent you and the rest of the RAF pilots who crash here back home, they would have to send the Germans back too. Would you want that?"

He opened his mouth, hesitated, and then closed it again, throwing his hands up in a gesture of surrender. "Why do I bother trying to argue with Irish logic? We are fighting for your freedom."

Kate sighed. "It's not that simple as you have just seen from Mrs. Scanlan's reaction. Up to twenty years ago, the English were our enemy." He rolled his eyes, his reaction telling her he'd heard that excuse before. She persisted, keen to get him to understand. "How would you feel if... say, the French invaded... what did you call your home again?"

"Colorado."

"Colorado." Kate tested the new word on her tongue. Then she remembered the point she was trying to make. "So the French invade Colorado and they throw you all out of your houses."

"They wouldn't."

"Just imagine they did. They give the best houses and the richest land to French people and expect people born and reared in Colorado to live on dirt farms where you didn't know from one year to the next how you would survive."

"But, Kate—"

"Let me finish. To add insult to injury, these French invaders refused to let you speak English, you had to speak French. They refused to let you practice your religion and they refused to let your children attend a Catholic school. They reduced the population of your country by four million, between emigration and death during the famine."

"You're talking about hundreds of years ago. This is 1942."

"And there are still Irish people living on farms where they can't fish the water that runs through their farmland because it belongs to some English lord," Kate said, losing her temper. Tony inched back before she reached out her hand to touch his arm. "I'm sorry. I shouldn't have snapped. I was just trying to explain that it is all those years of history and memories making it hard for some Irish people to trust the British, never mind fight on their side. My brother is with the Allies fighting, so is my cousin. I would be too if I was a man."

The admiring look in his eyes made her catch her breath. He put his hand on hers where it remained on his arm. "I dare say you would." He leaned in closer, his hand now caressing her hair.

Her stomach melted at his nearness, her pulse racing. He smelled of soap and something else.

Kate rose to her feet. "Is that the time? I'd best get back I'll be needed."

She pretended not to see the disappointed look on his face, never mind admitting she felt the same. This was silly, they didn't know one another, yet she was feeling something for him. That scared her.

"I guess I'll see you next time you and your friends come into the bar," she said. "Take care."

"Wait, what? I'll walk you home. I still have my legs, you haven't talked them off just yet."

EIGHT

As they walked past the church, they continued their conversation.

"So what's it like in the camp? I know there is a large stone barracks down there. Do you live in that?"

"No, that's where your army is based. The huts, where we sleep, are built on these stilt-like things. They said it's to stop us digging tunnels to escape. Not that there would be much chance of that as the lights are always lit up at night. Back in England they have a blackout, but you guys don't have that here."

"No need. Nobody should be bombing us. We're neutral, remember." She nudged him in the arm.

He didn't argue. "The British have a bar, not like your uncle's, it's just spirits and stuff. You sign a sheet to say how many drinks you've taken. That's it. Nobody checks on you. It's the British honor system. The same one that keeps us locked up."

Curious to know more, she leaned in toward him.

"What do you mean? I thought you said escape wouldn't be possible."

"The Irish soldiers can't shoot us as we're guests of the State. Some say they have blanks in their guns, not real bullets, but that's just a rumor. They're real, all right, but we're protected. A few have threatened to shoot some English officers and a couple threatened some Germans, but they can't do anything."

They were barely moving as they strolled together. Kate enjoyed chatting to him and wanted to make the short trip as long as possible.

"So why don't the men all escape? Do they want to sit out the war?"

"No, not at all," he retorted loudly, making her step away from him. "Sorry, I didn't mean to snap. We are desperate to get back to fight in the war, not sit it out like a group of old women. We're stuck here until the war is over."

His self-pity made her think of her da and what he would have given to get through the war safely. Joe was out there putting his life on the line along with thousands of others.

"At least your parents know you are safe. That must count for something?" She spoke sharply, and he responded in kind.

"How safe will anyone be if the Nazis win the war? I can't understand why the Irish don't fight on our side."

Kate couldn't understand either, not really, despite what she had told him about the history. She knew Ireland didn't have a proper army, the English having forbidden it when they were ruling. In the twenty years since the English had left, Ireland had fought a civil war and now their armed forces weren't large enough, at least not big enough to put up a fight and, being a small island, they were vulnerable. But it was funny that when she felt someone was insulting her country, she could defend it to the teeth, but in her own heart she wanted Ireland to come out on the side of the Allies. The Nazis were bullies, murderers and everything else she despised.

They made the rest of the walk in silence.

Mary was waiting at the door of the bar. "I was wondering where you got to, now I see you had company."

The admiring looks her cousin sent Tony made Kate blush. Mary was forward, at least that's how Kate's mother described it. But Kate knew her cousin was only being friendly. She was besotted with her fiancé, Ciaran, and they were saving like mad to get married.

"Mrs. Scanlan refused to serve Tony as she thought he was English. He was after a stamp."

"She's an aul witch, that woman. I know her husband was murdered but not everyone is like the Black and Tans. Come into the bar and I'll pour you a pint for your trouble."

"No trouble. I should be getting back to the camp. Nice to meet you, Mary, and you too, Kate."

Mary winked at Kate before addressing Tony. "Before you go, we're having a dance on Saturday night. You'll come, won't you? And bring your friends. It's the British night this weekend."

"The British night?" Kate mumbled.

"The dances are segregated. The Germans have theirs one night of the weekend and the English the other. Otherwise fights break out. Senseless really, as they're both locked up here for the duration of the war, but sure when would you expect men to behave sensibly? Too fond of killing each other for their own good." Mary turned back through the door, leaving Kate alone with Tony.

"Sorry," Kate muttered. "Mary didn't mean to be insulting."

"Don't be. I guess most women share that view. Mom certainly does. She said if wars were started by women there wouldn't be any." Tony fiddled with his collar. "Will you be going to the dance?"

"I'll be working the bar, no doubt," Kate replied, enjoying the look of disappointment on his face. "I'll get a few breaks, though. Mary will see to it."

"Good. Will you dance with me?"

Kate knew she should pretend to think about it. Men didn't like girls being forward, but she couldn't play games. She nodded, not quite able to say yes. He smiled and her butterflies exploded all over again.

"I'd best get inside." Her voice trembled. She wanted to stay chatting. "Mary's patience won't last forever."

He moved closer, the scent of Brylcreem wafting up her nose. Her heart raced before almost stopping when he whispered, "See you Saturday, Kate." She couldn't move as he walked away whistling, despite a few dirty looks thrown in his direction from a group of boys across the street.

A local man, Fergal Scanlan, strode straight over. "You shouldn't be encouraging them, Kate Ryan," he spat.

Her eyes narrowed as her temper flared. She snapped back, "Go away with ya, Fergal. I was only passing the time of day. I got work to be doing."

Kate pushed the door open and closed it quickly behind her, relieved Fergal didn't follow her. The last time she was staying with Uncle Pat, he'd forced her to kiss him. She could still smell his breath, feel his sweaty hands as they pawed at her body. She dreaded to think what would have happened if Uncle Pat hadn't shouted for her to get to bed. Hell would freeze over before she found herself alone with him again.

NINE

Kate hurried back from the farmers' market where she had gone to see if there was any seafood available, it being Friday and meat forbidden. In peacetime, the market always had a supply of fresh fish caught off the coast. Her mouth watered as she remembered the crabs, plaice and sole. But today there had been nothing available. Someone said the supplier couldn't get enough petrol to make the trip down from Howth in Dublin.

When she got back, wondering how she'd tell her uncle it would be just vegetables for dinner, Mark Donnelly was waiting at the door. By his side was a fishing rod and in his hand was a small parcel wrapped up in old newspaper.

He held it out to her, his eyes not meeting hers, as a scarlet flush made its way across his cheeks.

"I caught some trout and had some spare. Thought you might like it for dinner."

"Oh, Mark, I could kiss ye. I couldn't find anything at the market and Uncle Pat wouldn't be keen on just vegetables. Thank you kindly. Are you sure you have enough for your own family?"

"Plenty. And your uncle looks out for us. Least I could do." He all but ran away. Kate twirled around at the sound of Mary laughing.

"You got an admirer there, so you have. He's a bit young for ye though but a safer bet in the eyes of your mother than an American airman."

"Mary! Stop it, he'll hear ya. He's just a child and as he said, Uncle Pat has done a lot for the Donnellys."

"He might be a child but he has a man's love for ya." Mary poked the newspaper. "I hope he thought to gut it, I hate that part."

"I'll do it." Kate took the fish into the kitchen and set about preparing dinner, her thoughts consumed with a blond airman with the loveliest accent she'd ever heard.

Kate and Mary stood behind the bar, busy serving endless rounds of drinks. She was glad of the polished strong wooden counter between her and the crowd of men. Thank goodness her uncle had got Con in to collect the glasses, the young lad slipping easily between all the customers. He was earning a few tips as well as she saw his hand go regularly to his pocket. She smiled at him warmly as he placed more dirty glasses on the counter.

"Con, will you take these up to the lads, they must be getting thirsty with their playing." She indicated the musicians with a nod of her head.

"For sure. Paddy said his mouth was as dry as..." Con turned scarlet, catching himself before adding lamely, "The hay in the fields."

Amused, Kate looked back at the talented local musicians. Paddy could make almost any instrument sing, from the violin to the bodhran to the tin whistle. Uncle Pat said Paddy could draw tears from a stone when he had a mind to.

She wasn't comfortable serving so many Germans, feeling guilty thinking of Joe and Frank worrying about a Nazi torpedo ending their days. She didn't blame Uncle Pat for accepting their custom, times were tough and he could use their money to help families that desperately needed it, like the Donnellys, but she didn't have to be glad about being involved, did she?

"It's busy even for a Friday. The Germans' ambassador sent them some money so they have plenty to spend." Uncle Pat surveyed his pub, packed to the rafters with a crowd like from the days before the war. "The women seem to like the company, anyway. Makes a change I guess from the Irish lads with their two left feet."

"Nothing wrong with our lads, Uncle Pat. Aren't you one of them?" Kate laughed to take the sting out of her words.

"They are great dancers, aren't they?" Mary indicated the men on the floor. "Nice manners too. Hard to believe that they are fighting for a man like Hitler."

"Hmmm." Kate was torn. Her cousin was right, yet many of them insisted on wearing their uniform even with the authorities encouraging the camp *guests* to wear civilian clothes. The day after she'd met Tony at the post office, she had cycled out near the camp and had heard them marching, singing their songs and making the Hitler salute. How could such normal-appearing men support the murder of innocents? If only a fraction of the stories being reported in the papers were true, Hitler and the rest of the Nazi elite had no hearts. They were Satan's forces and they were the ones trying to kill Joe, Frank and other men just like them.

One of the Germans appeared in front of her. Like Tony he had blond hair but his eyes were a dark green color and his face more square than chiseled. "Will you dance?" he asked.

"Sorry, I'm working."

Just as she apologized, Mary spoke up. "Go on now, have a break, Kate. She's a wonderful dancer and you should hear her sing. Got a voice like an angel, she has."

Kate threw a daggered look in Mary's direction, but her cousin ignored her.

"Please, just one dance. It will make me very happy. My name is Franz." He bowed and clicked his heels.

Mary nudged Kate. "Go on, will ya. The poor man is barely out of short trousers."

Kate handed the dishtowel to her cousin, lifted the countertop and walked out. Franz offered her his arm to walk her onto the dance floor. He had lovely manners, if a bit formal given the tiny dance area of the pub.

Holding her at the waist, he expertly led her around the floor in a waltz. He made it seem easy and she wished Sister Marian from school could see her now. She always said Kate was as clumsy as an elephant dancing. Kate couldn't help smiling.

"You like to dance? I love it. Back home I dance every week. With Ingrid, my girl." The bleak look in his eyes spoke to her. Mary was right, he was very young.

"Do you write to her?"

"Yes, but she does not write back. It's a big disgrace to be taken prisoner and sit behind the wire during a war."

"It's not your fault. You didn't crash your plane on purpose, did you?"

"Crash a plane? I don't understand. I am not a pilot, I'm a navigator. It's my fault we landed in Ireland. My friend, he broke his leg. Another broke his back. They are in hospital and we are here." He looked like a lost puppy. She found herself feeling sorry for him despite what he represented. Maybe it was because he was wearing civvies so looked like a normal man rather than a Nazi.

He twirled her around in perfect pace to the music. "Try to write to Ingrid again. Maybe your letter went missing. She's probably missing you."

His step faltered but he recovered quickly. "It is not that simple. Her parents..." He shrugged. He looked so bereft she wanted to help him out.

"They don't agree with you being a couple?"

He nodded.

"Maybe they'll change their minds."

"I don't think so. Her parents do not like my family, their beliefs." He must have spotted the confusion on her face. "Her father is a Nazi, he loves Hitler."

"Aren't you all?" Kate immediately regretted her question as he stopped dancing and stepped back.

His eyes were like flint, his lips set in a thin line as he hissed, "I am not a Nazi. I fight for Germany but not for Hitler." He glanced around him, moving closer perhaps out of fear of being overheard. "What he is doing is wrong. Please excuse me, I do not wish to dance anymore. Good evening, Fräulein." He clicked his heels and walked away, leaving her standing staring at him. She was tempted to go after him but before she could, a regular customer spotted her. The band had stopped playing so his voice carried, across the room.

"Kate, sing 'My Bonnie Irish Lass'," he shouted.

Paddy moved with the speed of a young fella as he grabbed his fiddle and started playing the haunting melody, demanding over the sound of the music, "Kate, get over here and sing like the angel ye are."

Kate walked over and stood in front of the band, as the lyrical music washed over her.

Come over the hills, to your bonny blue-eyed lass
Come over the hills to your darling
You choose the road, love, and I'll make the vow
And I'll be your sweetheart forever.

She gestured for the crowd to join in with the chorus, smiling as the roof nearly came off the top of the pub with the volume of singing. She was surprised to find tears glistening in the eyes of some of their German visitors.

Red is the rose that in yonder garden grows
Fair is the lily of the valley
Clear is the water that flows from the Boyne
But my love is fairer than any.

As Kate finished the last line of the last chorus, the crowd went wild, breaking into thunderous applause.

"Kate, sing for us again," the man said.

She tried to protest but people started chanting. "Song, song, Kate, sing another song. Sing 'The Rocky Road to Dublin'."

They clapped their hands and stamped their feet. Paddy pulled out his bodhran, his skill raising the goosebumps on her arm, and started beating out the rhythm of the robust song, the crowd picking it up and clapping along. Kate sighed, not sure she'd be able to get to the end of the song without crying. She started to sing, her voice matching the tempo of Paddy's beat, closing her eyes as the words reminded her of Joe and his journey from Galway to Dublin. Everyone in the pub, young and old, knew the words. The Germans were the only ones not singing but they listened and clapped along.

Everyone cheered at the end of the song, apart from Kate, who fought to keep the tears at bay, the lyrics being too close to home, reminding her of Joe. When would he be home again?

Once the singing had died down, Kate retreated behind the bar and didn't venture out dancing again.

"What did you do to poor Franz?" asked Mary. "He left here like his butt was on fire."

"Mary, do you have to be so coarse? I insulted him but I didn't mean to. I should have kept my big mouth shut."

"Ah, go on with ya. Don't worry about him, he'll have forgotten about it tomorrow, you wait and see. Anyway, I thought you only had eyes for the American." Mary flicked the edge of the dishcloth at Kate. Kate smiled but turned back to washing the glasses. She didn't want her cousin to see the effect even Tony's name had on her. It was silly. She didn't even know him.

Despite herself, Kate's stomach fluttered at the thought of the dance the next night. What would it feel like for Tony to hold her in his arms?

TEN

Kate shivered as she stripped off her clothes and gave herself a quick top and tail wash at the basin in her room. She'd heard of some houses up in Dublin having indoor plumbing and bathrooms upstairs. What would it be like to be able to run a bath by turning on a tap? Or using a toilet that didn't involve a trek across the backyard?

Mary knocked on the door before walking in. Kate grabbed the towel to cover her embarrassment. Not that her cousin noticed.

"Kate, wear this one." Mary held up a navy-blue dress with a polka dot bodice and bolero jacket. Kate had never seen anything so pretty.

"I can't. It's gorgeous, Mary. Where did you get it?"

"Da's friend up in Belfast sent down the material—it came from an old ball gown, but nobody around here would know. She sent the dress pattern too and old Mrs. Hennessy made it up for me. Lucky she was a rebel in her youth, there aren't many of the old women around here would sew it. They think it's immoral but it's the latest fashion. I saw it when I went to the films. Da nearly keeled over when I wore it the first time. It's a bit tight around the waist for me but on you it'll be perfect. Go on, try it on."

Kate fingered the material. "It's very fitted, Mary. I'm not sure Mam would approve."

Mary rolled her eyes, poking Kate through the towel, aiming for her stomach.

"She's not here, is she? Go on, you're only young once. Just try it and see what it looks like. Then if you want to wear that old dress of yours again, I won't say a word."

Kate returned her cousin's grin. She knew her old dress wasn't suitable for dancing but it was the best she had. Her mam didn't see fit to waste money on new clothes. Mary turned her back and, throwing caution to the wind, Kate tore off the towel and slipped on Mary's gorgeous dress. The material clung to her like a second skin, the skirt feeling like it had been made for her. She put on the shiny black Oxford-style leather shoes, wondering how she could walk in three-inch heels.

"I never knew you had such a small waist," said Mary, eyeing her cousin up and down. "I'll ask Mrs. Hennessey to take it in a little for the next time you wear it. But otherwise, it's perfect. You look like a younger version of that Hollywood actress, Carole Lombard—you know, the lady who died flying around America trying to sell bonds or something. Lucky thing was married to Clark Gable."

Kate's eyes bulged. "Mary, she's dead."

Mary shrugged, walking around Kate, pulling at the bodice a little bit. "You do look like her. Apart from your hair color."

"I don't know about that but I don't look like me. Not at all." Kate gazed at the reflection in the mirror.

Mary pulled her hair back, styling it around her face. Then she pinched Kate's cheeks, making them flush.

"Wait there. Don't move."

Within seconds, Mary rushed back and twisted Kate away from the mirror. Without asking, she put a slick of red lipstick and a little eye make-up on her cousin, making Kate's eyes look even bigger. "Just a lick of mascara and your mam wouldn't recognize you. See?"

She twirled Kate around to look at herself. Struck dumb, Kate could only stare at her reflection.

"Mary, you're a genius. But the skirt is a bit short, isn't it?"

"Ankle-length dresses haven't been fashionable for about twenty years, my darling cousin. That mother of yours has you dressing like a nun. Yes, I know that's what she wants you to become but what about you? Surely you have your own dreams. Even if you do want to join the nuns, why not live a little first? With that dress, you're going to have to fight them off tonight."

Kate tried to argue but Mary wasn't listening. Her cousin disappeared only to return shortly with her father in tow.

"Aren't you a sight for sore eyes, Kate Ryan," her uncle said upon seeing her. "Reminds me of what your mother looked like the first time your da set eyes on her. Lost he was, from that first look."

Kate tried—but failed—to imagine her mother looking stylish. She was always dressed in an old wrap-around apron, apart from when she went to Mass wearing a long black dress and a lace mantilla over her head.

"Thanks, Uncle Pat, but I don't think Mam would have worn anything like this."

"You'd be surprised. Your mother was quite a lively young thing back in the day. Before she got consumed by that religion of hers after your da got injured. Pity as she was a right looker. Relax, girl, there is no point in wearing a fabulous outfit if you look like you are wearing someone else's clothes. You look beautiful." As Kate's cheeks heated, her uncle continued, "Only wish that mother of yours had the sense she was born with and knew how to treat you to appreciate the gifts God gave you."

"Listen to Da," chimed in Mary. "He wouldn't let you out looking like a strumpet, would you?"

Uncle Pat glared at his daughter. "Don't be using that sort of language, young lady. You may be an adult, but you still live in my house." Then he turned his focus back to his niece. "Kate, wear the dress with pride. There's no sin in looking pretty. You're a beautiful Irish rose. If I had a camera, I'd take a picture and send it to your da. That would pick him up better than any medicine."

Uncle Pat mopped his eyes with a hanky before gruffly reminding them it was getting busy down in the bar. Kate hugged her cousin.

"Thank you, Mary. You are so good to me."

"You're like the little sister I never had. Here, go down. I'll be there in a few minutes."

Kate walked down the stairs and into the bar, turning scarlet as the patrons of the bar whistled when they saw her.

"Leave the girl alone now, lads. You see her every day," Uncle Pat admonished the crowd but he beamed at his niece.

"Not dressed like that. You scrub up well, Kate, if only I was ten years younger." Paddy held his whiskey up to her. Everyone laughed.

"More like fifty, Paddy, and that's being kind," Uncle Pat replied, with a wink at him. "Kate, put on an apron and wash up those glasses, there's a good girl."

"Yes, Uncle Pat." Kate moved slowly, getting used to the higher heels, but by the time the airmen arrived, she was gliding along, thrilled by the number of compliments coming her way. She had never been vain but it was nice to be appreciated. Then her eyes locked with Tony's and everyone else faded into the background.

"You look stunning. I heard all Irish girls were beautiful, but you are absolutely gorgeous." He reached out a hand to pick up a tendril of her hair. "Never seen such a glorious color."

"Thank you, kind sir," she joked back, a thrill running through her veins at the look in his eyes.

"Will you keep all your dances for me?"

"Sorry, you're too late, my book is full." She tried not to laugh at the look of despair her words caused. "I'm joking. Nobody has asked me to dance."

"Nobody? Are they all blind?"

"I may have been moving too fast to hear them," she confessed, giggling at the expression of relief on his face.

"Your book is full now. I want every dance."

"I don't think my uncle would like that. He needs my help behind the bar."

Tony glanced in Uncle Pat's direction. "How about you work behind the bar for some of the time but for every waltz, you dance with me? Deal?"

Kate nodded, not trusting her voice to stay steady. She dipped behind the bar, grateful for the barrier the countertop provided. She needed to gain control of her racing heart. A few customers wanted serving and she busied herself pulling pints, pouring whiskeys and fetching water or soft drinks.

The crowd chanted for the band to start, so Paddy knocked back his drink and with a swipe across his mouth courtesy of his jumper, jumped up onto the stage and with his fiddle under his chin, played the first gig of the evening. The gig got faster and faster as the couples danced around the floor, their speed increasing to keep pace with the music. Kate beat out the rhythm on the bar counter, clapping with everyone when the dance ended. Afterwards, Tony stood waiting for her at the counter and, with a wink, Paddy picked up the fiddle again to play the first waltz.

Uncle Pat turned to her. "Off you go and dance, Kate. This young American was brought up properly and asked me for permission. Don't keep him waiting."

Kate smiled at her uncle as he lifted the counter for her to slip out. Taking her hand, Tony led her to the dance floor where other couples were already dancing. The airman held her politely and kept a proper distance between them but she was all too aware of his body so near to hers as he moved gracefully.

"You know how to dance properly. Did you have lessons?" she asked.

He leaned in closer, speaking softly. His breath tickled her skin, sending delicious tremors through her body.

"Mom insisted I know how to treat a lady properly. She said it's difficult to wear high heels with bruised ankles."

Kate couldn't imagine her mam having such a conversation with Joe.

They glided around the small floor, whispering about this and that, but even when they fell silent, there was no awkwardness between them. All too soon the music ended and everyone stood back to clap. The next dance was a lively jig. Another airman asked for a dance, but she declined, citing the need to return to her duties behind the bar. As she walked past the customers, Fergal Scanlan grabbed her arm. "Dance with me."

"Not now. Uncle Pat needs me to help out."

"He can manage the bar. Come on, let's show them how to dance."

Fergal's grip tightened. She looked around but Uncle Pat was distracted, the crowd at the bar three deep. By the determined look in Fergal's eyes, she knew his temper would explode if she refused again.

She let him lead her to the dance floor but despite her best efforts to stay out of his range, he insisted on dragging her close even though the jig didn't call for it.

"Fergal," she hissed, not wanting her uncle or, worse, the other customers to come to her aid and make a scene, "keep your hands off me or I will walk off the floor."

"You weren't so fussy with your airman, were yea?" he sneered. "All tarted up like a dog's dinner for the English and won't even let one of your own dance with yea."

"I'm not dressed for anyone but myself. Stop it." She glared at him as he pulled her close again. Catching Mary's eye over his shoulder, she gestured for her help. Her cousin nodded, walked to where the band was playing and announced a change in the program.

"You've been begging for Kate to sing for ye tonight. Now you get your wish. Come over here, Kate, and sing something for us."

Fergal's grip on her arm tightened. She tried but failed to pull loose.

"Let me go," she muttered.

"You heard the lady. Let her go." Tony stood to her side, his hardening eyes fixed on Fergal.

"Nothing to do with you. Mind yer own business."

"You heard the landlord's daughter. The customers have asked for Miss Ryan to sing. Let her go. Now."

"Will you make me?" Fergal dropped Kate's arm. As he pushed her behind him, her heel caught in a groove in the flagstone floor, and she stumbled. Tony caught her before she fell but his gallant action put her right in line of Fergal's fist, which crashed into her face. Stars burst into life as the pain burned through her cheek.

"Kate, are you okay?" She heard Tony's voice but couldn't seem to respond. The pain in her face receded as a black cloud enveloped her, and her legs gave way under her.

She woke later, lying on her bed, fully dressed. Doctor Sixsmith stood by the side of the bed, while Mary, on the other side, applied a wet cloth to her cheek.

"You're back with us, Kate. You gave us a fright, young lady, passing out like that. I thought you'd been hit in the temple." The doctor took her hand, eyeing his watch with his fingers placed on her pulse. "It's lucky for you, I'd just dropped in for a medicinal whiskey." He winked as he placed her arm back on the cover.

Kate tried to sit up, suddenly feeling dizzy. The room swam around her. Mary put her arm around her back to help her.

"My cheek... feels like it was burned."

"You'll have a bruise for a few weeks but your bone wasn't broken, amazingly enough. Luck was on your side. The same can't be said for young Fergal. By the time the men had finished with him, he was lucky to be alive."

"Tony?"

"Is that the name of the young man you were dancing with? No, he wasn't involved. He carried you to this room and took his temper out on the wall outside. I think your uncle will be sending him a bill for new plaster."

"Paddy and a couple of the regulars took Fergal outside and taught him a lesson," said Mary. "He'll think twice before he puts a hand on a woman again. About time too."

"Paddy?" asked Kate, shocked.

"You'd never think it but he can move fast when he wants to. Despite his reputation as a ladies' man, aul Paddy can't bear two things. Bad manners and lack of respect. He said Fergal needed a lesson. It'll be a while before that lad shows his face around the town. Da barred him from the pub."

"I don't think he meant to hit me. I stumbled and—"

"Don't you dare tell me you fell onto his hand, Kate Ryan." Mary plumped the pillow behind Kate's head. "There were plenty of witnesses. Fergal had more than a skinful and his lesson was coming. The men dealt with it. Let that be the end. Now, do you feel up to visitors? There's a young man outside who has waited patiently until the doc said it was okay to see you."

Kate blushed but nodded, and Mary opened the door to admit Tony, his eyebrows drawn together over a pained expression in his eyes. While the doctor left, Mary hovered in the background for propriety's sake. Even in her injured state, Kate couldn't be left alone in a bedroom with a man not related to the family.

Tony ran his hand gently down her arm, his eyes drawn together, concern fighting with anger in his expression. "I couldn't believe it when I saw you fall and then his fist hit your face," Tony said softly. "How do you feel? You should have a steak on that bruise."

"Waste of a good steak at the best of times never mind during rationing. Uncle Pat loves me but not that much," Kate tried to joke but dropped her act when he didn't smile. "Mary put some salve on it, can you not smell it?"

His nose crinkled as he laughed. "Is that what the stink is? I thought it was an Irish custom to have piglets share your bedroom."

"Oi you, any more of that and you will be out in the pigsty," Mary said with a smile.

Kate looked from one to the other, loving how easy they were in each other's company. Tony was like that. He made whomever he was talking to feel as if they were the most important person in the room. She sighed, not realizing she had made a noise until his gaze locked with hers, making her flush.

"Is the pain bad? Did they give you something for it?"

"I'll be grand. I've had worse although maybe not on my face. The state of me. Was the dance stopped?"

"Half the musicians disappeared out the back of the pub. For a second I thought they'd called the camp guards but it was something else." He shifted uncomfortably from one foot to the other.

"You can relax, they told me what happened to Fergal. I don't like him, but I can't condone violence. It won't solve anything. He'll just take it out on someone else."

"Wise words from a young head," Tony replied. "Has he tried something like this before?"

She was tempted to lie, given the look in his eyes, but it wasn't in her nature. "He tries it on with most girls. Never seen him hit one. I think he may have been aiming for you."

"I think so too. That's why I feel so guilty." He moved from one foot to the other, as if he had an itch he couldn't scratch. He looked everywhere but at her face.

"Tony?"

He darted a glance at the clock. "I'm sorry but I have to get back to the camp or I'll be posted as AWOL. Can I come visit you tomorrow? Please? If you're up to it, we could go for a walk or something."

"I'd like that."

"Why don't you come to dinner?" said Mary. "I can't promise it will be as good as Kate's cooking but Da is partial to roast chicken with potatoes and two veg. There's plenty if you want to join us."

"Don't mind my cousin," replied Kate with a grin, "she's a wonderful cook."

"I'd love to, Mary. Thank you."

"See you about one then. We eat early as we're all starving after being at Mass. Will we see you there?"

Tony colored.

"Mary, will you leave him alone?" said Kate. "You'd swear you were my mam."

"I don't attend Mass," replied a pink-cheeked Tony. "Not anymore. I did as a child but not recently. Is that a problem?"

"Not to me," said Mary, "but you might keep it to yourself. Father Burke will be after you—he likes to save damned souls and there's nothing more sinful than a Catholic who doesn't attend services."

"Mary!" chided Kate, her eyes widening. "Tony, I'm so sorry. Father Burke isn't like that, at least he isn't like the parish priest back home in Galway. Now, he'd march you off to church whether you liked it or not."

"Don't be. I like women who speak their mind. See you tomorrow then." He put his hand over hers and squeezed, sending a thrill up her arm. His eyes met hers and it felt like he could read her mind. "I loved dancing with you tonight. You felt at home in my arms." The last words were whispered and Kate smiled back, unable to put her thoughts into words. He had scrambled her brains and she couldn't think straight.

The Sunday sermon dragged on even longer than normal. The church was packed and the heat stifling, but Father Burke didn't appear to notice. During the service, Kate saw the locals staring at her, whispering behind their hands. She spotted Fergal sitting toward the back, his mother's face a picture as she glared at every person who dared glance their way. The priest continued talking—if he noticed the atmosphere in his church, he wasn't going to let it get in the way.

After church, the men gathered in circles outside while the women chatted as they headed back home to get Sunday dinner on the table. Children darted here and there, enjoying their freedom after hours spent on their knees during Mass.

Kate hurried home, not wanting to listen to any more gossip

about what happened to her face. Hopefully nobody would write to her mam or she might insist on Kate coming home. She hadn't gone far when a shadow emerged from behind Mrs. Scanlan's store.

"Fergal, you put the heart across me jumping out like that."

"Kate, I just... Listen, I'm sorry. I didn't mean to catch you with my fist. You know I'd never hurt you." His cheeks flushed, sweat dripping from his brow. He impatiently swiped it away before stuttering, "Not just 'cause you're a woman, but you... well, you probably guess how I feel about ya."

"I know you didn't do it on purpose. I didn't agree with what happened to you either. But it was too late for me to do anything to stop it."

"I knew you didn't send them after me. You're too kind and thoughtful to do that." His fingers pulled at his shirt collar. "I was hoping... I mean, when you feel better would you like—"

The hairs on the back of her neck stood on end. She didn't want to embarrass him any further.

"Is that the time? I have to hurry or the dinner will be burned. Uncle Pat will never forgive me. Look after yourself." Kate rushed off so he wouldn't get to ask his question.

Once back at the bar, she checked the chicken and the potatoes. She peeled and cut the carrots, washed the cabbage and put both on top of the stove. She loved cooking in Pat's kitchen; it was so modern compared to her mam's. Despite Mary's protests, Kate insisted on cooking because her cousin slaved away in the kitchen all year around. There was nothing wrong with Kate but for a bruised cheek.

As Mary set the table, Uncle Pat came in from the bar, sniffing his nose appreciatively. "My stomach thinks my throat was cut, I'm that starved. I thought Father Burke would never stop talking this morning." Pat looked at the table. "Are we having guests? Not Father Burke, for the love of God. I mean, he's a nice man and much easier on the ear than most priests, but I've had enough talk to last me the day."

"No, Uncle Pat, it's Tony. The airman who I was dancing with last night. Mary invited him as a thank you for looking after me."

"I don't think he expects any thanks. Think he'd walk to the ends of Ireland for you for a smile. He has it bad, the poor fella."

Kate caught the grin on Mary's face as her cousin checked the table settings.

"Uncle Pat!" Flustered, Kate tried to distract herself by checking the chicken wasn't burning. She wanted the skin crispy not charred.

"It's not that long ago when I was chasing your auntie around the country. She made me prove myself over and over before she agreed to marry me."

"Da, stop it. You're embarrassing Kate with the marriage talk. They only danced the once. Don't be talking like that when Tony arrives."

"You mean he hasn't asked you to be buried with his people yet?"

Kate nearly dropped the dish when she heard Tony laugh, not believing he had heard her uncle's teasing.

"We use a more romantic turn of phrase where I come from, Mr. Ryan. Is it all right to come through? I knocked but Paddy said you wouldn't hear me." Tony stood in the doorway, his cheeks flushed but a determined look in his eyes. He carried a bunch of wild white lady cushion mixed with yellow cowslips, purple clover and some heathers in one hand, a bottle of whiskey in the other.

"Come in and sit down, lad."

"This is for you, even if it feels funny giving a publican a bottle of drink." Tony glanced at Kate. "I tried to get wine but there's not much call for it in the camp."

"I'll take the flowers." Uncle Pat kept his face straight, leaving Mary to rescue Tony.

"Thank you for the whiskey. Don't mind me da, he's only teasing you," said Mary. "Come away in. Kate insisted on cooking dinner. Will I take those from you?" Mary indicated the flowers, which Tony handed over without dropping his gaze from Kate's face.

"Thank you for the flowers and everything," said Kate. "Dinner is almost ready. Do you prefer the brown or white meat?" What was she saying? Uncle Pat would carve the bird at the table and he could have asked that. Of course, Pat didn't miss the chance to embarrass her.

"What she's asking is, is it the breast or the leg you prefer, lad?"

Mary shrieked. "Da! That's enough out of you. Get back into the pub and we'll call you when it is served." She shooed him out of the kitchen, sending a look of apology in Kate's direction. They could hear Uncle Pat still laughing from the other side of the door.

As Kate felt Tony's eyes on her, she looked up and they exchanged a smile, his cheeks looking as hot as hers felt.

"Why don't you sit down while I just finish off the gravy?"

"Can I not do something to help?"

Kate stared at him for a second before dragging her eyes back to the gravy. A man offering to help in the kitchen. That was a new one.

"No, just sit down and make yourself comfortable. I hope you're hungry. I feel a bit guilty having all this food when so many have so little but Uncle Pat works so hard, he needs his strength."

"Seeing as he either grows or rears everything you're using, I think you should be proud of yourself for your cooking skills. It smells delicious." He took a seat at the opposite side of the table so he could still see her. "I remember the lines for soup kitchens during the Depression back home. Is it as bad here?"

"It's worse in the cities like Dublin where some of the children haven't seen any fruit or vegetables in months. Doctor Sixsmith says there's been an increase in rickets. That's where the children's legs are bowed. As if things weren't bad enough after the Depression."

"Kate is always worrying about everyone else, she's like her da like that," said Mary. "Would give the coat off her back to someone who she thought needed it more."

"Would you stop, Mary. I'm no saint."

Mary winked at Tony but Kate pretended she didn't see.

"I agree with Kate. It's nice to help others. Mom would say that it's our duty to give to those who need help. She was always sending food baskets to those who were ill or lost their jobs. The Depression hit our neighborhood hard. In Colorado and other places in the States, lots of people who worked in the factories lost their jobs and their kids went hungry. Dad had his own store, so we had it easier than most, I guess."

Mary carried the roast chicken on a wooden platter to the table as Kate dished up the carrots, cabbage, peas and roast potatoes onto the plates.

"Da?" Mary called out to her father. "You can come back in now."

Mary sat at the foot of the table as her father walked into the kitchen, sniffing the air appreciatively. He took his place at the head of the table just as Kate placed a full plate in front of him. She gave Mary and Tony theirs before taking her own and sitting opposite Tony.

Uncle Pat picked up the carving knife and cut into the roast chicken, passing a plate around with the various cuts of meat. Kate grinned as Tony sighed as the lovely scent of cooked meat filled the air.

"Thanks be to God I don't have to eat that black loaf they call bread," said Uncle Pat. "There is no wheat in that thing at all. Serving that in the cities they are, while in some parts of the country there's talk of people starving like they did in the famine years. Churchill did us wrong when he said Ireland wouldn't get a bit of the foodstuff that made it over on the merchant ships. And sure, many of those very shipmen are Irish lads. But we got our own back on him."

Tony swallowed the food in his mouth before asking, "How was that, sir?"

"Guinness, lad, the pint of the black stuff. When Churchill made his announcement, our government did the same. They stopped all export of Guinness until the end of the Emergency, as it's called around these parts."

Uncle Pat shoveled another huge helping into his mouth, chewing loudly. Kate couldn't help but compare his lack of manners to the way Tony ate, slowly and quietly as if savoring every bite. The airman caught her looking at him and smiled, opening his mouth to say something but Uncle Pat got in first.

"Sure, it almost led to riots on the streets of Belfast when they heard they weren't getting any more black Irish gold up there. That soon changed their tune. We might be a small nation but there's a reason we've been a thorn in the side of the English since time began. We're a stubborn, contrary race and that's the truth, lad. Best to know that before you get serious about one of our women. Beautiful and kind she might be, but Kate has Irish Fenian blood running through her veins. Dangerous combination with her red hair."

"Uncle Pat!"

"Da!"

Kate and Mary spoke at once.

"Tony, don't mind my da," carried on Mary, laying her cutlery on her clean plate. "He's the one who gets ornery just like the donkey in the backyard. Kate and I are saints to put up with him, isn't that right, cousin?"

Ever the peacemaker, Kate changed the subject. "Anyone like anything else? There's more potatoes and vegetables going spare."

"No, thank you, Kate," replied Tony. "The meal was delicious, but I've eaten too much."

"Uncle Pat?"

"I'll have another piece of meat if you have some gravy. You're a grand cook, Kate. Another one of your many talents." Uncle Pat stared at Tony, who turned scarlet. Kate pushed back from the table, the noise of the dishes shaking breaking that moment.

"I've got stewed apples and cream for afters. I couldn't make a crumble as I used the last of the flour in the gravy. Will you have a cup of tea with it, or after?"

"Make a pot now, will you, Kate? Mary keeps telling me I need to start living on the rations rather than paying the high prices on the black market. I guess I should listen and do my bit for the war effort." Uncle Pat looked so reluctant everyone laughed.

"I'll make up a pot but first, I just want to make up a plate for Paddy to bring home to his wife." Kate cleared the plates from the table before wiping her hands on her apron. "I saw Mrs. McCormack in the village and she's skin and bones. Times are tough for a lot of people. I know her children in America were sending home packages to her, but I guess the war has stopped that for now."

"Paddy's married?" Tony asked, his expression doubtful.

Mary nodded. "Coming up on fifty years, isn't it, Da? He said his wife was a child bride."

"She's a saint, that's what she is," said Uncle Pat. "The poor woman spends more time alone than she does with her husband. I didn't realize they were so short of money; he'd drink more than I can give him. You should drop the food into her house, love. If you leave it to Paddy, it's likely to end up on the street. My bar would fall down if anything happened to him. It's got used to him propping it up."

"Never stopped you serving him though, did it, Da?" Mary winked as she teased her father. Kate loved the easy-going relationship they enjoyed but it also made her wish that things were different in her family. She dished up the dessert and tea and everyone was silent while they enjoyed it.

"Kate, why don't you take a walk with your young man?" said Uncle Pat. "Enjoy the fresh air after all that hard work. You can drop off the food to Paddy's wife on your way."

Tony's eyes lit up and his grin nearly split his face in two. "Thanks, Mr. Ryan, we'd like that wouldn't we, Kate?"

"Taking the reins already, lad. Just watch your behavior around my niece. Like another daughter she is and I don't want to have to dig out the shotgun I shouldn't have under my bed upstairs."

"I saw the gun over the bar, sir."

"That one is just for show." Uncle Pat held Tony's gaze. "The powerful one is hidden under the mattress. It has a real kick to it, if you take my meaning."

"Uncle Pat!" Mortified, Kate hid her flushing face from Tony's view. She grabbed the basket she had prepared and headed toward the back door, not waiting to see if the airman was following. She heard Tony say his goodbyes before he joined her out in front of the pub.

"Slow down a little, you'll give me indigestion. It's been a long time since I ate so much food. I feel like a turkey before Thanksgiving."

"Before what? Is that the American word for Christmas?"

He shook his head, his eyes dancing with amusement. "Haven't you heard of Thanksgiving? Don't you have it here in Ireland?"

"If we did, I wouldn't think it was Christmas, would I?" She took the sting out of the retort by nudging him gently.

"I guess you wouldn't. It's a national holiday back home where families get together to give thanks for all the good things they have. Mom cooks the traditional turkey and lots of side dishes such as green beans, mashed potatoes, creamed corn and then, for afters, we have pumpkin pie. That's my favorite." He rubbed his stomach.

"Pumpkin pie?"

"Yes, you know the thing you make lanterns out of at Halloween."

She grabbed his arm to stop him walking into a pothole full of water. "We carve up turnips for Halloween and if you say you'd like a dessert made from turnips I think you must have hit your head when you fell out of your plane."

"You just wait, Miss Ryan. One day I will take you for pumpkin pie and you will eat your words."

He stopped to stand in front of her, his gaze lingering on her mouth before returning to her eyes. She couldn't breathe, couldn't think of anything but the fact he was so close to her.

He leaned in, whispering, "What would you do if I told you how much I'd love to kiss you right now?"

She closed her eyes, wondering if he would. Then she heard

the sound of a child laughing, bringing her back to her senses. They were on the main street of the village where anyone could see them.

She moved away from him. "I'd give you a slap just like any other well brought up young lady."

"Maybe it would be worth it."

His words make her skin tingle.

Tony took her arm and together they walked on down the street.

"Watch out, Kate Ryan, I shall steal a kiss soon enough."

Kate giggled as he waggled his eyebrows. It was silly but she felt so comfortable around him when it was just the two of them.

Paddy's house was a mile or so outside the village, down a lane almost overrun with bushes and gorse. Reluctantly, they broke apart to walk single file, Tony walking ahead holding back the worst of the brambles out of her way, saying, "Someone could do with cutting these back."

"Aye and clearing the road too. But look at that view."

They both stopped to gaze down at the view. The McCormack house was built on a hill overlooking the village. They could see the camp in the distance to one side but to the other they spotted a lake and behind it the Wicklow Mountains. "Isn't it beautiful?"

"Not as beautiful as you."

With that, Tony pulled her close and kissed her. She should have pushed him away but she was powerless to resist him, and she clung closer. He had his spare hand at the back of her neck, his other holding the basket for Paddy's wife. After a few minutes, they broke apart, breathing heavily. She couldn't speak, running her fingers over her lips, feeling shy.

"Sorry I couldn't wait any longer. I've wanted to kiss you since the first time I saw you, standing in the middle of the crowded bar."

"You were too busy arguing with Paddy to notice me," she

teased, almost frightened at the expression in his eyes mirroring how she was feeling. "We'd best get on."

She led the way a little further up the lane until they came to the house. She heard his intake of breath.

"It was once so beautiful," she explained. "Mary says Paddy's father planted the orchard for his wife and it was his pride and joy. When Paddy's children were small they used to play in the trees. Mary remembers climbing them and picking the best-tasting apples. But now... it's gone back to nature. Paddy lost interest years back and I guess Mrs. McCormack can't cope on her own. Not at her age."

She knocked on the peeling front door, the paint coming off as she rubbed against it. She tried to hide her shock when Paddy's wife opened the door. Mrs. McCormack's sunken cheeks and glassy eyes suggested she was fighting a fever. But when she spoke her voice was crystal clear and strong.

"Kate Ryan, what brings you up this way?" She put her hand to her hip. "Not that it isn't lovely to see ya, of course."

"We were out for a walk. We cooked too much for dinner—I don't think Uncle Pat likes my cooking as much as Mary's." Kate tried but failed to lighten the mood. "Rather than let the food go to waste, I... I mean, Uncle Pat thought you might enjoy it."

The woman hesitated, her hand half out, her forehead wrinkling as she shook her head. Kate kicked herself; she had hurt the woman's pride, which was all she had left.

"As payment for Paddy's musical services, of course, if that's acceptable to you. I know hard cash would be better but that's difficult these days. Uncle Pat said to tell you, Paddy's idea to add on space for a dance floor will pay off in future profits."

The relief on the old woman's face told Kate she wasn't fooled but at least she kept her dignity.

"Oh, in that case, we'd be delighted, thank you."

Tony coughed. "Would you like me to carry it inside for you, ma'am?"

Mrs. McCormack rubbed a tear from her eye, as she shook her

head. "No, I can manage. Blessings of the Lord above on ye both. 'Tis an awful bad thing this war, stops my children from sending little things home. A few dollars went a long way. Still, I guess I shouldn't complain. Not with you being so far from home, young man. Where is that accent from? My children are in Boston. I believe it's a lovely place."

"Never been, ma'am. I'm from Colorado myself. That's a bit like Ireland, in that we have plenty of green spaces, when it's not the height of summer that is. We have mountain ranges too and plenty of rivers."

"Really? I thought all places in America were big, much bigger than anything we have in Ireland. Won't you come in and have a cup of tea?"

"No, thank you, ma'am. We are off for a walk to enjoy the sunshine. Another day, perhaps."

Kate watched as his kindness allowed the old woman to keep her pride. She doubted Paddy's wife had enough tea to make a cup for herself, never mind guests.

After they said goodbye, they walked down to the river running through the village. They stopped, throwing some sticks into the water on one side of the bridge and then racing over to the opposite side to see who had won. Tony cheered on his stick as if it were one of the royal yachts, making Kate laugh. She loved his smile, and the way it made his eyes crease up. When he turned to brush a strand of hair out of her eyes, the touch of his hand on her skin made her toes curl. She blushed but when he held out his hand for hers, she gave it to him. Hand in hand, they walked down to where the river widened.

"Will we get in trouble if we take a pew here?" Tony asked.

"A pew?" Kate queried.

He took his jacket off and placed it on the grass on the side of the hill facing the camp. Gesturing for her to sit down, he put an arm around her shoulder, drawing her close. Looking into her eyes as if to ask permission, he leaned in and once again their lips met. She couldn't imagine being anywhere but here in his arms.

But after a while, her mam's voice rang out in her ears. *Nice girls behave themselves.* It sounded so loud in her head she jumped apart, as if her mother had appeared right beside them.

"Sorry, I didn't mean to get carried away. It won't happen again." He moved away before giving her a sheepish look. "Not that I can say I don't want it to."

"'Twas only a kiss. But I think we should talk for a while, get to know one another better. Don't you?"

For a second their eyes locked and she thought he'd refuse. Half of her wanted him to. But instead, he nodded. He picked a daisy from the grass beside them, pulling off the petals as he stared into the distance looking toward the camp.

"I hate being locked up here. I want to be back up there. Fighting back, bringing this war to a faster end."

"What will you do when the war is over? Can you go back to America? I read somewhere that pilots who joined the RAF before the US joined the war couldn't."

"Yeah, that's true but we're hoping they will forgive us. Now the USA is in the war it shouldn't matter, but technically it was illegal for us to join up and by doing so we forfeited our citizenship. But I saw what was happening in Europe and I just couldn't sit back and do nothing. So I went to Canada and joined the Eagle Squadron. Lots of us did. We fought in the Battle of Britain, made a good showing too. When America joined the war in December '41, lots of us applied for transfers to fight Japan but that didn't happen. Not quick enough for me. I was supposed to transfer over to the US flying forces." He threw the daisy away and took her hand in his. Looking as if he was about to kiss her again, he murmured, "If I had, I wouldn't be sitting here."

This was too dangerous. Any more and she would crawl into his arms herself. She moved a little to put some distance between them. "So you just went to war because of what was going on in Germany? Nothing to do with wanting to fly?"

He laughed. "Guilty. I love flying. You must get up in the air one day to understand—there's nothing between you and the rest of the world. Just you and the clouds and so much space. It's just the best feeling ever."

Kate stared up at the cloudless skies, wondering if she'd ever be brave enough to get in a plane. She wasn't at all sure she liked the idea of there being nothing between her and the world. She shook her head. "I think my feet are best kept firmly on the ground."

At the expression of adoration in his eyes, she gulped fleetingly, thinking a truer word was never spoken, even as she surrendered to his kiss.

ELEVEN

August, 1942

"Kate!"

Mary's scream brought Kate running from the barn, Mark, John Joseph and Con Donnelly following close behind her. As they entered the kitchen, Kate came to a standstill, spotting the telegram in Mary's shaking hand.

Heart thudding in her chest, she whispered, "Joe?" even as the voice in her head said the telegram about Joe would go to her parents in Galway.

"HMS *Eagle* was hit by a torpedo, Frank's missing." Mary staggered as she read the words. Mark jumped to her side but Kate's feet felt like they were encased in stone.

"Here, Mary, sit down. Con, go fetch Ciaran. He's working over at Brown's farm. Kate, where is Pat?" Mark took charge. "Kate?" His shout got her attention.

"Sorry, yes, of course. Uncle Pat."

"He's away over to see Kate's parents, went early this morning. How am I going to tell him? He'll worry when your parents get a telegram. Please God they are just missing, maybe they were picked up by another ship or something. What about you, Kate? Will you go home or wait for my da to come back?"

Go home. Kate's first thought was of Tony. She didn't want to leave him but her parents needed her. Joe could be... no, she refused to believe it. She'd know if something had happened.

Kate went into the bar and put a drop of brandy into a glass. Coming back into the kitchen, she handed it to Mary. "Drink that for the shock. I'll ask Mrs. Scanlan if she can place a call to our post office in Galway. They'll send someone to tell Uncle Pat and..." Kate's resolve broke.

Mary jumped up from her chair and wrapped her arms around her. Mark went out muttering about getting water from the well. "Kate, they have to be alive. They just have to be."

Ciaran arrived, his boots bringing half the bog with him. He'd been stacking turf, taking advantage of the sunshine. Kate heard Mark say, "She's inside with Kate, both crying. I didn't know what to do."

"You did grand, son," Ciaran replied softly, his respectful composure telling Kate he believed Frank to be dead. She had to get away.

"Thanks for coming, Ciaran, Mary is in the kitchen. I'm away up to Mrs. Scanlan to ask her to ring Galway. Hopefully someone will know if my parents got similar news."

Ciaran nodded. "I'd say sorry for your—"

Kate interrupted him before he could finish his sentence. "They're missing, not dead." She put her hand out to touch his arm. "Sorry, I didn't mean to snap. I just... well, you know."

"You go on, love, and leave Mary to me. Watch your step."

Kate smiled, trying to stop the tears from falling as she walked away from the house heading for the shop. She wished Tony was with her; he'd wrap his arms around her and make her feel better. She didn't believe Joe or Frank were dead—they were too young, too full of life.

As she drew nearer the shop, it seemed that there were more people than usual hanging around. News traveled fast in a small town. Several women commented along the lines of "Kate, 'tis sorry we are to hear the news."

Father Burke walked out of the shop just as Kate was about to enter.

"I was heading down to the bar to see you and Mary," the priest said. "I know Pat went to Galway this morning. Have you any more news?"

"None, Father, I was about to ask Mrs. Scanlan to put a call in to Galway. Maybe they could tell me more."

"I can do better than that. I've a friend up in Dublin with a contact in the forces. Will I give him a call?"

"Yes, please, Father."

"You go away home. I will put a call in to the camp and ask for Tony to be told. He'll be of comfort to you at a time like this."

Kate's lip trembled at his kindness. "Thank you, Father."

She turned on her heel, heading back to the bar, keeping her head down so as not to engage with any more neighbors. She couldn't bear to listen to their condolences. Not until they knew for sure.

Tony arrived shortly after she did, throwing the bicycle against the barn wall much to Mark's disgust. "Ye'll scrape all the paint."

Kate heard Tony's apology as she pushed open the kitchen door and ran into his arms. "Thank you for coming."

"I came as soon as I heard. How are you feeling?" He shook his head, a wry smile on his lips. "That's the dumbest question ever."

She hugged him in response.

Linking arms, they walked back into the kitchen where Ciaran and Mary sat at the table over another pot of tea.

"Will you have a cup of tea or do you want something stronger, Tony?"

"Water is fine for me, thank you, Mary. I'm sorry about the telegram."

Mary nodded, wiping a tear from her eyes with her hanky. Ciaran glanced at his watch.

"Go on with you," Mary told him. "The turf won't stack itself on the back of the wagon and the weather isn't likely to hold."

"I can do it tomorrow. I'll stay with you," Ciaran protested.

"Why don't we all go? I never gathered turf before but you can show me how it's done and maybe the work will take the girls' mind off things for a while," Tony suggested.

Mary didn't look enthused. "What about the bar?"

"Nobody will expect you to open now. Come on, a couple of hours outside in the sunshine will help. We can't do anything here but wait. Might as well give your man a hand with his chores."

Kate squeezed Tony's hand. His optimism was just what they needed.

"Mark, will you come with us or stay here?"

"I'll stay. I told yer uncle I would clean out the pigsty. If there's any news I will come find you."

Kate saw Tony slip a coin into Mark's hand before they walked in the direction of the bog. It was hard to keep moping in the blazing sunshine. It didn't take long for Tony to get into the swing of things and together they stacked the cut turf in the back of the wagons.

"We'll be glad of all this when Jack Frost comes to visit this winter," Mary commented as she wiped the sweat from her brow.

"Mam will be gathering in the turf too. Some of the local lads will help her as Da can't do much lifting." Kate exchanged a look with Tony. She wondered where they would both be this coming winter.

The sun had fallen, the wind rising by the time they finished. "Look, that's Father Burke. He can't be coming to help, can he?"

Mary and Kate didn't wait to find out. Picking up their skirts, they raced across the bog to meet the priest, who waved at them.

"It's great news. I couldn't wait for ye to come back. Both boys are safe. Joe managed to telegraph your parents, Kate. Mary, you'll get another telegram but my contact in Dublin confirmed there was serious loss of life, but some crew were picked up by other ships nearby. Frank has a concussion." Mary paled so the priest added hastily, "He will be fine after a brief spell in hospital. They may even send him home on leave."

Mary grabbed Kate and together they did a jig. Ciaran and Tony shook the priest's hand, having caught up with their girls.

"I knew they would both be fine, Mary. I told you, they are too young to die," said Kate, beaming.

Mary didn't answer but hugged her close before turning to Ciaran and burying her head in his chest as the tears overwhelmed her.

"Kate, your uncle had more news for you. He said to tell you that your parents said yes."

Mystified, Kate looked to the priest for clarification.

"Pat decided to stay a couple of nights in Galway to celebrate the news with your parents. He asked, Ciaran, if you'd help the girls in the bar." Ciaran nodded, his arm around Mary's shoulders. Father Burke turned to Kate. "Your uncle says your parents have given permission for you to stay until Pat can find new workers to take over from the Donnellys, who are moving to Dublin to live with Siobhan's sister."

Kate knew the Donnellys were leaving but she hadn't realized her uncle intended asking her parents if she could stay. Heart racing, as Tony squeezed her hand, she thanked the priest.

"Thank you, Father, for bringing us the news about the boys. Would you like to come for dinner tomorrow? It's to say goodbye to Siobhan and her family. Mark caught two rabbits so there's plenty to go around."

"I'm bringing a little something to keep the chill from your bones, not that you'd be needing it today." Tony wiped his forehead on his arm. "I'm not sure gathering turf is something I'll miss about Ireland."

Everyone laughed. "Come on, Tony, let's get back to clear the last of it. The girls can head home and put the dinner on." Ciaran gave Mary a peck on the cheek, before nodding to the priest and heading back to the wagon. Tony followed suit.

Father Burke walked Mary and Kate home. "I'd love to come for dinner tomorrow. I'll be sorry to say goodbye to the Donnelly family, but sure at times like these you need to be with your own flesh and blood. Speaking of which, your uncle had another message from your mother for you, Kate." Kate looked at him expectantly. "She said to mind your manners, but sure you always do, don't you?"

Kate was sure the priest had a twinkle in his eye but maybe it was the way the dipping sun was hitting his face. She flushed thinking about Tony and how she felt when she was near him. But her mother had warned her to be a good girl and that's what she was.

TWELVE

ASHEVILLE, NORTH CAROLINA

May 8, 1943

Carol ran her hands down her skirt again. Despite wearing gloves, her hands felt clammy. Josh grabbed her hand and held it tight. "Don't fret, darling. How could they not think us perfect candidates? A wounded war hero and his beautiful wife."

"But, Josh—"

He gave her a quick peck on the lips, stopping her mid-sentence. She pushed her foot against the floor, trying to stop her legs from shaking. She didn't lean against the wall—the color and smell suggested they had painted it in the last century. The flooring was scuff marked too and the pile of papers scattered all over the secretary's desk made her itch to go over and straighten things up. She caught the woman looking at them again, the cigarette hanging out the side of her mouth as she typed away on the rickety old typewriter. Clack, clack, clack, clack. Carol rubbed her temples, the pounding in her head mirroring the sound.

The door opened and a man, dressed in a suit straining over his belly, came out to greet them. He smiled but didn't meet her eyes. He focused his attention on Josh.

"Mr. and Mrs. Andersen, so nice to meet you. My name is Benjamin Williams. A true honor to meet a war hero. My son is over in Northern Africa. Busting those Jerries to pieces."

"The newspapers are full of the victories. Looks like we may have broken their hold in that part of the world at long last. Good news for your son and his friends."

Carol squeezed her husband's hand. He was always so good with people, knowing exactly what to say.

"Come into my office. Madelaine will fetch us fresh coffee, won't you, dear?"

The typist barely looked up but grunted. Josh put his arm around Carol's waist, guiding her ahead of him. He limped in behind her. He should use his crutches, but refused. Stubborn, that was her husband all over.

They took a seat in the office, the empty desk a marked contrast to the one outside. Carol glanced around her. The entire room was freshly painted, the carpet was new and, while not luxurious, was an improvement on the scuffed tiles outside. A crucifix adorned one wall with a picture of Pope Pius XII on the opposite wall.

"I heard you were severely wounded over Berlin, Mr. Andersen. Lucky to make it back." The man offered them both a cigarette, before lighting up.

"Yes, sir. I was lucky to land in Switzerland. I doubt the Jerries would have been too welcoming. They don't like American bomber crews."

"With good reason. I heard it said Goering had told everyone that if an Allied bomb fell on Berlin, they could call him Herr Meyer. A joke that rather backfired on him, don't you think?"

Carol didn't want to waste time talking about Nazi generals and their bad taste in jokes. She wanted a baby, and this man had the power to give her one.

A knock on the door admitted the secretary. The coffee

slopped over the rims of the cups as she set the tray on the desk. She withdrew without an apology.

"Please excuse us. Can't get the staff these days. The munitions and other war work pay so much better. So you expect to make a full recovery?"

"Yes, Mr. Williams. The doctors at the Swiss hospital didn't believe anyone could survive his injuries, but they hadn't counted on Josh's strong will," she replied. "He was walking, albeit with crutches, six weeks after the accident. The doctors at Moore General are confident with time he will be as good as new."

"That's right, Mr. Williams. I intend re-joining my buddies. I'll be back in action by the end of the year."

Carol froze. She hated the thought of Josh back flying bombers. The doctors had warned him any further injuries could exacerbate his existing wounds. And even the most confident had given little credence to him making a full recovery. Not that she was about to argue that point in Mr. Williams' office. She wanted nothing going against their application, least of all her husband's injuries in the service of his country.

Mr. Williams coughed before grounding out the cigarette in the overflowing ashtray.

She nudged Josh with her knee.

"Mr. Williams, how soon will we get the baby?"

The man's head jerked up, his surprise clear. "What baby?"

Josh and Carol exchanged a glance. "We, my husband and I, thought that was why you called us in. You'd found a baby for us."

He shook his head, picking up a brown manilla file from his desk. "I'm afraid that won't be possible."

"You don't have a baby available at the moment? That's disappointing but we can wait." She let her words trail off as she glimpsed disdain in his eyes before he blinked it away. She looked at Josh. Had he seen it?

"Mr. Williams, is there a problem with our application?" Josh held her hand tight as he spoke.

"There is nothing wrong with your application. A war hero would make an excellent role model, a wonderful father."

"So? What are you not saying?"

Carol held her breath. She recognized Josh's clipped tones. He was angry. His injuries had shortened his temper because of the almost continuous pain he was in. But he was too well bred to show it.

"It's rather delicate; perhaps it would be best if your wife were to wait outside."

Carol gaped at the man as Josh put his hand around the back of her chair and placed it in the middle of her back. "My wife is a grown woman and a perfect mother for any child lucky enough to be given to her. She is full of love and would do anything—"

"That's all very well and good, Mr. Andersen, but given your wife's recent medical issues... it's not possible to grant an adoption. Not now, not ever."

Carol stared at the man, taking in everything from the dark hairs protruding from his ears to the shirt straining over his stomach. He was missing a button. What was she doing thinking of mending at a time like this?

"Mr. Williams, my wife was under severe pressure. They gave my father the impression I wasn't coming back. They didn't see a chute, you see. So the report was that although officially missing, I was probably dead." Josh's voice faltered, his emotions not under as much control as usual. "Our son was killed..."

"We're aware your wife suffered a miscarriage after a motor accident. She was driving."

Carol's blood rose. "The man driving the other car was out of his mind on drink. I couldn't do anything. I was the victim. Regarding... the other matter, my parents-in-law made a mistake. They thought I was... I had... when, in fact, I had only taken two pills to help me sleep. The hospital discharged me."

The odious man opened the file. "Only after administering electric shock treatment and other cures used for those of a... shall we say nervous disposition." He snapped the file shut.

Carol wanted to tear the file from him.

"I'm sorry, but I'm afraid the decision is final. Thank you for your time. Your mother's position on several charities warranted I see you in person to deliver the news. Usually, a letter would suffice. I am a very busy man. Please excuse me."

He stood up, but it took Carol and Josh a few seconds to follow suit.

"You haven't heard the last of this, Mr. Williams. I don't use my family's name or position lightly, but my wife and I, we want a child and we will have one."

"Not by adoption. At least not a child you'd want. Perhaps you could find one from your wife's charity work."

Josh lunged, but Carol grabbed his arm just in time. "Come on, Josh, let's leave. Thank you for your time and your consideration, Mr. Williams."

She turned on her heel and marched out of his office, not willing to give him the satisfaction of crumbling to pieces.

Once back home, Josh headed to their bar in the living room and poured a whiskey, which he downed in one. He then poured another one. "Want one?"

"No, thank you. Drinking will not solve this."

She ducked as he threw a glass against the wall opposite to where she was standing. Shocked, she stared at him; he looked as surprised as she felt. He'd never done anything like this before.

"I wanted to punch his lights out. How dare he judge you, us, like that?"

Myrtle arrived, eyes bulging as she took in the cut glass littering the carpet.

"Be careful you don't cut yourself on the shards, Myrtle." Carol forced her voice to sound level and confident. She held Josh's gaze until the servant withdrew.

He flopped onto the sofa and ran his hand through his hair.

"Gosh, Carol, I'm such a grump. I shouldn't be taking things out on you. I should keep a hold on my temper. Forgive me?"

She laughed as he made puppy eyes at her. Shivers ran down her spine at the thought of how close she'd come to losing him in that bombing raid. He pulled her close and ruffled her hair with one hand, the other holding her tight against him.

"We'll find a way. Mother may know someone."

She jerked away at the mention of Priscilla.

"Your mother put me in that asylum. She ruined our chances."

"She was worried about you."

"Don't give me that. She hates me, always has. She never thought I was good enough for you. Now that I can't give you a precious son, she thought it was the best way to get rid of me. You could divorce the madwoman in the asylum."

"Carol, you're hysterical. Catholics don't get divorced. And you were the one who..." His voice trailed away, a sheepish expression on his face.

She stood up and paced the carpet.

"For the last time, I took two pills. I let the rest fall and knocked over the bottle of whiskey. Isiah saw how upset I was and I know he only acted out of genuine concern, but he should never have telephoned your parents. If they hadn't come back, I wouldn't have ended up in that place." She wrapped her arms around herself. Even now, the weeks she had spent in Highfield Asylum gave her nightmares when she wasn't sleeping. Hell on earth didn't come close to describing the electric shock and other treatments they had subjected her to. But it was the price they had paid as a couple that was the worst to bear.

"If your precious mother hadn't interfered, we wouldn't be childless. You heard that man, we could have adopted. You'd make an ideal father. That was what he said. But for the minor issue of me being an ex-asylum inmate."

"Honey, come here." He patted the seat beside him. "Please, darling, don't make the invalid get up and walk again."

She smiled despite herself and walked over and sat at the end of the sofa, but he pulled her close, and kissed the top of her head. "Honey, he was wrong. You'd have been a wonderful mother. I love you, darling, I'd do anything to make this better."

"I want a child, Josh. I can't bear to think of living the rest of my life without a family."

"I know you do, so do I. What do you expect us to do? If you think Mother can't help, I don't know who will."

She whispered, "Josh, there are other children who need a home."

He pulled back, putting his finger under her chin to force her to meet his eyes. "That isn't the answer. We both know it. Think about it, sweetheart. Neither community would accept us adopting a child of another race. That's just the way things are. You know how things are."

"It doesn't mean I agree with it," she spat back.

"I don't either. We didn't make the system but we live within it."

She laid her head on his shoulder. He was right. She was being silly. It wouldn't be fair to anyone, least of all the child.

"They'll never give us a child, Josh."

THIRTEEN

KILDARE, IRELAND

August, 1943

Kate and Tony walked hand in hand through the village, laughing at the children as they ran around shrieking.

"They're full of life today, aren't they?" Tony gasped as one young boy ran straight into him.

"Sorry, mister," the child mumbled before heading back to his friends, kicking the ball.

"What are they playing with?"

"A football made from the inside of a pig." Kate wrinkled her nose with distaste. "Uncle Pat slaughtered a pig yesterday, the lads helped."

Tony put his arm around her waist as they stopped to watch the improvised match. "I'm glad I was confined to barracks. I like bacon as much as the next man but my stomach isn't fit for farm work."

Kate put her head on his shoulder, enjoying the warmth of the sun on their backs.

"How many children do you want?" His whisper made her laugh as his breath tickled her ear. Then she heard the words.

"What?"

"I'd like at least two but I know you Irish like big families."

She pulled away from him. "Have you been out in the sun too long?" she teased, trying to distract herself from what he was saying.

He kneeled down on the grass beside her, causing the children to stop and cheer. Kate looked around; the women cleaning their steps looked up, their eyes alight with romance.

"Tony, stop. You're making a show of me. Of us."

"Maybe I do have sunstroke but I have to do this now before I lose my nerve. Kate Ryan, will you marry me?"

"Tony, get up. Everyone's staring."

"Is that a very unromantic yes?"

His eyes caught hers as her stomach turned over, the excitement racing through her veins. "Yes. Yes, Yes," she shrieked. He stood up and, picking her up, whirled her around. "Kate Burton. It's got a nice ring to it, don't you think?"

FOURTEEN

October, 1943

Kate could sense the mood in the pub. Despite the beautiful autumn day, everyone was inside drinking whatever they could get their hands on. Something was up; the aircrew were in high spirits and it wasn't down to alcohol. At least not all of it.

"Mary, have you heard anything? Why is everyone acting like Father Christmas is due any second?"

"I've no idea what you are on about, Kate. Can you get those glasses sorted? I'll run out if you don't get a move on." Mary wouldn't meet her eyes, which only intensified the feeling there was news.

The door opened, admitting Tony and some of his friends. He made his way straight for her. "Can you take a break? I need to speak to you."

"It's too busy." Although she wanted to see him, she had a feeling that she didn't want to hear what he had to say.

"Tony, be a dear and take those glasses through to the kitchen and wash them for me, will you?" Mary thrust a rack of glasses into Tony's arms. "Kate will help ya."

Her heart pounding, Kate held the door open as Tony walked through to the kitchen. He put the dishes on the table and took her in his arms.

'I don't want to hear it," she said, putting her hands over her ears.

"Kate, you knew this day would come. We talked about it. I have to go back. It's my duty, what I signed up for." He reached out to push her hair behind her ear, his loving gaze holding hers. "They are still short of pilots."

Stabbing pains hit her stomach. He was leaving. Her lips trembled, but she refused to cry. "What about me? Us? Or don't we count?"

He kissed her fiercely. "I love you, my red-haired Irish beauty. You're the only woman for me, you know that. I want us to get married when the war is over. I'll come back and then, I want you to come home to Colorado with me."

"Tony, don't go. Please don't go." She knew she was begging but she didn't care. She couldn't bear the thought of life without him; the last eighteen months had been the happiest of her life.

He drew her into his arms again and kissed her until all thoughts of anything but him disappeared.

Breathing heavily, they broke apart at a sound from the bar. They both glanced at the partition door but it remained shut.

"Can you meet me later?" he asked. "I need to be with you. Properly."

Kate knew what he was asking, and she knew it was wrong. But she didn't care. She felt exactly the same. What if this was the last time she saw him? What if he was shot down or he crashed? She grabbed his face in both hands and kissed him hard on the lips.

"I'll meet you at our special place in about an hour. Now help me with these glasses first so Mary won't ask me to work through the afternoon."

Together they washed the glasses in silence, both caught up in their own thoughts. Every so often she caught him looking at her just as he caught her when she glanced his way. She saw her love reflected in his eyes.

After they were done, Tony took the clean dry glasses back in to Mary as Kate fled upstairs. She changed into a dress and at the last minute wrapped up a small blanket and hid it under her coat.

With a call of goodbye to Mary, she strode out the back door, heading for the river. She nodded to different neighbors but didn't stop to chat. If anyone had asked, she'd have said she was going to see Paddy's wife. Only when she reached the turn would she take the route to the river.

He was waiting for her when she arrived. Suddenly shy, she stared at the ground as she moved closer to him. He took her in his arms, his finger gently forcing her chin up so she was looking into his eyes.

"I want you with every fiber of my being but this has to be your decision, my darling," he whispered. "I love you and that won't change."

Any resolve she had dissolved that second. She loved him too, and this could be a goodbye forever. She moved out of his arms, took the blanket and laid it on the grass. Then she sat and reached up for him to join her.

"I love you too, Tony, and, in my heart, we are married. We would have been if things were different."

With a smile that lit up his eyes, he kissed her slowly at first, stirring up feelings like she'd never experienced before.

They lay in each other arms after, using their coats as an overblanket. "Kate, if I don't come back..."

"Shush, I don't want to hear that," she said quietly, resting her head on his shoulder.

He pushed himself up on one elbow, looking down at her. "I love you and I will be back. But, just in case, I've written to Mom and Pops and told them all about you. How much I love you and my plan to marry you." He kissed her deeply again. "I love you more than anything, Kate. Never forget that."

As they walked arm in arm back to Uncle Pat's bar, Kate finally asked the question. "When do you go?"

"Tomorrow morning. A bus to the Phoenix Park in Dublin and from there we head to Northern Ireland, I assume Belfast. From there I don't know if I will be reassigned to a US airbase or back to Britain to an RAF one. But I'll write as soon as I can."

"Tomorrow, tomorrow?" she asked, eyes widening. She couldn't believe it was that soon.

"This isn't goodbye, my darling. I will be back. I promise." He folded her into his arms, laying his head against hers.

"Just stay safe. No heroics or showing off, you hear me?"

He saluted. "Yes, ma'am."

She raised her tear-stained face for another long lingering kiss, not caring who saw them. Then he left, taking her heart with him.

FIFTEEN

February, 1944

Kate didn't have time to go to the outside privy, but pushed the hair back from her mouth as she crouched over the chamber pot. That was the third time in as many days. She put a hand on her stomach. Could she be...? No.

"Kate, sorry there's no post for you this morning. I'm sure Tony will write back to..." Mary came up the stairs and into the bedroom. "Are you sick again? Jesus, Mary and Joseph, what did you eat that has you this unwell? Da's worried the patrons will stop eating the food we serve in the bar..." Mary fell silent, her eyes meeting Kate's, an expression of dread on her face. "Oh, Kate. You haven't fallen for a baby, have you?"

Kate stayed silent.

"How could you have been so stupid? I told you to be careful. If I get my hands on Tony, I'll skin him alive."

"What am I going to do, Mary?" She hated how her voice trembled. To her mother and most Irish people, being unmarried and pregnant was worse than being dead. "Tony had to go, it wasn't like he could refuse to be released and sit out the duration of the war in Ireland. He's coming back for me though, when it's all over." Kate held a hand over her mouth as her stomach heaved again.

"Unless Hitler surrenders in the next month or so, it will be too late for that. How are you going to hide the fact you're expecting? Your mam will kill you and... me too. She'll blame me and my da. You know she will."

Kate blinked away the tears her cousin's harsh voice caused.

"I'm sorry, Mary. I didn't mean to cause you any trouble. It's just we're in love and..." She fell silent at the look her cousin gave her.

"Save me the speech, Kate. I know what it feels like to be in love. Haven't I been walking out with Ciaran for the last four years? We never got carried away, although heavens knows we've been tempted, but nice girls don't. You know that." Mary paced back and forth. "I'll have to tell Da, he'll know how best to handle this."

Kate gulped back her fear of what her uncle Pat would say. She knew he'd be hurt but would he turn his back on her? He'd have the right to, given how she had betrayed his trust.

Mary sat on the bed for a second and then jumped up. "Maybe we can send you over to one of your sisters in England. Would they take you in? You can have the baby over there, get it adopted and come home. No one will know any different."

Horrified, Kate crossed her arms over her stomach. This was her baby, hers and Tony's. If he died, he would live on in their child—how could she give a part of him away?

"I'll know," she replied.

"Obviously. I meant the gossips, the priests and your mam. She won't have this, Kate. Not when she has you all set to go to the nuns. You'd be in that convent now if it wasn't for your da and Joe asking mine to take you for one last summer. He hoped to work on your mam. He knows the life of a nun isn't for you, but there was no way he saw this happening. You were always the one nobody had to watch, the one who obeyed the rules. I can't believe this." Mary glared at her. "I can't even look at you."

Mary turned on her heel, ignoring her cousin's cries for her to come back and leaving Kate curled up on the bed, feeling utterly alone. If Joe were around, he'd help her but her darling brother was on a ship somewhere in the Atlantic. Maybe Mary was right, one of her sisters might help her. If she just turned up on one of their doorsteps, surely they wouldn't turn her away. But just as quickly as the thought came, her hope died. None of her sisters cared enough to write to her. They weren't likely to open their arms to a pregnant unmarried sibling, were they? What was she going to do?

Mary didn't mention her condition again and neither did Kate. She did her best to hide her morning sickness, blaming the ration bread or anything else she could think of. The weeks passed and there were still no letters for her. Was Tony dead? No, he couldn't be. He was too young, vibrant, alive. Then why hadn't he written back to her? He loved her, she knew he did. Didn't he?

Joe hadn't written back either but his letters often took a month or more what with being at sea.

"Are you moping again?" Her uncle thought she was heartsick, missing Tony. "I know it's hard to understand being a girl," Uncle Pat said, "but Tony had a duty to return to the fight. He knows the Allies have to win this war and they need qualified pilots with experience. Lost too many over the years. He's a good man. If it's to be between the two of you, he'll be back. If not, you'll find a new man someday." He put his hand on her arm and squeezed before going back to pulling another pint. The guilt ran through her as she thought of how betrayed this wonderful man would feel at what she and Tony had done.

A few days later, her worst nightmare came to fruition. Walking back from the privy after being ill again, she came face to face with Fergal Scanlan.

"I thought it was an animal making those noises. Do ya need

the doctor? What have you been eating?" He wrinkled his nose, a suspicious look on his face. "You've not taken to the drink, have ya?"

"Go away, Fergal." She turned away but at that moment the wind blew her skirt closer to her belly, outlining her figure.

His eyes widened as his gaze ran from her head to her toes and back up to her face.

"You've fallen for a child, haven't ya? Makes sense now. Mary kept saying you were ill from eating bad food. As if the Ryans would have to eat rancid meat." He moved closer and instinctively she moved away. That was a mistake; his lip curled with distaste. "That's what you get for hanging around with foreigners. Might as well give us a taste of what they got." He grabbed for her but she was too quick for him and ran screaming back to the pub. Uncle Pat met her at the back door.

"What's wrong with you? Those screams made me punters think the banshee was on the loose."

Before Kate caught her breath, Fergal's menacing tone broke the news to her uncle.

"Not death you have to be worrying about, Pat Ryan, is it, Kate?"

Kate willed the ground to open and swallow her. It sounded so sordid coming out of Fergal's mouth.

Uncle Pat's nose flared, his eyes glinting as his temper rose.

"What do you mean by that, Scanlan? Have you put a hand near my girl?"

"Not me. I don't go for other men's leavings. I've more pride than that. Just wait until Father Burke hears about this."

Uncle Pat's eyebrows knitted. "Father Burke? What has he to do with anything?"

Scanlan ran off before her uncle could grab him. Kate tried to duck past her uncle too, but she wasn't quick enough.

"Kate, what was all that about? Do you have something to tell me?"

She stilled, her heart beating so fast she thought it might break out of her chest.

"Kate?" he almost whispered, he spoke so quietly.

"Fergal heard me being sick," she whispered back. "The wind caught my dress and then he saw. He put two and two together and..."

"And?" Despite the question, the knowledge was written all over his face. "No, don't tell me. I don't want to hear it. Not you, Kate. Your da will murder me and as for your mam, she'll damn my soul to eternal hell. I was supposed to be looking after you. I trusted you. Both you and Tony. I thought I was making things easier for my brother's family, having you here, lessening his burden. Not adding to it. And now Tony has gone, the news comes to light. I guess it's his?"

"Of course. I'm not a—"

"That's exactly what you are and worse words you will hear to describe what you've done. Get to your bedroom. Now!" He raised his hand, then lowered it quickly. "Go before I lose my temper and give you the back of my hand."

Red-checked, Kate ran, but not in the direction of her room. She raced out to the lane, heading for their special place near the river. An ache in her side reminded her to slow down for fear of harming the baby. She knew she'd hurt and disappointed her uncle, but he knew what it was like to be in love. Hadn't he adored his wife? Couldn't he understand how she felt about Tony? Tears rolling down her cheeks, she was too distressed to hear the voice calling her at first, but then she recognized it as Father Burke. All the years of training kicked in, and she pulled her features into something resembling calmness before turning to face the priest. She waited, trying to adopt an expression of composure as he walked toward her, his black cassock billowing in the slight wind, the hem covered with mud from walking across the fields. Her features froze despite his wide smile, until the kindness in his eyes made her tears fall once again.

"I thought it was you, young Kate, but you were racing like

demons themselves were after you. Oh, you've been crying. Here, dry your eyes, it's clean," he said, passing her a crisp white hand-kerchief. "Mrs. Scanlan gives me a new set every six months or so. She even embroiders my initials on them so I don't lose them or give them away as gifts to others." He smiled at his own joke but his eyes were wide with concern. Up close he didn't seem a bit like Father Devine, the Galway parish priest back home who never smiled, not even on Christmas morning.

She rubbed her eyes. "Sorry, Father, you caught me at the wrong time. I had a row with my uncle. I'm feeling guilty for upset-ting him, he's been so good to me and my family."

"He has, but so have you, child. I've never seen such a willing worker. If you aren't out with the cows, you're behind that bar. Not that I agree with women serving in the pubs, well not officially anyway. Don't be telling the bishop but if a woman has to work to help support her family these days, who am I to stop her?"

Kate stared at him, hearing the words but not quite believing them. Weren't priests meant to obey the bishops like children did with their parents?

"Yes, I'm a bit of a rebel at heart," he said, seeing the question in her eyes. "How could I be anything but coming from a family like mine? As Mrs. Scanlan will tell anyone that listens, my whole family have been involved in the fight for Ireland for as long as our country has been occupied. Not that I condone violence. Hate to see anyone fighting, even if they don't use weapons. So come walk with me, Kate, it's a little bit fresh to stand around without getting a chill. I love these crisp mornings even if the wintery sun gives little warmth, don't you?"

She mumbled something, not quite feeling up to discussing the weather. She couldn't care less if the heavens opened and the whole year's supply of rain fell on top of her.

"Tell me what you and your uncle Pat fell out about. A problem shared and all that. Maybe I can help to resolve the issue." He gestured to her to walk alongside him. She couldn't really refuse but was thankful he wasn't heading in the direction of the river. They walked in silence, every so often their feet squelching as the barely frozen ground melted beneath them, until he glanced at her one too many times.

"You can't, Father," she finally answered, "but thank you for trying."

"You seem very sure of that, Kate. An older head may have some wisdom to offer. Why don't you try me? If I promise not to tell, will that make it easier?"

She stopped walking, turning to face him so she could hold his gaze. "Like in confession?"

"That wasn't exactly what I meant but if you feel the need for confession, of course I can hear that. Though would a friendly ear do for today?"

Kate walked on, the priest joining her without comment as he let the silence linger. That helped make her mind up. She might as well tell him before Fergal got to him. It might be better if she told him how much she loved Tony, how she hadn't planned for it to happen but when it came to losing him she... Even the thought of what they had done made her blush; how could she put it in words to the priest? She risked looking at his face, expecting condemnation but only saw understanding. Her stomach fluttered as she wiped her hands on her skirt a couple of times, biting her lip trying to think of the right words. Before she lost her nerve, she blurted out the news.

"Father, I've committed a sin, at least in the eyes of the church, my uncle, and my mam but I don't regret it. Not one bit."

He raised an eyebrow but stayed silent and continued walking. She couldn't bear the quiet any longer.

"Are you not going to say anything?"

"I don't need to, do I? You seem to have it all figured out. You did wrong but you feel it was justified. Is that about it?"

His frank way of speaking took her by surprise. He wasn't being judgmental. At least he didn't sound like he was.

"Sort of. I guess I did let people down and I betrayed their trust, but I had good reason. I'm in love, Father."

"Sure, that's not news to me, Kate. Everyone in the village knows you are besotted with Tony. And he with you, if I was to listen to gossip, which I don't. Not with me being a priest." His eyes glittered as he made fun of his position.

The back of her neck prickled; had he not understood her? Blushing furiously, she put it more plainly. "Father Burke, I'm having a baby. And Tony has left for England so he's not here to marry me and make it right." Her nerves failed her, and she couldn't look up from the ground.

"Getting married after getting pregnant wouldn't make it right anyway, Kate, the sin being the same, but I take your meaning. You mean you aren't in a position to make your situation respectable."

Kate waited for him to start berating her but instead he remained silent, his kind eyes waiting.

"So, I assume you told your uncle Pat and he was rather disappointed?"

Disappointed? That was one word for it. "I didn't tell him. Fergal Scanlan said some nasty things about wanting... well, he tried to... I ran away and we bumped into Uncle Pat. Fergal told him."

The kindness in the priest's eyes disappeared. "I bet he did and a whole lot more. That lad needs dealing with." Father Burke hesitated. "But not today. Today we need to concentrate on your situation, Kate. How are you feeling? Have you been to see Doctor Sixsmith? It's important women in your condition get proper treatment, the correct vitamins and what have you. Especially now with the shortages, although it has to be said your uncle looks after his family properly."

"Doctor? No, Father." She could barely believe what she was hearing. "Apart from Uncle Pat and Mary, I haven't told anyone. Mary guessed as well. She is that angry with me. I think she's worse than her da and that's saying a lot."

"They are hurt, dear girl, and feeling betrayed and probably a little guilty. They had a duty of care toward you, and they will feel they let your parents down. So, what do you think your parents will do? Will they provide you with a home for you and your baby?"

Tears pricked her eyes. If only her mam followed this man's version of Christianity. "My da might if he was on his own. But Mam, well, she had her heart set on me joining the convent. She wanted me to start with the Sisters of the Bon Secours in Tuam this past year but Uncle Pat talked her around. He knew I didn't have a calling, no disrespect intended, Father."

"None taken. It's not a life for everyone, that's for sure. And for good reason. Ireland needs its mammies and daddies so our future generations can blossom. Isn't that God's plan? If everyone became nuns and priests, the world would die out soon enough."

Kate hadn't thought about it like that. She wished she could introduce her mam to Father Burke.

"So assuming your uncle won't keep you, and we can understand why he wouldn't, what are your plans? I take it your uncle won't have told your parents yet."

"He only just found out but, no, I don't think so. We don't have a telephone and he knows Mam wouldn't want to hear that news secondhand via the local shop phone. He may write to her," she stuttered as she thought of how her mother would react to a letter like that. Even as she said the words, she knew Uncle Pat would expect her to tell her mam in person. Her heart raced at just the thought of it. She swallowed hard before whispering, "I imagine he'll ask me to do it."

"Maybe we could do better than that. We should speak to your parents together. It's their duty as good Catholics to look after their children. What is it the good book says? He who is without sin cast the first stone."

Her mother's shocking words about Shane and the other orphans the Cumiskeys had used for labor came into her head.

"Forgive me, Father, but you haven't met my mother. She might not agree with you."

He sighed, his eyes full of sadness.

"She probably won't. I haven't met your mammy but I've met

my fair share of Irish mammies. Perhaps she will surprise you. It won't be the first or last time a young girl comes home with a baby on the way. These things have happened since the time of Deirdre and Naoise, if not before."

Kate gave him a half smile as he brought up the story she had told the youngsters on the beach that last day in Galway. Little had she known what fate had in store for her.

"Father, you are being kind and, well, if you forgive me for saying so, you aren't like a usual priest. I want you to know I am a good girl, usually, I mean. I didn't mean for this to happen. I love Tony and he loves me. It was just too hard, with him leaving and me never knowing if I'd see him again. I didn't doubt him when he said he'd come back for me, but pilots die all the time in the war. I just... well, what I mean is..." Her cheeks were scarlet as she sought the correct words.

"It's all right, Kate. I have some idea. Let's just leave it at that and save both of our blushes, shall we?" Father Burke tapped her hand awkwardly. Then he turned about to walk in the direction of the pub. "Let's be getting back to your uncle's before that rain cloud turns into a downpour. I imagine he is feeling bad too for letting his temper flare. He's a good man, a kind man, who has lived a lot of years. He probably understands more than you realize. He's hurt and when somebody is hurting they lash out to their nearest and dearest. Try to remember that in the days and months ahead."

She smiled, grateful for his kindness. "Yes, Father."

They walked in silence back to the public house. She couldn't help but notice the flower boxes were bare now unlike when she'd first arrived. The flowers would bloom again, so long as the frost didn't kill them. They didn't enter by the bar door, instead making their way into the backyard and entering via the kitchen, both welcoming the warmth from the range. Kate heard Father Burke's stomach growl in response to the scent of rabbit stewing on the stove. In contrast, Kate found the smell made her feel ill.

Mary, who was standing by the range, turned and saw Kate

first. "Where have you been and what did you say to my da? He's like the— Oh, hello, Father Burke, I didn't see you there."

"That's all right, Mary, I know today has been one of those days. Perhaps you could find your father and we could have a sup of tea? Paddy might mind the bar rather than drink it for once."

Mary looked dumbfounded but she left to find her da. Meanwhile, Kate picked up the bucket and ran to the well to fetch the water, not wanting to meet anyone else. She filled the kettle and put it on to boil over the stove. Opening the fire door, she threw on a couple of bits of kindling, the flames crackling in response. The priest sat down at the table as if today was the same as any other. Kate busied herself with making the tea and setting the table with cups and plates.

It took a while for Uncle Pat and Mary to return; no doubt Mary had to talk her father into coming into the kitchen. He didn't even glance at Kate before he took a seat opposite the priest. Kate poured the tea and milk into the cups as Mary cut some slices from an apple cake she'd made earlier. Then Mary took a seat beside her da, leaving Kate to sit opposite her uncle.

"'Tis a bad day, Father, and no doubt about that."

"I'm sorry for your troubles, Pat Ryan, but you can get that look off your face. No point in berating the girl now."

At that, nobody tried to hide their surprise.

"It's a priest I am, not the judge, jury and executioner. I see my role to help people in their hour of need. Kate already feels guilty for upsetting you fine people and for betraying your trust. She's sorry for that and will confess her sins and seek God's forgiveness. He'll forgive her, so why wouldn't we?"

Her uncle almost spat out his tea; Mary set her cup on the table so hard the liquid slopped out over the side.

"Father, forgive me for speaking frankly, but can you hear yourself? The girl didn't steal a potato or a loaf of bread." He glanced over his shoulder as if afraid the patrons in the bar could hear through the thick stone walls, before dropping his voice to a whisper. "She's carrying a baby, an illegitimate brat who will shoulder that shame for the rest of his or her days."

Kate held her breath, her lungs hurting. She couldn't even look up at anyone. She dug her nails into the palms of her hands.

"I know that, Pat. I am aware of how our unmarried mothers and their babies are spoken about but that doesn't mean it's right. This is my own opinion, not that of the church. God tells us to love his children, meaning all his children, not just the ones that fit perfectly into our rules."

Uncle Pat stood up just as Kate exhaled. She wanted nothing more than to run and had to force her feet to the ground to remain sitting at the table.

"That might be your view, Father, but it isn't that of Archbishop McQuaid or his followers. It won't be Emer Ryan's view either. Kate knows what her mother believes. Sure, she had this girl down for the convent almost before she was born. This news will put her and us to shame."

Kate risked a look at the priest, who was nodding as if in agreement. But when he spoke, his words were a surprise.

"That's as may be. I would like the chance to talk to Mrs. Ryan and, of course, to Kate's father. I will accompany Kate home to Galway. By train, I'm afraid, as I can't drive my car due to the petrol shortage. I know they give us priests extra rations but it's not sufficient to get to Galway and back. It's a real burden, don't you know." His eyes twinkled again and Kate was sure he knew what the gossips had to say about his love of driving and his car.

Uncle Pat hadn't finished. "I never thought I'd see the day where a priest condoned a mortal sin."

Father Burke's eyes flew to Pat's. "I never said I condoned her sin. I said it wasn't our place to chastise her. There is a difference. God himself said *'Everyone who believes in Him receives forgiveness of sins through His name.'*" The priest took a sip of his tea before continuing in a gentler but equally firm tone. "We are all sinners. There is only one judge and that is our Lord. I ask for charity through my prayers. I also ask for the good Lord to give me the skills I need to help those who have sinned or fallen away from the teachings of our church to find their way back to God."

Uncle Pat sighed heavily. "I apologize, Father. The way you talk, well, it's not what we are used to."

"More's the pity in my book. But we digress. So, is it agreed I will accompany Kate home to her village in Galway? You will not write to her parents in advance. It may help if we have the element of surprise on our side."

"You'll need that and more if you talk to my sister-in-law the way you just talked to us. She may forget you are a priest, Father, and throw you out of her house. She gets on famously with her parish priest, Father Devine. He's definitely not reading the same books you are."

The priest stood taller, an unfathomable expression in his eyes. "We both read the Bible but our interpretations may be different. Won't be the first time I have a different theological argument to my fellow priests, won't be the last either. But let me worry about that. For now, can you at least give Kate the chance to apologize? We all know she wasn't thinking about the hurt and upset she would cause to you. She loves you, that's obvious to everyone including a blind man. Kate, I will have to organize a few things in the parish before I can leave. Shall we get a train on Wednesday? Will that give you enough time to pack?"

"Yes, Father, thank you, Father," Kate replied, struggling to find the words as she walked him out to the door. When she returned, she found her uncle and cousin still sitting at the table in silent contemplation.

"Uncle Pat, Mary," she said, finally finding her voice. "I'm sorry I brought trouble to your door and shamed you in front of your friends and neighbors."

Uncle Pat slammed his fist onto the table, making his daughter jump. Kate stepped back, for a second worried he was going to hit her.

When he spoke, his voice shook. "You think that's why I'm upset? I don't give a monkey about what the people around here think. It's filled with sadness I am at the life you have chosen for yourself, Kate. I love you like a second daughter. I wanted more for ye than... well, than this. I can't help but feel I am to blame for not keeping a closer eye on you. You can bet your mam will blame me."

"She might but she'd be wrong. Uncle Pat, you've always been so kind to me. Thank you and to you too, Mary."

"Come here, you." Mary pulled her into a hug. "I couldn't stay mad at you for long. I just hope your mam listens to Father Burke."

"Miracles can happen. Maybe I should light a candle." Uncle Pat shrugged his shoulders as he walked back into the bar with Mary following behind. Left alone, Kate scrubbed down the kitchen table—she always thought better when she worked. She had written to Tony to tell him her news. Time would tell if he really meant everything he said...

SIXTEEN

Word had spread, no doubt thanks to Fergal. Most of the villagers gave her a wide berth, ignoring her presence. Mary insisted she do the shopping while Kate did the cooking, cleaning and any other chores that kept her out of sight. She didn't venture into the bar.

On Tuesday evening, Paddy and his wife surprised her by calling to the back door. The rain teemed down from the dark black clouds dominating the sky. It was a day not even suited to hardy animals and the pair of them were drenched. She should have invited them in but instead stood staring at them until her upbringing caught up to her shock.

"Paddy, Mrs. McCormack, what are you doing here? Did you want my uncle? Only he's in the bar."

"No, child, it's you we came to see. Can we come in for a second?"

She saw pity mixed with determination in the old woman's eyes. Although dripping water everywhere, Mrs. McCormack looked so much better than that day she and Tony had called to see her.

"Of course, where's my manners?"

Paddy stood back to allow his wife in the door first. He looked around him as if worried he'd be seen before he followed her inside.

"Will you have a cup of tea or something?"

"No, thank you, Kate, we won't be staying. We heard you are away back home in the morning. We wanted to give you this."

Mrs. McCormack opened her leather bag and handed her a soft package wrapped in brown paper. "Go on, open it. I know you should wait until the baby comes but you won't be here." Mrs. McCormack eyed Kate's stomach. "You're small but it's early days."

"Almost five months." Tears pricked Kate's eyes as she opened the package. Inside was a crocheted pair of fine white wool booties, a matching bonnet and a cardigan.

"Mrs. McCormack." Kate swallowed to try to steady her voice. "It's beautiful, such fine little stitches. Thank you."

"I made it for our last baby, buried above near the graveyard, God rest his young soul—the priest, he wouldn't baptize him, you see." Mrs. McCormack's whole body shuddered as if reliving that horrible moment. "It's never been worn. I hope you don't think we're intruding or..."

Kate put her arms around Paddy's wife, kissing her tear-stained cheek. "Thank you. For being kind to me."

The woman squeezed her in return. "You and your young man were so nice to me. I'll pray you are reunited one day. Until then, be strong. If I could, I'd offer you a home but..." She glanced at her husband, who stared at the floor. "... that's just not possible."

Paddy coughed and without looking at Kate turned to his wife. "Come on, love, we need to get going. Before..."

Kate saw the look Mrs. McCormack gave her husband and was amazed to see Paddy flush. She held out her hand to the old man.

"Thank you, Paddy, for coming."

He hesitated for a fraction of a second before shaking her hand and wishing her well. Then they were gone.

Kate folded the gift back into the brown paper, wondering how much it had cost Mrs. McCormack to come to see her. Mrs.

McCormack had been the only person who acknowledged her love for Tony. Paddy obviously didn't share his wife's understanding or charity. Was this the one time Mrs. McCormack had stood up to her husband? Kate climbed the stairs to her bedroom, relieved Mary didn't follow her. She undressed quickly, before lying in the bed, holding the precious parcel to her chest. The kindness, from such an unexpected source, made Kate cry herself to sleep.

The train pulled into Galway town, allowing them to get out and stretch their legs. Father Burke suggested they walk to Kate's village but Kate spotted one of the local farmers driving a cart.

"Mr. Cumiskey will give us a lift, if you ask him, Father. He won't say no to a priest. I'll just stand back a little until he agrees. He's not too fond of my family."

Father Burke didn't get a chance to answer as the cart drove closer. He held his hand out and Kate heard Cumiskey tell his horses to halt.

"Can I help you, Father?" asked the farmer.

"I hope so. I need a lift out the road. Would you be heading that way?"

"I am indeed, Father. Hop up beside me. The back isn't too clean." Kate stepped out just as Mr. Cumiskey saw her, the warmth disappearing from his gaze and tone. "You're back then."

She held his gaze, thankful the coat Mary had given her hid her condition. "Yes, Mr. Cumiskey."

He flicked her a look of disdain, obviously not having forgiven her for going to the aid of Shane. "You can get in the back."

Kate didn't argue but sat on the cleanest part of the dirty cart, thankful it wasn't full of manure but just dirty hay. She let the men chat as she went over what she'd say to her parents with a churning stomach. No matter how often she practiced the words, there wasn't an easy way to give them her news. Thankfully Mr. Cumiskey didn't ask Father Burke what was bringing him to this area. In fairness, the priest didn't give him a chance as he kept the man talking about his farm.

"So before the war you concentrated on the dairy side but with all the shortages caused by the war, you've branched out into producing larger quantities of potatoes and root vegetables?"

"Aye, Father. There's a lot of hungry people about."

"That showed wonderful foresight, Mr. Cumiskey."

Was it her imagination or did old man Cumiskey sit up straighter as Father Burke praised him?

Kate hopped off the cart at the end of the lane to her parents' farm. How she wished Joe was here. He'd be able to talk her mam around if anyone could. Father Burke shook out his skirts and together they walked down to the house. He didn't speak and she was grateful for his silence. Her mouth grew drier as the house loomed nearer, where her mam was outside, polishing the front brasses. Flustered at the arrival of Kate with a stranger, a priest no less, her mother was caught short of words. Her face flushed as Kate introduced her to Father Burke. Her mam's gaze flickered over Kate before she called for her husband as they went inside.

"Father Burke, would you like dinner?"

"No, thank you, Mrs. Ryan. A cup of tea, if you have it, and a slice of that delicious-smelling bread will do just fine."

Keeping her coat on, Kate watched her mam's face as her lip twitched—she was nervous and curious, yet too much of a lady to show it.

"It's not the tea you're used to, Father. I've not had time to collect the rations for this week."

After what seemed like hours, her da came out of the back bedroom. Tears sprang into Kate's eyes as she saw he'd tried to dress in his Sunday best. From the knowing look he gave her, she knew he suspected something was up. She'd never been able to hide things from her father.

"Welcome to my home, Father. Have you come about Joseph?"

Father Burke looked slightly confused.

"My brother, Joe, is with the British navy. He hasn't been

home in some time," Kate hastened to explain. "Daddy, it has nothing to do with Joe. Why don't you and Mam sit down. I'll pour ya a cup of tea."

Her da sat down next to his wife, whose hands were fluttering.

The priest set his cup back on the table. "My name is Father Burke, I'm a parish priest and honored to call your brother Pat Ryan a good friend of mine. Over the last year and a half, I've had the pleasure of getting to know your daughter better. She's a hard worker, a kind girl."

Her parents exchanged a look, wondering what the priest was leading up to.

"I won't keep you waiting. I'm here because of Kate. Her news will come as a shock to you, but I hope—"

Her mam's eyes widened, darting to Kate's stomach.

"How dare you come back here and show your face as if you were a decent girl," Ma yelled, her face turning various shades of purple. "I knew it. It was a mistake to send you to your uncle Pat. He couldn't take care of a—"

"Emer! That's enough. Father, please excuse my wife's outburst. Kate, what do you have to tell us?"

Kate struggled to speak past the lump in her throat, and wiped the tears from her eyes. Her father's gentle voice was one thing, but the look of reproach in his eyes was another.

"Da, Mam, I'm... I'm going to have a baby." Kate curled her hands together, rubbing the palm of one with the fingers of the other. "I'm sorry. I... we didn't mean for it to happen but... well, it did. Tony, he's the father, had to go back to the war so he can't marry me."

Da paled and his hands shook. "Does he know?" His voice was so quiet, she barely heard him.

"No, Da, he doesn't. At least I don't think he does. I wrote but I haven't had a reply. I don't really know where he is."

"Get out," her mother boomed, wide-eyed.

She jumped at her mam's shout.

"Go on, get out. I don't care who you brought with you.

Nothing changes the fact you are sinner, Catherine Ryan. You were all set to join the convent. The neighbors are going to have a field day at my expense."

"Mrs. Ryan, let's calm down," said the priest. "We are all sinners and while it is true Kate has made a mistake, she hasn't lost her calling. From what I have seen and been told, Kate is a natural-born mother. It wasn't her dream to join the good sisters. There are many ways to serve the Lord."

"Are you telling me you condone what she's... what they have done?"

"Obviously not. They committed a mortal sin, but Kate has sought forgiveness from our Lord. I do not condone their actions, but it is not my place to condemn or judge your daughter. She's a sinner but so am I. As indeed so are you."

"What sort of priest are you?" she yelled, before turning on Kate, pointing her finger at her chest. "Just wait until Father Devine hears about this. He'll call your name from the altar and then where will we be? Laughing stock. That's where."

"Emer, hush up." Her da stood up. "I don't care what the neighbors say or whether they laugh or not. Kate, what will you do, child? Go to your sisters in England and have the baby adopted? You could stay over there and get a job. Give the neighbors some time to find something else to gossip about."

"I want to keep my baby, Da." She tried to take his hand but he moved it out of her reach. Instead, she covered her belly. "I love my baby."

"Love! 'Tis talk of love that got you into this fine mess. Didn't I warn you what would happen but when have you ever listened to your mother?" Her mam turned on Da. "This is all your fault, you've always been soft with her. Letting her have her own way and sending her off to your brother. You Ryans, you haven't a clue."

"Emer, I told you to hush," replied her father. "I won't have you showing such disrespect not only to me, but to our guest and our daughter. Father Burke, I share my wife's surprise at your views. They aren't what we are used to." Before Father Burke could protest, her da continued. "Although our country might be better off if the version of the church you seem to follow were in charge. Now, Kate love, you can't keep the baby. That's daft talk. Sure, how would you keep it fed and clothed? Unless this young man steps forward to marry you. We can't take on the baby either." Her father coughed and the red stain was evident on his hanky. "If I had my strength, I could offer both of you a home but... Well, that option just isn't available."

"I won't share my home with a Jezebel. That's my final word on the subject." With that her mam grabbed her shawl and stalked out the door.

Da sighed heavily. "She's away to fetch our local priest no doubt. Come across him in your travels, Father?"

"No, Mr. Ryan, I can't say I have."

"You'd remember him. All fire and brimstone he is. Everything is pure evil in his eyes. He has a knack of turning the most innocent of things into a sin, if you don't mind me being frank with you." He glanced at his daughter. "Dear God above, Kate, what have you done?"

Kate stood up. "I'm sorry, Da, I didn't mean to disappoint or hurt you."

He held his arms out to her and she ran into them, almost knocking over the seat he sat on. "*Alannah*." His use of the Irish term brought more tears. "Your mam is right about one thing. I've always had a soft spot for you. You're my baby girl. I wanted to protect you, look after you. I did a poor job of that." His tears hit her cheek. She'd never seen her da cry before.

"Ah, Da, don't. You're the best daddy anyone could have. I'm so sorry. I didn't mean to let this happen, but I love Tony. I swear, Da, I love him. And he loves me."

"'Tis more than love you will need now, child." He hugged her before pulling gently away. "Father Burke must be hungry. Heat up that soup for him before he loses his appetite when the other one arrives back with your mam."

Kate did as she was told, while Father Burke and her da

chatted at the kitchen table like old friends. She was surprised to find the priest had served during the last war, and knew what it was like for her da. They even laughed a couple of times. Kate couldn't eat herself but dished up the vegetable soup and fresh-made soda bread for the men. While they ate, she changed into older clothes and went out to catch up on a few chores for her mam.

Joe's absence was even more pronounced in the farmyard, where her da had clearly fallen behind in the chores. The barn door didn't close properly, damp having warped the wood. Walking inside, her nose wrinkled with distaste, the lingering odor of animal waste and dead hay turning her stomach. Tears pricked her eyes as evidence of her father's deteriorating health mounted. She should have come home sooner to help her mam.

Glad of the hard work, she pulled on Joe's old jumper, his scent still lingering in the Aran wool. It made her feel he was with her. Feeling slightly calmer, she collected eggs, fed the animals and was about to change the straw in the horse's stall when she looked out and saw her mother coming back down the lane, Father Devine walking tall beside her. She shivered at the look on his face, slipping out the back of the barn and running to the kitchen door. "They're here," she gasped as she washed her hands, pulled off the jumper and was sitting down just in time before the door opened.

"Bless this house," Father Devine greeted them as he stepped inside, taking off his hat. His florid face contrasted sharply with the crystal white starched stiff clerical collar around his neck. His black cassock, appearing spotless despite the mucky roads he had traveled, flowed behind him but it was his eyes Kate fastened on. Her nails dug into her palms in a bid not to shake at the coldness in his expression. Chairs screeched against the floor as Father Burke and her da stood up.

Father Burke held out his hand to the priest in greeting, which Father Devine pretended not to see as he turned to put his hat on the hook just inside the back door. Kate held her breath at the insult but Father Burke didn't react. Her da sat back down, breathing heavily, his handkerchief at his mouth. Father Devine turned to face them.

"Thank you for bringing Kate home to her family, Father Burke. But we mustn't keep you. No doubt you have business in your own parish, awaiting your return." The meaning was clear: *Get out of my business.* Kate gasped at his rudeness but Father Burke spoke in a moderate tone.

"I'm actually heading to Galway for a couple of days. Bishop Michael Brown was my theology teacher at Maynooth."

"Perfect. I've no doubt the bishop will have a stern discussion over your views on sin and sinners. Good evening to you, Father Burke." Father Devine took out a chair and sat down at the table, his dismissal evident.

Kate looked to her da to object but he said nothing. Instead, he seemed to grow smaller looking in his chair. Father Burke picked up his hat and his little case and nodded in the direction of Kate's parents.

"Perhaps you could walk me to the top of the lane, Kate?" Father Burke turned to Father Devine. "Father, please remember Kate and her as yet unborn child are both God's creatures and deserve love and kindness."

Father Devine hrumpped. Kate followed Father Burke out the door, willing him to stay but knowing he was just as powerless as she was. Father Devine was the parish priest, a position on the same level as the President of Ireland as far as the local community was concerned.

They walked to the top of the lane. Turning, Father Burke took Kate's hand in his, placing his second hand on top. He sighed deeply before saying softly, "I think I may have overestimated my abilities to speak to your parents, Kate, and for that I am sorry. I should pray for forgiveness for the sin of pride. I hope Father Devine will do his best to help you all. I will pray for you." He tugged his collar as if he felt it was stifling him.

"Thank you, Father, for being so kind. You can't help what Mam is like or what she believes. Please pray for Tony as well and my brother Joe to both come through the war safely. Someday I want us all to be together again."

Father Burke put his hand under her chin, forcing her to look into his eyes. "Kate, you will need every ounce of strength you have to look after yourself and your baby. It's probably for the best if you put Tony out of your mind."

"Never, Father. I love him." Kate spotted Mrs. O'Hara in the distance and waved to their neighbor. "That's Mrs. O'Hara, Father, she is a nice lady. If you walk her way, she'll probably invite you in for a cup of tea and Mr. O'Hara might give you a lift back to Galway. I'd best get back."

He smiled but it didn't dim the pity in his eyes. "Goodbye, Kate."

With a pat on her shoulder, he walked in the direction of the O'Mara homestead. Kate watched for a couple of seconds, her stomach plummeting, ignoring the sleety rain now falling, before turning back home. At the door, she forced her shoulders back, ready to do battle for the sake of her baby.

"Is the father of the child a Catholic?" Father Devine greeted her as she walked into the kitchen. He was sitting at the table as if he owned the house, a plate of scones in front of him and the best china.

"Yes, Father." Kate crossed her fingers at the half lie. Tony had been born a Catholic. His current views were none of Father Devine's business.

"Where is he stationed?"

"I don't know, Father. He hasn't had a chance to write to me yet."

"More like he's never given you a second thought. He got what he wanted." Her mother struck her across the face. "My daughter. A trollop."

Holding her stinging cheek, Kate tried to remonstrate with both of them. "It wasn't like that. Tony loves me. He'll write as soon as he can. You'll see. Mary will send on his letters."

"No, she won't," her mam replied. "You are not to have any

correspondence with your cousin, your uncle or this Tony again. Do you hear me? From now on you will behave yourself. Father Devine will make some enquiries. There are places for women like you. You can have the baby and then we will see what the future holds for you. The baby will be adopted."

"No!"

"Don't talk back to me, Catherine Ryan. There is no way for you to keep the brat even if we were to agree to it. Child of the devil you are carrying. Let it be someone else's problem. It isn't going to be ours."

"Mam, this is your grandchild," Kate said in a raw voice.

She didn't like the way the priest was looking at her. Like a cat that had swallowed a canary.

"'Tis nothing to do with me. Or your father."

Kate looked beyond her mam to see her father's head resting on his chest. There was no help going to come from that quarter. Despair threatened to overwhelm her.

"I'll go to England. Orla will help me."

"Orla can barely look after her own brood with that good for nothing husband of hers off fighting a war we have no business being a part of. No, my girl, there is nothing for it but for you to stay here. Inside, mind, as I don't want you talking to the neighbors. Father Devine will need a little time to sort things out but it will be done within the next two weeks. And that will be all that is said about this." Her mam held one arm across her chest, pointing one finger at Kate. "Do you hear me?"

Despite knowing her mam wouldn't react well, the last vestige of hope that she'd been wrong disappeared. Tears streaming down her face, she begged, "Da, please help me. Don't let her do this, please."

"Your da agrees with me. You saw how everyone treated those orphans the Cumiskeys fostered; even the kids of the parish threw stones at them or beat them up in the schoolyard. Everyone knows a baby born out of wedlock carries the devil's mark. Do you think I will stand back and watch the Ryan name be dragged through the mud? Not on my watch, young lady. Now excuse yourself and go to your room."

"Mam?"

"Your room!" she shouted.

Knowing it was pointless trying to talk to her mother, Kate climbed the stairs to her small space in the loft. Compared to the room she had at Uncle Pat's it was tiny, with barely enough head-room for her to stand up straight and a tiny bed under the eaves. But something about the familiarity made her feel better. She picked up her copy of *Gone with the Wind*. Da had given it to her the last Christmas before she'd left for the Curragh. A shell sitting on the shelf was one Joe had collected for her. Tears caught at the back of her throat. Why hadn't Joe answered her letters? Surely, he'd had shore leave by now. If he was here he'd stand up to their mam. Wouldn't he?

The temptation to eavesdrop grew too much and she lay on the floor trying to hear the conversation taking place below her. Father Devine mentioned somewhere called Bessborough in Cork, New Ross in Wexford and another place in the Navan Road. With her ear pressed to the floorboards, she could hear them discussing convents. If the nuns would help her with her baby, maybe it wouldn't be as bad as it sounded?

SEVENTEEN

A week later, Kate woke to a touch on her forehead. Her mam had sent her to pray in her bedroom and she must have fallen asleep. "Da, what are you doing?"

"Time to go, child. Father Devine is downstairs. Don't keep him waiting. He's driving you to the home."

Kate jumped out of bed, throwing herself at her father, wrapping her arms around him.

"Da, please. I'll do anything, don't send me away. I'm sorry."

He held her close briefly before releasing her as he took a fit of coughing, his tears aggravating his chest. He gasped, "Don't take too long. You don't want the priest coming up here."

The drumming of her heartbeat almost drowned out the sound of his descent down the stairs.

Kate dressed as fast as she could, her hands shaking so much her dress fell to the floor. It took an age to tie her shoes; her fingers wouldn't obey her command. The scent of fried bacon and eggs wafted up to her room causing her stomach to rumble. Morning sickness had been replaced by almost continuous hunger. She'd had nothing to eat since breakfast and then only a slice of yesterday's bread.

Coming downstairs, her mother wouldn't even turn around.

The table was bare but for the yolk-stained plate and china teacup in front of the priest. His chair screeched on the stone floor as he pushed it back to stand up.

"Come along. I've a dinner to attend in Galway City this evening so I will have to drop you at the gate of the convent. Mother Superior is aware you are coming, we mustn't keep her waiting."

Kate knew she was gawping at him but surely she could have dinner. She looked to her mam, but she turned away.

Kate took a step toward her but her da shook his head. He took her arm and walked her outside, following in the wake of the priest.

"Mind yourself and do what they tell you. I'll work on your mam so you can come home after..." Her da's eyes dropped.

"I can't give up my baby, Da. You wouldn't want that. It's your grandchild."

Her da shook his head, whatever he was about to say drowned out by a roar from the priest to get in the car.

Kate waved to her da long after he had disappeared. Closing her eyes, she could see him stooped over as if he'd aged twenty years overnight. The drive took place in silence. Kate closed her eyes, trying to hold back the tears.

The car drew to a stop outside a large wall, the top of which was covered in broken glass. Kate knew there was a convent behind the wall but had never been inside. Was the glass a deterrent to those trying to get in or was it to stop those inside getting out?

The priest blinked rapidly. "You can get out here. Go straight inside or the guards will be after you. Don't bring any more shame on your poor parents. Do you hear me?"

"Yes, Father." The car door slammed shut just as the car moved off. If he'd been any closer, he'd have shaved her legs.

Kate walked down the long drive, sweat dripping down her back and her forehead, not that anyone would have noticed in the streaming rain. She cradled her stomach with one hand, the second holding a small brown case. The baby kicked. "I know, I don't like it much either, but we don't have a choice." Kate couldn't remember when she'd first started talking to her unborn child.

The large Georgian property, covered in ivy, stood facing south overlooking a large lake, surrounded by picturesque gardens. The vivid green grass lawns edged with beautifully manicured shrubs were a riot of color in the otherwise gray day. She wondered how many gardeners were employed on keeping the grounds so pretty.

Feeling eyes on her, she glanced at the windows as she approached, hoping to catch a friendly face. Shielding her eyes with her hand, she stared, but couldn't see anyone, yet she could sense that somebody was there. She slowed her walk, dreading the last few steps to the large oak door. She looked behind her but there was no point in going back that way. Her mother would inform the priest and local guard, neither of whom would be pleased to escort her back to this place.

Putting her case on the ground beside her, she pushed the hair out of her face and knocked on the door. As she stood waiting, the seconds ticking by, she couldn't hear anything. Despite knowing there were over a hundred people living in the home, there wasn't a single sound apart from the rain hitting the ground.

She raised her hand to knock again when she heard the screech of metal on the door as the bolt was slid across; the black door opened inwards. Kate hesitated as nobody came out. Was she supposed to just walk in or wait for an invitation?

"Sorry, child. What am I like, leaving you outside? Come on in. Just dry your shoes on the mat there. That's it. Can I take the case?" The nun held out her hand. If it were not for the stiff coif framing the youthful nun's face and the white wimple covering her from under her chin and down onto her chest, Kate would have assumed she was simply a postulant not a fully-fledged nun. Her long black veil, attached to the coif, swirled around her giving an impression of a young girl dancing. Delight in life filled the nun's eyes. "I'm Sister John Bosco and, like yourself, a new arrival to this home. We could have shared a ride to the convent. And you are?"

Kate exhaled; this was going to be all right. The young nun smiled, her eyes full of gentleness, not the condemnation her mother's held.

"Kate, I mean Catherine Ryan. Thank you, Sister, but I can manage. I'm sorry for dripping all over the floor. I had to walk from—"

"Don't apologize. Come along in. Reverend Mother is waiting in her office. Let me close the door behind you."

Kate tried to make herself slimmer, rather difficult at five months pregnant, but Sister John Bosco was able to squeeze past her to close the door.

The water dripped over the wooden floor as she followed Sister John Bosco down the long white-walled corridor with its incredibly shining wooden floor. Despite it being early evening, there wasn't a sound from any room inside the convent. She'd expected to hear babies crying or laughing or something. If you said there wasn't anyone else in the building, she'd believe it.

"I'd imagine you are cold and hungry, Kate. When Reverend Mother dismisses you, I will take you to the kitchens for something to eat and find you some dry clothes." Sister John Bosco smiled and then nodded at the door. "Go on in, she's expecting you."

Kate wanted to ask the nun to come with her but decided she was being silly. She knocked and pushed the door open, the heat of the roaring turf fire inside a stark contrast to the freezing cold corridor. Immediately her clothes started steaming and the smell of wet wool filled the room. The door closed behind her as Kate moved closer to the figure sitting behind a large wooden desk, a picture of Pope Pius above her head. She kept writing as Kate watched, wondering if the woman was even aware Kate was in the room, let alone standing in front of her. You could almost see the nun's face in the sheen from the mahogany desk—there wasn't a speck of dust in the whole room; even the hearth around the fire had been freshly swept. Kate could feel a puddle forming around her feet but was too intimidated to do anything other than cough. Yet the nun continued to write.

Eyeing the straight-back chair in front of the desk, Kate wondered if she should just sit down. Her aching feet would thank her. She lifted one foot at the same time as the nun put down her pen, raised her eyes and pierced Kate to the spot with a glare. In stark contrast to the kindness shining from Sister John Bosco, this face was cold, drawn into a mask with eyes so blue they were almost opaque.

"Ryan. You're late."

"Sorry, Sister..." She kicked herself; the proper term of address was Mother not Sister.

"Don't speak unless I ask you to. Father Devine wrote to me and told me all about you and your sins. You won't get away with your wanton behavior anymore."

Kate's stomach rumbled. She hadn't eaten since breakfast and that had only been a rushed piece of bread. The noise gained her another reproachful look.

"I expected better manners from a girl of your background, but I see we have our work cut out for us. While you are here you will learn new ways. But first our rules. You are a penitent; that's what we call all the fallen women here."

Kate wasn't sure if she was supposed to say anything so chose silence. It seemed the right choice as the nun continued.

"Penitents are expected to conduct themselves in silence. There is to be no talking unless you answer a question from one of our sisters. There will be total obedience."

Kate wondered if the silence meant she should answer. She opted for a nod and was rewarded with one in return.

"You will, of course, know of the story of Mary Magdalene from the Bible."

This time she was expected to answer. "Yes, Mother."

"Just like Jesus saved Mary Magdalene, so too shall you be saved through a combination of prayer, discipline and hard work. The outside world may refer to the women who work in our laundries as Maggies but that is not a term you will ever use."

Again Kate knew a response was expected but this time she

wasn't sure what was appropriate. She scratched her neck, wishing the rain hadn't made the material so itchy. The nun might think she had fleas.

The nun didn't utter another word but reached for a large bell on her desk. She rang it, bringing the sound of footsteps running down the corridor before they heard a knock on the door.

"Come."

The door opened so slowly, increasing the tension. Kate couldn't hold back her gasp at her first glimpse of the new arrival. The young girl looked half starved, her cheekbones jutting out prominently on her face, reminding Kate of young Shane.

"You rang, Mother?" the girl whispered, speaking to the floor. Kate couldn't take her eyes off the new arrival's shorn hair and shapeless dress.

"Take Fidelma to room twelve. See to it she has a bath and a change of clothes. And no running."

The girl nodded, almost curtseying to the nun, her gaze never leaving the ground. She turned to leave.

"Fidelma, what are you waiting for?" said the nun to Kate. "Follow Irene."

"My name is—"

The nun's cold tone cut her off. "Your name is what we tell you it is. From now on you will answer to Fidelma and you will forget all about your past life of sin. Follow Irene, she will show you around and outline the rules. They are simple enough even for someone like you to understand. Good evening."

The Reverend Mother picked up her pen and recommenced writing as if there was nobody in the room. Kate opened her mouth but caught a glance from the other girl, who shook her head slightly.

Picking up her case, Kate followed the girl in silence down the corridor. The walls adorned by religious pictures and crucifixes seemed to press in on her, the eyes in the picture of the Sacred Heart following her.

"Irene, wait. Do you have to walk so fast?"

"Shush. We're not allowed to talk," Irene sputtered, glancing around the dark corridor as if expecting someone to jump out at them. The young girl took off her shoes and put them in a cupboard to the right of the staircase. She indicated Kate do the same before turning and heading up the stairs. Kate took off her shoes, and put them in the same cupboard all the time resisting the urge to run back to the front door and make a break for freedom. She looked up to see Irene disappearing up the stairs, so she followed, trying to dampen the panic rising in her chest. On and on they climbed until they'd reached the fourth floor.

"Leave your case there and follow me." Irene pointed to the corner where two of the white walls met, before pushing open the door to a room. Kate followed, nearly walking into Irene's back as she took in the view. There was a bath full of scalding water and two women—although not thin like Irene, they were dressed in the same shapeless outfits, their heads shaved, their facial expressions frozen—stood waiting for them. Instinctively, Kate backed up, but Irene had already slipped out and closed the door behind her.

"Get undressed and be quick about it," said one of the women. "We're hungry, don't have time to be waiting around for the likes of you."

Kate held her coat tighter against her. "I had a bath last night, I don't need another one."

The younger of the two well-built women flexed a muscular arm. "You'll have a bath. Sister's orders and nobody disobeys the rules. It's easier if you just do as you're told."

Kate stepped back, until she reached the door, looking frantically around the room for some sort of escape. But the one sole window was too small even if she wasn't several floors above ground level.

The older woman advanced with a look in her eye showing she meant business. "As Nora says, it's easier to work with us than against us. Take off your clothes now."

Relenting, Kate unbuttoned her coat before shrugging it off and everything else she was wearing. Stepping forward, she didn't attempt to hide her nudity. The women didn't look at her, not as a person. Trembling, she put a hand in the steaming bath. "Please, the water, it's too hot." Her mind spun. Wasn't a scalding tub and a bottle of alcohol a way to get rid of a baby? She wrapped her arms around her stomach. "I'll go to hell if I do anything to my baby."

Nora rolled her eyes. "Nobody cares. It's illegitimate. Not wanted by anyone."

"I want it." As Kate said the words she realized they were true. Standing here, as naked as the day she was born, she wanted her baby more than anything else. Even Tony.

The older woman tsked but Nora picked up a jug and poured some cold water in. It didn't change the temperature too much, but Kate got in regardless. She didn't want these women to help her. Her skin stung as she held her breath, trying not to cry out. Eventually, the water warmed her chilled body. She relaxed slightly until Nora handed her a white flannel and a bar of evil-smelling soap. It was even worse than her mother's carbolic soap.

"Every inch needs to be scrubbed. You have to wash off the evil of your sins." Nora mimicked the Mother Superior's voice perfectly, exchanging a grin with the older woman. "Was the five minutes of pleasure worth this?"

Kate ignored them, gingerly scrubbing as much of her legs and body that she could reach. Her baby kicked out, his foot clearly visible under the mound of her stomach.

"Is it true you're carrying an English bas—"

Kate cut the woman off, retorting, "That's none of your business." Her mother had asked the same question. Kate closed her eyes, remembering the harsh tone and hatred dripping from her mother's eyes. Which was worse, being unmarried and pregnant or lying with the enemy?

Only Tony hadn't been the enemy. He was American, wearing the uniform of the RAF with pride, just like the other lads had. He was just the same as Joe and Frank. If she concentrated hard enough, she could hear him whispering to her, telling her how much he loved her, how he was going to marry her as soon as he could. First, he had to survive. After the war was over, he'd be back to find her and together they would tell her mother they were getting wed.

Kate screamed as a large clump of her hair landed on the floor beside the bath. She didn't have time to react before the woman cut more, her reddish-brown curls covering the wooden floor. Trying to get up, she slipped on the side of the bath, sending water flushing over as she struggled to leave.

"What did you do that for?" she spurted through the water.

"Sister's orders," Nora replied. "All your hair has to be removed to get rid of nits."

"I don't have lice."

"Can't be vain now, can we? If you settle down, I will cut it carefully, try not to injure you, but either way you will look just like Irene when you leave here. It's up to you how much it hurts."

Kate massaged her bare scalp with her fingers, catching the look the women exchanged and accepted defeat. For now. She didn't resist another second but allowed them to shear her head right down to the scalp. A pail of freezing water washed the last pieces of hair from her shoulders. Shivering, she stood up, drying herself on the hard towel and putting on the clothes they gave her, a pair of bloomers her grandmother would wear tied with a string, rough woolen tights and a shapeless shift. There was no mirror, but she guessed she mirrored Irene, the blue coarse fabric like a shroud covering her from her neck to her knees.

She couldn't cry, rail against her treatment. She could barely move one leg in front of the other, too shocked by it all. Irene arrived so fast that Kate wondered if she'd been waiting outside the door the whole time. She glanced around for her case, but it had disappeared.

"I'll show you where we sleep and then we have to hurry downstairs, or we will miss supper," said the girl.

At last, she'd get some food although her stomach wasn't grumbling anymore. She followed Irene down to a dormitory with ten identical beds. There wasn't a single personal item in sight.

"That one is yours." Irene pointed at the bed in the far corner. "Come on, we'll be late."

The girl walked out and hurried down the stairs, leaving Kate with no option but to follow. The oppressive feeling intensified as they were joined by others, all wearing the same uniform of shorn heads and shapeless frocks, filing down the stairs in complete silence. She noticed nobody was wearing shoes. She sniffed the air but there was no scent of cooking. She tried to catch the eye of a girl walking near her but to no avail. As they walked into the dining room, she was staggered to find there were almost forty pregnant girls standing at the tables, all totally silent. On the dais in front of the hall, a long table was fitted with a white tablecloth and set with silverware. The glasses shone in the light. Kate saw the nun who'd first greeted her, Sister John Bosco, smile at them all as they walked in. Her gaze dropped when her eyes met those of Kate but not before Kate saw the shame—or was it shock—in the nun's eyes. Then she met those of the Reverend Mother, not mistaking the gloating expression. Kate picked up the message. She was nothing, this was the Reverend Mother's domain, and her word was law.

Kate stood next to Irene until a signal was given and they took their seats, a loud scraping noise overtaking the room. Once everyone was sitting, a gong indicated grace. Reverend Mother led the group with a prayer for forgiveness for their collective sins, especially for those of their latest joiner, who had fraternized with the enemy.

Kate kept her eyes open; she wasn't prepared to let that woman show the hurt her words caused.

Supper arrived in the form of bread and margarine soaked in milk. "Goody" was the name her mother gave to this vile concoction, reminding Kate regularly how lucky she was not to live in the tenements in Galway City where children were fed this muck at every meal. Silently, Kate waited for the girls around her to start eating. But nobody moved. The reason why soon became apparent when the scent of pork chops made Kate's mouth run with saliva.

The nuns were served a proper meal, meat and two vegetables, peas and carrots, if her nose was anything to go by, followed by a large, heaped mound of mashed potatoes. Even in this light, she could see the gold puddle glistening on top of the white mash and could bet it was real Irish butter not margarine gracing the nuns' plates. She glanced around her table but not a single girl looked in the direction of the nuns.

At another signal the girls picked up their spoons and started eating the meal in front of them. Kate took a taste and almost spat the revolting mixture back onto her plate. She pushed it away but a sharp nudge from Irene made her take it back.

"They will beat all of us if you don't eat it," Irene whispered out the side of her mouth.

Kate looked at her in disbelief but then after everything else that had happened in the short hours since she'd walked through the oak door, she couldn't take the chance. She didn't care what the nuns did to her, but she wasn't going to be responsible for any more brutality to the girls surrounding her.

EIGHTEEN

After the worst meal of her life, a rotund nun with bulging eyes, called Sister Anne, directed Kate back to the dormitory where she would sleep. Her teeth rattled it was so cold, the stone floor causing her stocking feet to freeze. Laid on the bed was a nightgown. It had been patched several times but at least it looked clean.

"The other penitents will be up here soon enough. You'd best be in bed fast asleep when they arrive. Remember we hold a vow of silence here, so no talking to the other girls. They won't answer you so best not to try." The nun's pinched expression turned the innocent remark into a threat. "There is no getting out of bed at night so use the facilities now."

Sister Anne indicated a door to the left outside of the room. Inside was a single toilet and basin but at least they didn't have to go outside to a privy. Following the nun back to the bedroom, Kate's widening eyes were drawn to the barred window, nailed shut and covered in chicken wire.

The nun left her to it. Alone, Kate stripped off the scratchy, horrible uniform, putting on the old nightgown. She tried to find a comfortable spot on the bed but the mattress was somehow both thin and lumpy. The sheets were rough and the blanket smelled of detergent. How she missed her warm bed at Uncle Pat's with the quilts her Granny Ryan had made. How was she going to last living in total silence?

The sound of feet on the stairs announced the arrival of the other penitents, accompanied by the same nun. As they filed in, Kate kept her eyes squeezed closed, hoping the sister would believe she was sleeping. Once the other girls had undressed and got into bed, the nun left. After a little while, once her heartbeat had stilled, Kate opened her eyes to find several girls staring at her. They crept out of their beds and gathered around hers.

"My name's Agnes, in here anyway. Irene said your hair was magnificent. Like a horse's mane in all sorts of reddish brown, chestnut and autumn colors. Those witches had to make you remove it. They don't like us looking or acting like anything but sinners."

"That's why they keep the men away, worried they will get so worked up by our lovely *gúnaí* they'll jump us." The girl held her shapeless dress out either side and pretended to curtsey. "I'm Maura." She held out her hand in greeting, her eyes sparkling with mischief. "Even Father Flanagan is never allowed to be alone with us."

Irene glanced fearfully at the closed bedroom door before hissing, "Shut up, Maura. Fidelma doesn't want to hear your stupid comments."

"You shut up." Nora, the girl who had cut her hair, threw Irene a dirty look. "Do you think she wants to hear your nonsense? About keeping your head down and doing everything they tell you so you can do your three years and go home to live happily ever after with your Paddy? You're a fool."

"I'm not. Paddy said he'd wait for me." Irene bit her quivering lip before directing her next words to Kate. "As long as it took, he said."

Nora sneered. "Sure, and what's he doing every Friday and Saturday? I'll tell ya. He's off chasing any other woman who'll let him into her knickers. That's the truth."

Irene moved faster than Kate would have thought possible

given her emaciated frame. She had her hands at Nora's throat. "Shut up, you mean old witch. Just because—"

A tall, slim girl with beautiful eyes spoke firmly. "Nora, Irene, stop it. Fidelma doesn't want to hear your petty quarrels." The girl held out her hand to Kate. "My name, here at least, is Geraldine but everyone calls me Ger when the nuns aren't around."

Kate responded to the gentleness emanating from the girl. "Kate Ryan. How long have you been here?"

"I've been here six months now. I was in hospital and then the Gardai brought me here."

Kate couldn't resist asking, "The police? What did you do?"

"Nothing. I was working in a shop and someone broke in. I was attacked and badly injured. I was in the hospital for months. When they fixed me up, it was obvious I was pregnant. My parents wouldn't have me home so there was nowhere else."

Nora caressed her red-marked throat. "At least you get out when yer brat comes. You're one of the lucky ones."

Kate couldn't believe someone thought a rape victim landing in a place like this was lucky.

She caught a fleeting look of pain in the other girl's eyes before Ger clarified. "She means I won't have to stay for three years after the baby is born. My parents paid the one hundred good old Irish pounds the nuns charge so I can leave early."

"What do you mean early?" Kate's heart hammered against her chest. Was this a way out for her and her baby?

Ger's next comment flattened her hope. "If you don't have the hundred punt, you must stay working for the sisters for the next three years to offset the cost of looking after you and your baby."

Kate's mouth opened but she couldn't get the words out. Three years? She would be trapped here for that long?

"The nuns don't offset the money they get from selling our babies against the huge cost of starving us." Maura's sarcasm didn't help Kate's nerves.

Ger shot Maura a dirty look before putting her hand on Kate's arm, saying gently, "The best advice I can give you is to keep your head down. It's bad enough without upsetting Reverend Mother. Good luck."

Ger went back to her own bed, leaving Kate feeling bereft even though they had just met. Agnes patted her arm, and this time Kate looked closer at the girl whose eyes were all-knowing, as if she'd lived a thousand years instead of the twenty she looked.

"Been here three months," Agnes said. "My da dropped me off on his way to the boat. He works in the merchant navy. If he was at home, maybe this wouldn't have happened."

"Leave off, Agnes." Maura gave Agnes a none too gentle poke. "This is her second time here, a second offender we call her. The nuns said they'd have to tie her legs together before they let her go home next time."

Kate cringed at the crude language, but Agnes didn't seem to take offense. She sat on the edge of Kate's bed. "So, what happened to you? Was it yer father?"

Kate felt the blood drain out of her face. "What? No, of course not."

"Good, 'cause the nuns they don't like those kids. Don't treat them right. Just ask Helena." Agnes indicated a girl lying on her bed facing the wall. Either the girl was deaf, or she was used to the horrible teasing as she didn't move a muscle. Then she turned back to Kate.

"Where's the da?"

Kate had planned on keeping Tony's details to herself but given the comments from the women who washed her and the nuns, it wasn't a secret. She refused to be ashamed of him. Putting her shoulders back, she spoke proudly. "He's a pilot. In the RAF."

Agnes' eyes widened as she leaned in closer. "Really? I bet he was handsome. Their uniform looks good on most of them. How did you meet a flyer?"

"My uncle owns a pub near the Curragh, the internment camp is there."

At the blank faces looking at her, Kate added, "The camp where they keep the British and Germans if they get shot down and land in Ireland. We're supposed to be neutral, so we must keep them in a camp until the war is over. But last October, the British forced their hand and made the government release them."

"So, your flyer knocked you up on his way back to fight for England?" one girl sneered.

Agnes hit her sharply. "Shut up, Bernie, let her talk. I like her accent and want to hear her story."

"Tony and I met in April 1942. The prisoners come and drink in the pub. Not on the same night, of course, as then there would be fights. The Germans come some nights and the RAF on the others."

Bernie, heading back to her bed, hissed, "I wouldn't let an Englishman come within an oar of me."

"They wouldn't bother coming near ya, Bernie. They like them pretty and young."

Some of the girls laughed but Kate didn't. She hated bullying of any type.

"Tony is American not English. He and his English friends were nice lads, heroes fighting against the Nazis. If it weren't for them, we could have bombs dropping on us as well."

A couple of the girls looked impressed until Bernie added, "So you didn't serve the Germans then, or did you keep them warm at night too?"

"I'm not that type of girl," Kate protested, but even to her ears those protests sounded hollow given where she was. But it was true, she hadn't lain with anyone but Tony and only on that last night before he left. They shouldn't have, she'd known it was wrong, but she couldn't bear the thought of him going back to war and maybe not coming back.

"Quick, she's coming," Nora hissed, racing back from the direction of the bathroom.

The girls didn't need telling twice and they dispersed quicker than Kate thought possible, all jumping under their covers and assuming positions of sleep. They managed it just in time as the dormitory door opened, admitting a nun carrying a light. Kate squinted through her lashes, recognizing Sister John Bosco. She exhaled, only then realizing she had been holding her breath.

The nun glanced around the room. Whether she was taken in by the sounds of snoring, Kate didn't know. The nun looked behind her as if wondering if someone was following her before she carefully made her way to Kate's bed.

"Kate," she whispered, bending down. "I just wanted to say I'm sorry. I didn't... I hadn't... I never thought it was like that. I only arrived this morning. I know you're not asleep but I don't blame you if you don't believe me. I'm sorry. I just... I can't even find the words to explain. I'll do all I can to help you and the other girls here. Please believe that. No matter what the next few days and weeks bring."

The nun was gone before Kate, her heart pummeling, allowed her eyes to open. She sounded genuine but given everything that had happened, how could she believe her?

NINETEEN

It was still pitch black outside when the girls got up the next morning. Filled with dread, Kate pushed back the covers and joined them. First, they had to attend Mass. She shivered in the cold and didn't feel like praying but went along with the motions. Her stomach rumbled, her mouth watering at the smells filtering through to the chapel. A hot cooked breakfast was just what she needed.

When Mass finished, the girls walked in single file toward the dining room. This time Kate paid more attention to her surroundings. The large room had two long tables with benches either side. The girls queued down each side but nobody sat down. Another door at the top of the room opened and the nuns filed in, their black habits contrasting sharply with the crisp white linen tablecloth covering the table on the raised dais. The silverware glinted in the weak sunlight as they took their seats.

Only then could the girls sit down at the wooden tables, the ridges and pockmarks evidence of a long history of use. The penitents ate from chipped and cracked tableware using discolored metal utensils.

But Kate didn't care. The smell of bacon rashers, sausages—

and was that black pudding? —wafting under her nose made her stomach grumble.

Irene put a bowl of cold oats in front of Kate. Burned toast and cold weak tea accompanied the horrid mush. Each penitent got the same. Despite this, some fell upon the dishes like they were eating their last meal. Kate picked up her spoon, risking a glance at the top table where the nuns feasted.

Tears smarted at the unfairness, but she wisely held them back and forced herself to eat. There was little sympathy and even less charity within these walls.

At the end of the meal, they carried their dirty dishes to a big pot at the end of the hall. Any waste was scraped into a bin for the pigs, which currently stood empty.

Ger whispered, "Nobody dares leave anything on their plates. If they do and get caught, they have to eat the contents of the bin."

Kate believed her.

Kate followed the lines heading towards the back of the convent. A door opened and the smell of carbolic soap combined with bleach hit her immediately.

"That stinks." The stench of starch caught the back of her throat. She reckoned she'd still smell it long after leaving the laundry room.

A beady-eyed nun, her glasses hanging around her neck, roared at her. "Silence! There is no talking. You will work in silence. You are the new girl so I will excuse you this once. I am Sister Ita."

"But—"

"You are fallen women, dirt ye are. While you work you will think about your soul, pray for guidance, for redemption."

Kate looked around the room dominated by three large machines. There were four girls working each machine with another two on hand to fold the freshly ironed sheets. The sweat poured down her back and arms and she had yet to move. Some of the girls around her were little more than children. They looked like twelve-year-olds, with skinny bodies, hair forming clumps on the top of their heads. But it was their eyes that shocked her most. Each girl was the same, their expression dulled and dead.

She watched as two girls fed the material into the calendar, mesmerized by the crumpled white sheet traveling between the red-hot steel roller and sheet of metal, coming out on the other side perfectly ironed.

"What are you waiting for? Help the others." Sister Ita pushed her forward. She picked up the sheet and took her place among the four. The other girls didn't even look up, never mind speak.

The heat was unbearable, the work tiring and difficult. What would it be like in the summer months when it was warm outside? Kate hoped she wouldn't be there long enough to find out.

As they worked, she watched the girls closely. If the sheet didn't go through the roller correctly, the creases would be in the wrong place. Again and again they lifted wet sheets and put them through the giant rollers until they were dry. Her throat was as dry as sand. She glanced at the other women; some of them were obviously pregnant but others were older—a few of them even had gray hair. What were they doing in here?

Distracted, Kate fell forward, hitting her arm on the hot steel. She watched as her skin blistered from the burn, only vaguely aware this was happening to her and not someone else. The pain registered, the tears pricking her eyes as the skin seemed to bubble in front of her. Stunned, she walked toward the nun, holding her arm out, biting her lip to stop the scream escaping from her lips.

"Why did you stop working?"

"I burned myself, Sister." She held out her arm for inspection, but the nun barely glanced at it.

"Get back to work and stop shirking. That will heal in no time."

Shocked, she stared at the woman, but the nun's eyes remained cold. Turning in defeat, she went back to her place at the calendar.

Ger leaned in closer and whispered, "No point in expecting any sympathy. They don't have hearts, none of them."

"What was that you said, Geraldine?" barked the nun.

"Sorry, Sister, I was just saying to Fidelma to ask the Sacred Heart for a blessing on her burn."

"Our Lord has much better things to be doing with his time, Geraldine. Now get back to work, girls. You're behind enough as it is."

The heat made the burn sting even more but Kate had no choice but to bite her lip and get on with it. Geraldine's act of kindness helped her feel less alone and when the girl came around later with a bowl of water, Kate was glad of it. Only later did she find out the girls took the water from the toilet bowl as it was the only source of water.

They finished working hours later when the gong went. Soon after it was the dinner gong. Kate filed into the dining area in a line, following the other girls to their respective cubbyholes where they found their cutlery. They took a seat in silence and ate the meal—lumpy mashed potato and boiled cabbage. Kate found she didn't care this time. She finished every morsel, being so hungry.

"Dinner is potatoes and cabbage every day. Some days we get a piece of fatty meat, nothing you'd recognize but you'll eat it. It's that or starve. On a Wednesday, it's dessert day," Geraldine whispered at her side.

"Pardon?" Kate muttered under her breath.

"That day we get a dessert, either bread and butter pudding, rice pudding or custard. But don't get excited. They give us the dessert without the meal. How do you think I got this figure?" Geraldine stuck out her stick-thin arm and leg.

A painful dig of an elbow in her side warned her a nun was watching. While they ate, a nun read a prayer before the girls marched out of the room in silence, splitting into two groups.

"The mothers go to the orphanage to spend an hour a day with their children. We get to do some sewing."

Kate screwed up her mouth in distaste; she hated most domestic crafts but sewing was the worst. She followed Ger into a smaller room furnished with tables and chairs. Sitting beside Ger, she watched as her friend chose a piece of fabric to work on. Kate followed her lead and picked a smaller piece. Looking around, she saw the girls sewing the garments used by the priests for Mass, the long-embroidered altar cloths. The material was so white Kate was afraid she'd get it dirty, but she didn't dare comment.

An elderly nun peered over her shoulder, tsking her displeasure.

"Make the stitches smaller, it's not crochet you're doing, Fidelma. Look at Geraldine, try to follow her example."

Ger gave her a look of sympathy once the nun's back was turned. The fear in the room was palpable, almost worse than it had been back in the laundry. It was as if they were waiting for something to upset the nun.

After two hours of pricking her fingers more often than the cloth, the nun clapped her hands. It was time for bed. Kate looked around for a clock but couldn't see one. Not that she cared, she couldn't wait to get into bed.

Her legs dragged, the pain in her back competing with the burn smarting on her arm. She was so tired, she simply followed the row of feet in front of her down the corridor and up various flights of stairs. Every step got harder, so it was a relief to finally reach the dormitory.

"Hurry up, girls, and get ready for bed."

Kate stripped off, fighting the temptation to climb into the bed fully clothed. The temperature in the room dropped as she became aware of an unsettling stillness. The booming voice made her jump.

"You are a brazen hussy. Do not lower the moral tone, Fidelma."

Kate spun as she realized she was the one the nun was shouting at. She glanced around, realizing the other girls had put on their nightgowns over their uniforms to remove their clothes for bedtime. The nun bore down on her, her black habit swishing with the wind generated by her speed.

"Have you no shame? Flaunting your body like a Jezebel?" Each word earned Kate a thump.

"Sorry, Sister, I didn't know." She pulled on her nightgown as fast as she could to put the thin barrier between her and the sharp slaps Sister Anne was dishing out. The other girls continued to undress in silence. Nobody came to her aid. She had never felt so alone.

TWENTY

After a week in the convent, Sister Anne stopped Kate on her way to the laundry.

"Fidelma, I need you in the orphanage this morning. Two of the girls who usually work in there are malingering, staying in bed claiming a fever."

Kate knew the girls had flu; they were babbling in their sleep, the sheets of their bed drenched in sweat. "Yes, Sister."

Nobody argued with Sister Anne given she liked to punctuate each syllable of reprimand with a slap. The nursery had to be an improvement on the laundry, especially on a beautiful day like today.

She followed the nun through a maze of corridors waiting for her to open each door and then lock it again behind them. Finally, they arrived at the orphanage. Where were the shouts and cries from the children? It was unnaturally quiet for a place where children lived.

"The babies need to be bathed. I assume you know how?"

"Yes, Sister, I helped our neighbors look after their younger ones."

The nun didn't respond but directed Kate into a room, before turning on her heel and retreating back the way she came, black skirts billowing out behind her.

Stepping inside, Kate shivered at the combination of gray walls and open windows. Surely nurseries were supposed to be bright, cheerful and warm? Fresh aprons hung on a wooden peg just inside the door. Furniture was sparse; one tiny tin bath hung on the wall above a shelving unit holding fresh napkins and some towels. Kate ran her fingers over one, not surprised to find it as scratchy as the ones the penitents had been given. Kate expected more staff but it was only her and four babies, all lying quietly in their respective cradles. From their sizes, she guessed they ranged in age from three to nine months. There were no names on anything, just a series of five numbers. She had no idea what that meant.

After putting on an apron, Kate set about getting ready, singing as she worked. The babies seemed to enjoy her renditions of different songs.

She picked up the first baby, cradling him gently in one arm while testing the bath water with her elbow, just like Mrs. Kelly had shown her years ago, with the other. It was just right. She lowered the child into the water, watching him carefully. The touch of water on his skin startled him at first, and he waved his arms around, but he didn't cry. She lowered him down and he smiled. His legs and arms kicked out, splashing water over her. Laughing, she scooped up some water with her free hand and ran it over his chest. He looked up at her, the complete trust in his expression melting her heart. She sucked in her breath as her own child kicked inside the womb. Would she bathe her own baby? The nuns didn't like you to get too close. If anything they seemed to take perverse pleasure out of keeping you and your baby apart.

"Now, little one, we have to get you dry. That's it, I'll wrap the towel around you just like this. Sorry it isn't as soft as you deserve but it's the best I could find. Lift your chin, that's a good boy. I've to dry all the creases as we don't want you getting any sores or a rash." She chatted away in a sing-song voice, hearing her mam in her head as she bathed the latest village newborn. She brushed a tear from her eye with her shoulder. What was she getting upset over? Her mother had always adored the babies; it was the older children she didn't like.

She glanced out the French windows to find a girl not much older than herself staring back at her, a look of longing on her face. She held the baby up so the other woman could see him.

"Is he yours?" she mouthed.

The girl looked around her before nodding. She stared at the child with such yearning that Kate knew she had to help. She moved as close as possible to the window, cradling the baby in the crook of her elbow to give the mother a better look.

"Look, baby, that's your mammy. She loves you to bits, she does. She'd do anything to keep ya so don't you listen to anyone who tells you different." The child giggled, trying to pull at her hair. She looked up again but the girl on the other side of the window had gone. In her place stood a nun, not anyone she recognized, but the cold look on her face with her expressionless eyes was similar to that of the Reverend Mother. She turned away, putting the child down on the canvas-topped table to dress him. *Please don't come in, please don't. Just leave,* Kate silently begged. She expected a harsh word any second but miraculously it didn't come. When she was brave enough to look up, she saw the nun retreating down the path in the direction of the kitchen field.

"Maybe she has a heart after all, little man. What do you think?"

The baby gabbled away in his own language, making Kate laugh. Only later did she find out the number above his cot was what the nuns used to identify him.

The weeks came and went with no word from her family or—ice crawled along her veins—Tony. She knew the risks aircrew took every day but pushed away those fears. Tony had to come back, for the sake of their child and her own heart.

She'd written to Joe but hadn't heard back from him either.

Was her brother even alive? The losses the navy had endured in the North Atlantic had made the newspapers almost every day before she'd landed in this place. He'd survived one sinking, but would he be so lucky next time?

Kate cried herself to sleep every night. She tried to keep her spirits up during the day so as not to bring the other girls down, but it was challenging. Ger, now her firm friend, did her best to make her smile.

"You can't frown today," said Ger on Easter Sunday. "It's the resurrection of Jesus and even the Reverend Mother cracked a smile this morning. We get to rest all day, no chores until tomorrow. So come on, tell us a story or sing us a song. Every girl has to do a party piece. Show the old battleaxes they haven't won." Ger patted her bump, so large it seemed to have taken over her body. "I'd do a jig but I think I'd fall flat on my face."

Despite their worries, the girls managed to forget about their troubles for a little while. It didn't last though.

Later that night, after everyone was asleep, Kate heard Ger crying. She got out of bed, careful not to make a sound and crept over to the girl's bed.

"I'm sorry, I kept you awake, didn't I?" her friend whispered. "I'm just being silly."

"What's the matter? Well, aside from living in this palace with the best clothes, finest food and kind guardians?"

Ger laughed and then covered her mouth in case she'd been too loud.

"I wish I had your spirit, Fidelma."

"Kate, that's my name. You do; after what happened to you, you still care enough about the others to keep things to yourself. You don't crow about getting out of here even though most of us will be in for at least three years. You do the worst jobs in the laundry. I've seen you protecting the new girls or the younger ones."

"Someone has to try. What does a thirteen-year-old know about babies? The nuns treat her as if she had a choice."

"They do the same to you, Ger. You shouldn't be in here either. The man who attacked you, did they do anything to him?"

Ger shook her head. "They didn't seem interested."

"Is that why you were crying?"

"No. I was thinking of my boyfriend. He says he still loves me and wants us to get married when I get out of here."

"That's great. Isn't it?"

Ger shook her head. "I can't marry him. I love him so how could I ruin his life? Nobody will ever forget what happened to me. You heard the Reverend Mother, once a Magdalene, always a Magdalene. We're dirt, Kate. Ruined women. He has a good job, he could go places."

"You aren't dirt. None of us are. We aren't criminals, you least of all. Ger, he loves you. If you love him..."

Ger shook her head. "Thank you, but you don't understand." The girl had turned away from her, so Kate took the hint and went back to her own bed. Yet sleep wouldn't come as Ger's words played over and over in her mind.

TWENTY-ONE

ASHEVILLE, NORTH CAROLINA

April, 1944

Carol pulled open the drapes, allowing the sunlight to flood the room. Her feet sank into the plush pile carpet as she opened the window, savoring the scent of the trees and flowers in full spring bloom. She loved nature, especially at this time of year, as the budding flowers opened their blooms and the apples blossomed on the trees.

"Miss Carol." Myrtle nearly fell through the bedroom door. "Miss Priscilla is downstairs demanding to see you." Myrtle flushed. "She's not happy, Miss Carol. She's spitting feathers, as Mammy would say."

Carol sighed. What did her mother-in-law want this early? The woman rarely rose before noon.

"Myrtle! Don't make comments like that, it's rude." No matter how true it was.

"Sorry, Miss Carol. Mammy always says I talk too much. I never know..." Myrtle put her hand over her mouth. "I be doing it again."

Carol smiled at the girl, whose very presence brightened up her life. No matter what challenges Myrtle faced, and there were a lot, she was always smiling or singing.

"Please offer Miss Priscilla some coffee and tell her I will be down in a minute." Carol pulled off her cotton dress, changing into a linen outfit her mother-in-law would consider more appropriate. Pursing her lips, she took a deep breath before heading downstairs.

"Good morning, Priscilla. How nice of you to call." She dropped an air kiss near her mother-in-law's cheek but managed not to touch the highly coiffed dyed blonde hairstyle.

"Don't you good morning me. Is it true?"

Carol turned her back to pour some coffee into a cup. Adding cream, she stirred it.

"Carol?"

"I assume you're talking about my job."

"Job? The Andersens do not have jobs."

"Stop it. There's a war on and as I don't have children"—*thanks to you.* Carol pushed that thought away—"and my husband is overseas, it was only right I answered the call."

Priscilla's finely chiseled nose wrinkled, as she sneered. "The call! Working as a dance hostess? Flaunting yourself at all types of men."

"Those servicemen are heroes and I don't dance with anyone. I serve food and drinks from behind the counter. I listen to the men who need someone to talk to."

Priscilla patted down her wrinkle-free skirt. "Need someone to talk to. That's not what those men are thinking about. Think of your position. You are an Andersen now."

"These men are just like Josh. They have served their country or are about to ship out to serve. It's an honor for me to work with them and their families. I help the wives and children too. Do you know how difficult it is for some of them to find food?"

"Will you listen to yourself, Carol. Anyone would think you were a communist. When my friends talk about you, I just want to die of shame." Priscilla held her hand to her heart as if she was about to faint.

Carol ignored her antics and concentrated on trying to keep cool and rational.

"Priscilla, you and your friends have never had to worry about food for a single second. Rationing hasn't even affected you."

"You can't say that. Dean limits the amount of times I can take the car out and we weren't able to travel to the—"

Carol cut her off. "You can survive without taking an afternoon drive downtown. I'm talking about food and people going hungry. Rationing makes it difficult but the allowance for each state was based on an old census. It takes no account of the number of people flooding into Asheville and similar areas where the military have set up hospitals or recuperation centers. Do you know there are pregnant women who can't find enough eggs to supplement their diet, children who don't have milk to drink, never mind three meals a day."

Priscilla rolled her eyes before picking up a magazine and flicking through the pages.

Carol hesitated; she didn't want to alienate her mother-in-law completely but Priscilla needed to be told. "Not that it matters what you and your friends believe. Josh encouraged me to do it. He knew it would be better for me to be occupied than sitting here alone waiting. Waiting for his letters to arrive, waiting for him to come home on leave." She took a deep breath as her voice started to tremble, and she sat down beside Priscilla. "I can't bear the thought of another telegram. I worry about him flying bombing raids again."

Priscilla sniffed. "Josh never mentioned it."

Carol's blood rose despite her efforts to stay calm but Priscilla didn't notice her discomfort.

"Dean would have told me if he said anything to him. I should write to him, remind him of his duty to keep his wife under control."

Carol stood up and walked over to stare out at her beautiful garden, hoping the tranquil scene would help to calm her.

"Frankly, Priscilla, it's none of your business. I thought you and your society friends would be glad I found something more suitable to do."

"I can't speak to you when you are in this mood. It was bad enough when you went to work with..." Priscilla lowered her voice, "women of low morals and their offspring. But this? I don't know what you are thinking."

"The doctors at Highfield," Carol said, noticing how Priscilla winced at the name of the asylum, "said I should find something to do. A way to help others to take my mind off my own problems. It was too difficult for me to be surrounded by babies. A constant reminder of my loss." Taking a breath, counting backwards from ten, she put her coffee cup back on the tray. "At least now I am helping the war effort. Now, if you don't mind, I must get on. I have to change for my next shift and tonight I might even go dancing." Carol walked over to the door, holding it open.

"I haven't finished—"

"Priscilla, you're Josh's mother and you deserve my respect, but please don't try my patience. You have your life and I have mine."

"Well, if that's how you want it." Priscilla picked up her fur wrap and flounced out of the house.

Isiah closed the door behind her. "Mr. Josh be mighty proud of you, Miss Carol."

Her eyes filling, she squeezed them shut, picturing Josh. She wished with all her heart he hadn't re-joined the war, but that was his job. He had a role to fill and now so did she. Smiling at Isiah, she climbed the stairs back to her room and changed. Not that she would dance with anyone; the only man she wanted to hold her was Josh.

TWENTY-TWO

CONVENT, GALWAY, IRELAND

June, 1944

"Kate, we're on garden duty today." Agnes handed her a dirty apron; it looked like it had more mud on it than you would find in the garden.

It wasn't raining, nor cold, the wind only a little brisk for a June day. After her experience in the hot, sticky, smelly laundry, anything was an improvement.

The kitchen garden grew everything from potatoes to carrots, cabbage, lettuce, scallions, even strawberries. All this food and yet none of it ended up on their plates. Their diet never changed, cold porridge in the morning, a broth and stale bread at lunch, with a dinner made up of some indescribable meat and potatoes. Apart from Friday, when it was bony fish.

Determined to take advantage of their time outside, the girls chatted quietly, talking about their dreams of what life would be like when they got out. Kate kneeled planting the lettuces with Ger on the opposite side. Together they weeded the patch, disposing of any slugs who'd eat the leaves.

Ger whispered, "Do you think you will find your Tony, Fidelma?"

She wanted to say yes but after months in here, her belief in their love was shaky. What if Agnes and some of the other girls were right? Had he only been interested in one thing and forgotten all about her once he'd left Ireland?

Beside her, Agnes snorted. "How would she? He doesn't know where she is. The nuns don't advertise our presence; why do you think they change our names?"

Ger, a pained look on her face, stuttered, "That's to protect us. So when we get out, nobody will know we were once Magdalenes."

Agnes rolled her eyes up to heaven. "If you believe that you believe anything. Since when did the good sisters ever care about us? If you ask me, it's so they can hide our babies. If anyone comes looking for us in the future, they won't be able to find us. Our children won't even know our real names."

Kate wanted Agnes to stop talking but the girl spoke the truth. It made Kate more determined to take her baby away from this place. Nobody was taking her child away from her. She didn't care what anyone said.

Ger moaned under her breath. Kate sent her a questioning look but her friend shook her head. Gentle as ever, Geraldine never wanted to impose on the others.

Kate thought of the conversation she'd had with Ger on Easter Sunday, the paleness and terror on Ger's face reminding her of that night. It was clear something was wrong with Ger. The girl was pacing back and forth, her hands alternatively rubbing her back or abdomen.

Ger groaned. "The labor pains are bad, girls. I feel like my insides are going to fall out. My head hurts something awful."

One of the girls sniggered. "The baby doesn't come out your head."

The comment earned her a dig from Agnes, who stood up to check on Ger. "Walk up and down."

Ger tried to stand up straighter, her hands cradling her bump.

"The baby won't fall out. Just keep walking, it will help," Agnes said. "Believe me, I should know."

Maura giggled. "You should know better than to end up in this place twice. What sort of a silly cow... ow." Maura held her arm, a red mark appearing from where Agnes had hit her.

"Enough of that talk, you're not helping Ger. Keep walking, just one foot in front of the other. You don't want to end up in front of Sister Ita until you are well past the first stage." Agnes held Ger's elbow trying to make her walk. "She's an evil wagon, that one. She'll have you sitting on the chrome commode for hours."

Maura glanced at her own bump. "Why? Does that make the baby come?"

"No, genius. She can look in the reflection of the chrome without having to look directly at your bits. That's how she knows how far advanced you are."

Kate thought this was a load of baloney but wasn't about to argue with Agnes. When Mam saw to Mrs. Kelly when she was pregnant, Mrs. Cumiskey or any of the other women who lived around about their farm, they stayed upright until they couldn't bear it any longer. Then they got on the bed with plenty of newspaper covering the sheets. Lots of towels and hot water were involved but no chrome commodes.

Ger groaned again, sending all thoughts of anything but panic from Kate's mind. "I think she should see someone. Maybe we should take her to the labor ward."

Agnes retorted, "Are you out of your mind? Haven't you listened to a word I said? She's better off waiting till the night nurse comes on. If she's lucky it will be that new nun, Sister John Bosco. I heard she's much nicer than the others."

"But what if the baby is coming right now?" Kate insisted.

"Ger, cross your legs before you let that happen."

Ger didn't look capable of doing anything. Her forehead was clammy to the touch and Kate didn't like the flush to her cheeks or her swollen hands and legs. "I'm going for someone. This isn't right."

She was gone before they could stop her. Picking up her skirt, she tried to walk as fast as she could, cradling her own bump as if the baby would fall out. Her breasts hurt, chafing against the rough material of the dress. The nuns refused to let them wear bras, for some reason she couldn't understand. Maybe they thought it would cause sinful thoughts. Not wearing one certainly did; she wanted to murder whomever had made the decision. She'd just reached the kitchen door when she bumped quite literally into Sister John Bosco.

"Are you all right?" asked the nun. "You gave me a fright. You shouldn't be rushing around, not in your condition."

"Sorry, Sister, but it's Ger... I mean Geraldine. I think there's something wrong. Her pains have started and the other girls told her to walk around for a bit, but she's pale yet her cheeks are flushed, her forehead is clammy to the touch and she seems all swollen or something. It's not just her legs but her fingers too. I don't know but I think there is something wrong."

"Labor isn't a pretty sight. Where is she? In the labor ward?"

"No, Sister, they wouldn't let her go there. She's down there, near the lettuce patch. We're working there today, weeding and planting lettuce."

Sister John Bosco plucked up the skirts of her long habit and headed in the direction of the garden. "You go to the labor ward and tell them Geraldine is on her way. Stay there. Don't try to get back to the garden. I want to examine you once I check on Geraldine. That running at such a late stage might have started your labor."

Kate cradled her bump, watching the nun take off toward the garden. She went through the kitchen and, taking the back stairs, headed toward the labor ward. Sister Ita appeared to be doing some stocktaking.

"Fidelma, what is it? You look rather flushed."

"Geraldine is in labor, Sister. I was told to come tell you and ask you to prepare the..." Kate wasn't sure what Sister Ita was supposed to prepare. She glanced helplessly at the nun.

"Where is Geraldine? Why didn't she come with you or rather come herself and let you get on with your work?"

"She's not well, she was in the kitchen garden, walk... working and came over a bit funny. I left her there to go and find someone. I was afraid if she tried to walk here, she might faint or something."

"You expect me to deliver a baby in the kitchen gardens?" Sister Ita's incredulous tone sent a shiver of fear through Kate although she did her best not to show it. "Have you lost your mind?"

"No, Sister. Sorry, Sister. I wasn't thinking... I..."

"That's correct. You weren't thinking. Go back to the garden and tell Geraldine to come here at once. Then you are to finish your work and hers as well. I know you girls. The first excuse you can get to avoid doing any work and you'll grab it with both hands."

"But, Sister—"

"Did you not hear what I said?"

The steely expression in her eyes told Kate it was pointless arguing. She turned on her heel and walked back the way she had come, down the stairs and out through the kitchen. Sister Ita was vindictive to the point of viciousness. She'd no wish to get on her bad side, or any further on it. The nun would find a way to make her pay for what she saw as her transgression today.

She'd barely reached the kitchen door when she met Agnes. "Sister John Bosco told me to find Reverend Mother. Where have you been?"

"Labor ward." Breathless, Kate could barely talk. "Sister Ita won't come."

Agnes swore under her breath. "You go back to Ger, I'll go find Reverend Mother."

Kate continued down the gardens until she was almost at the lettuce patch.

"Fidelma, find someone to help me," Sister John Bosco cried from Ger's side. Maura and the other pregnant girls stood around, their faces pale with shock. "Geraldine's lost consciousness. Try to find one of the gardeners. I need someone strong to carry her inside."

"Yes, Sister." Kate moved off quickly toward the garden sheds where the gardeners worked. She hadn't much contact with the gardeners, none of them did, but they seemed to be nice, at least from a distance. They often left out fruit like apples and other treats on the benches around the garden when the girls were let out for a walk.

Waving her arms, she attracted one man's attention.

"What's wrong?" he asked as he came running.

Kate panted. "Sister John Bosco is in the back garden kitchen. One of the girls collapsed and she needs help lifting her up to the ward."

"John," the gardener shouted over his shoulder, "come and help me. Girl, you sit down and catch your breath, won't do anyone no good with you breathing like a steam train."

Kate sat where she stood, all the energy drained from her. She watched the men race to the back garden. *Dear God let Geraldine and her baby be okay*, she silently prayed. *Please God, she's a lovely girl.*

It took a few minutes before her heartbeat returned to normal and she slowly made her way back to the kitchen garden where the others were still weeding as if nothing out of the ordinary had happened. "Any news?" she whispered as she took her place, careful not to catch the eye of Sister Anne, who was now supervising them.

Maura hissed, "No. But I saw Reverend Mother go up the stairs a few minutes ago. She never goes to the labor ward."

"Shush, girls, get on with your work." Sister Anne rapped her cane on the ground.

Kate plucked at the ground, removing the weeds, making a hole and shoving in the lettuce plants. It made her think of Mary, who despite living on a farm squealed at the sight of slugs. She missed her cousin more than anyone, aside from Joe and, of course, Tony. Mary always knew how to make her feel better. She'd tried writing to her but there was no response. Surely now after all these months her cousin had time to forgive her?

She knew some of the other girls hadn't a clue and didn't differentiate between a plant or a weed, but the nuns didn't seem to notice or maybe they didn't care. It was hard to kill lettuce and potatoes, in fairness. You didn't need to be a genius to grow them.

From the convent building, Ger's screams carried on the air and a couple of the girls made the sign of the cross. Kate begged, "Can't they give her something? She sounds like she's in agony."

"They want you to be in pain." Bernie wrenched a weed from the ground. "The worse it is, the better. Sister Ita thinks it will remind us of the sin we committed. She won't even give you an aspirin. The doctor sometimes insists but it's rare. She won't allow stitches either even if you are left with a—"

"That's enough of that talk. Get back to your work." Sister Anne rapped Bernie on her back with the cane. "Geraldine knew there would be consequences for her actions."

Kate stared at the hard-faced nun. How could she be so callous? If that was an animal screaming in distress you would try to help it, never mind a human being.

"Fidelma, your work!" the nun railed.

"Yes, Sister."

She bent to the weeding again, a dart of pain through her back making her whimper. She tried to stop the sound from escaping but didn't quite manage it.

Sister Anne scowled. "Don't try me, Fidelma, my patience has been tested enough for one day."

"Sorry, Sister."

Kate bit her lip at the next pang of pain and the one after that. She tried to breathe through them as one of the second offenders had suggested but that didn't work. Was her baby coming? The thought thrilled and terrorized her at the same time.

Geraldine had fallen quiet now, or else they had closed the window. There was nothing to be heard from the labor ward.

The sun fell lower in the sky but it was almost dark before the nun called time on their efforts. They all got to their feet, taking Kate almost twice as long as the others, before they headed indoors to wash their hands before dinner.

"Fidelma, please take the basket to the kitchen," said the nun, indicating a basket full of broccoli, onions and other vegetables.

Another girl stepped forward. "I'll do it, Sister, Fidelma isn't feeling too well. Her time may have started."

"I told Fidelma to take it. Now go on, the rest of you, or you'll miss dinner."

The girls trooped off with an apologetic look at Kate. Refusing to give the nun any satisfaction, she grabbed the heavy basket and lugged it to the kitchen. She had to stop several times as she stumbled under the weight but she got there eventually, panting from the effort of it.

"Lord above, what are you doing carrying that thing on your own?" Brenda, a long-time inmate at the convent, moved towards her. Ger spoke to her sometimes and told Kate that the woman had been at the convent since 1930. "How many times do I have to tell you girls to carry it between two of you?" The older woman indicated the table where Kate gratefully set down her load.

"Sister Anne insisted I carry it over."

Brenda rolled her eyes before quickly pouring out a glass of milk. "Drink that, my poor flower. You look done in. Quick now, before someone sees ya and reports both of us. You look like you are about to burst. Is your time near?"

This was the closest she had stood to Brenda, who wasn't as old as she appeared. Her gray hair didn't match her youthful eyes, now full of sympathy.

"I think I may have started." Kate punctuated every word with a gasp. "My back hurts and my stomach keeps going hard and then soft again."

"That will be it. Mine went on for a long time so don't be worried that you won't have time to get to the labor ward."

"You had a child?" Kate managed to ask between pains.

"I did indeed although the poor thing didn't last the night. A boy he was, I called him Peter but the nuns named him something else. He's buried up there where they put all the little ones."

Kate followed the woman's gaze to the back wall of the far garden. "You never left?"

"I couldn't leave him alone. Not here where nobody else cares. I don't know exactly where they put him but he is here somewhere." Her voice sounded gruffer, her eyes traveling in the direction of the old wall, near where Kate had seen people digging at night. She hadn't given it much thought before. Was that where the babies who died were buried? Her stomach lurched at the thought.

"Were you not at the funeral?" Kate asked hoarsely.

"Child, there was none. There never is for our babies. And for that they will live in..." The woman hesitated before continuing. "Never mind about me, can you walk to the labor ward or will I come with you to make sure you don't pass out on the way?"

Kate wanted to hug Brenda, the pain in her eyes making her want to cry, but she couldn't.

"Thank you but I don't want you to get into trouble. Sister Anne told me to go in for dinner first. Best do what she says as the mood isn't good today."

"When is it ever?" the woman whispered before taking the now empty glass and washing it under the water in the tap. She caught Kate staring. "Want some water?"

"Yes, please. We've been out in the gardens since lunchtime."

Brenda muttered before she filled the glass and handed it back to Kate. The chilled water tasted better than anything she could remember. With tears in her eyes at the unexpected kindness, she handed the glass back. "Thank you."

"You look after yourself, dear. Don't worry about labor. Women have been having babies since Moses came down from the mountain. You'll be grand."

Unable to speak, Kate nodded and left the kitchen and kindness behind her.

As soon as she entered the dining room, she could tell something was wrong. The usual silence in the hall was disturbed by the sound of girls crying. She looked to the head of the room where Sister John Bosco rubbed her red eyes with a hanky. Kate's skin prickled and, looking up, she caught Agnes looking at her, the fear on the other girl's face causing the terror in the pit of her stomach to soar.

Reverend Mother walked in and all crying ceased. "I see the news has spread," she said coldly. "We shall pray for the departed soul of Geraldine."

Kate screamed, the pain in her stomach as vivid as if she had been punched. Ger couldn't be dead. Not her dear kind friend who'd gone out of her way to help everyone else. Closing her eyes, she saw Ger help the younger pregnant girls face the reality of life in the convent, taking on the worst of the tasks in the laundry. Her dear friend had made this place somewhat bearable.

And they'd killed her. She screamed at the nuns. *"Murderers. You murdered her."* She kept screaming, the animalistic sound tearing from her, until Sister Anne slapped her across the face.

"Show some respect, Fidelma, and stop seeking attention. You will kneel in silence while we eat."

Kate staggered onto her knees, forcing her mouth to move as the others ate. Only she wasn't praying. She kept repeating the same words over and over. *One day someone will pay for what happened to you, Ger, I'll see you're not forgotten.*

TWENTY-THREE

Within twenty-four hours of Ger's death, Kate knew for definite her time had come. Crippled with the pains in her back and stomach, Kate paced back and forth across the bedroom like a caged animal. The other girls were already away in the laundry, leaving her alone. Or at least she would have been but for Agnes being sent to find her.

"Fidelma, you have to go to the labor room. Your baby is coming."

"No. They'll kill me just like they did Ger and her baby."

Agnes pulled at her arm. "If I must leave you to get Sister Ita, I will. You know I will. You can't risk giving birth on your own. You need someone to help."

Kate whirled around, grabbing both Agnes' hands in hers.

"You help me, you've done it before. You're a second offender. You know what to do."

Agnes shook her head, pulling her hands away. "Don't talk soft. I can't help, I'm no nurse."

"Neither is Sister Ita, least not that we know."

As the pain ripped through her, how she hated Tony at this moment. Why had she fallen for his gentle words, his caresses that set her skin on fire... Stop. She couldn't think of him now. She had to breathe. She panted through the agony, waiting for it to subside. The pains were coming faster now and the pressure between her legs was increasing.

"I can't let you do this. I'm sorry," said Agnes, watching Kate double over in pain. "I have to go find someone."

Kate was beyond caring. She struggled to get to her bed and lay on the stiff mattress trying to hold her stomach. *Please God let my baby be born alive and healthy. Please God look after my child, don't blame him or her for my sins.* Gritting her teeth, she tried to count backwards as the pain slammed into her. Someone, she couldn't remember who, had said if she started at a hundred, it would take so much concentration to remember what came next it would take her mind off the pain.

"They lied!" she roared into the empty room, before screaming as the pain hit a crescendo. Her breathing stopped as she tried to escape her own body but that didn't work.

The bedroom door opened, admitting Sister John Bosco, with Agnes following close behind.

"That's it, girl, pant through the worst of it. Come on, up you get, you can't give birth here. We need to get you to the labor ward."

"No, can't move," Kate said between pants. "It's coming. Help me, please, for the love of God, help me."

Kate didn't care who saw her. She swiped up her dress while Sister John Bosco shouted for towels.

"Agnes, I can see the head. The baby has crowned. Get me scissors, and a towel. A clean one." Agnes stood frozen to the ground.

"Agnes, go or the child will land on the floor. Run."

At that Agnes fled, her footsteps echoing as she retreated. Sister John Bosco stroked Kate's stomach, telling her when to breathe and when to push.

"You're doing great." The nun palpated her stomach. "Its head is down, Fidelma. You'll be fine. Now just follow your body. Mother Nature is wonderful. Let her guide you."

Kate couldn't concentrate, the pain was too bad. She felt the urge to push and keep pushing. She dug her nails into the sheets and mattress of the bed as she pushed her child out.

"Don't let my baby die, promise me you won't," Kate begged between gritted teeth as the pain engulfed her.

"Of course not. Nobody is dying on me today. You just concentrate on what you have to do. Leave the rest to me. Where is that Agnes?"

Agnes arrived just as Kate delivered the baby. The nun grabbed a towel and covered the child, wiping the newborn down before handing her to her mam.

"Congratulations, Kate, a baby girl."

Kate held her baby, all pain forgotten as the vivid blue eyes stared back at her. Tony's eyes and his blond hair.

"She's beautiful, Kate. Look at the head of hair on her, no wonder you had heartburn."

Agnes' use of her real name brought Kate back to reality. "You called me Kate."

"Sister John Bosco did. It's a pretty name, much nicer than Fidelma. What will you call the little one? I know they will change it but what would you pick?"

"I like Eva."

Agnes kneeled by the side of the bed and kissed the top of Eva's baby head. Kate had never seen this side of Agnes before. There were tears in her eyes. "She's just gorgeous. Prettiest baby I've seen."

Kate didn't care whether she meant that or not. As far as she was concerned Eva was perfect. Filled with love for her daughter, she counted her toes and her fingers. She examined her from head to foot but there was nothing amiss. Her little girl was just perfect.

Neither of them spotted Sister Ita marching into the room until it was too late. "What's the meaning of this? Agnes, get back to work this instant. Fidelma, what are you doing in bed and you, Sister? Look at the state of you."

"I just had my baby," whispered Kate, feeling the need to stand up for the woman who'd given life to her baby. "Sister John Bosco didn't have a chance to get an apron."

"I was talking to Sister. Silence. Agnes, take the child to the nursery." She turned her icy glare on Kate. "You get into the bath and clean yourself up. Then you will strip this bed and clean the floor. This place is a pigsty."

Kate clenched Eva tighter, causing her daughter to wail in protest. Sister Ita's eyes bulged at Kate's disobedience but as she reached for the baby, Sister John Bosco stepped between the other nun and Kate.

"Forgive me, Sister, but Fidelma will have to stay in bed a while yet. Her blood pressure may be rather high. I'm on the way to fetch my instruments. Leave the baby with her for the moment. I've yet to check her. Might as well do that here rather than have a mess in the nursery as well."

Sister Ita opened her mouth but without a word, she turned on her heel and marched out. Sister John Bosco winked at Kate before following her.

Kate cuddled her daughter. "See, Eva, not all the nuns are evil," she said to her baby. "Some are kind. Just like all human beings."

Her daughter nuzzled closer, her eyes closed. Kate watched, fascinated, as her baby snored slightly. The faintest of sounds but it was definitely a snore. "You're a Ryan all right. Da and Uncle Pat would be dead proud of ya."

Sister John Bosco returned to escort Kate and Eva down to the newly delivered mothers' ward. Agnes and Maura followed behind her.

"The girls have a new set of clothes for you and have offered to clean up so I can get you down to the ward and examine both of you properly. Are you ready to walk?"

"Yes, Sister. Thank you for delivering Eva safely."

Agnes held out her arms. "Let me hold her while you get yourself decent. Isn't she adorable, Maura?" Kate reluctantly handed over her little bundle, watching as Agnes expertly cradled the little girl.

"Don't go getting attached to her, it only leads to heartbreak," Maura muttered as she started cleaning up the floor and changing the bed.

Kate pulled the replacement dress over her head, the old one covered in stains. She took Eva back into her arms, holding the blanket around her. "Nobody will ever take my daughter from me. I'll never let them have her."

Maura rolled her eyes, causing Agnes to give her a dig. "You just take Eva down to the ward with Sister here and stay out of the way of Sister Ita and Reverend Mother. You'd think you committed another mortal sin by having the baby in your bed rather than the labor ward."

"Thank you, Agnes." Sister John Bosco's tone held a gentle rebuke. "Come along, Kate, both baby and mother need to rest."

She carried her daughter as she gingerly walked down the stairs, gritting her teeth as each step reminded her of the delivery.

Kate had never been in the new mothers' ward, but it looked much the same as their bedroom did. "A lick of whitewash and some new curtains would really brighten this place up, wouldn't it?' Sister John Bosco commented as she took Eva from Kate. "You get into that bed nearest the window while I examine baby."

Kate gave in to the overwhelming tiredness and climbed into the bed but didn't take her eyes off her daughter. She trusted JB, as she christened the nun in her mind, but she wasn't about to let her daughter out of her sight.

"She's a bonny baby. Look at those blue eyes taking everything in. She's so alert for a newborn." Sister John Bosco continued her

commentary as she examined the child. Then she handed Eva
back to Kate. "Have you tried feeding her yet?"

Kate shook her head, her cheeks burning.

"Don't be like that. Sure, it's as natural as the sun rising and
setting every day. Let her lie against your bare chest and you'll find
she does most of the work."

Kate watched in awe as her daughter nuzzled into her. A warm
tingling filled her chest as her baby fed, the connection between
her and Eva deepening with every second. This was what pure
love was and it didn't come close to anything she'd ever felt before.

Once Eva had finished, the nun showed Kate how to burp her.

"That's it. You're a natural mammy. Now, let me put her in her
cot as I need to examine you and check your blood pressure." At
those words, Kate and the nun locked eyes.

"Thank you for helping me, Sister. I don't know why you went
against Sister Ita but I'm grateful."

Was it her imagination or did the nun's eyes fill up? She turned
away to put Eva in the cot, busying herself with the child's covers
for a few seconds. When she returned her attention to Kate it was
all business, even calling her by her convent name.

"Now, Fidelma, let's see how you are doing. I don't have any
aspirin; it's not allowed in the convent but these gauze pads will
help with the bruising down below."

"How long will they let me stay here with Eva?" Kate
whispered.

"That depends on Sister Ita, but I will do my best." Sister John
Bosco spoke softly as if afraid of being overheard. As she gathered
the dirty linen to her, she said louder, "I shall be back later. Try to
sleep. You need your rest."

"But if they come when I'm asleep?" Kate couldn't put her
fears into words, that someone would steal Eva away.

"Nobody will disturb you. Sister Ita is away on a few days'
leave from tomorrow so she's gone to pack. She is going to visit one
of the other convents. It's just me, and Agnes as my helper, to deal

with the new mothers. Sister Anne is busy with the laundry. You chose a good time to have your baby."

With a smile the nun left, shutting the door behind her. Kate stared at her daughter, resisting the urge to pick up the sleeping child and take her into the bed. Exhaustion filled every bone. She contented herself with looking at her beautiful little girl. *Tony, we have a baby daughter. She's just as beautiful as can be and has your blue eyes. How I wish you could see her...*

TWENTY-FOUR

Ten days later

"Get out and get dressed. No more lying around in bed for you, my lady." Sister Ita pulled back the curtains. It was still dawn, the sky a picturesque array of pinks, blue and purple. Kate couldn't concentrate on the beauty. Sister Ita's short holiday hadn't helped her mood. She was still a vindictive aul—

"Fidelma, what are you waiting for? A written invitation?" The nun glared as Kate jumped out of bed, her breasts swollen as Eva had yet to feed.

"I'm coming, Sister, I just have to feed Eva."

"Delia is the child's Christian name. You should have done that earlier." Sister Ita walked over to the cot, snatching Eva and thrusting her to Kate. "Take her to the nursery and report to the laundry."

"But, Sister, she's star—" A swift slap across her face stopped her mid-sentence.

"Don't cheek me. Do as you're told." The nun glared around

the room, picking on another penitent. "You go with her and report straight back to me or it will be you next. Take this key."

"Yes, Sister." The girl jumped out of bed despite only delivering her baby the day before.

Kate's milk flooded her dress, adding to her humiliation. Eva roared, smelling her breakfast, not understanding why she was being denied. Kate's escort hurried ahead.

"I'm sorry but I have to think of my baby," the girl whispered. Kate barely acknowledged her; she knew the person to blame was the nun they'd just left behind.

They walked through several doors, Kate watching as the girl opened and then locked each door after they passed through. On arrival at the nursery, Kate was surprised Eva was the only baby screaming. The quietness of the children's area was unnerving. A harried-looking nun greeted them. "What have you done to that brat? Shut her up."

The hairs on the back of her neck stood up. "Eva isn't a brat. She's starving and Sister Ita wouldn't let me feed her."

The nun's eyes focused on Kate's wet dress before turning to Kate's escort. "What are you doing here?"

"Sister Ita told me to accompany Fidelma and report back immediately," the girl stuttered, holding out the key. "I have to take this back."

"And her?" The nun pointed at Kate.

The girl flushed. "Sister Ita said Fidelma was to go to the laundry."

"You heard the girl. Off you go. Put the brat in that cot."

Kate stood, unable to move, gripping Eva to her, which only made her scream more.

"Don't annoy me, girl. Put her down and get to the laundry or you will live to regret it."

Tears blurred her vision as she laid her wailing daughter in the cot. With a last kiss on her forehead, Kate left. Her escort followed; she had to unlock and lock the doors again.

"I can't believe they did that. They're so cruel. That's what they are."

Kate ignored her, crossing her hands against her chest. The pain was unbearable but it was nothing to that in her heart.

Every morning, Kate had to turn up at the laundry. She worked harder than before, giving Sister Anne nothing to complain about. All she focused on was the half hour visit she got with Eva every evening. She fed her, settling her down to sleep with a kiss.

"You'll regret the choice to keep feeding her. Your milk won't dry up for ages," Sister Joseph, the same nun who'd called Eva a brat, taunted her.

Kate didn't respond.

Several times Sister John Bosco visited the laundry, taking Kate and some of the other mothers out on some pretext or other.

"Why do you keep helping us?" Kate asked one day as she gave Eva an extra feed while Sister John Bosco kept an eye out for Sister Joseph's return.

"Sister Joseph asked me to cover for her siesta as she calls it. She knows Reverend Mother wouldn't approve so she turns a blind eye. I try to help as many of you as possible. It's not right to deprive a child of her mother's milk, not to mention love and cuddles. But, Kate..."

Startled by the use of her real name, Kate paid attention to the nun. Her eyes darted all over the place, making Kate shiver. Something was wrong.

"Are they taking Eva?"

"No. At least they haven't told me."

Kate's shoulders relaxed but she held Eva closer all the same.

"I'm going away, Kate. There is much need for nursing sisters in Europe and I've volunteered. I'm weak. I can't stand it here. Feeling helpless amongst such misery."

Kate's chest hardened. "But you have a choice. You can help

us, offset the worst of what goes on here. How many more Gers will die? How many babies?"

Sister John Bosco kept her eyes averted, her hands stuck in the deep pockets of her habit. "My hands are tied here. I have to go where I can make a difference. I'm sorry." The nun looked at the clock. "Hurry now, she's due back any minute."

Kate finished the feed, wiped her daughter's mouth and kissed her before laying her back in her cot.

Sister John Bosco escorted her back in silence to the laundry.

"Have you anything to say to me, Kate?"

"I thought pride was a sin, Sister."

TWENTY-FIVE

May 9, 1945

Kate turned the heavy mangle again and again, her arm feeling as if it would fall off despite having developed muscles she never knew she had. She rubbed her forehead on her arm, but as soon as she wiped it clean, the sweat reappeared. It streamed into her eyes, down her back and underarms. The heat, always bad, was much worse today. She glanced at a couple of the pregnant women working near her. They had it even worse. It was no joke doing laundry while heavily pregnant.

"Kate, look. The war is over. Do you think your Tony will come looking for you now?" Agnes whispered as she shared the newspaper with Kate. They were taking an enormous risk. If Sister Anne caught them reading rather than working in the laundry, the cat would be among the pigeons.

"The Germans surrendered. It's over. Really?" Kate swiped the day-old paper from her friend and skimmed it.

"Says there were riots in Dublin. Some fools at Trinity College burned the tricolor. Why would they do that? Should be shot for

defaming our flag, so they should." Agnes took her frustration out
on the sheet she was scrubbing.

Maura looked up from her tub. "They are Protestants that lot
and pro-Britain too. Just like our Fidelma."

"Shut up, Maura. Leave Fidelma alone." Agnes glared at
Maura, but she didn't move from her workstation. Getting into a
fight while Sister Anne was on duty was a stupid move. She'd
punish everyone who was working, even if they'd played no part.

"I forgot how chummy you two were. Anyone would think you
were—" Whatever Maura was about to say got drowned out by
Sister Anne.

"What is the meaning of this chatter? Don't you have enough
to do? Fidelma, why are you reading the paper? Where did you
get it?"

Kate's heart jumped as she heard the nun's voice, not having
seen her come back into the laundry. "Sorry, Sister, it was at the
bottom of a pile of laundry. It was the war news that got me. My
brother, Joseph, he's in the navy and now he can—"

"Your brother is not any of my concern. Or yours. Get on with
your work." The nun swiped the paper from her hands and shoved
Kate back toward the mangle. She put a hand out to save herself
from falling, immediately regretting it as the metal singed her skin.
She bit her tongue, trying not to cry out. It was pointless, as Sister
Anne would only gloat. She stuck her fingers in her mouth, trying
not to cry as the pain seared through her.

Agnes pulled her toward the tub and shoved her hand into the
cold water. The relief was immediate, but disappeared as soon as
she took her hand out. "You wash the sheets and I'll do the mangle.
Use the cold water to rinse them off."

Kate flashed a smile at the other girl. They'd become closer
since Agnes had helped deliver Eva, though not friends like she
and Ger had been. Kate closed her eyes, picturing Ger's face.
Nearly a year had passed since her death, yet her presence in the
convent was still missed.

. . .

When it was time to go to dinner, Agnes fell in beside Kate as they walked to the dining room.

"How's the hand?" Agnes whispered.

"Better, thanks to you."

"Kate, I'm going to get out of here. I can't stand it any longer. They don't care what happens to us."

"How, Agnes? They will not let us just walk out."

"John said he'd help me."

Kate's mouth fell open. "The gardener?"

"How many other Johns do you know?" hissed Agnes.

"Silence!" Sister Ita called with a glare in their direction.

They stood at their chairs until everyone had entered, and they were given the command to sit. As usual, inedible vegetables and a bit of gristly meat filled their plates. The scent of roast beef made Kate's mouth water, but she refused to give the nuns the satisfaction of glancing in their direction. She could tell exactly what they were eating. Roast beef with boiled carrots, potatoes with melted butter and... yes, some cauliflower with bread sauce. Her stomach growled with hunger, but with so many other Maggies having the same reaction, nobody called her out. After they said grace, she picked up her fork and tried to pretend she was eating from a nun's plate.

After dinner Agnes volunteered them both to bring in coal from the shed outside. For once, Kate didn't mind the dirty work. She was dying to hear more about Agnes' plan.

"Tell me more about John," she said as soon as they were clear of witnesses.

"He's a lovely man, Kate. He's going to help me get out of here."

Kate piled coal into the buckets, not wanting to do anything to burst her friend's happiness.

"You don't believe me, do you?" Agnes put her hands on her hips. "I'm sorry I said anything now. I shouldn't have opened my mouth."

"Keep your voice down and fill the coal buckets or the nuns

will be out to us," Kate hissed. She thought her friend's eyes were suspiciously bright, but Agnes never cried. "Agnes, you haven't... done anything to make him..."

"Give over. Do you think I'm going to risk landing back in here a third time? I've learnt my lesson, believe me. Not going to be any of that business until I have a ring on me finger. John isn't interested in that. He says he loves me."

Kate opened her mouth but closed it again. Who was she to tell Agnes to be careful? She'd believed Tony's every word, and while she'd never be without Eva, she couldn't say she'd ever trust a man again.

"I hope it works out well for you. I really do. But make sure you don't get caught. The nuns will kill you if you escape and they catch you."

"You won't tell, will you, Kate?"

Kate shook her head. "Don't be daft. I won't say a word. Just be careful."

"Aren't I always?" Agnes nudged her and they both fell over into the coal dust, bursting into howls of laughter. Hearing a door bang, they quickly came to their senses, throwing the coal into the buckets at record speed.

"Good grief, girls. I didn't send you out to take a bath in the coal dust."

"Sorry, Sister Anne, it was my fault. I didn't see the bucket and tripped over it, grabbing Fidelma as I fell. It won't happen again."

Kate marveled at the angelic expression on Agnes' face. She belonged in Hollywood if anyone did.

TWENTY-SIX

June, 1945

Kate tried to stand still outside the Reverend Mother's office but it was difficult. She glanced at the bolted front door, so close yet in reality it could be a million miles away. What did Reverend Mother want with her? It was never good news to be singled out by the head nun.

She pushed the fear down to the pit of her stomach—nothing would allow her to let these nuns see how scared she was. She rubbed the palms of her hands on the side of her dress and knocked on the door. The nun's voice called to her to come in.

On entering she saw a broad-shouldered man dressed in a shop-bought suit. Her gaze traveled from his black shiny shoes to his head and back to his face. Joe. Her brother. Warmth radiated through her body. She hadn't seen him since 1942 and here he was standing in front of her. Her eyes flew over his face; he looked older, his eyes haunted, but his smile was still her Joe.

She rushed to his side, about to throw her arms around him.

"Joe, oh how I wished..." Her emotions caught in her throat, and she found that she couldn't speak.

"Fidelma, stop shouting and carrying on," said Reverend Mother. "Mr. Ryan, please take a seat. Fidelma, sit there." She indicated the seats in front of her desk. Neither of them sat. Joe put his hand out but failed to reach Kate's arm as if afraid to touch her.

"What has happened to you? You're skin and bone. Good Lord above, what type of a place is this?" her brother asked.

"Mr. Ryan, remember your place. This is a convent and only for the letter you hold, you wouldn't have seen the inside."

"I've served my time in the war, seen death and destruction all around me. I'm not one of your congregation too scared to mutter a word against you and your church."

Reverend Mother put her hand to her chest, her face turning scarlet. "Mr. Ryan!"

Joe's eyes turned to flint as he demanded, "I wish to speak to Kate in private."

"Her name is Fidelma and it's not seemly to leave you both alone."

"She's my sister, for goodness' sake. Kate, go and get your things. We're going home."

"With Eva?"

Her brother's eyes hit the floor along with her heart.

"Joe, I can't leave Eva here. They'll sell her, to cover the cost of me being here. But I worked hard for them. Don't let them take her." She grabbed his arm, squeezing it through his jacket, her voice breaking. "I'll never see her again."

Reverend Mother glared at her. "Compose yourself, Fidelma. We don't sell children, we place them in good Catholic homes with married parents who can give them a decent example and everything they need to become successful individuals. If you loved your child like you claim, you would recognize it's the best way."

"Not for my daughter. She's mine. Joe, please don't make me leave her behind."

He stared past her. She moved closer to him, taking his calloused hand.

"Joe, please. I love her. If Mam saw Eva, she wouldn't turn her back, she's the prettiest child in the nursery. She's well behaved too, not a bother to anyone. And her smile..." Her brother wasn't listening, and she saw the closed expression take over his face. In that second he looked just like her mam. But this wasn't Mam, it was Joe. The brother she adored and who loved her.

"Joe, please," she begged, squeezing his hand tighter.

"I can't." His voice trembled as he stared at a point behind her head. "It's for the best, Kate."

Her heart sank. When Joe wouldn't look at her, she turned her back on him and walked to the office door. "I won't leave without her. It's both of us or neither."

"Kate, I can't. You don't understand how hard it was to get Mam to agree to you leaving here. I've got to get back to my ship; my landlady in England has space for you but she has a no-child policy. You must think of the child. Let her grow up without the stigma of being a..." Joe reddened.

"Just get us out of here, please, Joe. Mary will help me." She caught the look in his eyes. "What? She will, I know she will. She doesn't care what Mam thinks."

"Don't you know?"

"Know what?"

"Frank died. Mary's grieving for her brother. Her and Pat both."

Kate's legs gave way beneath her, but somehow Joe managed to catch her in time. He held her while she sobbed.

"I can't believe it. He was such a fun, happy man who dreamt of seeing the world. His last words to me were that he was lucky. What happened?"

"He was injured during the D-Day operations and despite being ordered to seek treatment, stayed at his station. You couldn't imagine the chaos of that day, not just in the waters but on the Normandy beaches. We saw so many heroes that day, the sea water turned red with their blood. Frank, he was like a maniac, determined not to let anyone who could be saved, die. There are many men alive today because of his bravery. Uncle Pat has the medal he was awarded."

"Oh, poor Mary. She adored her brother. Has she got married yet? She said she was hoping Frank would make it back on leave for her to get wed."

"Yes, she married Ciaran in March, 1944. Frank was on leave and Father Burke said the Mass. Haven't you had any letters?"

Kate shook her head, trying to swallow the lump in her throat. She'd missed so much.

"I know Mary wrote to you about the wedding." He looked away. "I don't think Mam did."

"Joe, why didn't you write back to me? I wrote so many letters, to you, Mary, Da." *Tony.* "Nobody wrote back."

She watched as the red tint on his neck spread to his face. He'd got her letters, or at least some of them. "You were angry?" She shrank back from the flare of temper in his eyes.

"I wanted to kill Tony with my bare hands and you..." He caught himself and gentled his tone, reaching out to her. "Kate, imagine how I felt so far from home reading that you... my baby sister was having a baby. Without a ring on yer finger. I never expected that. Not from you."

Kate pulled away from him. She hadn't expected censure, not from Joe.

"I needed you," she whispered, her voice choked with emotion.

His scarlet cheeks could have heated the room. He didn't look at her.

"What does Da feel about me now?"

Joe stiffened. Surely her da hadn't turned on her as well?

"Da is dead, Kate," Joe said hoarsely, staring at his feet. "He died less than three months after you came here. Mam said it was too much, his heart was broken."

She felt her own heart crack in two as her legs gave way, and she fell back against the wall. "He can't be dead, Joe, not Da. I never got to say I was sorry for disappointing him." She looked at her brother, begging him to say he was lying but he just stared back, his eyes glistening.

"No, Joe, no. He never got to meet Eva. He'd have loved her, I know he would. I never got to say goodbye." She held her hands across her chest. "It was my fault."

"We both know he had limited time ahead of him. He was a victim of the last war just as surely as if he had died over in Flanders. You can't... you mustn't blame yourself. I'd stay away from Mam though."

She wanted to scream. If Da had been in his full health, he wouldn't have sent her to this place. He'd have stood up to everyone, his wife, the priest, the village, everyone. She knew he would have; he loved her no matter what she'd done.

"Joe, please help me. I have to get out of here and see Mary and Uncle Pat. Maybe Eva will help them in their grief."

She ignored the doubtful look on his face and the hurt it caused. For all his traveling around the world, he was still the son of a Catholic farmer.

"I'll not leave here, not without my baby," she said, turning away from her brother. "Thank you for coming, Joe. Take care of yourself."

With her heart racing, she moved to the door, opening it before hesitating for a second. But when he didn't call her back, she kept walking. Only then did he come after her. He pulled her arm and led her out the front door into the large garden with its perfectly kept vivid green lawn, the flower beds in full bloom, alive with color. She could see the bees flying from one plant to another. How could such beauty exist in this house of horrors? By rights, nothing should grow or live surrounded by such cruelty.

"Kate, you can't be serious. How can we get the baby out? It was hard enough getting in here to see you." She stared at him. He threw his hands up in the air. "Why did I think you would come? You always were the stubborn one."

"She's my daughter. Your niece. Do you really expect me to

leave her here, at the mercy of them? They killed my only friend, Geraldine. I don't even know her real name. She needed help getting the baby out but they refused to believe she was in agony." Kate indicated the convent with a shake of her head. "You have no idea how they treat the girls in here and the babies aren't treated much better. The nuns only let them drink milk for the first three months then they force them to eat solid food. When the poor child can't swallow properly and keeps being sick, they still insist on doing it. I'm lucky, Eva is made of strong stuff." She didn't mention she sneaked in to feed her daughter herself when she could.

"The weaker babies, they just let them... they die, Joe. Nobody cares, well no one apart from us mothers. We try to look out for the poor mites whose mothers have left, those whose families paid the hundred pounds to get out of here. But with so little time, no food... well, you know yourself. They haven't any toys and spend all day in the cot. Sometimes they don't even change their—"

"Enough, Kate. You said they sell them?" The disbelief in his voice spoke volumes.

"The rich parents who drive up here make large donations to the convent. Then they leave with the child of their choice. It's just like the cattle market in Galway Da took us to when we were kids. Only instead of animals, it's our babies that are sold."

"Who takes them, Kate?"

"Americans and rich Irish folk who can't have their own children. The nuns don't care. So long as they pay, the parents could be Hitler himself. Only he'd have to be Catholic."

His eyes widened as he took a step back from her. "Kate, I know you want your child but you can't be talking like this. I've no time for the nuns, especially ones like her indoors, but if people hear you throwing stuff like that around, they'll lock you up."

"They've done that already. I can't walk out of here, can I? This is my prison. It may look pretty out here but there is nothing good about the laundries where we slave our guts out. See that grass—do you know how it gets to look so nice? We cut it, Joe. By hand with scissors. On our hands and knees, the whole lot of us work from one end of the lawn to the other. If it's not done to their liking, we do it again. And again. It doesn't matter if the sun's high in the sky or it's torrential rain, the grass has to look good. Appearances matter to our holy sisters."

She saw the disbelief on his face. Who could blame him, standing in the fine gardens of the beautiful convent?

"There are constant punishments for our sins. Total lack of medical care at the birth, never mind afterwards. If anyone complains, they are told it is penance for the fifteen minutes of passion." Her brother flushed at her words, pulling at his collar. "Joe, I loved Tony, you have to believe me on that, but there are women in here who were forced, attacked and the like. They didn't have a choice, but the nuns don't make any exceptions."

Joe hesitated. She saw he was starting to believe her.

"There is one nun," Kate carried on. "She isn't like the others. Her name is Sister John Bosco. She was kind to us, especially to me, at least until she volunteered to work in Europe. If you find her, she'll tell you the truth, confirm what I am saying."

"Kate," Joe said, releasing a sigh, "I believe you. You've never lied to me but what you are saying, it's just so..."

"I swear every word is true and I haven't told you the worst of it. Some is too horrible to talk about." She squeezed her eyes shut.

"You have to save Eva," she begged her brother. "If you can only take one of us, take her, please. She's your flesh and blood."

"Don't be ridiculous. What do I know about babies? That's women's stuff."

She bit her lip rather than call him out. Why did men behave as if they had no input in creation?

"What will it take for the nuns to give you the baby?" he asked.

"They won't allow us to take her. We'd have to escape."

"Kidnap the baby? From the nuns? They'd put the Gardai onto us, we wouldn't get away."

"Eva is mine. I can't kidnap my own child. Joe, there is a

gardener. He's keen on one of the girls. You could bribe him to take us. I know you can."

His cheeks flushed. "I'm not made of money." When she stayed silent, he repeated himself. "I'm not flush with cash."

"I'll pay you back every penny, just try, please. You have no idea how bad it is here, Joe."

He ran a gentle hand over her shaved head. "I think I have an idea."

"What? Really? To get us both out of here? Because I'm telling you, Joe, if I leave here without Eva, I'll never see her again. I can't let that happen. Tony said he'd find me. After the war."

"If I got my hands on that English—"

"American," she corrected him quickly. "I loved him and he loved me. We didn't do anything wrong. We didn't plan on Eva but I know Tony will love her just as much as I do."

"You don't even know Tony survived the war. Will you listen to yourself?"

"I hope he did but if not, I won't fall apart. I survived this place. I'm not losing my baby."

Joe paced back and forth. She knew she'd won him over before he said a word. "I never could say no to you. All right, what's this fella's name and are you sure you can trust him?"

"John Hanlon's his name. I can."

"How are you so certain?"

"Because we are going to bring his girl, Agnes, out of here at the same time."

Joe rolled his eyes. "Might as well be hung for a sheep as a lamb."

"I'll find a way to speak to him during the week, tell him to meet you in the Mucky Duck pub, he likes it there." She leaned in and kissed his cheek before hugging him. "I'm so glad you came back, Joe. I prayed you would. I knew you wouldn't desert me."

"Never, Kate. You're my baby sister and nothing changes that. You'd best get back before that old wagon does something else to hurt you. I'll go in and have a pint every night until I meet John. I'll get it sorted. You'll have to work out how to get the baby."

"Her name is Eva."

Joe nodded. She thought she caught a hint of a tear in his eyes, but he blinked rapidly and it disappeared.

"I'll be back on Sunday. After Mass, maybe she'll be in a good mood then." He nodded in the direction of the Reverend Mother's office. Kate followed his look and saw the nun staring at them. She swallowed hard to dissipate the fear filling her. The hate on the woman's face was almost personal.

"See you Sunday, Joe. Thank you."

Kate didn't wait to watch her brother walk down the drive even though every ounce of her longed to. She didn't want to tempt fate. Instead, she picked up her skirt and headed back to the laundry where she threw herself into the tasks assigned to them. She wasn't going to give anyone any reason to complain about her, not between now and Sunday.

TWENTY-SEVEN

The hours passed slowly in the laundry room, as she waited to be summoned but none came. Maybe Reverend Mother would let the confrontation pass without discussion. She couldn't believe that but perhaps the nun had other things on her mind. But there was more activity around the convent and the nuns were rattled about something. You could tell by the way they whispered to each other and barked at the women.

"What has you looking so happy?" Agnes whispered as she passed yet another sheet over to Kate.

"I've got us a plan to get out of this place. You, me and Eva."

"You never? What we going to do? Fly?"

"Shush. You don't have to believe me but I said I'd get out of here and I meant it. You tried to help Ger and were the only one who helped me. I owe you and I always repay my debts."

"There's something you're not telling me."

"You're too suspicious. But I guess I should tell you, the plan involves your boyfriend or more precisely John's truck."

Agnes stood staring at her until a whack on the back alerted her to Sister Ita's presence. "Something wrong with you, girl?" barked the nun.

"No, Sister, I was just stretching out the ache in my back. Sorry, Sister."

"Get back to work or you'll have more to worry about than a back pain."

Kate didn't dare catch Agnes' eye after that warning. Instead, she went over the plan that John had managed to whisper to her in her head.

When Sunday morning came around, Kate leaped out of bed. Glancing out the window, it looked like it was going to be dry if cold. That was better than rain as it would bring more guests to the convent—local families currying favors with the nuns, as well as family members visiting their favorite religious relative. Hopefully everyone would be too busy to worry about the Magdalenes.

Agnes inched closer, before whispering, "Are we on?"

"Yes. John said to wait at the side gate. I've to get Eva."

"Jesus Mary and Joseph, you're not serious are ya? There's no way you'll get out of here with a child. The nuns aren't going to let you walk out of the door with one of their money bundles. They might not care about us, but they will see the donation Eva could bring them."

"I will or we'll all be stuck here. Last chance, you coming or not?"

"Course I'm coming." Agnes rolled her eyes but temptation won. "Good luck taking Eva, you mad thing."

Kate walked toward the orphanage, believing she would be better hiding in plain sight. If she looked like she should be going somewhere, the nuns would assume she had been sent on an errand. Once inside the orphanage, she went to the nursery section, the babies lying in their cots, some asleep but all too quiet for their age.

"Eva, my darling girl," she whispered to her daughter. "We're getting out of here today, so we are. Come on, put this on for Mammy. We don't want you getting a chill."

Kate pulled on a coat a mother had knitted, which the nuns used when they took the children outdoors for fresh air. Eva gurgled, waving her arms and kicking her legs. Kate couldn't resist enjoying a few precious seconds playing with her little girl.

"Just wait until you meet your uncle Joe, he's a lovely man. Now, shush, my darling, you must be quiet. We must play a game so pretend you're asleep. Nobody can see us leaving together. Don't want to upset any of the bad nuns."

Holding her daughter close to her chest, Kate headed in the direction of the side gate where Agnes should be waiting. To her relief, Agnes was there wearing a headscarf and holding out a spare for Kate.

"Good thinking." Kate grinned at Agnes, swapping Eva for the headscarf, before taking her baby back in her arms. Where was the van?

Suddenly Joe appeared at her side and kissed her cheek. "Change of plan, we're taking a car instead. John thought it would be less conspicuous. You'll have to put Eva in the boot."

"Are you soft in the head? She's a baby not a suitcase. I'll hide on the floor with her on my lap. You sit in the back seat and Agnes can sit up front. That way you'll look just like one of the visiting families."

White as chalk, Agnes whined, "They'll see us. We can't just drive out of here."

"We can. It's the last thing they think we will try to do." Kate tightened her arms around Eva. "What have we got to lose?"

Agnes exchanged looks with Joe, who simply shrugged.

They watched as John drove in the gate and parked to one side; now all they had to do was walk down the main driveway and meet him.

"Joe, give us your coat so I can hide Eva."

Joe took off the coat and put it over her shoulders, a look of admiration on his face. "You've some neck, Kate Ryan."

They walked down the drive, heads up. Agnes looked behind her once but Kate resisted. Her stomach churned as she waited for someone to shout but they didn't. Not a word. Nobody looked at them apart from one female visitor heading up to the convent, a basket of baked goods on her arm for the good nuns. Kate looked away in disgust, but not before she saw Joe wink at the woman. The saucy mare winked back.

John started the car and the engine rumbled to life.

"Drive slowly, please," Joe said, squinting over his shoulder. "The last thing we need to look like is escaping felons. Will the Gardai not question why you have petrol?"

"No, sure this is the priest's car. He asked me to repair it. He won't miss the petrol and if he does, I'll tell him I had to test it out."

Agnes giggled but it came out like a strangled cry. Kate saw her hands shaking. She leaned over the seat and put her hand on her shoulder. "The worst part is over. Off we go."

As her heart thrashed in her chest, she lay in the hollow behind the front seats, taking care to cradle and not crush her daughter. John drove out too slowly, every agonizing second felt like an hour, but she resisted telling him to hurry up. They drove for about fifteen minutes before he pulled up at the side of a deserted road. "You're safe to sit up now, nobody will take a blind bit of notice of a car with two men, two women and a baby."

Nobody argued least of all Kate, whose legs had turned numb from the crouched position. She took a seat next to Agnes in the back, leaving Joe in the front. After another ninety minutes, John pulled over by a bus stop. "The next bus is scheduled to stop in about fifteen minutes if it isn't running late. It'll drop you right outside your uncle's bar."

She hugged Agnes, wishing her luck as they bade goodbye. "If you have any sense, you will put as much distance between you and those nuns. If you turn up a third time, they'll probably send you to Castlepollard or Sean Ross and they are both even worse than our place. At least that's what the nuns always say."

"No fear of that happening." Agnes grinned at John. "We're off to London, aren't we, love?"

John just grunted, evidently keen to be off. The car roared off down the road, leaving them without a backward glance.

As they stood waiting for the bus, watching the rear car lights disappear into the distance, she hugged Eva close to her chest as Joe rooted in his pocket and produced a gold ring.

"Best put this on. You can't get on a bus carrying a baby without a wedding ring. The game would be up in no time. Give me Eva."

She handed over the sleeping bundle, who didn't even whimper. "Where did you... it's Granny's, isn't it?"

"Just wear it, and stop giving me earache."

She put her ring on her finger, forcing it over her swollen knuckles. Her nails were almost non-existent, the skin cracked and burned from the chemicals. And the nuns considered her the sinner. Eva woke, holding her hands out to Kate. She settled easily and when the bus eventually pulled up, thankfully it was fairly empty. They climbed on, and once they were moving Eva fell asleep with the rocking motion of the bus, and Kate nodded off soon after.

"Kate, wake up, we're here," came her brother's voice what seemed like seconds later. She thanked the driver and followed Joe down the steps from the bus, allowing it to pull off before making her way over to her uncle's pub.

"You wait over there at the outhouse, I'll get Mary."

Kate nodded, keen to keep to the shadows—she didn't want to run into anyone, especially Fergal Scanlan. She could still hear his words taunting her.

Mary arrived out with Joe, dressed to the nines as usual in a fitted dress with a skirt ending just at her knee, a head full of gleaming healthy hair and a wide smile on her face. But the smile faded when she hugged Kate.

"Kate, oh my goodness you're skin and bone. What have they done to you? Is this her?" Mary took Eva in her arms; the child simply stared at the new face. "Ah, Kate, she's gorgeous. What a little beauty. I've no idea where to shelter you. The outhouse is too cold in this weather. But Da is in foul humor, you know, since Frank." Mary faltered for one second before continuing, "You wouldn't recognize him. He's not the same man you knew."

"I know someone who will help. Paddy's wife, Mrs. McCormack. She said as much when I left here with Father Burke."

"If you're sure?" Mary looked doubtful. Joe didn't comment; he didn't know the people as well as the women did.

Kate wasn't at all sure, but she headed down the street in any case and prayed her instincts were correct. "Joe, are you coming? Mary, you'd best get back inside or your da will think something is wrong."

Mary hugged her, kissed Eva on the top of her head and disappeared back into the pub. Joe took Eva in his arms and carried her as they walked down the street, keeping to the shadows before they came to the lane up to the McCormacks' house.

"You didn't tell me she lived so far away from the village."

"That's a good thing, isn't it? Give Eva to me and you knock on the door; watch the paint, it tends to peel off."

Joe gave her a funny look before he knocked and then stood back behind her.

Mrs. McCormack opened the door. "Lord above, Kate Ryan. You're the last person I expected to find standing on my doorstep. Come inside before you catch your death. You're chilled. Come in, the fire's lit. My daughter's package came through from America, thank the Lord the post is working again now the war is over. I've some money in my pocket, hidden from Paddy. I love your uncle, but I've paid enough into his coffers over the years." Only then did she seem to notice Joe. "Is that yourself, Joseph Ryan? Come away on in, don't be letting the heat out the door."

"No, I won't, thanks all the same. I'll stay with Uncle Pat back at the pub. Try to cheer him up and talk him into looking after my sister." Joe took off his cap and nodded to Mrs. McCormack. "Thanks, missus. Kate, talk to you tomorrow."

Kate winced as she hadn't had a chance to ask if she could stay yet, but Mrs. McCormack just ushered her inside and shut the door.

"Did you run away?"

"Yes. How did you know?"

"You wouldn't be on my doorstep unless you were desperate. Now you feed the poor child and change her nappy. She doesn't smell the best, poor thing."

"I don't have another one, I couldn't pack properly."

The old woman muttered something but indicated the couch while she went upstairs. Kate fed her baby, to both their relief as her breasts were painful.

Moments later, Mrs. McCormack came back down holding several items, all old but clean. She rubbed her hand over the knitted cardigans and the little booties, a yellowed crocheted blanket, her voice trembling with longing. "I kept them in case my girls came home with their babies. You use them."

"Thank you, I don't know what to say."

"You don't have to say anything at all. Kate, you're welcome to stay here, both of you, but Paddy, he won't like lying to your uncle. I can't trust him to keep it from Pat or Mary."

"Mary knows. She'll help. It will only be for a few days. Please, Mrs. McCormack. Look at her, how beautiful she is. Eva doesn't deserve to grow up in that place, none of those poor children do." She clutched her daughter closer to her chest. "Please, you're my only chance."

The woman nodded. "Eat some soup, it's only vegetable but it will keep the hunger pangs at bay. I'll try to get food tomorrow."

Mrs. McCormack held Eva, cooing to her as Kate swallowed the most delicious soup she'd ever tasted. Then they heard singing.

"That's Paddy. Quick, let me show you," she said, leading Kate down to a basement. "It looks like a pantry and I guess that saved them in the old days more than once. My Paddy's family had what we'd call a history. They ran guns and whatever else was needed in the fight for freedom. It's not the cleanest but it's warm and dry. Free of vermin too apart from the odd spider. I'll bring you down a quilt and a box for the babe. You'll have to keep her quiet if anyone visits or when Paddy's in, not that he's here often. Most of the time he's in the bar or he's upstairs sleeping it off."

The woman scurried off to fetch the quilt and other items. In the darkness, Kate tried to keep the tears at bay. She told herself that this was better than being without her child.

"I'm sorry, Eva darling," she whispered to her baby, "but Mammy will do better soon. For now, we have to take what we can get."

Eva sighed, as if she was in agreement, her eyelids fluttering as she slept.

Hours later, heavy footsteps thundering overhead woke Kate with a start. She held Eva close to her breast to stop her daughter crying. The floor above them shook, dispersing dust and plaster down on top of them and Kate pulled a coat over her shoulder to protect her baby girl. She clenched her teeth, trying to stop the fear from taking hold.

She wasn't sure who it was, but she heard them thundering up the stairs, shouting at Mrs. McCormack, who kept telling them to get out of her house. She could hear the woman roaring. Goodness knows she was loud for a woman of her age.

"This is my home. I didn't invite you in, now get out, you bunch of heathens. You can go and all. Nobody asked a priest in here."

A priest. Did that mean Father Devine? Surely he hadn't come all this way just to fetch her back, had he? The sweat ran off her back, drenching her clothes as she strained her ears trying to hear his voice. But she could only hear the older woman. "Your kind aren't welcome."

"Now, Mrs. McCormack, you must understand..."

"I understand all right. You, with your fancy clothes and good meals living in decent houses, standing up at the top of the church every Sunday looking down on the likes of me. I'm a decent woman, Father. I've never stolen a thing in my life, nor broken any of the ten commandments but I don't stand for what you preach. All fire and brimstone, the God you talk about isn't my God. My God is a kind man who loves everyone regardless of how much they put in the parish collection. Where were your kind when my baby was coming? I was sick and needed the doctor but I didn't have a penny to pay for him. My baby died just as he was born so your kind, they wouldn't baptize him. Said he was a sinner. A wee babe who didn't even take their first breath. He's buried at the back of that field under that tree out there. 'Cause your kind wouldn't let me put him with my parents in the churchyard. I haven't stepped into a church since and I won't. When I die, they can put me in the ground with my son. Now, I won't tell you again. Get out of my house or I swear I'll throw the contents of the chamber pot over all of ye. Get out."

Eva, hearing the noise, flailed around but Kate held her tight. She couldn't let her cry. Then they would know someone was hiding under the floorboards.

"We're going, Mrs. McCormack, but we'll be back. Believe me, Kate Ryan and her brat will be back where they belong before long."

Kate held Eva closer to her chest, trying to calm her own racing heart. Her mouth was so dry, she desperately needed some water but she couldn't move a muscle.

"Why can't you leave that poor girl be? Haven't you tortured her enough? Starved she is, looks worse than a famine victim. We expected that from the English but how can you, an Irishman, treat your own like that? Where's your heart, your compassion, your Christianity?"

Kate wilted. The kind old woman had just confirmed she'd seen her and baby Eva.

A door slammed and Kate could only hope that was the priest leaving. She put Eva on her shoulder, trying to placate her, but she could see her daughter's temper was up. Her face grew redder as the child squeezed her hands into fists. That was the Ryan spirit all right but now was not the time.

"Eva, don't cry, please not now," she whispered in desperation. "We must find a way out of here. Poor Mrs. McCormack. No wonder Paddy drinks himself to death." Kate kept murmuring to Eva as she listened to the house above, which seemed to have settled back to normal—but for how long?

Moments later, the door rattled before Mrs. McCormack stuck her head in. "Is the little one all right?"

"Yes, I thought she was going to scream her head off. You were magnificent, thank you. I'm sorry to bring this trouble to you."

"You didn't, child. But that priest, he'll be back. I've seen men like him before. Can't bear anyone to be happy. Is he from your neck of the woods?"

"Father Devine. Yes, he's one of my mam's favorite people." A thought crossed her mind. Had her mam told Father Devine where she was likely to head if she ever escaped? Could her mother be that vindictive?

"That says a lot about your mammy. I'd best get my Paddy back from the bar. I want him here if that boyo tries anything again tonight."

Kate panicked again. "Won't he tell them where we are?"

"My Paddy talk to a priest? That will never happen. Even Father Burke, and he is as kind a soul as ever lived, couldn't get a word out of my Paddy. His heart broke in two when we lost our boy. He said the only way he survived was because I did. I wish I hadn't. Then my Paddy would have died a decent man not the ridiculed town drunk." The devastation poured out of the woman's eyes. Kate yearned to comfort her but what could she say?

"I'll be away. I don't have to tell you to stay put and keep quiet. I wouldn't trust that Devine man as far as I could throw him."

Kate retreated to the hiding place to wait. She cradled her baby close, jumping at every sound even when the cat meowed above her.

"Your mam will be hearing the banshee next," she said to Eva, who just gazed back at her, a dreamy expression on her little face. Then the sound of thundering footsteps rumbled through the house again. This time, she recognized the voices. Father Devine was the leader but with him were Fergal Scanlan and another voice she didn't recognize.

The men came straight for the door to her hiding place. Someone must have told them about the basement, she thought, as her heart almost burst out of her chest. She held Eva as close as she could, trying to press herself against the wall but it was no use. As she screamed, they dragged her out of the basement as if she was a sack of potatoes.

"Mind my baby, Fergal Scanlan, don't you dare hurt her," she screamed above Eva's terrified wails.

Father Devine looked down his nose at her. "Now, my girl, it's back to where you belong and the brat with you. Garda, escort her to the car."

The young garda hesitated, his face flushed. Fergal showed no such reluctance as he grabbed Kate's arm and dragged her to the Gardai vehicle. Kate couldn't fight back, much as she wanted to. She held on to Eva, who screamed.

It was pointless trying to protest. If she made a fuss, they might take it out on the old lady and she couldn't bear that. She huddled in the back of the police car, trying to stop Eva crying, but she wasn't about to feed her child. Not with Father Devine sharing the back seat. She didn't even get a chance to say goodbye to her brother or Mary.

Poor Mrs. McCormack would blame herself but there was nothing she could do about that. It took hours for them to drive back to the convent, by which time Eva had screamed herself to sleep and Kate was completely numb. She couldn't rest, not with the priest sitting beside her, glaring at her. His hate for her and her child seeped from every pore.

Reverend Mother waited until the priest left before she turned to Kate, a gloating expression on her face. "You'll regret trying to run away. Didn't I tell you that obedience to our rules is non-conditional?" The nun rang the bell on her desk. This time, it wasn't a girl who arrived but Sister Ita. Kate barely stopped herself from groaning aloud. The one nun whom everyone hated almost as much as the Reverend Mother.

"Sister Ita, take the child to the orphanage and tell them under no circumstances is she to have contact with Fidelma. That includes any stories the other penitents may wish to share. Make it clear, there is to be no communication whatsoever."

"No, you can't do that." Kate held Eva so tightly the baby screamed.

"Yes, Mother."

Kate managed a quick kiss on her daughter's head before Sister Ita pulled the baby from her arms. Tears ran down her cheeks as she watched the nun take her baby out of the room, the door closing behind her with a final bang. All the fight drained out of her. She didn't care what punishment the Reverend Mother had in mind.

"You will be locked in one of the unoccupied nun cells. For a week. You will not be allowed out for any reason. Is that clear?"

Kate didn't answer. What was the point? The nun had won and they both knew it. She had all the power.

The nun rang the bell again and this time it was Nora and one of the other women who escorted Kate to the cell. It was smaller than she expected and covered in cobwebs. Shuddering, Kate tried not to think of the other creatures sharing the small space.

Nora gave her a sad smile as she locked the door. Kate heard her retreating footsteps but didn't look up. She was beaten. She'd lost the chance to save her daughter.

· · ·

The time passed slower than Kate ever believed possible. She tried to avoid using the chamber pot until she couldn't hold it any longer. Her breasts hurt, the milk she should have used to nourish her baby flowing down her chest and into her dress. She was given bread and water but after two days, she couldn't manage to keep it down. Her tongue seemed to swell within her dry mouth. Her whole body ached and at one point she believed she was sharing the cell with her da, Tony and, for some reason, young Shane. She was slipping into insanity and there was nothing she could do about it. There were moments where the darkness passed, and she remembered that Eva was still in the convent orphanage. There was a chance, however slim, she would see her daughter again. They wouldn't win. She held on to that thought until, seven days later, the key turned in the lock.

The Reverend Mother scrunched up her nose, her voice sounding muffled as a result. Or was that just Kate's dulled senses?

"I assume you have learned the error of your ways, Fidelma."

Kate forced out the lie. "Yes, Mother, sorry, Mother."

"If you attempt to see your child again, we will send you to Dublin or to Cork. Don't you forget it."

She held the nun's gaze.

"What do you say?"

"Yes, Mother."

But Kate had no intention of keeping her promise. Nothing would keep her from her child.

TWENTY-EIGHT

Christmas, 1945

Father Devine's voice droned on and on. Around her, some of the women shifted on their seats but Kate sat straight, shoulders back like an army general, a perfect example of a penitent. She'd become the model inmate since Eva had been torn from her arms, hoping against hope the nuns would give her another chance. She hadn't mentioned Joe or Mary once, never complaining about not getting letters although she was sure they had written. She volunteered for any extra duties that needed doing. Sister Anne had even given her a compliment the other day.

Ignoring Father Devine's sermon, she prayed the Reverend Mother would find her heart. The other mothers had been promised a visit but Kate was still forbidden from any contact. She squeezed her hand against the pocket of her dress, feeling the soft gift she had made in anticipation of a reprieve. Surely she'd done enough. She could feel Eva's small body nestled against her neck.

Gwen, the newest arrival to the convent, pulled Kate's dress, alerting her to the fact the sermon was over. She'd been so caught up in her memories she'd almost ruined everything. Her rescuer was someone she hadn't even bothered speaking to, too engrossed in her own troubles. She eyed the shaven-headed girl kneeling beside her, eyes full of fear. She could only be about fourteen. *How could I have ignored the poor girl? Ger wouldn't have done that.* Kate clenched her hands, determined not to cry over the loss of her friend. One day the nuns would pay.

Father Devine held his hands up for silence as the Mass finished, not that the Maggies would dare to breathe a word. The locals took a second or two to comply.

"Thank you, everyone. Reverend Mother has graciously invited us all to stay at the convent to celebrate the birth of our Lord and the end of the war. This is the first Christmas during peacetime and it's fitting we gather to mark such an auspicious occasion."

"Did he swallow the dictionary?" Bernie whispered but her voice carried, earning her a ferocious glare from Sister Anne. She'd pay for that later. Kate kept her face void of expression.

Reverend Mother led the way through to the convent, with Father Devine and local guests following her, then the nuns and the Maggies bringing up the rear. Reverend Mother coughed discreetly before saying, "Thank you, everyone, for your generous gifts. We shall have tea, coffee and cake now shortly and then the children will come over. Mrs. McEvoy, you and Father Devine can distribute the gifts."

Mrs. McEvoy, the widow of one of the biggest landowners in Galway, bowed her head in acknowledgment. Kate's stomach turned over with excitement. This was her chance.

"Fidelma, go downstairs and help Brenda get the trays. Take Gwen with you." Sister Anne looked to the girls. "Maura, go with them and make sure everything is as it should be."

"Yes, Sister." Maura led the way to the kitchen with Kate and Gwen following in silence. Kate refused to let the disappointment crush her. She would find a way back into the room to see the children get their gifts if it was the last thing she did.

Down in the kitchen, plates of dainty sandwiches and slices of fruit cake greeted them. Kate's stomach growled in unison with Gwen and Maura. "Look at this, not a hint of rationing. I know the war is over but rationing continues. Where did they get all this food?"

Gwen's eyes were out on stalks, her reed-thin arm reaching out as if to take something.

"None of that is for you lot." Sister Ita pounced from behind the kitchen door. "This is for the good citizens who came to celebrate the Lord's birth with us. I've counted every slice and if I find any missing, you know who will pay the price."

"Yes, Sister," Kate replied as Gwen lost her voice. The poor girl shook with fear. "Brenda, what should we do to help?" Kate hoped to avert Sister Ita's attention. She pushed Gwen toward the aprons. "Put one of those on and fill the kettles."

Brenda, perspiring heavily from the warmth of the ovens, directed them on their tasks. "I need more turf for the fire. Take that new one with you. She's no use to me, she'll drop everything," Brenda barked, but Kate saw her glance at Gwen with concern.

"Yes, Brenda, come on, Gwen."

They pulled back the lock on the back door, pushing it open, each inhaling sharply at the freezing temperature. The brisk cold wind tore through their thin dresses. Kate held onto Gwen's arm directing her toward the shed where the turf had been stacked.

"What do you think Sister Ita will do to punish me? I didn't mean to reach out only I'm that hungry," Gwen muttered through chattering teeth.

Kate pushed her inside the shed, the walls providing a little shelter from the biting wind. "Forget about her. She'll soon have others to worry about. Thank you for what you did in church. If you hadn't pulled my dress, I think I'd still be there now."

"What were you thinking about? You had a lovely smile on your face. Was it food?"

Kate shook her head. "My daughter. She's over in the nursery and I haven't seen her in almost four months."

Gwen's face lost whatever color it had, as she put her hands over her protruding belly. "I thought we could see the babies."

"You can, usually. I upset the Reverend Mother; her punishment was to forbid me to be near Eva." Tears filled her eyes so Kate busied herself by throwing turf into a large bucket. "If we fill this one, we can carry it together back to the kitchen. It will save Brenda a couple of trips."

Gwen followed Kate's directions and soon the bucket was full. Kate added some wooden kindling on top. Together they hauled the bucket to the back door. "If I can, I will give Eva a kiss from you. Sister Anne said I was to work in the nursery after Christmas."

"Thank you, Gwen, but you should know anyone who gives me messages about Eva will be punished too."

Gwen leaned closer, whispering despite the howl of the wind, "Only if they find out."

They pushed the door open and dragged the bucket inside. Kate filled the range fire with turf, while Gwen washed her hands.

"Sister Ita is away upstairs with Maura and a couple of trays. Drink this while you can." Brenda pushed a glass of milk into Gwen's hands. "You've got to be careful, child, around the nuns. They have eyes in the back of their habits."

Gwen's eyes rounded, making her look much more like the child she was. She drank every drop before handing the glass back to Brenda. She refilled it and gave it to Kate. "It'd look suspicious if I had three empty glasses down here. Quick now, I hear footsteps."

Brenda had a sixth sense as, despite the silence, sure enough Sister Ita appeared just as Kate placed the empty glass in the sink.

"Put on a clean apron and follow me upstairs with those trays. The visitors must be starving."

Everyone was, given they hadn't been allowed to eat since yesterday, but wisely the girls kept their mouth shut. As they followed Sister Ita up the stairs, Kate's butterflies had butterflies.

She almost expected one to fly out of her mouth. Was Eva already in the room?

Before they entered, Sister Ita held up her hand. "The refreshments are for the guests only. The penitents will have their share later today. Understood?"

"Yes, Sister," Kate, Gwen and Maura replied.

Sister Ita opened the door into the main reception room. Kate had never been inside and relished the feeling of her feet sinking into the lush dark carpet. Exquisite rose and pink shaded wallpaper adorned the walls. The mahogany furniture glistened under the electric lamps located on each wall. The guests mingled freely, chatting among themselves. Sister Anne looked totally different as she smiled and laughed with the locals. Kate walked to the large table with its pristine tablecloth.

"Probably one we washed in the laundry," Maura whispered as they laid their trays on top.

Kate didn't answer, the hairs on the back of her neck standing. Turning, she found Father Devine glaring at her as if she was the devil himself. Keeping her gaze on the floor, she made her way to the back of the room where the Maggies had gathered.

Reverend Mother clapped and the door opened, allowing the children from the nursery to come in. Kate's shock was mirrored on the other women's faces; the children were dressed in the finest clothes she'd seen, their faces and hands scrubbed clean. She watched as each child walked up to Father Devine and Mrs. McEvoy to receive a present. The joy on their little faces made more than one person cry. Kate saw several villagers wiping tears from their faces; even a couple of men coughed into white hankies.

"I can't believe the change in the nuns, they look almost human, smiling and laughing and chatting like me mam used to do on the street with the neighbors," Maura whispered, but Kate was concentrating on the door. More nuns and some postulants, recognizable by their lack of wimples and plainer black dresses, came in carrying babies. The group oohed and ahhed over the precious bundles. Kate strained to see. A woman stepped forward to take a baby from one of the nuns. It was Eva. Kate took a step forward, but Gwen pulled her hand, reminding her where they were. Kate's nails pierced her skin as she clenched her hands so tightly in an effort not to move. She bit her lip to stop herself from crying out. *Eva, look over here, please look at me*, she begged silently as her eyes raked her child's body. She was too thin, the chubbiness of her little arms having disappeared. The woman held Eva up, tickling her under her arms. Eva's giggles tore through Kate's heart and she almost lost her composure.

"Watch but don't touch, remember," Gwen whispered into her ear.

Kate's lip wobbled as she struggled to contain her emotions. Then Eva looked up and held her gaze. *Tony's eyes*. She could see him in their daughter's face. Where was he? Had he survived the war and if so why hadn't he tried to rescue them?

"Kate, Maura, take those empty trays back to the kitchens. Gwen, help with the babies."

"Yes, Sister Ita," they chorused again. Gwen leaned in to Kate. "I'll give her a kiss, I promise."

Kate glanced around; nobody was paying any attention to them. "Give her this, will you, it's for Christmas."

Kate passed the white bunny she'd knitted from scraps of wool to Gwen, who shoved it into her pocket without looking at Kate. "I will. Now go on."

Grabbing a tray, Kate headed to the kitchen. Sister Ita had gone ahead so by the time they got there, she was sitting at the table, a mug of tea in one hand, a slice of cake in the other.

"Help Brenda rearrange the leftovers on plates for supper. If I catch you taking as much as a sniff, heaven help ye."

Maura muttered, "Yes, Sister," but Kate couldn't bring herself to speak. She returned to the room several times to collect plates, cutlery and trays but Eva had gone. So had the children and now the remaining villagers were being escorted off the premises. Kate headed back to the kitchen and washed dish after dish, all the time praying she would get to hold her daughter later.

"All finished, Sister."

Sister Ita stood in response to Brenda's comment and walked over to inspect the dishes.

"Haven't they worked hard today, Sister?"

"They have, Brenda. They will be rewarded later. Back to the sewing room, girls, now."

Kate and Maura exchanged a smile as they left the kitchen in silence. They could taste the fruit cake slathered with fresh butter.

They arrived to find some of the women in tears, including Gwen. Children's toys and clothes were stacked on the table as the girls worked around them, wrapping presents. Kate moved as fast as she could to Gwen's side but waited until Sister Anne left the room to ask, "What's wrong?"

"They are such a pack of witches. They only took back the presents from the wee children. As soon as the villagers had left, Sister Anne arrived at the nursery and removed their gifts and brought them back here."

Kate picked up a doll. "Why?"

"We've to wrap them and put them away for next year. Oh, you should have seen the little mites' faces. It's cruel, they are. Those vicious witches. What would make them do such a thing?"

"Shush, she's coming back," Nora warned.

Kate couldn't find any words. She sat down heavily at the table, thanking God Eva was too young to know of such a horrible trick. They worked in silence until the gong went for supper.

"At least we get cake today. I can just taste it." Maura rubbed her stomach as they made their way to the dining room.

Gwen whispered to Kate, "I gave Eva a big kiss from you and put the bunny into her cot. She was cuddling it when I left."

Kate squeezed her friend's hand in thanks. Gwen smiled back but then the smile slid from her face. Kate followed her gaze, staring at the bare tables in the hall. She couldn't look at the surrounding women but heard Maura swear softly. Reverend Mother addressed the hall.

"Father Devine suggested you all fast tonight and ask for forgiveness on this special day. Let's pray."

The girls kneeled as one as the rosary started. Kate closed her eyes, her lips moving in time with the prayer, her mind filled with images of her daughter. *I will find a way out of here, my darling. I promise.*

TWENTY-NINE

ASHEVILLE, NORTH CAROLINA

Christmas, 1945

Carol lay on the rug beside the fire, watching Josh sleep. She still couldn't believe the war was over and he was back with her. The Christmas tree lights danced in the reflection of the fireplace as the last log collapsed into red ashes. She should really fetch more fuel, having sent Isiah and Myrtle home for Christmas. Myrtle's mammy insisted Isiah spend the day with them, him having no family of his own.

Buddy whimpered as he turned around in circles. "Shush, boy, I'll let you out now. Give me a second."

Moving slowly so as not to wake Josh, Carol pulled the blanket from the sofa and covered her husband. Shivering, she pulled her light robe closed as she let Buddy out the door into the kitchen and from there into the backyard. The dog sniffed at the snowflakes falling heavily. He whimpered again, looking at her as if she was torturing him on purpose. "Go on, you aren't doing your business in the house. Go on." The dog barked in protest but then, spotting something, darted outside as fast as he could. Carol laughed as she closed the door and then screamed as Josh surprised her with a warm hug.

"Sorry, darling, I thought you heard me."

"You were fast asleep just seconds ago. Buddy needed the rest room."

"That dog. Who thought a pet made a great present?"

Carol kissed him on the nose. "You did and you were right. I love Buddy but not sure the feeling is reciprocated. He really didn't like going outside."

"Can't blame him. It's freezing out there."

Carol stared out the window as Josh cuddled her from behind. "We're so lucky to have plenty of food and live in this big warm house."

"Carol..."

"Josh, I mean it. You should see some of the houses people in our community live in."

"Not today. Please. Let's just enjoy having the house to ourselves. Listen..."

She waited. "I can't hear anything."

"Exactly." He smiled before nuzzling her neck. "Myrtle isn't singing or talking and Isiah isn't shuffling anywhere. Do you have any idea of how many times over the last few years, I dreamed of this moment. Last Christmas I was flying raids over Germany. This year, the war is over and it's just you and me."

The dog whined and barked as he scratched at the back door. Josh rolled his eyes.

"And Buddy." Josh left her to go and open the door, allowing the dog inside, who then shook his coat, spraying them with freezing water.

"Ah..." Carol escaped back to the fire, leaving Josh to dry the dog out with his blanket.

Staring into the fire, Carol tried to count her blessings. She was beyond lucky her husband had returned in one piece from the war, especially after he'd been injured. So many other servicemen and women had died or been horribly injured. They had this lovely home, plenty of money, a dog but...

"Carol, sweetheart, stop brooding. You'll make yourself ill again."

She turned to face him. "I can't help it, Josh. I know I'm lucky. My husband is home. I love you. But..."

"You want a child."

"Yes. So much. I can't stop myself. God knows I've tried."

Josh pulled her into his arms as she muttered, "It's all my fault. If I hadn't taken those two pills and been able to explain to your parents I wasn't going to do anything stupid, they wouldn't have..."

"Carol, don't."

"It's true, Josh. If I hadn't been committed to Highland and been subjected to electric shock and bathing treatments, they'd have let us adopt. Because of me, you'll never have a child."

"Now that's enough. Do you hear me? I love you and you are all that I need. It was my fault for leaving you alone so soon after the accident. Stop blaming yourself. You have got to get over this, honey, or you will tear yourself apart."

She knew she shouldn't keep going on but she couldn't help herself. "You know they are never going to give us a child. Even with your contacts, you couldn't get that horrible Ben Williams to change his mind. Even with your mother contacting that friend of the Kennedys, Archbishop Spellman, nothing's happened. Everyone knows he is one of the most powerful men in your church." She waited for him to argue but he remained silent. "Josh, I just want to be a mom. I'd be a good one, I know I would."

"You'd be the best." Eyes glistening with unshed tears, he pulled her closer. "The best."

THIRTY

CONVENT, GALWAY, IRELAND

1948

Josh Andersen shuddered, despite being used to the freezing temperatures of Berlin. He'd been stationed there with the Allied Forces, facing a new enemy, that of the Soviets. It had been six months since he'd seen Carol but rather than head back stateside, he'd opted to visit London and from there found himself in Ireland. Could Father Armstrong deliver what he'd promised?

He paced around the room in the convent, pulling at the collar of his uniform. He could deal with Nazis and all sorts of crooks, but this group was something else. He shivered, although it wasn't from the cold, it was from the complete lack of human warmth in the room, in the whole building. Closing his eyes momentarily, he pictured his wife, Carol, the day that Williams man had shattered their dreams of adopting a child. Carol blamed herself, saying it was her lapse in judgment that led her to be admitted to an asylum. He didn't believe that. It was his and only his. He was the one who'd left her alone, vulnerable after her accident so he could go off and fight in a war. She was the reason he was here.

When Father Armstrong had driven up the long drive to the convent, the building had risen out of the mist ahead of them. There wasn't one redeeming quality he could see in the whole place. Even the trees were bent over as if weeping under the weight of sadness surrounding them. The gray stones themselves seemed soaked in misery. Entering through a large double-locked door, into a long corridor with statues spaced out at meter intervals, gave him the creeps. The floor was so highly polished that he wondered if he took off his shoes would his socks skate straight across it. This room, the chief nun's domain, was marginally better. The white walls didn't offset the feeling of damp, the only decoration being a wooden crucifix and a picture of the scared heart. The plush carpet was nicer to walk on but any potential warmth it exuded was drowned by the woman in charge. Her expression seemed frozen in a mask of distaste, mean narrow eyes, with a mouth to match. She was taller and straighter than most ladies he'd met; she reminded him of one of the night witches he'd met from Stalin's army.

"Gentlemen, have a seat and I will send for some tea. It's a cold one out there today. Thank you for coming to see us, Father, and you, Mr. Andersen, so unusual to have a real-life war hero in our midst. I gather you served together in the war."

Josh sat and didn't bother correcting her use of his civilian name. What did it matter if she didn't address him by his rank as the wearing of his uniform dictated? He listened as Father Armstrong outlined their connection, how it was his brother who had served with Josh. They'd met after the war when Father Armstrong had come to counsel those who had lost their faith. It was hard to believe in a God after seeing the horrors in Europe.

The nun couldn't leave quick enough when the priest started outlining what they had seen. Josh waited until she closed the door behind her and left to organize the tray before pushing himself off the chair to stand. His old injury, irritated after the long car journey, made sitting more difficult than standing, which was a feat.

"These dames are cold, Father. Did you see the girl hiding

behind the door when we came in?" said Josh. "Skin and bones she was, worse than the women in Germany and they've been at war for years. I don't like it."

"Calm down, Josh. You said you wanted a child for Carol. This is the best place to find the perfect one. Reverend Mother isn't used to dealing with men. I'm sure she is more comfortable with the poor unfortunate women in her care." The priest picked a thread from his black robes. "Ireland has been at war too, you know. The Emergency led to rationing and lack of supplies; it has affected lots of people."

"The nuns appear hale and hearty. Isn't there another way?"

The smile on the priest's face disappeared and for a second Josh thought he was once again a thirteen-year-old altar boy being chastised by the parish priest.

"Josh, do you want the child or not? There aren't many places who will provide you with a little girl with no questions being asked. All you must do here is prove you are a Catholic, hence my presence, and make a substantial donation. Then we leave, child in tow, and you can head back to the USA and make your beautiful wife smile again. The child will have a better life, the nuns will be happy, so everyone wins."

Josh paced the room, tormented by the question running through his mind. Should he ask and potentially ruin his chances? Or stay silent and always wonder?

"What happens to the child's mother? The baby girl is three; hasn't she formed an attachment to the child? Are you sure she wants the baby adopted?"

He watched the priest's face closely, seeing his questioning had annoyed him.

"Josh..."

"I want the mother here. I want to explain to her why I am taking her little girl home to my wife. I want her to know she will be loved, adored, never want for anything ever."

"You don't get to dictate the terms. We are here on the sufferance of the Reverend Mother."

"You expect me to believe that? You're a priest. In the church the men always rank above the women, same as the services. That much I do understand."

Before the pink-cheeked priest could reply, the door opened, admitting the nuns. Josh wondered how much they had heard given their glacial expressions. What did he care? He wanted Carol to be happy, to be the smiling carefree woman he'd married, the lady she'd been before the baby and the operations. But was he prepared to break another woman's heart to achieve that?

"We are lucky, gentlemen." The Reverend Mother beamed as if bestowing a great honor. "Sister Monica has been baking; if she hadn't been a nun, she'd have been the best cook Ireland produced. Her scones fly off the plate with their lightness." She handed Josh a plate with two scones cut in half and liberally spread with cream and red jam. He was tempted to ask her to feed it to the girl he'd seen at the door. He pretended to listen as she went on. "Our strawberry jam is made here at the convent with the fruit of our gardens and the cream comes from our own dairy herd. We try to be as self-sufficient as possible. I admit the sugar isn't from our own beet—we swap vegetables with a local farmer in return for bags of sugar."

Josh made what he hoped were the appropriate noises. He didn't want scones, jam or anything else but he had to be polite. He forced the hot tea to his lips. What was it the Irish and English saw in this drink? Give him his mother's sweet tea any day of the week.

"Reverend Mother, thank you for your hospitality." Father Armstrong removed some crumbs from his chin with a hanky. "The food is delicious. You are very lucky to have such fine cooks in your convent. I might suggest to the bishop you have an unfair advantage and Sister Monica be sent to look after us priests."

"Father Armstrong, you are always a tonic, cheering up an old nun on a day like today. I wish you luck with the bishop but as he is a regular visitor, I think you'll find Sister Monica remains here."

Round one to the nun. Josh took a bite of his scone so he couldn't comment.

"Mr. Andersen, congratulations on your achievements. Your local bishop wrote to tell me you are to be awarded the Medal of Honor on your return to the USA."

Gee, the newswire between the convents is faster than most Allied Forces communications.

"Thank you, Sister, but I don't deserve it. My men do. They were the ones facing the enemy; some paid the ultimate price."

"Your humility serves you well but all regiments, orders, communities need leaders. Your bishop also tells me of your wife's... challenges."

He bristled as the tone of her voice changed but he didn't interrupt.

"I'd say a family like yours finds such a condition especially difficult given your prominent position in society. I believe your parents and the wonderful Irish family, the Kennedys, are mutual friends."

"Yes, ma'am. My father and Joe are old buddies. Mom and Rose get along well too."

"And your wife? I hear she spends a good deal of time in the hospital." The look of false sympathy on her face reminded him of his mother.

"Carol, my wife, is a wonderful, charitable lady. She stays at the medical center some days but when home, she never stops helping those less fortunate than we are. She volunteers at several local schools and communities to help both the children and their parents."

She scowled. "Unmarried mothers, I believe."

"Pardon, ma'am?"

"The bishop writes that your wife gets involved in other communities where there is a significant number of fatherless children."

"That's rather impossible, don't you think? I mean all children start with two parents."

The priest coughed, the nun flushed and the Reverend Mother

looked like he had walked dog dirt into her best carpet. He realized he'd better make some friends, at least temporarily.

"What I mean is, yes, Carol works with the single moms and their children. Just like she helps all the families in need. She doesn't ask to see a marriage certificate if people are starving and in need of basics, like a roof over their head. Before the war, our state was hit bad by the Depression and although things are improving, they are slower to improve for some communities than others."

He smiled his most charming smile, the politician's smile his father perfected years ago. *That told you, you spiteful old battleaxe.*

Father Armstrong stood up and walked to the fire, his hands open to the flames.

"Reverend Mother, we have had a good relationship over the years. The bishop suggested you had two girls you thought would suit the Andersens. Is that the case?"

"Yes, Father. A three-and-a-half-year-old and a two-and-a-half-year-old. The second child is a little darling, a sweet-natured child. The elder child would benefit from joining one of our own schools for such children."

Josh couldn't hold his tongue. "What type of school takes in three-year-olds?"

"She will be four soon enough." Her tone could have given him frostbite. "Thanks to the war, she is here longer than she should have been. There are several, Mr. Andersen. St Vincent's, or Goldenbridge, as it is more commonly known above in Dublin, and others like it. There the child will be taught how to behave, and she will also learn skills beneficial to the life ahead of her."

Josh knew he was missing something. "How can you know what her life will be like? She is only three."

The nun looked at him disdainfully over the top of her glasses. She obviously thought he was missing a few brain cells. "She is illegitimate. Those poor unfortunates must be treated carefully to prevent their sins corrupting our society. Special measures are taken to ensure they don't turn out like their mothers."

Josh clamped his lips together. Could the woman hear herself?

She was talking about children, mere babies, completely innocent. They didn't ask to be born. They didn't choose their parents or the circumstances of their birth. The need to get out of this place was overwhelming. He closed his eyes and saw Carol's face. This was her last chance to be a mother. The adoption societies in America wouldn't help them due to her health issues. They thought she was too mad to have a child. His own mother believed Carol should be placed back in an asylum. But Carol wasn't mad, not insane anyway. She was grieving, not just for the baby she'd lost but the future babies they couldn't have. She blamed herself for the hysterectomy, which was ridiculous. For his wife's sake, he swallowed hard before he spoke.

"Reverend Mother, forgive me. I'm nervous and probably letting my nerves get the better of me. Could we please meet with the girls? Is that allowed?" He held her gaze, smiling until she blushed and looked away. She wasn't that old. He hid his triumph. His dad would be proud his training had paid off. Dad always said the way to any woman's heart was through a smile that made her feel like she was the center of your universe.

"Sister Anne, could you please fetch child 1167 and child 1544."

Josh stared at the floor, willing himself not to react. This was like being in a camp with the inmates having numbers not names. He closed his eyes, saw Carol's face when she told him they would never be parents, held on to the hurt those words had impacted. The silence became oppressive, but he didn't make any attempt to break it. Let Father Armstrong speak if he wanted to. He was done trying to understand this setup. He wanted to escape as fast as possible.

After about fifteen tense minutes the door opened, admitting the nun holding the hand of a dark-haired girl with violet eyes. The second child, a little taller with blonde hair the exact shade of Carol's, followed, her chin up in the air as if to tell people she didn't care what they said or did. But he caught the wary distrust in her dazzling blue eyes when she briefly looked up and their gaze locked. Tears came to his eyes. Apart from her expression, she looked very like his wife. Or what Carol had looked like when she was young.

"Children, what do you say to the two gentlemen?"

'Pleased to meet you." The dark-haired girl bobbed up and down but the older girl remained silent. The nun glared at her, but the child still didn't open her mouth.

"This is the child I told you about." The Reverend Mother pointed at the younger child. "As you can see, she is a little angel. I'm sure your parents would approve of your choice. I have her documents all here, signed and ready for off."

"Thank you, Sister, but I want to talk to them." Josh walked over to the girls, bending down onto one knee as he got nearer so he was more at their height level.

"Hi there, I'm Josh. What's your name?"

The girls didn't answer but he saw the younger one look to the Reverend Mother over his shoulder. The blonde-haired girl held his gaze as strong as she'd already grabbed his heart. "They call me 1544 but Mammy calls me Eva."

"Eva is a lovely name."

She glared at him. "I don't like you."

Josh smiled at her spirit. "Why not?"

"You want to take me away. Mammy told me to kick hard if anyone called me out of the room. I tried but she hit me." The child pointed to Sister Anne. Josh clenched his hand.

"What if I told you nobody will hit you again? If you come with me, that is. My wife, her name is Carol. She really wants a little girl to love and spoil and play games with."

The child glanced up at him, her bright eyes glowing with intelligence.

"And you? Do you want a child too?"

He laughed sincerely for the first time in ages. "Yes, sweetheart, I want a little girl too. My wife and I can't have children of our own but we have a lovely home, a good life and lots of love to give. Do you think you could talk to your mom and ask her if you could come with us?"

The child leaned in closer. "Can you take Mammy too?"

He held her gaze, not wanting to lie to her, but he couldn't hurt her either. "I don't think that would be allowed, but I promise to let you write to her as often as you want. She can reply to us too. Then, after you've grown up a bit, you could meet her. If she wanted to."

The girl stared into his face before nodding slightly. She held out her hand. "Pleased to meet you."

He clasped her hand and squeezed it. "My pleasure, Eva." He didn't want to let her go but the Reverend Mother interrupted their moment.

"Sister Anne, take the girls back to their dormitory. Thank you."

Josh opened his mouth to protest but the nun silenced him with a look. Once the children had left and the door closed behind them, she launched into her tirade.

"Mr. Andersen, you can't go making false promises to the child. Her mother doesn't want her anymore, that's why she signed the papers allowing her to be adopted. In those papers, she signed away all future rights to the child and promised she'd never to attempt to find her. That's the way it must be, otherwise there will be hearts ripped apart on all sides."

"But—"

"Think about your wife, Carol, isn't that her name? What would it do to her if a child she loved started talking about going home to see their real mother? Is that the relationship you are looking for? If that's the case, you'll have to go elsewhere. The adoptions we arrange are final. Once you take the child there will be no further contact with anyone." She glared at him. *Gee, if they'd rolled her out to deal with Hitler the war would have been over long ago.*

She coughed, gaining his attention once more. "Do I make myself clear?"

"Yes, Sister, but—"

"Father Armstrong, I think you should take Mr. Andersen home now. There has clearly been a misunderstanding. I wish you luck in finding a child. Goodnight."

The dismissal was final as the woman walked back to her magnificent mahogany work desk. She sat and opened a large ledger, totally ignoring their presence. The priest stood and indicated Josh follow him to the door, but Josh wavered. He couldn't bear the thought of an intelligent, charming young girl like Eva being locked away in some industrial school. If the rumors he'd heard about them were true, nobody belonged in them, let alone a girl like her.

"Reverend Mother, I'm sorry," he finally relented. "You're right, I didn't understand and spoke out of turn. My only saving grace was the fact I did it in the belief it would make things easier on Eva."

"No child carries that sinful name in this house of God. She was christened Delia."

"Delia. Please let us adopt her. My wife will adore her as much as I do. I can write you a check right now." Immediately he wished he could retract those words. The atmosphere in the room chilled even more.

"Mr. Andersen, I am not in the spirit of selling children."

"Reverend Mother, Josh meant he would like to make a sizeable donation to the convent." Father Armstrong moved back into the room, his genial tone lifting the atmosphere. "Not to buy the child, nobody thinks like that. A gift, if you will, to help cover the costs of the incredible work you do helping these fallen women, those unfortunate souls who need this convent so badly."

The nun put her head to one side as if calculating something. Josh was tempted to just hand her a blank check and leave her to fill in the amount. He sent the priest a beseeching look.

The priest walked closer to the nun, his voice lowered. Josh barely heard him.

"Perhaps two thousand dollars would be acceptable? In cash,

not check, as it is almost impossible to negotiate a US check here in Ireland."

Josh didn't take his eyes from the woman's face. Would it be enough? Her eyes widened at the amount but this wasn't the first time she'd negotiated payment, of that he was certain. He'd spotted the greed in her eyes before she closed them and clasped her hands in front of her bodice, her mouth moving as if in prayer. After a few seconds she opened her eyes and spoke directly to the priest.

"I'd like to think about this and pray for guidance. Perhaps you could return on Friday?"

Josh shook his head. He didn't want to wait any longer. He wanted to take Eva and run away from this place.

The priest put a restraining hand on his arm. "We would be delighted, wouldn't we, Josh?"

"Yes, of course, but I am due back in the USA next week so there is a little bit of pressure coming from the top. The President has a date set for the ceremony to award the Medal of Honor. There are other recipients." Josh crossed his fingers. He'd no idea if that was true but he didn't want this old woman stringing them along for weeks.

"Till Friday then. Goodnight, gentlemen." She picked up a bell from her desk and rang it. Almost immediately the door opened, and another nun dressed head to foot in black appeared.

"Sister Joseph, can you please escort these gentlemen to their car, thank you."

"Yes, Mother." Sister Joseph nodded her head and moved to the door, expecting the men to follow her.

"Thank you, Mother, as always it's been a pleasure." Father Armstrong doffed his hat; Josh just followed in his wake. He was barely controlling his anger and disgust at this place.

As soon as they got into the car, he exploded.

"I've seen more charity in the eyes of a Nazi than in that woman's. Don't go all priest on me, *Father* Armstrong, you must have felt it. The atmosphere in that place, it's almost evil. Those poor women must be terrified of that old bat. Someone should do something."

"What would that be? The place isn't perfect but where would you have all the pregnant women go? Their own families send them here, Josh. Not the so-called 'wicked' church."

Josh spent the next three days touring the countryside on a bicycle. It was too difficult to find petrol and he didn't want his friends using up their precious rations. Despite the end of the war, some things were still in short supply. He liked being on the bike, away from other people, just him and his thoughts. His legs and back hurt like anything but the surgeon said he needed physical therapy to get back to his pre-injury fitness levels. If that was even possible. To see him now you would think he was seventy or older, not a man in his early thirties.

He stopped at a village on the road to Athenry outside Galway. The public house, Egan's, looked inviting, with red flowers in pots outside, the walls looking like they'd stood since the last century. He went inside and ordered a pint and something to eat. The place wasn't busy, with just a few regulars by the bar. Everyone was eager to talk when they heard the American accent. They told him stories about their friends and family over in America. The hours passed without him noticing and it was too dark for him to get back to his accommodation.

The landlord solved his problem. "Sure, stay here the night. I'll lock the doors just to stop the local superintendent getting ideas. He might call in later himself if he's in the mood. Will you have another drink?"

Everything and anything was discussed as the drink flowed. Josh couldn't remember getting to bed and the next morning he woke with the worst hangover ever. A full Irish breakfast awaited him, complete with the usual hot tea.

"Bridget, that's the wife, she makes a mean breakfast. So what has you in Ireland, Josh? Looking up old family, was that what you said last night?"

Something about the man made him tell the truth.

"Something like that. I came to see if I could adopt a child and bring them back to America."

He waited, not sure if he expected censure or encouragement.

"That's a grand thing to do altogether. There's so many poor children around these days. A few dollars never went astray and I'm sure the family will be delighted the child is going to a good home. I've a nice place here, a good wife and my children are producing grandchildren to beat the band. Nothing warms a man's heart than having a family around him."

"You're a lucky man, Barry. We can't have children of our own but we'll love the child we get as if it was our own blood."

"I'm sure you will. Bridget, will you give this good man one of your medals." Bridget nodded, stood and walked over to the wooden dresser at the corner of the room. Opening a drawer, she rummaged around for a few seconds before returning to sit at the table. She handed Josh the medal as her husband said, "The wife's sister is a nun over in Africa; when she comes home some of the nuns from the convent in Galway visit. They leave us a good supply. For the child, like."

Josh fingered the silver medal, tears in his eyes at the man's words and kindness. He blinked rapidly to get rid of them.

"The child lives at the convent on the Galway road. It's also a home for mothers and babies."

Barry exchanged a glance with his wife, and Josh's breath slowed.

"Those poor women deserve better than they get." Barry shook his head. "The shame of it. Someday Ireland will look back at the way we treated those poor girls, as many of them are just that, and hopefully see how wrong we are. It takes two to make a baby but you don't see any men in those places."

Bridget placed her hand over her husband's. "Barry, don't be getting worked up now."

"I'm grand, Bridget, don't fuss. My wife will tell you where her sister, the nun, is, they don't lock the women who fall pregnant in houses. The families look after them if the man isn't willing or is unable to make things right. And they call them who live in the third world countries uncivilized. Methinks it's us that are needed to be taught lessons. Bridget, tell him what your sister told you."

"I don't think our new friend wants to hear about that."

"Please, Bridget, do tell me," replied Josh. "To be honest, I feel a bit uneasy taking a child from the home. Not for any other reason but the girl wanted me to take her mother with us. My understanding was the children rarely knew their parents. At least that was the way it was explained to me by the bishop."

Bridget snorted. "That's the way is it for those girls lucky enough to come from families willing to pay one hundred Irish pounds over to secure their release."

"Sorry?"

"When an unmarried mother lands in the convent, she has to work to pay off her debts. The cost of bed and board plus any additional medical costs incurred with her condition." Bridget blushed as she told Josh the horrid reality.

"So what happens to the girls who don't have the one hundred pounds? I don't mean to be crass but it seems that would be a lot of money for many families."

"It is, a small fortune, and far more than it would cost to house those girls properly. It's sinful, a disgrace, but sure who is going to speak out about the nuns or the priests or any of them? Have you ever seen a poor church? Even in the worst-off parishes out on the coast where people are starving, there is plenty of gold and jewels to be found in the local church. The priest isn't starving, of that you can be guaranteed."

Bridget glanced around her as if she feared the local priest would walk in. "What people from abroad need to understand about Ireland is that we never secured our freedom when the British left. The Catholic Church, aided and abetted by several in our government, took over. The people don't have any power, at least the ones that don't have money. They are afraid. Of the local priest, the bishop, the Gardai—sorry, police as you call them—the teachers, even the cruelty man."

"The what?" Josh struggled to believe what he was hearing. This wasn't the picture drawn by all his friends and neighbors who claimed Irish heritage back in the USA.

"The National Society of Prevention of Cruelty to Children. It's an organization set up to protect children but the poor call the officers the cruelty men for good reason. They arrest children as young as two years of age and take them away to schools."

"What crime can a child commit at that age?" Josh asked, his eyes rounding. "They can barely walk and talk."

"Vagrancy. The mother may have ten children and a one-roomed hovel to call home. So the children play on the street with an older sibling in charge. If the family falls foul of the authorities for some reason, talking back to a priest, having an issue with the drink, make a complaint against an employer taking advantage, the cruelty men come along and arrest the children. They are put away for years at a time. They are promised an education but I've yet to meet a child out of one of those places that could write their own name. They're put to work, doing jobs, the girls to the laundries, the boys to farms." Bridget fell silent, her eyes clouded by memories. Barry reached over to put his hand on hers.

"You sound like you know a lot about these places."

"I should do," replied Bridget softly. "I was in one from the age of three until I ran away when I was fifteen. I met Barry and have been here since. His mother, God rest her, took me in and, when I was of age, we got married. So, I tell you, Josh, if you can save a child from one of those places of hell, please don't think twice about it."

Stunned to his core, he could only stare at her.

"I know I've shocked you. That wasn't my intention. I didn't commit any crime other than the fact I was deemed to be an orphan. My father died, my mother couldn't cope. Not with six children and her barely thirty. Mammy would never have given us up willingly. She'd have done her best to keep us. But it wasn't possible." Bridget gulped before continuing, her voice strengthening. "I think whatever child you pick, they will be lucky to have a father and mother who can give them a decent home. Love and understanding means more to those poor unfortunates than anything else. My sister, she joined the convent as a youngster, a brother joined the Christian Brothers when he was thirteen. A lot of children end up in the clergy in some way or another. Anyway, Frances, my sister, she's still a nun but she couldn't stay in that place in Galway. She'd kill us for telling you but she said she'd seen animals treated better."

Josh's throat hurt trying to contain his emotions. "And her mother? Is there anything I can do for her?"

"If she's still in that horrible place and her child is three and a half, she could end up there forever. No doubt she has repaid her debt but nobody will make that call. They will keep the free labor for as long as they can. If you can afford it, pay for her freedom and send her the money for a ticket to England. I've heard of other Magdalene girls starting afresh over there. With the end of the war, she might get a job in a hospital, maybe a chance to train as a nurse if she has an education. From what I read in the papers, there's a lot of opportunities over there for men and women looking to start again."

"What did you call her? A Magdalene?"

"Yes, that's what they call them. After Mary Magdalene, the..." Bridget shifted in her chair, her cheeks flushing again. "I'm sure you know the story. If she goes back to her village, or her town, the locals will never let her forget where she was. A Magdalene girl is always a Magdalene. It's like they get tattooed with that name. Nobody will give them a chance. Not in Ireland."

Hours later, Josh asked Bridget for a pen and paper. Then, with a heavy heart, he wrote a letter.

Dear Eva's mammy,

I don't know your name and for that I apologize. But I wanted you to know that I already love your daughter as if she was my own child.

Eva begged me to bring you with us but I can't. The Reverend Mother told me you gave all claim up to Eva. You wish to be free of your daughter and have asked not to hear from her again. I am not a hundred percent sure this is the truth. From what Eva said, you two have a close bond. I enclose my address should you wish to contact Eva. I also enclose the sum of one hundred pounds to pay the convent should you wish to leave and a further fifty pounds to help you start over.

Thank you for the gift you are giving my wife and I. We will be the best parents we can be.

In gratitude,

Josh Andersen

Josh folded the letter before saying his goodbyes.

"Bridget, could I leave this with you? I'd like Eva's mammy to be able to leave and go to England if she wishes. I will send you the money in a few days as I don't carry that much cash. In two weeks could you get the money to the convent?"

Bridget's eyes filled up. "You're a rare man, Josh Andersen."

He blushed as she reached up and kissed his cheek, retreating quickly to stand by her husband.

"Maybe someday I can bring the wife and our daughter back here to see you and Bridget again."

"We'd love that, wouldn't we, Bridget? Now I'd best get the pub sorted, clean the glasses and what have you. I have to open on time; thirsty men are never happy to be left standing." Barry shook his hand before he put his arm around his wife's waist. "We wish you the best of luck. Please write and let us know how you are getting on. Maybe one of these days, we could take a trip across to America."

"You can go all you like, Barry Egan, but you'll never get me in one of those planes and I get seasick crossing the Shannon. No, if you want to see me again, Josh, you will have to come see us."

"I'd like that. Thank you both for your kindness and giving me an understanding of what Eva's been through. And her mother."

He got up on the bike and cycled away from the public house, turning as he left the village to wave one last goodbye. Then he cycled as if the devil himself was after him. Forget about his injuries, he could handle physical pain. It was time to collect Eva and get back where he belonged. With Carol.

THIRTY-ONE

Singing as she walked to the nursery, Kate couldn't wait to feel her baby girl's little arms around her neck. No matter how horrible a day they had in the laundry, she could handle it if it meant she got to see her daughter. The nuns had finally found a way to control her. Kate knew if she defied any more instructions, her permission to visit the orphanage would be withheld.

Eva—although the nuns insisted on calling her Delia in official records, and child 1544 when addressing her—was almost four now. Her intelligence shone from her blue eyes and she never stopped asking questions. Kate clenched her hands, remembering the last punishment her daughter had endured for asking why she couldn't be with her mammy every day. The nun delivered a sharp slap across Eva's face and then made her kneel for so long, she developed welts on her legs. She was supposed to pray for forgiveness. For what? Using the mind God gave her?

Kate pushed open the door, greeting the women working with the children.

Where was Eva? Usually, the girl spotted her coming and came running straight over. A pit formed in the depths of her stomach, sweat running down her back.

"Eva? Where are you? Come here now, darling girl." She

walked then ran from one room to the other, panic mounting. "Where's Eva? What have you done to her?" she called out to the nuns.

"Compose yourself, Fidelma. What is all this racket?" Sister Joseph, the nun in charge of the orphanage, moved toward her.

"I want to see Eva... Delia, I mean. I can't find her anywhere."

"She's gone." Kate didn't miss the gloating expression in the nun's eyes. She was enjoying this.

Sister Joseph crossed her arms across her chest, clasping her hand just under her wimple. "You shouldn't be here. Get back to your quarters."

"Gone? What do you mean gone?" Kate knew the answer but still she asked, torturing herself.

"Delia has been adopted by a lovely Catholic couple who will give her an excellent future."

Kate's temper rose, her heart racing. "You evil cow, you can't do that. I didn't sign any papers. I want my daughter. Get her back. I'll get the guards. You can't do this. I won't let you." She was yelling now, unable to stop herself.

Reverend Mother walked up behind Kate, her rustling skirts and the sound of the rosary beads clicking together the only warning Kate got before the slap across the back of her head.

"Calm yourself this instance, Fidelma," she hissed. "You are not fit to be a mother. That's why you were sent here. You knew the plan is for all children to be adopted. What life can you give a child? You couldn't keep yourself out of trouble."

Kate's tears ran unchecked down her face. "She's my daughter, my flesh and blood."

"If you care about her, you will forget her. What child wants to be reminded of the disgusting circumstances of her birth, conceived in sin and forced to carry the consequences for the rest of her life?"

Kate's fingernails dug into the palms of her hands as she struggled not to grab the woman and strangle her with her own rosary beads.

"I will never stop looking for my daughter. Never. No matter what you say or do, I will find her. She will know I loved her from the first minute I felt her move inside me."

"You will never see her again." The nun held her hands together as if in prayer, a satisfied smile hovering on her lips. "She's not even in Ireland anymore."

Kate stared at the woman trying to comprehend the words. Not in Ireland? Had they taken her to England? Where was she?

"You're lying."

"I never lie. Now compose yourself and get back to your quarters. You should beg God for forgiveness for your selfishness. Your daughter will forget all about you; you're only her birth mother. Her real mother will be the one to rear her, read her stories, kiss her goodnight, take her to school, Mass and raise her to be a—"

Kate screamed as the nun continued her tirade, sinking to the ground, pulling out her hair, scratching her face, her arms, anything she could reach. Reverend Mother and some of the other nuns tried to quieten her, to grab her, but to no avail.

"Let me near her. I can help." Gwen, one of the mothers working with the children, pushed past. "Kate, it's me. Come here to me." Gwen put her arms around Kate, stopping her from lashing out. She pulled her into her arms, laying her head on her chest and allowing her to cry. She held her while Kate sobbed and sobbed. Reverend Mother stepped forward but Gwen snapped, "Leave her. For the love of God, you've done enough. Let her cry it out."

The rebellion must have taken the nun by surprise as she didn't reprimand Gwen. Instead, she clicked her fingers at the other two nuns and together they withdrew, leaving Kate sobbing on Gwen's shoulder. As soon as the nuns left the room, some of the other girls came forward and tried to comfort Kate as best they could. But she didn't hear them. She couldn't hear anything other than the cries of her daughter.

"Gwen," said Kate, "she must be so upset. She needs me just as much as I need her. She's not yet four, God love her, but who is going to look after her, help her sleep," she said through her whimpers.

"I know, love, I know. My Matthew hasn't stopped crying, you know how much he loved Eva."

"How will I find her? I must get out of here. I have to..." Kate looked around her wildly, trying to figure out an escape but with the barred windows and locked doors, who was she kidding?

"Kate, listen to me. I gave her the bunny you knitted. I made sure it was in her coat, hidden in the pocket. She has it. Don't say a word to the nuns, they'll take it out on both of us."

Kate shrugged off her friend's arms, the truth she didn't want to acknowledge hitting her between the eyes. "You knew! You knew they were taking her and you didn't stop them. You let them take my daughter. You? You're supposed to be my friend."

Gwen bowed her head before whispering, "I am."

"If you were, you would have found me. If they tried to take your Matthew, I would have walked over hot coals to stop them. You know that. We promised each other to help one another." Kate pushed the girl away. "I hate you. I hope they take Matthew off you. Then you'll know how I feel. Get your hands off me, never touch me or talk to me. I may hate the nuns, but I despise you."

Kate pulled herself off the floor, ignoring the outstretched hands trying to help her. Kate brushed past Gwen, heading for the door. There had to be a way to escape eventually, and she'd find it.

THIRTY-TWO

WASHINGTON, D.C. AIRPORT

"Wake up, Eva, we're home."

"Mammy?"

The child's plaintive cry was enough to break Josh's heart as he picked her up and carried her off the plane and into the terminal building. Yet again he questioned the wisdom of what he had done.

"I'm not a baby, I can walk."

He let the child down. A baby would have been less challenging yet this girl had captured his heart. "Come on then, sweetheart, let's go meet Carol."

His father must have called on his friends as they were ushered through security in no time at all. Then he spotted his wife, the woman he adored. She was standing by the wall, her eyes trained on the new arrivals. She looked drained, as if worried about something. He groaned inwardly; she'd been expecting him days ago. She must have thought he'd had another accident or his injuries had caused problems. He could be so thickheaded at times. He was trying to please her and he'd done the exact opposite. He waved, attracting her attention. Immediately relief lit up her eyes as she smiled.

"Josh, you're here. I thought there was something wrong when your dad..." Carol stopped talking, her eyes fixed on the little girl at his side. "Josh..." Her eyes held his, questions lurking in their depths.

"Meet Eva. Eva, this is Carol, the wonderful woman I told you about."

"Are you going to be my new mammy? I don't want you. I want my real one." Eva burst out into noisy tears. Josh glanced around. Some children could cry nicely but his new daughter wasn't one of them. She roared and wailed as if she was being tortured. Even candy didn't work. He tried to pick her up but she turned rigid.

Carol bent down to Eva's level. "You poor child, you must be so tired after your trip. My name's Carol and I'd like to be your friend. Can I do that?"

He watched as Eva stopped wailing, her eyes surveying Carol from head to foot.

"Are you going to take me to your house?"

"I will but first we have to stay in a hotel as the drive to our house is a long one. I think a hot bath and some food would be nice. What do you think?"

Eva put her head to one side, taking a few seconds to respond. "Can Mr. Rabbit come too?"

Carol glanced at Josh. He shrugged.

"Of course he can," replied Carol. "Is he with you or in your case?"

"He's right here." The little girl pulled a bedraggled piece of wool from her pocket. "I like you." Eva put her hand in Carol's. "Let's go. I need a bath and so does he. He smells."

Carol giggled, a sound that almost destroyed Josh's resolve not to cry. The woman he loved more than anything in this world had laughed. Everything was going to work out just fine.

"Carol," said Eva. "I have another friend called Matthew back home. He's a boy, he's one. So a baby really but he gets upset if you call him that. He'd like you too."

"He would?" Carol glanced up and met his eyes. Oh no, he knew that look.

"Have a little patience, darling," he said gently. "I'm not sure I'm ready to do battle again that soon."

Carol gave him a questioning look but before he could explain, Eva said, "Are you going to call me Eva or 1544?"

"Why would anyone call you by a number?" Carol's voice shook with emotion.

"The nuns did. I don't like it; I like being called Eva."

"What about Eva Andersen? How does that sound? That way you always have the name your mammy gave you," Josh said.

She put her little hand in his. "I like that a lot. When Matthew comes will you give him a new name too?"

"Yes, of course, darling." Carol ruffled Eva's hair before giving him a loving look he hadn't seen in such a long time. "He'll be an Andersen too."

THIRTY-THREE

CONVENT, GALWAY, IRELAND

Barely a month had passed since Eva had gone yet it felt like forever. She'd thought Mary or Joe would be in touch but she'd heard nothing. It was as if the outside world had ceased to exist. She wrote to them both once a week but it seemed to be a futile exercise.

The days dragged by despite her throwing herself into the work to become so exhausted, she passed out at night. Maybe then she could sleep. But it never worked. Every time she closed her eyes, Eva was there calling for her, screaming for her mammy. Several times, Kate jumped out of the bed thinking she heard her daughter's voice. Every morning for a split second she thought Eva was waiting for her in the orphanage, but then the reality hit, shattering her heart all over again.

Gwen had tried to reconcile, to explain her actions, but Kate ignored every attempt. She didn't have any energy left to hate the girl but she couldn't bear her being near her. She had to get out and that's what consumed her—the drive to escape and find Eva. She was determined to get out there, beyond the gardens and walled enclosure of the convent.

She volunteered for the laundry on the basis the work was the hardest so she'd be spent by the time she got to bed. She didn't talk to the other Maggies but kept herself distant. Not because she didn't care; she cared too much.

Today, she pounded another sheet on the scrubbing board, sweat clinging to her like an extra skin. Sister Anne called her. "Fidelma, Reverend Mother wants to see you."

"Why? I haven't done anything." Her cheek earned her a belt over the ear. She glared at Sister Anne before she threw off her apron and headed out of the steaming laundry, up the stairs and through the door with the chicken wire over the window. It was like the difference between night and day but her feet barely felt the wooden floors rather than cement. She continued walking, ignoring the statues and holy pictures, the smell of incense coming from the chapel and found herself outside the office. She knocked, waiting for the instruction to come in.

Once inside, she froze. Reverend Mother sat at her desk, her ledger open on the desk in front of her. Another woman sat at the desk, with her back to the door. At first, Kate was paralyzed. Was it her mam? The woman turned and her smile lit up her face despite the habit she wore. She was a nun. She stood and came toward Kate.

"Hi again, remember me?" the lady said.

"Sister John Bosco, please sit down. I will explain to Fidelma why you are here."

"Yes, Mother, of course. Please excuse me."

Sister John Bosco retook her seat. Kate remained standing as nobody told her to sit down. On closer inspection of the desk, she saw the nun had a letter in front of her. As she squinted, she thought she could see that it was addressed to Eva's mammy.

Her heart rate quickened as she glanced at Sister John Bosco again. "You know who has my daughter?"

"Fidelma, stay quiet," the Reverend Mother ordered. "Sister John Bosco doesn't know anything of the contents of the letter I received. She kindly came to visit on her return from our sister house in Germany. She's been helping the displaced persons settle after the war. She asked after you and I suggested she come to meet with us. The letter I've had put me in a predicament."

Totally confused, and feeling like she was a squirrel caught between two dogs, Kate wanted to run. But that letter had been addressed to her. After all this time, someone knew about her daughter.

"Can I see the letter?" Kate asked, using her most polite voice. She saw that failed to impress the nun. "Could you please read it to me? Please."

The Reverend Mother nodded in a gesture of what could only be interpreted as triumph. Kate knew the nun believed her to be beaten, and she would play that game all day long if pretending to be got her information on her daughter.

"Dear Eva's mammy."

Kate swallowed back a cry as she knew the Mother Superior was watching her closely. She'd play the games but she wasn't going to give away the whole house. She stayed silent, waiting. After a few seconds, the nun continued to read.

"I don't know your name and for that I apologize. But I wanted you to know that I already love your daughter as if she was my own child.

I enclose the sum of one hundred pounds to pay the convent should you wish to leave and a further fifty pounds to help you start over."

Kate couldn't stop herself; her head jerked up as she stared at the nun. The writer had paid her debt; she was free. Wasn't she? Could she believe it? Something in the nun's expression made her wary. She knew better than to trust the cruel woman, so she waited to hear more.

The silence continued growing heavier with each tick of the clock.

"I'm sure you can see my dilemma, Kate."

Kate tried but she couldn't think of the right answer to that question without seeing a trap. To her the answer was obvious. She was free. The nuns had taken her child and now had the money they said she owed as well. But that wasn't how it worked in here. The nuns didn't play by the rules, at least not any rule book she'd heard of. She risked a glance at Sister John Bosco.

"I believe I can help you, Mother Superior," said the kind nun. "I am on my way back to London to re-join my sisters overseas. My order has connections to St Thomas' Convent in London. They are in dire need of nursing staff, assistants and other roles. I remembered Fidelma from my time here; she had an excellent report from her work in the laundry and with the children in the orphanage—"

"Fidelma." The Reverend Mother spoke over Sister John Bosco as if she hadn't been mid-sentence. "Your future has caused me many sleepless nights. Despite our best efforts, you haven't lost your pride and your lack of humility given your circumstances is concerning. You have a negative impact on our other penitents. For that reason, I think it may be God's plan for you to travel with Sister John Bosco. Maybe you can become a nursing assistant or work in a laundry over in London. I believe their standards to be lower than ours."

Kate forced the retort back down her throat. She could escape. Once out of here, she would look for Eva. There was no way she was going to London.

"In order for me to agree and sign the release forms—those forms that prevent the Gardai from arresting you on sight and returning you to our care—you must agree to the terms of the offer. You will leave Ireland immediately, nor will you return at any point in the future. Should you break these conditions, I will revoke your release, report your absence to the authorities and you will be returned to live in another Magdalene Institution."

Kate stood, feet wide apart, teeth bared. "You can't stop me looking for Eva."

"You won't find her. Believe me. She is long gone, her name changed. Her official papers are now in her new name. There is no trace of your daughter, no way for you to track her down. Of course, if in the future she was to come here looking for you, we

would know what address to give her if you take Sister John Bosco
up on her kind offer."

Her stomach plummeted; the evil old wagon had thought of
everything. There was no way for her to find Eva.

She stared at the floor, wondering what to do. Was it better to
tell the nuns to forget their offer and work off her debt or was it a
chance to start over? Instead of a Magdalene for a mother, Eva
would have a nurse or even a matron. Because if she was going to
London, she wasn't going to be anything but a real nurse. She'd
study and find a way to qualify somehow. Then when Eva came
looking for her, and she had to believe her child would remember
Galway and her real mammy, she'd be someone to be proud of.

Looking up, her gaze locked with Sister John Bosco, who
seemed to be trying to communicate some message.

The Reverend Mother pushed her chair back and stood up.
"Well, what have you decided? I'm losing patience and I'm sure
Sister John Bosco has other things to be doing with her time. I
know I do. So your decision, Fidelma?"

"My name is Kate Ryan. Thank you, Sister John Bosco, I'd love
nothing more than to get out of this place."

Sister John Bosco smiled at her, her eyes filled with kindness.

Reverend Mother looked like she'd been given a dose of castor
oil like they reserved for the women about to give birth. She
handed Kate a letter to sign, stating that she had no claim to any
monies due because of her stay in the convent. Kate rolled her
eyes; it sounded like she'd been here on a religious retreat, not
worked as a slave. Kate read it carefully but before she signed it,
she said, "I'd like my letter. The one addressed to me."

"There is no such letter, Fidelma." The Reverend Mother
cleared her throat.

"You just read it out to us. It's addressed to Eva's mammy."

"Yes, but you aren't a mother, are you? You are a Maggie and
always will be. At least in Ireland."

The threat was potent. Kate scribbled her name and flung the
letter on the nun's desk.

"Go to your room. You will find your old clothes on your bed. You will wait outside the front door for Sister Bosco to collect you. Goodbye, Fidelma."

"My name is Kate. If I ever see you again, Sister, it will be too soon."

Kate spun on her heel and marched out of the room but not before she saw the glimmer of admiration in Sister John Bosco's eyes before it was quickly covered.

There was nobody in the bedroom, and it seemed even colder and forlorn than usual. She dropped the hated uniform in a heap on the ground and changed into her own clothes. They were too loose, hanging off her skeletal form, but she didn't care. She tried to look at her reflection in the window but the dreary gray day outside didn't help. She picked up her bag, her eyes glistening as she spotted the book her da had given her on leaving the house to go to Uncle Pat's. She hadn't seen it in the four years she'd been here. She touched it, immediately seeing her father as he gave it to her, the feel of his arms as he hugged her. "Sorry, Da, I never meant to hurt you," she whispered to herself.

She picked up the uniform, folded it and placed it on the bed. She wanted to rip it to pieces but her da had brought her up better than that. Without a backward glance, she left the room and headed down the stairs toward the front door. She didn't speak to anyone along the way, ignoring the nuns and other girls alike.

She'd just reached the front door when she heard Gwen calling her. She stood for a second and then opened the door and walked outside without a backward glance. Gwen followed.

"You're leaving and you weren't going to say goodbye?"

Silently, Kate stared at the view down the drive out of the convent. As far as the eye could see, there was green grass, bright flowers and a blue sky. No more gray. Gwen came to stand beside her.

"Fidelma, I swear there was nothing I could do. I couldn't get to you and risk Eva leaving without her bunny. I decided to be the one friendly face she saw before she left. Would you prefer I had left it to Sister Anne?" Kate stiffened. "So be it. You're still my friend and I'll never forget you. Thank you for being my friend when I needed one." Gwen put her hand on Kate's shoulder and turned away.

Kate bit her cheek, trying not to cry. Gwen hadn't any power, no more than she had. They were both victims of this horrible place but the difference was Kate was getting her freedom. She was leaving. Gwen didn't have that luxury.

"Stop. I'm still your friend," said Kate softly.

Gwen turned around, tears streaming down her face. Kate dropped her bag and took the first step, finding herself wrapped in Gwen's arms, who whispered, "I'm sorry I didn't stop them."

"No, no. Please don't say that. You couldn't have done anything and because of you, Eva has a piece of me. Thank you. I'm sorry what I said about Matthew. I hope you find a way to be with him."

"We both know that isn't going to happen, Reverend Mother says they have found a family who want to take him." Gwen hugged her again and then with a last squeeze released her, racing back inside, almost knocking over Sister John Bosco. Thankfully there was no sign of Reverend Mother. She hoped that she would never see that hateful woman again.

A car drove up to collect them. Surprised, Kate waited for Sister John Bosco to get in.

"Did you think we'd be walking to Dublin?" the nun asked with a slight smile.

"After this place, Sister, I don't think anything would surprise me."

Sister John Bosco laughed, the sound so infectious the driver and finally Kate joined in. Then she was crying and the nun cradled her until the tears were spent.

"Kate Ryan, from the moment I met you I knew you were strong, intelligent and you have done nothing but prove me right.

My advice to you is to put these years behind you. You can achieve anything you want. In London, nobody will know you. You can change your name if you wish. But it's your choice. I want you to sign up to do your nursing training. Whomever your donor was, he or she gave you sufficient money to do that and have a little to put by in case of an emergency."

Kate asked even though she knew the answer, "Do you know who he or she was? Did you see his name on the letter? Do you know who has Eva?"

"No, Kate, I don't. But I do know that God is looking after you."

Kate rolled her eyes. "God put me in that place."

Sister John Bosco put a finger under Kate's chin. "Never believe that. God has nothing to do with what goes on in that place and all the others like it. Now come on, let me tell you about St Thomas' and London. It's a great big world out there. Just waiting for someone like you."

THIRTY-FOUR

LONDON

1948

Kate couldn't believe her eyes as she walked around the East End of London. She'd read about the bombing and the destruction caused by the war but it wasn't until she arrived at St Thomas' and saw for herself the scale of the devastation that she understood the full horror. On the road, there were bomb craters big enough to almost swallow a car. Children played on bomb sites, made all the more poignant by the remains visible of the family home those bricks and mortar once formed. Kate stood staring at one such property; it looked like it had been sliced in two. The exposed half bedroom with its faded pink wallpaper, a bookcase with some books lining the back wall, a few on what remained of the floor, the rest of the room having dissolved into rubble on the earth at the foot of the building.

She heard of numerous casualties involving children finding live explosives and playing with them.

Sister John Bosco accompanied her to the hospital and signed as her referee but only after Kate had a holiday. Sister John Bosco insisted she needed a companion to aid her recovery and the two of them went to Bournemouth for a week. The seaside town reminded her of Galway Bay, although the tide was a lot gentler and the wind was warmer. She spent her days sitting on the beach staring across the water wondering whether Eva was happy and where she was now living.

"Kate, you can't torture yourself forever," Sister Bosco had said. "You did the only thing you could do. The family that adopted Kate are good people. They proved that by paying for your freedom." The nun had leaned across and squeezed Kate's hand. "You will never forget your baby, but don't let the pain of her loss turn you bitter inside. You have so much love to give and, believe me, the world needs as much of that as it can get." The nun's eyes had darkened, telling Kate she was thinking of the concentration camps and the evils she had seen there. She had told some stories but Kate knew it was much worse than what she described. Hellish nightmares kept the nun awake; she often heard her crying in the hostel room next door.

"I'm going to be a real nurse and keep a diary. In it I'll write to Eva every day or as often as I can. I will tell her what I am doing, seeing and also about her father. Maybe, someday I will see her again and I can give it to her. To prove I never forgot her." Kate had brushed away a tear.

"I think that's a lovely idea. Never give up hope, Kate. That's all we have sometimes. Just hope."

After a week of sightseeing, sleeping and eating fish and chips, they both returned to London. Sister John Bosco had to leave for Germany while Kate had to start a new life. With the money she had, Kate bought her uniforms, books, pens and other essentials. She lived in the nurses' home to save money. She also bought writing paper and some stamps, spending her first few days in London catching up on correspondence with her family.

One day she was called by the ward sister and told her brother was waiting at the hospital door, that there was a family emergency and she was needed urgently. She almost ran through the corridors and out the door to find Joe waiting for her. He swept her into his arms, holding her tight.

"There's no emergency. I didn't know what else to say to see you." Joe held her away from him. "I couldn't believe it when I got your letter. I just happened to be home. I called up to that convent but they wouldn't let me inside the door. You should have seen the state of me, Kate. I stood on that drive screaming your name. They called the Gardai and only then did I leave."

She hugged him again, not caring that tears were streaming down her face. "I have to get back to work but I finish at eight. Can you come back?"

"Just try and stop me. It's that good to see you, Kate, and you looking so well. See you this evening."

The ward sister took one look at her tear-stained face and must have assumed it had been bad news as she left Kate alone for the rest of the shift. She worked hard, allowing herself to smile.

An elderly male patient complimented her. "You should smile more often, nurse, you got a real pretty face. Look like an angel, you do. Doesn't she, Doc?"

Kate whirled around, mortified to be caught by a patient's bedside by a doctor during ward rounds. The ward sister would have a fit.

"Sorry, Doctor, I just refilled George's water bottle. He seems to be very thirsty. It's the third time I filled it for him in the last four hours."

"Excellent observation, Nurse. George has some medical issues and his continuous thirst is a cause of concern. Keep a close eye on him for me."

"Yes, Doctor." Kate beamed at George. Things were looking up and she could hear Sister John Bosco's words. *"There is always hope."*

THIRTY-FIVE

GALWAY, IRELAND

August, 1949

Carol hooked her arm with her husband, enjoying having him to herself for once. Not that she didn't love Eva, their daughter. She did, with every fiber of her being, but it was nice to have some adult time.

Josh interrupted her musings. "Did you see that? I think it was a dolphin, I wonder if it was. Do they really come this close to shore?"

Carol stared at the ocean; she could only see waves, large powerful ones that made her glad they were walking on the sand. "Bridget and Barry will spoil Eva rotten."

"Yes, they will and why not, she is utterly spoilable." Josh laughed before grabbing her and kissing her with such passion her toes curled into the sand.

"Josh, put me down before someone arrests us!"

"Isn't a man allowed to kiss his wife?" He hung his arm around her shoulders. "Come on, out with it. What's that pretty little mind of yours worrying about now?"

"What if Matthew has been adopted already. Eva will be so disappointed. We shouldn't have promised."

He pulled her around to face him. "Darling, I've written to the Reverend Mother and Father Armstrong has given us a glowing recommendation again. That and the cash I donated means Matthew will be there. I guarantee it just as I can promise we need to take cover now."

She glanced at the sky, the clouds did look darker.

"Do you think it will rain?"

"I don't care about the weather, but I want to make love to my wife and I don't think she'll want that to happen on a beach in Ireland, no matter how beautiful the coastline."

She giggled like a young bride as together they made their way across the road and back to their hotel.

The next morning Carol's nerves were giving her butterflies. They drove in silence; she could tell something was bothering Josh but he wasn't in the mood to share. As they got nearer, his frown deepened. He pulled over just before the gate, loosening his tie and undoing his shirt button.

"Carol, I don't want to go back in there. The last time, I barely held on to my temper and came closer than I've ever come to hitting a woman. If things haven't improved for those children, well..." He clenched his fists so tight his knuckles shone white.

"Joshua Andersen, you have never hit a woman in your life and you are not about to start now. If you find your temper rising, just call me honey bun and I will take over."

His eyes widened. "Honey bun?"

"Well, if you ever call me that in public, you know I'll hit you so it's a good word to use. Now let's get this done, find our son and bring him home to his sister. I miss my daughter."

"Yes, ma'am." He gave her a mock salute before starting the car.

She could have swallowed her own bravado as they neared the

end of the long drive. The place had looked picture perfect; every blade of grass was almost the same length, for heaven's sake. As they drove closer, she started as the building seemed to appear out of nowhere. She could sense the misery and sadness.

"Bridget said the stones in Ireland leach the sadness from over the years. I think this place has leached the entire world's."

Josh nodded. "I had the same feeling. Wait until you get inside."

He parked in silence, opening his door before walking around and helping her out. She took his arm as they walked up the steps and rang the bell. A young nun, wearing a very simple uniform, answered. "Come in, please. Reverend Mother is expecting you."

Carol sensed Josh falter on the step, but she didn't think his war wounds were to blame. Her heart surged with love for this gentle giant of a man who ordered men into battle but couldn't bear to see a child in need.

She squeezed his hand and together they walked through the door.

She shuddered as she looked at the long white-walled corridor with its holy statues dotted along at regular intervals. Her gaze took in the shiny wooden floors, so glossy you could almost see your face in them. Totally impractical for pregnant women to walk on. Her gaze flickered to the stairs at the far end of the corridor where she thought she glimpsed a shadow. Was that one of the mothers watching her, wondering was she coming for her baby?

Carol shivered. Maybe this was a mistake. If they didn't adopt Matthew maybe the nuns would give him back to his real mother. But then Eva's face popped into her mind. She was so excited, all chat about the friend she'd had to leave behind at the convent.

The meeting with the Reverend Mother went just as Josh had predicted only Matthew was waiting in the room for them. Carol's heart melted at the sight of his terror-filled face, the wet stain on his short pants. The poor child was rigid with fear. Carol took a step toward him, not wanting to make him feel worse.

"Hello, Matthew, my name is Carol and this is my husband, Josh. A friend of yours sent us to find you today."

He stuck his thumb in his mouth and gazed up at her.

Reverend Mother spoke sharply. "Stop that disgusting habit at once or these people won't want you."

The child pulled the thumb from his mouth, his eyes watering.

Carol faced the nun. "Where do we sign?"

"There are some formalities to go through." Although the nun was speaking to her, she saw her give the child a look that would freeze an adult to the spot.

Carol saw red. "Look, lady, we both know how things stand, now I repeat: where do we sign?"

For a second she thought the nun would keel over she went so pale, but instead she pushed the letter toward Josh. He offered Carol the pen but instead she turned to Matthew and held out her arms. "Would you like to leave here today?"

The child nodded but at the same time his eyes darted to the door. "Mammy said she'd try to say goodbye. Will she?"

Not if that old witch behind the desk has anything to do with it.

"I met your mammy outside, Matthew, and she asked me to give you the biggest hug and tell you she loves you so much. She said you are the best boy any mother would be blessed to have."

Matthew nodded and then he moved one step closer. Carol sensed that was all he was capable of given the dirty looks the nun kept sending his way. She reached down and lifted the child onto her hip.

"Mrs. Andersen, your beautiful coat. The cashmere will be ruined."

Carol looked over Matthew's shoulder as he snuggled his head into her neck as far as he could. "Coats can be replaced. Unlike children. Good day to you, Sister. Josh, I'll see you outside."

Carol marched as fast as her high heels would carry her. If she lived to be a hundred, she'd never step foot in this horrible place again.

. . .

Matthew whimpered the whole way back to Bridget's home. Carol tried to distract him, pointing out the birds or flowers through the car window. Nothing worked, causing the thirty-minute drive to feel like hours. They pulled up outside Bridget's pub. Bridget and Eva came running out.

"She heard the car, she's been fretting you weren't coming back," Bridget apologized, her eyes full of pity for the tiny boy clinging to Carol's coat.

"Matthew. Is it really you?" Eva rushed forward, enveloping the boy in a hug. "Do you remember me? It's Eva."

Matthew burst into noisy sobs.

"Mom, why doesn't he remember me?" Eva wailed.

Carol bent down to pick up her daughter, leaving Josh to carry Matthew. "Let's go inside, darling. Your poor brother is scared. It's been a long time since he saw you."

"I remember him!"

Carol smiled, her daughter's fire was amusing. Most of the time.

"Yes, but you were older, sweetheart. Why don't you try humming a song you used to sing to him? Do you remember any?"

Eva moved to sit beside the trembling Matthew. She sang a few words and they all saw the boy's eyes light up with recognition. He held his arms out to Eva. "Mom, see, he remembers." Eva's smile reduced Carol to tears but her words almost finished her.

"See, Matthew, I promised I'd come back for you. I never break my promise."

THIRTY-SIX

LONDON

1951

Kate peered out the window of her terraced home in South London. Where were they? She paced back and forth, picking up a duster and running it over the spotless furniture in the front room.

"Darling, you need to sit down." Alan ran his free hand through his dark curly hair, lifting the fringe from his eyes. She'd nagged him to get a haircut but his work came first. The demands on a National Health doctor far exceeded the time available in a day.

"The place looks lovely and they aren't coming to see the house. Have a cup of tea." Alan handed her the cup as he stared at the chair, waiting for her to take a seat. She lowered her heavy frame into it, glad to rest her back.

"How are my boys?" Alan whispered as he rubbed her stomach. "Don't be too hard on your mother."

Kate lifted her head for his kiss. "You don't know they are boys yet, darling."

"I guessed it was twins early enough, didn't I? Of course it's boys. I'm a doctor, I'm always right."

She knew he was trying to make her laugh, to relax, but she couldn't stop wishing he'd gone to work. *How could I be so mean? He is being supportive.*

As if he read her mind, he held her hand. "Kate, don't build your hopes too high. They may not have news."

Her heart jumped at the knock on the door.

"I'll get it. Give you time to get out of the chair and make yourself presentable," he teased as he gave her a quick kiss on the top of her head and went to answer. She pushed herself out of the chair, feeling as dainty as an elephant.

The door opened.

"Kate, you look amazing. Oh my goodness, you are huge." Mary put her arms around her or tried to. Joe walked in behind Mary, looking every bit like the Irish farmer he now was. He even wore a peaked cap like her da had.

"Kate, you're blooming. See, I told you, Mary, she was doing great. Has herself a fine man too, even if he is English." Joe elbowed his brother-in-law gently to show he was teasing.

"Mary, let me show you where to put your bags. You too, Joe, while Kate dishes up the tea. She's made enough sandwiches to feed an army. I think she's been saving the rations for weeks. I hope you like Spam!"

Mary made a face. "I forgot you were still on rations. Good job we packed a few goodies in our cases, right, Joe?"

Joe grinned before grabbing both bags and heading up the stairs after Alan.

Mary hesitated. "Will I give you a hand?"

"Go away up to the room and have a good look around. I know you're dying to. I'll dish this up and then we can talk till the cows come home."

"Kate, I'm so glad to see you so happy. Alan seems like a nice man."

"He is and I'm very lucky."

"It's me that should say that. An Irish beauty, a nurse to help me in my practice and about to deliver my sons any day now. What more could a man ask for?"

Mary's face flushed as she realized they'd been heard. "I'm so sorry we couldn't get away to come to your wedding. Ciaran was busy with the farm, and our three little ones were just too young to leave. Mrs. McCormack has taken up the role of granny. She's moved into the house while I'm over here. Ciaran may not want me to come back. She was spoiling him before I even left."

Kate couldn't speak, tears running down her face as Mary clenched her hand. Together, they sat on the sofa. Alan carried in a tray of sandwiches and some cups with the teapot and a jug of milk. Taking in Kate's emotional state, he turned to his brother-in-law.

"Why don't I show you the local and you can see if the Guinness is up to your standard. We'll come back in a while, let these two chat in peace."

Joe took one look at Kate's tears and he was out the door in seconds.

"Joe never could stand to see anyone crying. Even if they are tears of happiness, at least I hope they are." Mary gripped Kate's hand tighter. "I can't believe I'm sitting beside you after all these years."

Kate tried hard to get a grip on herself. Mary stood up. "I'll be mother." She poured the tea and handed a cup to Kate, before taking one for herself. "You haven't changed a bit, Kate. Still as gorgeous as ever and your hair is even more beautiful. It suits you in that style."

Kate ran a hand through her hair self-consciously. "It took a long time to grow out. You should have seen the looks I got when I first arrived here in London. I had to wear a scarf on my head for ages. People assumed I'd been working in munitions or lost my hair because of the war."

Mary shifted in her seat, drinking her tea and then getting up to look out the window. "How do you live surrounded by so much concrete? And the building sites? I can't believe how many shells of buildings still exist. They should have been cleared away by now. I saw children playing in what looked like remains of old houses."

"This area of London suffered terrible bombing during the Blitz and again when the V1 and V2 rockets came. There's a lot of poverty around here and, with rationing, there isn't a lot of spare building materials. The locals joke they would be better off in Berlin, with the Americans helping the Germans get back on their feet. The British are over there too, rebuilding the cities after their bombs. Our turn will come. At least the children are safer now. In the first few years, we had many come into the casualty department with injuries because of unexploded shells or bullets."

Mary nodded, but Kate sensed her cousin wasn't listening. Not really.

"Why don't you just tell me what's on your mind, Mary? You're like a cat on a hot griddle, can't stay still. What is it? Has Mam decided to visit me?"

Mary's lip curled with disgust. "Don't mention that woman to me. How a nice man like your da, God rest him, ended up with a mean aul witch like her is beyond me." Mary gave Kate a look. "Don't look at me like that. I know she's dying, and that's why Joe came back home. He'd never have done that if she hadn't black-mailed him into it. He's miserable in Galway, Kate. He puts on a good show but the life of a farmer isn't for him. He was happier when he was in the navy or even in the two or three years he spent over here. But this last year, he's been that miserable, he'd put the cows off their feed. You've got to persuade him to come back to London. He can get work on the buildings or even go back into the services."

"Joe's a grown man. He'll not do what I say."

Mary sighed before taking a seat again.

"You didn't come all this way to talk to me about Joe. Mary, spit it out. Whatever it is, I can handle it. Have you news of Eva?"

Mary shook her head, tears filling her eyes. "I've a path worn up and down to that convent. They won't tell me a thing."

"So why are you upset?"

"I have something to give you. I didn't want to send it by post. I'm not even sure I should give it to you. You're happy now with Alan and..." Mary stared at the floor and then the spot behind Kate on the wall but not at her face. What was she hiding?

"What is it?"

Mary stood up and went to her handbag, taking from it a bundle of letters. Kate's heart lurched. She recognized the American stamps. Tony? Was he alive after all this time?

"They aren't from Tony, at least not all of them. His mom wrote."

Kate repeated what she'd heard. "Tony's mom wrote to you?"

"No, she wrote to you. Da held on to them. I swear I didn't know, Kate. I found them after he died. But you'd sent word you were getting married and then you were pregnant. I couldn't send them by post... I don't even know if I should have brought them to you now."

Kate's hand shook as she held it out. "You opened them?"

"Yes. Not the ones from Tony, but I opened the last one. I know I shouldn't have but... Oh, Kate, I was so worried that it might be something to make you regret getting married. Joe said you were so happy, he was that proud to give you away. He said Alan loved the bones of you and you seemed to love him too."

Kate whispered, the lump in her throat increasing. "I do. Not the same way I loved Tony but Alan is a good man. I'm not that innocent seventeen-year-old anymore."

"Will I leave you in peace to read them?" Mary offered.

"Tony's dead, isn't he? I mean I thought he was but that's why his mom wrote, isn't it?" Kate's voice trembled, her hand shaking as she took the letters. "Tell me."

Mary nodded, her eyes glistening. "They shot him down in January 1944. The Dutch Resistance picked him up and tried to smuggle him back to Britain, but they were betrayed. They sent

Tony to a prisoner of war camp. He'd been injured. I guess the camp wasn't... yes, he died. But he knew about Eva, well, the baby, I mean."

Kate's head shot up. "He got my letters?"

"Yes. His mom knew he wanted to marry you and that you were having a baby. She's written asking if she can meet the child. She wrote again and again. The poor woman is in bits."

Kate let the tears fall. In her heart, she'd known he was dead. Guilt flooded through her as she remembered all the times she doubted him, thinking the nuns might have been right about him using her. But he'd loved her.

Mary stood up. "Why don't I go up and have a nap. Let you read these in peace before the men get back."

Kate nodded, leafing through the envelopes. She barely heard the door closing and Mary's step on the stairs.

Dear Kate,

How I feel I know you already, yet we've never met. Tony wrote to us about his Irish beauty so many times. He described not only a beautiful girl, but one with the biggest heart. He wrote to tell us he was going to ask for leave to go to Ireland to get married and then bring you back with him to the USA. He also told us about your pregnancy, which came as a shock with us being Catholics.

As you know, he never came home. It took a long time to find out what happened to him. We got notification the plane crashed, and they posted him missing in January 1944. We heard nothing for months and were going out of our minds with worry. Imagine our joy when we heard via the Red Cross that he was a prisoner of war. The Nazis captured him while he was hiding in Holland. We heard nothing more until the notification of his death arrived. We had no way to contact you until the war was over and they returned his belongings. In there was a half-written letter to you. I've enclosed it in a sealed envelope. I'm the only one who read it and only because I wanted your address. I've written now twice and can only assume you haven't received my letters. I can't believe you wouldn't write back. The girl Tony described wouldn't be that heartless. As you know, he was our only son. Please, Kate, if you read this can you write back and tell us about his baby. Did you have a boy or a girl? I'd love to meet my grandchild, but this isn't possible with you living in Ireland and us over here. My husband, he's rather set in his ways, but I don't care that you and my son weren't married. I believe the war was responsible, and I was so excited about becoming a grandmother. All I care about is seeing my son live on in his child.

Please write to me, Kate. I beg you.

Yours truly,

Evelyn Burton

Crying, Kate put the letter down and opened up the other letters from Mrs. Burton. In the second one, a blank sealed envelope fell out. Kate stared at it, not wanting to open it but also dying to know what he'd written. Her chest tightened. She swallowed to reduce the constriction in her throat. Her hands shook so much she couldn't read the words.

Darling Kate,

I'm going to be a dad. I can hardly believe it. Me and you are having our own baby. Do you want a girl or a boy? I know most men want a son, but I'd like a little girl for now, a replica of my beautiful Irish rose.

How are you? I hope Pat and Mary are pleased with the news. I guess that's a bit much to expect, but they know how I feel about you. We would be married if they'd let us.

How I wish I could hold you and tell you how much I love you. I miss you every day. I wish I had got your photo taken. I guess that would be hard for you to organize but if you could, it would be great. I'm going to talk to my CO about getting some of my pay sent to you. I know they do that for wives, but not sure about sweethearts. He's a good guy though, so he'll help if he can.

I hope you don't mind, but I wrote Mom and Pop already and posted it first thing this morning. They'll be annoyed we anticipated our vows, but they'll get over it. At least Mom will and she'll talk Dad around. She wants grandchildren, lots of them.

We are flying tonight. Don't worry, it's not a dangerous trip this time. We aren't bombing any major cities or anything. Just taking some pictures. When I get back tomorrow, I will finish this and post it. I've asked the CO if I can get to Ireland on my next leave. He's doubtful, but we'll see. I'll check in with him tomorrow before I send this. Fingers crossed, he'll say yes. He's a romantic at heart.

I love you, darling. Give our little bump a kiss from Daddy.

Yours forever,

Tony xxx

Kate sank back onto the sofa, clutching the letter to her. He'd loved her just as much as she'd loved him. For a second, she was glad he'd died. It would have been so hard trying to tell him she'd lost his little girl. The tears flooded down her cheeks as she rocked herself back and forth.

Mary came through the door and wrapped her arms around her. "Oh, Kate, I'm sorry. I shouldn't have given the letters to you. Do you want me to go for Alan? You can't get into this state, think of the babies. You are so near your time. What was I thinking of? I am a right eejit."

Kate couldn't stop sobbing. She held on to Mary like someone drowning. Mary soothed her, patting her on the back. "He loved you just as much as you said. We all knew it even if we were blind to it when he left. May God forgive me for swearing about him leaving you in the lurch with his baby. I feel dreadful."

"Shush, Mary, you did nothing wrong. We made our bed as Mam would say." Kate pulled herself together. "I'll have to write to his mother, but..."

"What?"

"How do I tell her I lost her grandchild?"

Mary put her hand under Kate's chin, forcing her to meet her gaze. "You didn't lose anyone. They stole Eva from you. You write to Tony's mother and tell her the truth. Maybe she knows a bishop or archbishop or even the Pope and they can tell those witches in that convent to tell us where Eva is."

Kate burst into laughter even as she cried. "The look on your face, you'd murder them yourself, wouldn't you?"

Mary nodded grimly. "I swear I don't know how Joe does it. You know he goes every Sunday without fail. Always the same question and the same answer, but still he goes back. That Reverend Mother must be the only woman in Ireland that didn't fall under the charm of our Joe."

Kate hadn't known her brother was visiting the convent. Her chest felt looser; he'd been supporting her all this time. "He should give up."

"I told him that, but he won't." Mary sighed. "He said something will change. She's getting old, so maybe the next one in charge will be kinder."

"And I'm about to dance up the street doing the can-can. There's not a chance of anyone kind ending up in charge at that convent."

Mary hugged her before bending down to pick up the letters now scattered across the floor. "Where do you want to put these? Alan and Joe will be back shortly. Do you want me to put them back in my case?"

"No. Leave them here. I don't have any secrets from Alan. He knows about Tony, the convent, everything."

Mary's eyes widened. "I know, but you're not going to let him read these, are you?"

"I don't think he'll want to, but I won't hide them. He's my husband, and he knows I love him. Keeping these a secret would make him doubt that. I've enough shadows in my life without adding to them."

Mary didn't have time to argue as the door opened, the men's voices announcing their arrival.

"Ew, you smell like the brewery." Kate wrinkled her nose as Alan kissed her on the forehead. She smiled at his anxious look. "I'm fine. Mary brought some letters from home. They're from Tony's mother. And there was one from Tony he didn't get to send."

Joe's eyes were on stalks, but Alan appeared unruffled. Only Kate saw the slight tensing of his jaw muscle. She pulled his hand. "Kiss me again." She offered her lips this time, and he grazed them with his, visibly relaxing. They exchanged a deep loving smile.

"Keep this up and Joe and I will go stay in a hotel. You two are a right couple of lovebirds, aren't ye, Mr. and Mrs. Hyland?"

"Never mind that lovey-dovey stuff. What's for dinner? I'm starved." Joe rubbed his stomach, making everyone smile. "What? Do you want me to go for fish and chips?"

"Great idea. I'll come with you. Be back soon." Mary grabbed Joe's arm, and they headed out the door.

"You all right, love?" Alan said, taking a seat beside her.

"I'm fine. It's a relief, you know. I mean, I guessed Tony was dead but there was a part of me that doubted, that believed maybe the nuns were right."

Alan growled. "Those women weren't right about anything."

"They aren't all bad. Look at JB and how wonderful she's been to me. She's like a mother, well, what a proper mother should be. And she can't wait for these two to arrive. I think she hasn't stopped knitting for them since we told her."

"Aye, you're right. I'm forever grateful for Sister John Bosco bringing you to London to my hospital. She'll be glad to catch up with Mary when she comes for tea tomorrow." He massaged her shoulders. "Joe was in excellent form in the pub, although he was talking about coming back here. I reckon once your mum dies he'll sell up and live in Britain. Brian was in the pub and a few of the other veterans. Joe was chatting about the good old days of the war until I dragged him home."

Kate rolled her eyes. "The war that killed millions." But Alan didn't hear her.

"He said they had little time for those who served in the forces, in Ireland he meant. I think he's lonely."

"He should settle down and have a family." Kate grimaced, thinking of how much like her mam she just sounded.

"I don't think it's just that, Kate. He finds living in a small community stifling. He says the local matchmaker is at his door, morning, noon and night. The only time she avoids the house is when Father Devine visits."

Kate stiffened. Even now, after all these years, that man's name had a similar effect. "Mam's favorite person in the whole wide world."

"He can't hurt you now, love. Nobody can. Not while I'm with you and I don't intend going anywhere."

They shared a kiss, Kate moving closer to her husband. He was her rock, but she'd never have expected his next question.

"What would you think about moving back to Galway?"

Kate gave herself a crick in her neck, turning to look at him so quickly.

"What? Why? What about your practice here?"

"One question at a time, darling." He skimmed her lips with his. "I was just thinking, it's a fine place for young children to grow up. Our family wouldn't have anything to do with your church or their schools. The Germans will march the streets of London before I'd let my children near the likes of that priest." Alan lit a cigarette, taking a deep drag. Kate watched the lit end as it flared up and died away again.

"The country air and wide open fields. No cement jungles. We could have a dog, a horse even."

"I never saw you as a farmer."

He grinned. "I wouldn't go that far. I'd still be a doctor. Maybe not now, but in a few years' time. Would you go back?"

Kate saw how much he wanted her to say yes. She knew he worried about the pollution in London. Food was scarce too with the rationing. They had a small patch on an allotment, but that wasn't the same as large green fields.

"I can't. Not while that woman who calls herself my mother is still alive. Anyhow, the nuns said if I ever returned to Ireland, they would have me locked up again. Me being a Maggie."

"Don't call yourself that name." Alan's knuckles whitened. "Nobody would touch a doctor's wife. Not even those precious nuns."

"Let's talk about it another time. Mary and Joe will be back soon. Best get the table set." She pushed herself to her feet with a little help from him.

"We're happy, aren't we, love?"

"Yes, Alan." She was being truthful. She was happy, or at least as happy as she could be when her baby girl was still missing.

THIRTY-SEVEN

ASHEVILLE, NORTH CAROLINA

1966

"Morning, gorgeous. How do you keep looking so good after all these years?" Josh kissed his wife, his hands cupping her face. "Hard to believe you are the mother of an eighteen-year-old boy."

"Josh! You're incorrigible. The kids are both home. They'll be expecting breakfast."

Josh grunted as he moved to his side of the bed. "Couldn't they have stayed in school another few days?"

Carol giggled. She knew he didn't mean it. They were both thrilled that Eva and Matt were home for spring break and their family was together once more. She pushed back the covers. Her son was like his father, he could eat his body weight in food and wanted all his favorites for his birthday breakfast.

Hurrying downstairs, she found Eva setting the table in the dining room and Myrtle fixing breakfast, the smell of fried chicken making Carol's mouth water.

"Morning, darling. Can you believe your kid brother is..."

Eva sniffed, her back still turned to her.

"Eva, what's the matter?"

"Nothing, Mom. Don't mind me. I'm just going to grab a shower and will be back down soon. Myrtle won't let me help her in the kitchen."

Carol watched her daughter go. Was it a fight with her boyfriend or problems at college? Eva hadn't seemed herself since she came home but refused to talk about it.

Carol pushed the door open through to the kitchen to find their housekeeper fixing biscuits with gravy. "Morning, Miss Carol. I done fried chicken, crispy bacon, and scrambled eggs. I knows that boy will want to eat the lot together. I got the gravy on too."

"What would we do without you, Myrtle?" Carol poured herself a cup of coffee. "Eva's upset this morning. She didn't tell you why, did she?"

Myrtle shook her head at the same time as muttering, "It be boys. They always makin' some girl cry. Now you get out of my kitchen, Miss Carol, and let me get on."

Carol took the hint and wandered back into the dining room. The rain prevented them from siting outside, but she didn't mind too much. The large double glass doors out onto the deck filled the dining room with light. Her roses, lilies and other flowers would benefit from the brief shower, it having been so dry lately.

Josh joined her as she poured the coffee into their cups, putting his arms around her waist from behind. "How did I get so lucky, Mrs. Andersen? A fine wife and two fabulous kids?"

"Dad, put Mom down. I'm starving." Matt burst through the dining-room door as he always did. Their son never did anything silently.

As her family ate, Carol kept her eye on Eva. Despite her daughter's valiant attempts to appear jolly, Carol could sense her sadness. She saw Josh glance a few times at Eva, sensing he'd picked up on her mood, but didn't want to ruin Matt's birthday. "Matt, you want to take a spin out to the stables. From what I hear, you need to practice your skills."

"Funny, Dad. You should be on the television." Matt grinned

back as his father teased him, secure in the knowledge he could have been born on a horse, he was so proficient.

"What do you want to do for your birthday, Matt?" Carol asked as she set her cup on the table. She caught the discreet cough from Eva and the look that passed between her and Matt.

Matt shook his head, but Eva rolled her eyes, ignoring him, and said, "Mom, Dad, today probably isn't the best day to ask, but we'd like to go to Ireland this summer, wouldn't we, Matt?"

Carol's heartbeat slowed, her breath coming too fast. Although they had never hidden the adoption from their children, she didn't want them finding their actual mothers. What if the women wanted their babies back? Not that they were babies now, but... Josh caught her hand and squeezed. "Breathe, Carol, take a deep breath. There you go."

"I told you to let me handle it, Eva, but you never listen," Matt berated his sister, who had tears rolling down her cheeks. "Mom, you all right?"

"I'm fine, I just felt a little dizzy." Carol forced her voice to sound cheerful. "Eva darling, what is it? Why are you crying? I'm sorry, I was just surprised."

"It's not you, Mom. Someone at college has been giving Eva a hard time. Calling her horrible names." Matt turned scarlet.

Eva spoke softly, her eyes glued to her plate. "They said I was a b—"

Josh interrupted quickly. "We can imagine what they called you, darling. People can be very cruel, don't worry about them."

Eva looked straight at Josh. "I'm not. I just want to go to Ireland. We both do. We want to see where we come from."

Carol couldn't look at Josh as she knew he'd be thinking the same as her. Their precious children didn't need to know about the horrible, unfriendly place where they had been born, or worse, meet the nuns that ran it. How much of the story was it safe to tell them without damaging them for life? Had Ireland changed much? From letters they'd exchanged with Bridget over the years, she didn't think so. It seemed unmarried mothers were still treated like pariahs.

Matt looked up from his plate. "Mom, Dad, the last thing we want to do is hurt either of you. You're the best, and Eva and I know we are lucky. But..." He glanced at Eva, who gave him a quivering smile of encouragement. "... it would be good to know where we came from. To see Ireland for ourselves. A vacation would be cool. The Kennedys loved it. You might too."

"Your mom and I have been to Ireland, and it's a beautiful country. Give us a chance to talk this over, son. Now, how about you take me out for a spin in your new car."

"Sure thing, Dad. Want to come, Mom?"

"No thanks, Matt, maybe another day. You and your dad have fun. Eva, are you going with them?"

Eva shook her head. "I'd like to spend the day with you, Mom."

Carol smiled through her tears. "I'd like that too, honey."

Later, Carol went upstairs to find Eva in her bedroom, a box of letters on her bed. Knocking on the door frame, she asked, "Can I come in?"

"Sure, Mom."

"What are you doing?" Carol sat on the bed.

Eva picked up some letters. "You know when I was little, and I wrote to my birth mom every birthday and at Christmas. But she never answered. I told Dad when I was sixteen that I wouldn't write anymore. And I didn't."

Carol nodded, unable to speak past the lump growing bigger in her throat. She put her hand on Eva's.

"I wrote again, a while back. I didn't post them. I used to tell her about things I couldn't speak to you about." Eva turned guilt-stricken eyes to look at her. "Not anything bad, just stuff about boys or when I was mad because you wouldn't let me cut my hair."

Carol ran her hand down her daughter's golden tresses. "I'm glad I won that argument."

"Me too. You were usually right, not that I was going to admit that." Eva bit her lip.

Carol hesitated, not wanting to ruin this lovely moment between them, but curiosity won.

"Why now, darling? Why do you want to go to Ireland?"

"I can't explain it, Mom. I love you and Dad and you are my proper parents, but we've been learning about Irish history and stuff at college. I was thinking I know nothing about Ireland, about where I came from. I don't just mean my birth mom and dad, but my country, my ancestors. All of that is a blank. I don't want to hurt you, Mom, but I need to know more."

Carol gathered her daughter into her arms and hugged her as Eva whispered, "I need to know why she gave me away."

THIRTY-EIGHT

GALWAY, IRELAND

Summer

The drive along the coast was wonderful, with the prettiest scenery imaginable. It was all so green, with quaint little villages dotting the horizon. Everyone they met had relatives in America and wanted to talk to them. They learned a lot of Irish history along the route, while keeping the reason for their vacation to themselves.

Matt stared out the car window. "Every village has at least three public houses and two churches, one for the Catholics and the other for everyone else."

As they drove down one winding road after another, they saw the sign for ten miles to Athenry. The next village would be their destination.

It was so green, that was their first impression. The one main street had a store, a couple of churches and, of course, the public houses. It also had a large grass area, perfectly mowed directly opposite the street. A river babbled along on the far side of the green area. Carol took a deep breath and felt the tension leave her body. It was just like it had been almost sixteen years ago. In her mind, she could see herself and Josh arriving with Eva in the back of the car, still sleepy after the excitement caught up with her.

Each house had a decorated windowsill covered in fresh flowers. The houses themselves were neatly thatched, and freshly painted. It looked like something from an advertisement for a box of old-fashioned candy.

They parked in the car park across from the pub and Bridget welcomed them with open arms, literally walking toward the car with her arms wide.

"I recognized ye from the photographs you sent. Matthew, you are much taller than I expected, Eva, you are just as beautiful as your father wrote me and Carol, Josh, you haven't changed a..." At that moment, Bridget's voice failed her and Carol couldn't find hers. She let the woman hug her. "I can't believe you are here. In the flesh. Finally."

After a few minutes, Matthew and Eva went ahead with the cases into the bar. "Barry is inside minding the lunch. I told him not to burn it, not that he'd know one end of a cooker from the other." Bridget laughed as she waved the youngsters off. "He couldn't greet you in public, he'd have made a show of himself. Irish men don't cry in public, not even tears of joy." Bridget sniffed. "Come away inside and get a bite to eat. Then I will take you on a walk of the village so you can see the sights. Or would you prefer a nap after your journey?"

Carol wasn't even sure they needed to answer as Bridget continued chatting as they walked through the snug and into the wide-open kitchen at the back. Barry stood and with two steps enveloped her in his arms. He held her so tight, she could barely breathe but it was exactly what she needed. He shook Josh's hand before Josh pulled him into a hug. "So good to see you, Barry."

"You too, son. Those children of yours are a credit to you both."

. . .

The day after their arrival they all sat down to discuss their plans. Eva and Matt wanted to explore Galway City. "I'll take the young ones on a trip and show them the sights," Barry confirmed, knowing Carol and Josh had their own plans.

"Can you take us sailing too, Barry?" Matt asked.

Barry ruffled the boy's hair. "I can, to be sure. I've plenty of friends who are fine fishermen. Will you come too, Eva?"

Eva screwed up her face as she shook her head. "I'd like to check out some Irish jewelry from the Claddagh area."

"Bridget can show you all you need to see. She might even pick up a small something for herself." Barry kissed his wife, causing both Matt and Eva to roll their eyes.

"Young ones today, they think they invented love," Barry grumbled as he headed into the bar. "Come on, you two, you can help set up the bar."

Carol watched her children leave before saying, "Thank you so much, Bridget, for entertaining them. Neither of us want to take them to the convent. They don't need that cold place in their memories."

"I still think you should invite Matt and Eva," said Bridget in a quiet voice. "They could see where they were born."

"No, Bridget, not until we've seen it again. I swore I'd never go back there; it was very grim." Carol shuddered.

Bridget's pursed lips told her that her friend didn't agree but she didn't argue. "I won't say a word to the children."

Relief flooded through Carol. "Thank you because I don't mind telling you we're both terrified of what we might find."

Carol glanced at Josh, whose face was an expressionless mask. "I'll go in and help Barry."

Carol watched Josh leave the room before confiding, "I think this visit is the hardest thing he's had to do."

Bridget took off her glasses, blowing on them and rubbing the glass with her blouse. "You don't think they will give you any information, do you?"

"Maybe if they see us again and finally accept that we aren't going to give up trying to find out."

"I wouldn't hold your breath. I know you Americans like to be optimistic but... Well, let's just see what you find tomorrow."

THIRTY-NINE

Josh drove slowly, not just because the roads weren't as big as those in the US but also because he was dreading what they'd find. He figured Carol felt the same; she was paler than he'd seen her in a long time.

"Honey bun?" He glanced at her, seeing surprise followed by clarity on her face. "Is that the name you still want to use if things get rough in there?"

"That was not one of my finest ideas." She giggled but the laugh fell flat. "Do you remember how I walked out last time? I'm not sure I have that same spirit."

"Carol, you have more. Back then you were collecting a child. Now we're fighting for our son and daughter. You'd walk over hot coals for those kids."

"What if they won't tell us anything?"

She put his fears into words. "We'll deal with that if it happens. Right, take a deep breath as it looks like we're here."

The same feelings overwhelmed him as he had felt the first time he'd visited the convent back in 1948. Nothing seemed to have changed; it was like taking a step back in time—only to revisit a nightmare. They drove to the top of the drive and like before the convent appeared, the sadness all but enveloping them both. After getting out of the car, they walked to the front door.

"It's so quiet, it's making me nervous." Carol reached for his hand; he squeezed it, seeking her support too. "The children should be playing out in this glorious sun although it seemed warmer on the road outside. Look at this place, you'd think it had been preserved in vinegar, not a place where real people lived."

Josh knocked on the door and they both stood back, waiting. And waiting. He knocked, harder this time.

They heard the grating sound of the lock being pulled back and then the door opened. A young girl, about Matt's age he guessed, stood dressed in black but without the white thing on her head.

"Can I help you?"

"We'd like to see the Reverend Mother, please."

"Do you have an appointment?"

Josh and Carol exchanged a glance. "Erm, no, but we've come a long way. From the United States. We want to talk to her about two children who were adopted from here in 1948 and 1949." Josh smiled, turning on the full American charm but the girl could have been blind for all the notice she took. Her stern expression remained unchanged.

"Reverend Mother is very busy. She can only be seen by appointment. Thank you for calling. Good day." The girl went to close the door but Josh wasn't having that. He stepped forward, blocking the door with his foot.

"I'm sure if you explain to Reverend Mother how far we've come she'll make an exception. Thank you."

The girl glanced at Carol, who smiled back.

"Wait, please." She indicated Josh remove his foot before she closed and locked the door.

Carol shivered. "Nothing's changed."

They heard steps, the door opened but the answer was the same. "Sorry for keeping you waiting but, as I said, Reverend

Mother cannot see you today. Perhaps you could make an appointment for next week."

"Next week we will be back in the USA," Josh almost snarled, and Carol intervened.

"Josh, go wait in the car." She turned to the nun. "Please forgive my husband; perhaps we could make an appointment for this Friday."

Josh saw the fear in the girl's eyes before she blinked. He left his wife to it and walked back to the car. Carol wasn't long joining him.

"That poor youngster is terrified of her own shadow. She's a novice, you know, a nun in training. I made an appointment with the Reverend Mother for Friday. Maybe we should bring Matt and Eva back with us. The young nuns might relate to them."

Carol looked at the imposing Georgian building and shivered. "Josh, can you feel a real sadness about this place? I've never felt anything like it."

Just then the skies opened and torrential rain hit them.

Josh's face was stony. He turned the key in the ignition before saying, "I have." As they pulled away, an elderly nun came out of the front door, waving at them.

"Josh, wait," said Carol. "I think that nun wants to speak to us."

"She's probably ready to read us the Bible. Let's go back to Bridget's home."

"No, please wait. She is trying to hurry but she's old." Carol opened the passenger door and walked toward the nun.

"Thank you, dear. I can't run, not at my age but I overheard you talking to the novice. Poor thing is totally unsuited to her chosen vocation, more likely her mother wants a nun in the family. Still I guess she'll be fine once she learns to trust herself."

Carol waited, thinking the elderly nun hadn't flagged them down to talk about the novice.

"You're from America asking about two children, is that right?"

"Yes, Sister. Do you want to sit in the car, get out of the rain?

This is a beautiful country but the rain is almost continuous, isn't it?"

"That it is. But then the grass wouldn't be as green if it didn't rain. I will take a seat with you. In fact, if your husband was willing maybe we could go for a drive. I'd like to talk with you." The nun glanced over her shoulder as if fearing someone would see her. "Away from here."

"I'm sure that would be fine. Take my arm, we'll take it slow over to the car." Carol led the way to the car. She hopped into the back, letting the nun take the front seat. Carol made the introduction.

"Sister, this is my husband, Josh Andersen."

Josh barely grunted a hello but he agreed to the nun's request.

"My name is Sister John Bosco. I've been away, in England and Europe for many years. I only came back to Galway last year. I'm afraid things haven't improved much in my absence."

Josh met Carol's eyes in the mirror but he didn't say a word. They kept driving back down the drive and out the gate. Immediately the atmosphere in the car lightened.

"Is there somewhere you'd like to go, Sister?"

"Anywhere you pick, Mr. Andersen, so long as it's private. I shouldn't like anyone to overhear what I have to say."

Josh turned at the sign for the coast road and drove for about fifteen minutes, Carol wished she knew what to say, the silence in the car more awkward than oppressive.

Josh parked up near a beach and the three of them stared at the Atlantic waves crashing onto the shore. Gray clouds hid the sun, threatening another downpour of rain. But it didn't stop the families walking on the beach or the children playing in the sand.

"I heard you ask about children who were adopted back in 1948 and 1949. Cecilia, that's the novice you met, she wasn't here back then. She wasn't even born. Of course, you'd know that. Our Reverend Mother, she is another story. She's been at the convent for years although she wasn't in charge when the children you speak about were born. She was plain old Sister Ita back then. We butted heads often, still do if truth be known." Sister John Bosco sighed.

Carol sensed Josh's impatience. "What has this to do with Eva and Matt?"

The old nun seemed not to hear her. She continued talking.

"I was in Europe in those days, trying to help displaced people find old homes or build new communities. We set up orphanages for the children, so many children... I miss it." She closed her eyes, obviously reliving her memories.

The silence grew, becoming uncomfortable, yet good manners wouldn't let Carol ask the nun what information she had.

Josh, on the other hand, didn't have any problem interrupting. "So you don't remember us visiting in 1949?"

"No, as I said, I was away."

Josh rolled his eyes. Carol was tempted to tell him to behave when Sister John Bosco added, "I wasn't there when Mr. Andersen came in 1948 either. I was very ill. I contracted typhus. It's a wonder I didn't die but the Lord had other plans for me."

Josh coughed, catching Carol's eyes in his mirror. Taking the hint, she tapped the nun on the shoulder, causing her to look at her.

"Forgive me, Sister, but why did you want to speak to us?"

"I think your husband adopted my friend's daughter."

Josh's mouth fell open as they both stared at one another and then back at the nun.

"Do you mean you know Eva's mom? Is she still alive? Where is she?" Josh asked. Carol couldn't form the words, the fear bubbling up in her stomach. Finding her children's birth parents had become all too real.

"She lives in London. I can't give you any more details than that. It's not my secret to tell."

"Come on, lady. We've had just enough of your lot telling us to wait or that you don't have any information. You can't announce our daughter's mom lives in London and expect us to leave it at that."

"Josh, she's old, she must be at least seventy-five," Carol hissed, before she turned back to the nun. "Sorry, Sister, patience isn't his virtue. Not since the war."

Sister John Bosco waved away her apology. "Your husband has every right to be angry. Everything he says is true. You have been kept waiting, and you have been lied to."

"So you'll tell us?"

The nun's head twitched as she pursed her lips. Carol didn't know whether she should be relieved or angry. This woman wasn't going to spill her secrets. "I can't."

Josh snapped, "You won't."

"You are correct, Mr. Andersen. I won't. Not until I speak to my friend. I think she will want to tell you her story in person."

Carol slumped back in the seat of the car. Not only was her daughter about to discover the details of her birth, but she'd meet her real mother too. What if she wanted to live with her?

Josh got out of the car, and, opening the back door, pulled Carol out and into his arms. "The children love us. Believe in that. Just that."

FORTY

Sister John Bosco was true to her word. A letter arrived at Bridget's home suggesting that the Andersens travel to Dublin. She would see them there on Friday at two p.m.

"She doesn't say she's bringing anyone with her." Carol looked up from the note. "Why can't she just tell us?"

"Who knows with these nuns. It all seems so cloak and dagger. That convent just reeks of secrets." Josh put his drink back on the table.

"Would you like the children to stay here with us?" Bridget asked. "It's no trouble. They've taken to the place like ducks to water. Matt sure loves his horses, doesn't he?"

Josh put his arm around Carol's shoulders as they moved to the window overlooking the backyard. Matt was fixing the saddle on a giant black stallion.

"You'd think he was a pony the way he's behaving, not a wild horse with burrs under his saddle. Won't allow anyone on his back for any length of time. Badly treated, he was." Barry stared at the horse.

Carol's heart was in her mouth as Matt mounted the horse. But to everyone's surprise, the horse allowed him to sit, even letting

Matt lead him out of the yard. Eva followed suit, but her mount was a smaller brown mare.

"Look at them," Josh muttered, his voice quivering slightly. "We should tell them about Friday."

"Let them enjoy the rest of their holiday. Friday will come soon enough. We can prepare them in the morning."

Bridget opened her mouth but shut it again at a look from Carol. These were her children. At least for now.

FORTY-ONE

Friday

"Who gives their baby away?" asked Matt just as the waiter arrived, filling their penthouse suite with the delicious fragrance of freshly ground coffee. The plate of pastries also looked appetizing. Afternoon tea was the cute name they used. Liberally tipping the waiter, Carol waited for him to leave before answering Matt.

"It's not that simple." She poured herself and Josh a cup of coffee that neither of them needed. The children helped themselves to their own drinks. "Things were different in Ireland back then, they still are. There is no allowance for single mothers to live on, no social security. Unless their families supported them, both emotionally and financially, there was nowhere for them to go but into the mother-and-baby homes. Most girls were forced into signing away their children; often many didn't realize what they were agreeing to. They didn't know they had agreed never to search for their babies. It would have been almost impossible for them to find anyone given the birth certificates didn't have their real names on them. Sister John Bosco has said the girls were given different names on entering the homes or laundries, Saints' names, in most cases. The nuns didn't tell anyone they sent children to the USA in return for large donations. It's still not readily spoken about. To this day, the mother-and-baby homes are thriving."

Matt blinked rapidly, his hand playing with his chin, shock evident in his tone. "You mean there are girls locked up in institutions and their only 'crime' is to get pregnant before marriage."

"It would seem so. Sister John Bosco told me a little when we visited with her the other day. She will explain more to you but, please, darling, remember she is old and not responsible for what happened."

"She was part of the system. She didn't help my mother or Eva's, did she? She allowed them to take the babies away."

"It's not that black and white, Matt." Eva gave her brother a disdainful look. "If they hadn't taken us, we wouldn't have Mom, would we? Who knows what type of life we'd have had if our birth mothers kept us?"

"Eva, don't be rude. Your brother is entitled to be upset. It's an emotional time for us all." Carol smiled at her daughter, hoping to take the sting from her words.

Matt stood up, giving her a withering look of disapproval. "I think we should visit the convent and demand to see their records. They don't have the right to stop us from finding our families."

Our families. His words cut deep even though she knew he wasn't thinking properly. Eva squeezed her hand, the look of understanding on her beautiful young face almost bringing Carol to her knees. She had to be strong for all of them. She'd known this day might come from the moment Josh had first arrived home with their gorgeous baby girl.

"Matt, you can't go charging in and ordering the nuns around. This is Catholic Ireland; the nuns and priests are revered, on pedestals, if you like. If you don't follow their rules, you'll find yourself with a Gardai police escort. Now act your age and stop upsetting Mom. This is difficult enough for her."

Carol gave her daughter a grateful look.

"Sister John Bosco said she'd try to help. We've agreed to meet her here in Dublin, it's a neutral venue. There are a lot of rules in place but I think if anyone can find out, she will. So let's give her the benefit of the doubt."

Josh gripped his cup so hard she was afraid it would break. He hadn't spoken a word. Carol tried to change the subject. "So what were the best things you saw in this city?"

"Mom, you should have come to see Trinity College." Matt turned to face her. "Did you know Bram Stoker, he wrote *Dracula*, went there?"

"Matt, I'm not that old. I know *Dracula* and Bram Stoker. Your dad isn't the only reader in the family. What else did you see?"

"We saw so much. The General Post Office on the main street has holes in the wall from the 1916 Easter Rising. Kilmainham Gaol is the place where the English took the leaders of the revolution and executed them. One guy had to be shot while sitting in a chair, he was so badly injured. Then we went on the bus out to the Phoenix Park. It's a bit like Central Park in New York, a massive area of trees and parklands, with deer and other wildlife roaming around. We saw where the Irish President lives, it has some funny Irish name and then we saw the American Embassy. I wanted to call in and say hello but Eva said we couldn't. President Kennedy visited here back in 1963. I told the tour guide you knew him but he just laughed." Matt looked insulted, causing Carol and Josh to exchange a smile. At home, he'd said their friendship with the Kennedy family was embarrassing.

Carol turned to her daughter. "What about you? What do you make of this city?"

"I like the hotel; if it's good enough for Audrey Hepburn and Grace Kelly, I guess it will do for us." Eva laughed before joking, "Maybe we should have insisted on a revamp before we arrived. Don't they know we're the Andersens?"

Eva and Carol shared one room, with Matt and Josh in the other. There were only two-bedroomed suites in the hotel and Josh hadn't wanted the children alone on another floor.

Carol grinned, knowing her daughter was using humor to hide her nerves. She took her hand. "Darling, please don't get your hopes up. It may be that Sister John Bosco isn't able to find out anything."

"I know, Mom, but what if she does? I have vague memories of her. The woman who gave birth to me, but that's all. You're my mom, the woman who raised me." She gave Carol a spontaneous hug. "I love you so much."

"I love you too. You will always be my daughter, darling, but you don't have to stop loving me to find your mammy. Remember what your dad told you." Carol prompted Josh with a look.

"Your mammy loved you very much. She told you to kick anyone who tried to take you. And you did, do you remember?" Josh's voice trembled so Carol took over.

"After hearing Bridget's story, and that of her friends, I'm glad you didn't grow up here where people could have been very cruel about the circumstances of your birth." Carol caressed her daughter's hand. "I am very grateful to your mammy and to Matt's. Without them I would never have shared my life with two of the most wonderful people."

Eva burst into tears and threw her arms around her. "I love you so much, Mom. Whatever happens, that will never change."

"I know that, baby girl." Carol sniffed. "I also know you can love more than one person. Your heart is big enough. You wanted your dad to take your mammy too, do you remember?"

"Yes, I did. I don't remember but he told me that many times. Every time I sat down to write her a letter, on my birthday and at Christmas but she never answered. Not even once. Who'd do that to a child they loved?" Eva coughed. "I tried telling Dad it was pointless writing but he insisted. He said he'd made a three-year-old a promise and he wasn't breaking it. I wrote twice a year until I turned sixteen and then I refused to write again. He argued but he couldn't excuse her behavior either."

Carol tensed; she hadn't known until this second just how much writing those letters affected her daughter. Even when Eva showed her the letters she'd written in the last few months, she hadn't told her this.

"Sweetheart, we have no way of knowing she got the letters."

"Mom, you always believe the best of everyone, but we sent them to the same address. The convent is still there almost twenty years later. Some may have got lost in the post but not all of them."

"But..."

"Please, Mom. Let's not discuss it anymore. I'm going to grab a shower and change." Carol watched her daughter walk across the room to their bedroom, her normally confident stride now a shuffle. Matt followed his sister back to his room. Once again, Carol wondered if she'd done the right thing in coming to Ireland.

Josh turned back from the window where he'd been observing the crowds. The Waterford crystal chandelier overhead shimmered in the sunlight. He beckoned her over and together they stared at the view. "We did a great job with those kids, Carol. No matter what happens today, we'll have the memories. And each other." He kissed her. The sound of the phone ringing made them both jump. Carol walked across the room, her feet feeling like they were encased in cement. Picking up the receiver, she said, "Hello?"

"This is the front desk, Mrs. Andersen," said the voice on the line. "Your guests are here. Shall I send them up?"

"Yes, please, thank you." Carol replaced the receiver.

Josh came to stand by her side. She put her shaking hand on his arm, prompting him to say, "I take it Sister John Bosco is here."

"Yes, but she is not alone." She saw her nervousness mirrored in his expression, his eyes blinking rapidly as his breath shortened.

FORTY-TWO

Kate stared at the floor as the lift flew up to the penthouse, feeling more than a little ill. Her heartbeat was too fast but nothing she tried worked at slowing it down. She wished she'd agreed to Alan coming with her. Could she race down O'Connell Street and across to their hotel to fetch him? *No. You can do this.* She put a hand up to fix her hair but immediately lowered it. She was visibly shaking.

"Kate, try to relax. It will be fine. I told you they are lovely, especially Carol."

Kate accepted a hug from her old friend, but she didn't feel any better. The floors disappeared fast, and the doors opened. The lift operator stepped out, indicating they should follow.

She couldn't get over the opulence of the room, the crystal chandelier, the glistening wooden furniture, the upholstered couches. This one room was bigger than the ground floor of her old home in London. She wanted to race back into the lift and leave.

"Sister John Bosco, how nice to see you again." She watched an extremely stylish lady, wearing a cream tailored dress cut just above the knee, with nine silver buttons down the middle—she could be Jackie Kennedy's double but with blonde hair—greet the nun. Then the woman extended her hand. "I'm Carol Andersen and this is my husband, Josh."

The doors to the bedroom opened as a young man stepped out. His brown hair flopped over his eyes, curling just along his collar. He wore jeans and a casual shirt, although they were expensive based on their cut. He wouldn't have looked out of place on Bond Street in London, although his sparkling white teeth suggested he was American.

"Oh, hello." He blushed as his gaze ran from her to Carol and back. "Are you my mother?"

"Matt!" Carol turned to her. "I apologize for my son, he's forgotten his manners."

"No, Matt. I didn't have a son." *But Gwen did and his name was Matthew; he'd be a similar age.* She stuttered, "I'm sorry."

He shrugged as if it was of no importance and walked over to sit on one of the sofas.

"Why don't we sit down, and I'll ring for tea or would you prefer coffee?"

"Either is fine, thank you." Kate forced her legs to move, her eyes darting around the room. Sister John Bosco eyed her carefully, but Kate refused to meet her gaze. Why hadn't the nun warned her about Matt? Did she suspect he was Gwen's? No, she couldn't. JB had left the convent by the time Gwen arrived. Kate felt the sweat gather on her brow. Was it really that hot in here? Where was Eva?

"Mom, what time was the nun supposed to... Oh."

Kate's eyes watered as her hands flew to her mouth. She was the female version of Tony, all legs and that glorious blonde hair. She had his brilliant eyes too; well, the color was his but the shape was all Ryan. She wore a short miniskirt and a multicolored blouse; her eyes were highlighted in black kohl.

"Eva?" Kate whispered. "Is it really you?"

The girl moved to Carol's side. Kate tried to hide her hurt, but she must have failed miserably if Carol's look of commiseration was anything to go by.

"Kate, this is Eva, our daughter."

Kate's legs gave way and she'd have fallen but for Carol's shout to Matt, who pushed the chair behind her just in time.

"Always was good at basketball," he joked.

"I'm sorry, I just... it's just you are the image of your father." The tears streamed down her face. She didn't make any attempt to get a hanky. She couldn't take her eyes off her baby. "You were nearly four the last time I saw you. When they took you away from me."

"You signed the papers to give me away." Eva's accusation caught Kate right in the heart.

"I didn't. I swear to God I never signed any papers. I refused. Didn't I?" Kate begged Sister John Bosco.

Everyone turned to stare at the nun, who rooted in her handbag. "I found some papers. I brought them. They are signed."

Eva sent her a dirty look.

Kate stood up and walked over to the nun, almost snatching the papers out of her hand. "This isn't my signature. That old witch. I knew she was evil, but I didn't think she'd stoop this low. I never signed my name Catherine Ryan. I was always Kate. See?" With a trembling hand, she thrust them in the girl's direction, but Carol intervened. She took them, reading them first, before passing them to the girl.

"Eva, don't you remember anything? I used to visit you in the orphanage behind the laundry. I probably stank of bleach or carbolic soap. I told you to kick anyone who tried to take you. Think. Please think. Can you remember?" Kate knew she was badgering the girl but she couldn't stop. She was desperate for recognition.

"I think it's best if we all sit down and discuss this as rationally as possible," Carol suggested, indicating the sitting room. "Or we can use the dining table."

"You stole my child!"

"Kate! Please." The nun's eyes shone with sympathy despite her admonishment. "I told you Carol wasn't party to Eva's adoption. Sit down and let's start at the beginning."

Only then did Kate notice there was a man standing by the window. He stepped forward, moving slowly as if unsure of himself. He limped, a war wound perhaps. "When I took Eva home, I asked the Reverend Mother if I could see you but they told me you didn't want anything to do with your baby."

Kate sobbed, losing control at his words. She took the hanky Sister John Bosco handed her. He moved to her side and helped her toward the sofa where she took a seat. "I'm sorry," he whispered; she wasn't even sure she heard him until she saw the truth on his face. She dried her eyes while Carol telephoned down for coffee. They sat in awkward silence until it arrived. She sensed Eva examining her, but she resisted catching her gaze. She needed to take things more carefully or she'd lose any chance of recovering her daughter.

They sat around the table while Eva played mother and poured the drinks. Matt joined them with a mumbled apology for his bad joke.

"I have twin boys not much younger than you appear to be. I don't think they would handle something like this as well as you have." Kate could have cut her own tongue out as she saw the look of hurt on Eva's face.

"You have other children? Ones you kept?"

The bitterness cut her to the quick. Yet this was just a child lashing out when she didn't know the truth. She opened her mouth to explain but shut it again at a look from Sister John Bosco.

She listened as Carol explained it was her husband, Josh, who'd traveled to Ireland to find a baby.

"You mean buy one." At the hissed intake of breath, Kate immediately regretted her words. "I'm sorry, that was uncalled for."

"I can understand why you might think that." Carol gave her a weak smile. She put her hands on the table. "If I am honest, that is exactly what we did even if that wasn't our intention. I was desperate for a baby, Kate. I hope you don't mind me calling you that. I was pregnant after years of trying for a baby and one night I drove down to the local store. Josh had asked me not to drive but he was away with the military. I hadn't long passed my test. But I was young and who listens at that age? Not me. Anyway, there was a wreck, not my fault although it took me years to admit that. A drunk driver hit me and as a result, I lost my baby. And the ability to have any children. Ever." Carol hesitated as if to gain control of herself. She spoke again, her voice less controlled. "Yes, we were rich but I would have given every dollar we had away if I could have a child. I became very ill; some would tell you I went mad. My mother-in-law for one." Carol smiled tightly and Kate warmed to her. "Josh went away shortly after as war was declared and he was needed. The Andersens are a long-time military family. Josh was shot down in 1942 and we thought he was dead. My life was over." Carol threw a quick look at her husband before continuing. "I was alone and that night I took two pills but I spilled the bottle of whiskey and my in-laws, they jumped to conclusions and I was admitted to an asylum."

"Oh, Mom, I had no idea." Eva stroked her arm. "I mean, Grandma said you were sick but she implied, well..."

"The ice-queen told us you were off your head." Matt directed his next comment to Kate. "My grandmother doesn't have blood in her veins, it's anti-freeze."

His comment earned him a slight rap on the knuckles from Sister John Bosco. "You're not helping your mom by being a smart alec."

Carol took a sip of her coffee and Josh took over. "Obviously I wasn't dead, but I was badly injured and shipped back to the States where I underwent almost a year of therapy and countless operations." He glanced at his wife and she took over.

"They told him he'd never walk again never mind fly, but they underestimated my husband's love of his men and his country. In January 1944, he flew off once more, this time to London. I never found out the full extent of his involvement in D-Day but he was awarded the Medal of Honor for his actions. When peace in Europe was declared, Josh decided he was going to bring a child back to America. He couldn't adopt an English child as the law changed to prevent Americans and other non-residents from adopting babies. One of his men had a brother in the priesthood, a Father David Armstrong who had contacts with the convent where you lived. Josh and Father Armstrong visited and, yes, some money changed hands. There he was introduced to two little girls, a blonde and a brunette. He said Eva"—Kate met Carol's eyes—"Eva captured his heart from the second she walked into the room. He said he'd never seen a child so brave at such a young age. She wasn't in the least bit interested in him or finding a home. When he asked her if she would like to go home with him, she asked if he'd take her mammy too."

Kate couldn't stop the sob escaping and Eva had the same reaction. Carol was staring at her daughter. "Josh said you told him your mammy had said to kick anyone that tried to take you. That she loved you and wanted you to stay with her."

Tears rolled down Eva's face. Carol took her hand in hers. Kate lifted her hand to do the same but returned it to her lap. She had to have patience.

Eva whispered, "I remember. I told him if I went with him, I had to write to you and tell you where I was so you could find me. And I did. Every birthday and Christmas. I even kept the name Eva—it was our special name. But you never answered. Not once. If you really wanted me, if you loved me, why didn't you find me? You had my address. I can't forgive you for that. I'm sorry. Bridget told us what happened in Ireland back then and even now, but that doesn't excuse you for not replying to your own child."

Kate stood up. "I didn't get any letters. I swear I didn't." She turned on the nun. "Did I?"

Sister John Bosco, openly crying at this point, shook her head.

"Did you keep them from me?" Kate resisted the urge to grab the nun by the shoulders and shake her.

"I didn't see any letters. My guess is the Reverend Mother destroyed them. She probably didn't even read them."

"How can anyone be so cruel?" Carol asked, still holding Eva's hand.

"You have no idea. While I was in that place, I saw things nobody would ever believe. They murdered my friend. Geraldine her name was but that wasn't her real name. I tried to tell the Gardai, but they weren't interested in a Maggie. Especially as I didn't know her real name."

Matt leaned in. "A what?"

"Magdalene girl, the laundry workers were given that name as we were so-called fallen women."

Sister John Bosco wetted her lips before saying in a shaky voice, "Ger died in labor. We didn't have the facilities to help her."

Kate glared at her friend. "Don't protect them now. You know she could have lived and her baby too if they had called a doctor. But instead, they made her work even though it was obvious she wasn't well. High blood pressure it was. I don't care what anyone says, those nuns killed her and many others. In time, the Irish government and the rest of the world will realize just how awful those places are. That's why I left Ireland."

Silence descended. Kate guessed they were all trying to process things. She certainly was; she couldn't get over the fact her daughter had written to her.

"Did you make any attempt to find me?" Eva whispered.

Eva's soft question might as well have been a dagger, the pain wouldn't be any less.

"I never gave up. I couldn't risk coming back to Ireland. Sister John Bosco helped me escape the convent, but I didn't trust the system. My own mother had me locked up with the help of the local priest. She was still alive and would have done the same again. It might seem crazy but, in those times, a single woman had very few rights. My brother, Joe, and my cousin, Mary, they both tried to find out what happened. Joe jokes he had a path worn up to that convent, but nobody would ever tell him anything. Mary suggested getting a solicitor, an attorney I think you call them, so I did. But he was as useful as a blunt butter knife. Nobody would take on the nuns, the church. They still won't."

Kate glanced at her friend, waiting for the nun to give her permission. She nodded.

"My friend gave me a second chance. Mr. Andersen"—Josh looked surprised as she addressed him directly—"paid off the hundred pounds the nuns charged for the release of a girl from the convent." Kate ignored their shocked reaction. She had to keep talking or she'd lose her nerve. "You also paid for my ticket to London and gave me the financial ability to study to become a nurse. That's what I did. I qualified at St Thomas' Hospital; they accepted me on a course after my friend wrote a reference." Kate flashed a smile at Sister John Bosco. "I qualified as a maternity nurse first, planning to become a community midwife. But fate had other ideas. My husband, Alan, he was a doctor at the hospital." Kate turned to hold her daughter's gaze. "He's known about you from the very start. We also told our twin boys about you as soon as they were old enough to know. When we moved back to Ireland, Alan came with me to the convent but they refused to tell us anything. Please believe me, Eva. You have been in my heart from the day you were born."

"And my father?" Eva darted a nervous glance at her. This time Kate held her gaze.

"Your daddy was one of the kindest men I ever met. He was American just like you. He joined the RAF before America joined the war; that's why he was in the internment camp when I met him. We knew each other for eighteen wonderful months. We didn't get a lot of time alone together—well, enough, obviously." Nervous laughter met her attempt at a joke. "Tony was the first man I ever loved. He loved you, although I didn't find that out until later."

"He came back?" Eva whispered.

Kate shook her head, taking a few seconds to find her voice.

Sister John Bosco put her hand over hers. "I can tell this part of the story. Kate's uncle still lived at the pub where Kate met your fath— Tony." The nun sent a look of apology in Josh's direction.

Kate wanted to tell her to hurry up and get to the point but maybe this was a better way.

"When her dad died, Mary found letters from your grand-mother, her name is Evelyn. She wrote to say she knew about you and Kate. Tony had written to them to say he was going to get married as soon as he got out of the forces. He was so excited, telling them how much he loved an Irish girl. He admitted he'd fathered a child and wanted to bring his family home. His parents being Catholic were upset and disappointed, but his mother claimed they were also very excited. They never got to tell Tony. He was killed shortly after he returned to the war. It took a long time for Tony's belongings, including Kate's letters, to be returned to his parents. I don't know why but that's what happened."

Kate picked up the story, confident she could keep her voice steady. "Mary and Joe, my brother, came to London to see me. Mary gave me the letters. I sent them a letter. It was the hardest one I've ever had to write, explaining how you were missing. I never received a reply. I'm not sure she believed me." Kate took a deep breath; this was her chance. "I swear everything I've told you is the truth, Eva. I tried so hard to find you. We all did, Mary, Joe and Alan when he found out. But nothing we did made any differ-ence. We had nothing to go on, no birth certificate or passport. Alan checked with the foreign office but they denied issuing a pass-port to a four-year-old child. We didn't know you were in America. You could have been anywhere." Kate bit back a sob. "Thank God JB retired to the convent or I'd never have found you."

"I was determined to right a wrong if I could," Sister John Bosco said. "More than one. I wish I could tell you things have changed. They have to a certain extent; there are no more babies being sold. Today, most of the babies born to single mothers in Ireland are adopted. That's just the way it is and the way it will remain until..." The nun stopped talking, just shrugged her shoulders.

Matt coughed, causing everyone to stare at him. If she was honest, Kate had forgotten he was there.

"So where do I fit in? You aren't my mother. We've established that, so where did I come from?"

Kate heard the pain behind his forced casual tone. Carol did too as she stood up and walked around the table to put her hands on his shoulders. His hand slid up to meet hers. Carol was an amazing mother. Eva was lucky with her adoptive family. "I'm sorry, Matt, when were you adopted?"

Carol answered, "August 1949. Josh and I both went to the convent and met the coldest woman I've ever come across. We have papers, but I guess they were forged too. Matt wasn't a baby either, he was a toddler and really Eva chose him."

Kate couldn't believe what Carol said. It confirmed her initial thoughts. "What? Really?"

"You know who I am?"

Kate saw his eyes widen with hope.

Kate shook her head, saying softly, "I knew your mam. She was, is I hope, an amazing woman. She looked after Eva, gave her a bunny I had knitted for her, when she was leaving."

"I had that for years. I threw it out when I had the tantrum at sixteen over the letters and have regretted it ever since."

Kate gave her a sad smile before focusing back on Matt, the pain now evident in his eyes.

"Gwen is the name she used in the convent, and I have tried to contact her but have come up empty-handed. She loved you so much, she was so excited about having you. She prayed every night you would go to a good home. She knew there was no way they would allow her to keep you. Sister John Bosco is still searching, aren't you?"

"I've also tried, but as yet we have had no real leads. She may have left Ireland, many women did. There is no easy way to tell you this, son. She was about fifteen when she gave birth."

Carol and Josh exchanged a look, but Kate saw this information didn't register with Matt.

"I promise you, Matt," Sister Bosco continued, "I will live at that convent until the day I die. In that time, it's my mission to reunite as many families as I can. I sit by the window so I can intercept, and some would say interrogate, anyone who comes to visit. It drives Reverend Mother nuts but sure we never got on. Even when we were both novices." The nun laughed.

Kate stared at Matt, hoping he would remember his mother loved him and was a lovely person. It wasn't the right result, but it was the best she could offer.

She turned her attention back to Eva. "Your brothers, Niall and Darren, are in Dublin too. Alan and the boys would love to meet you. If you were willing, of course." The last words cost her all she had, but they had to be said. Her baby was an adult now, not a child. She exhaled. That was the entire story. She had nothing more to add. Neither, it seemed, did anyone else. Silence reigned. Kate tried not to push.

Her hopes soared when Eva stood up and made a move as if to come over to her. She stood too, hoping to make it easier for her daughter.

"Get out. I never want to see you or meet your happy family. I have a mom and dad and a home in America. You're nothing to me." Eva turned on her heel and stormed across the room.

Matt jumped up. "Eva, wait." He moved just as fast as his sister, slamming the bedroom door shut behind him.

Kate picked up her bag, tears streaming down her face. "I'm so sorry. This was a mistake. Tell her I'm sorry."

She pressed the button for the lift. It opened. She stepped in, seeing Josh moving toward her as the doors closed. The lift descended and this time it was her leaving her daughter.

FORTY-THREE

Josh took control. "Where is she staying? What hotel?"

Sister John Bosco shook her head, tears wetting her cheeks, but despite his pity for the older woman, they did not deter Josh. "Sister, what hotel?"

"Wynn's Hotel. It isn't far. Please be kind."

Josh kissed Carol. "Look after our kids. I'll be back."

"Josh, my heart breaks for poor Kate. The look on her face when Eva said those words."

"Our daughter is hurting just as much, darling. Go to her." Josh strode across the room, called the lift and got in. Shifting from one foot to the other, he counted the seconds until the bell went and they arrived on the ground floor. Scanning the lobby, he didn't see any sign of Kate. She should have been easy to spot, given her distinctive red hair.

Josh ignored both staff and customers, pushing open the door onto the street, whistling for a cab. People stared at him but, ignoring them, he jumped into the back of the taxi, giving the driver the name of the hotel. "You could have walked, it's just around the corner."

Josh passed him a ten-pound note. "Get there as fast as you can."

"Mad Yank," the driver muttered. Josh held on to the seat as the taxi sped off. He spotted her just as he arrived, sitting on a bench on the street, her face drawn and gray. Exiting the taxi, he strolled up to her, not wanting to scare her. "Kate?"

She glanced up but appeared in a daze. Shock. "Kate, let's get you back inside. To your husband. You're shivering."

"I've lost her forever, haven't I?" Her flat tone worried him even more. Tears and recriminations he could handle, but not total defeat.

"Eva is sensitive, and it's a lot for anyone to take in, let alone a girl just turned twenty-one."

Kate didn't seem to hear him.

"Please go inside to your husband. We'll stay in the hotel. I'll postpone our return to the US. Give Eva, all of us, some time to process what we have learned today."

He held out his hand to help her to her feet. Instead, she opened her handbag and took out two dog-eared notebooks. Hesitating for a second, she thrust them at him.

"These are some of my diaries. I started them the day I left that place. I didn't write every day, but most. Perhaps you could give them to Eva. To prove I didn't forget her."

He coughed, his voice gruff as he pushed the words out. "She knows. She's older than you were when you had her, but she's not as mature. We have protected her all her life."

Kate held his eyes for the briefest of seconds before shaking her head. Ignoring his hand, she shuffled to her feet. It was as if she'd aged thirty years right before his eyes. "I worried about my boys seeing me cry. I'm fine now. Goodbye, Josh Andersen. Thank you."

She turned toward Wynn's Hotel.

He put a hand on her arm, making her turn her head. "Wait, lady. You fought to get her back for so long. You aren't giving up now." Her eyes widened at his harsh tone. He'd hoped to get through the shock, to make her fight, but she looked as if he'd punched her. Feeling inadequate wasn't something he was comfortable with. Why hadn't he brought Carol with him? He lowered his voice. "I'm taking you back to your husband. He's a doctor and will look after you. Give me time. You owe Eva that much. You owe yourself."

She appeared overcome. He held out his arm, and she grabbed it, her nails clawing him through his shirtsleeve as she held on so tight. "Let's get you back to your family." He spoke as one would to a wounded child. The child forced to give up her baby.

He ignored the curious stares of the hotel staff, asking them to call Doctor Hyland, requesting he come down to the lobby alone. Barely had they put down the phone when a dark curly-haired man ran out of a door toward them. "Kate darling, what happened? Who are you and what have you done to my wife?"

"She's had a shock." Josh glanced toward the reception desk where the staff were busy trying not to look interested. The doctor took the hint and, holding his wife around the waist, walked her to the lift. Josh followed, whispering, "Eva told her she didn't want Kate around. My daughter is hurting, they both are. We're staying at the Gresham and will be there for another week." Josh glanced at Kate's chalk-white face, her unfocused eyes. "All this pain. When will it end?"

FORTY-FOUR

Despite Josh and Carol's best efforts, Eva refused to read the diaries or even speak about Kate. She stayed in the hotel room and nobody could get through to her, not even Matt.

Josh and Carol asked Kate and Alan to join them for dinner in the hotel restaurant.

"We may be able to keep it civil in a public place. Otherwise, I'll end up crying," Josh commented as he tried but failed to straighten his tie.

"Come here, let me do that." Carol tied it quickly. "Hug me, Josh. Tell me it's all going to work out. Eva won't eat and she cries herself to sleep when she thinks I'm asleep. I can't bear it."

"Me neither. I wish we'd never come here."

Carol couldn't help but agree with him. They walked out of the room Josh shared with Matt to face their children. They'd elected to stay in the suite.

"I can't understand why you insist on meeting her. She's got nothing to do with your family." Eva's protruding lip took Carol back years to when she'd first taken her daughter to the dentist. The child had refused to open her mouth despite the bribes the dentist resorted to. Strong-willed didn't come close to describing her daughter. *That's how Kate survived.*

"Darling, we know you are angry, confused, upset and hurt. But you have to see none of this was Kate's fault. She didn't give you up. You were stolen from her, ripped from her arms. Won't you read her diaries? See what she says in her own private words?"

Eva shook her head, going over to turn on the radio.

"Turn that off and treat your mom with respect, young lady. You were reared better than this. I never thought I would say this but I am disappointed in you."

"Josh, please." Carol put her hand on his sleeve but he shook it off.

"No, Carol, this has to stop now. Eva, we love you and your brother more than words can say. You know that. But if I could go back to the day I chose you, I would insist on seeing your mammy. I would have given her our address so she could have come and lived with us." He ran a hand through his hair. "Or at least that's what I'd like to think I'd do. But the truth is I probably wouldn't. I loved you from the second I laid eyes on you. The last few weeks, thinking about meeting Kate and how you might react, have given me nightmares. What if you wanted to live with her?"

"Not a chance," Eva retorted.

"You aren't listening. What I mean is those nightmares were so real it gave me a hint of what your mammy must have felt losing you. I've been in some hair-raising situations but nothing, not even when the plane got shot down, comes close to the fear of losing you. Eva, please try to think of Kate. She's been to hell and back. Give her a chance. Get to know her." Josh choked up but pushed out the last words. "For us if not for yourself."

Eva stared at her father, Matt stared at the floor, while Carol waited for someone to break the silence. Noise filtered in from the busy street outside but in this room it was as if time stood still. She turned pleading eyes on her daughter but saw Eva turn away.

"Come on, Carol, let's get out of here. I need some air." Josh strode to the lift, leaving her to almost run to catch up.

"We're downstairs if you need us," she threw over her shoulder as she blew a kiss to the children. Then the lift doors closed. Josh glowered beside her, his rage making the small space feel claustrophobic.

"Josh, you can't expect her to have your maturity. She hasn't faced death or injury. We've protected her from everything."

"We've spoiled her, Carol. She's selfish."

"No, Josh, she isn't. She's hurting, and if you can't see that, you must have landed on your head when you fell out of that plane."

Carol marched out of the lift, her heels clicking on the tiled floor. She didn't care what people thought, she was that mad she'd take the head off the devil himself. She spotted Kate and Alan sitting at a table in the corner of the room.

Kate rose to introduce her to Alan. She shook his hand distractedly, seeing Kate focus on the room behind her. The hope in the woman's eyes died when Josh joined them.

"Sorry, Kate, we tried but she's still hurting."

Kate forced a smile, the edges of her mouth showing signs of strain. "I expected miracles. How can a child understand pure evil?"

Carol gave Josh a pointed look before ignoring him for the rest of the dinner. The conversation stopped and started, with awkward silences. Carol caught Kate looking from her to Josh and back again but pretended not to.

"I love your dress, Kate. Is that from a London store?"

"This? I bought it just before we left. We don't live in London anymore. After the horrible smog of 1952 we moved back to Galway to the farm I grew up on."

"Smog?" Carol queried.

"It's a type of pollution which killed four thousand Londoners in December 1952," Alan said. "It was on the cards and preventable." Kate put a hand on her husband's arm, causing him to smile. "I've just been told to get off my pedestal. No talking about politics in public. But, as Kate was saying, we now live in Galway. Our boys went back to the farm yesterday, to look after the horses. Kate's brother, Joe, needed to get back to London. There's only so much of the local matchmaker he can take."

Carol surprised everyone by clapping her hands. "I've got it. Please excuse the forwardness but thank you so much for your kind invitation, we'd love to come to your farm."

Kate paled, Alan grinned, but Josh looked ill. "Carol, what are you doing?"

"Eva loves animals and people. Matt worships horses. Let's take them to Galway and just see what happens. Nothing could be worse than the present situation."

Alan nodded. "It could work. I'm biased but our boys could charm the last sandwich from a beggar and have him thanking them. I think it's worth a shot. Kate?" He took his wife's hand in his, rubbing it tenderly.

Kate didn't answer, using her other hand to wipe tears from her eyes.

Josh put his drink down. "I think you are mad. This is madness."

Carol opened her mouth, but Kate got in first. "Maybe it is, but that's my baby up there and I'm going to fight for her love if it's the last thing I do. Just you try and stop me."

FORTY-FIVE

They didn't tell the children the plan but checked out of the hotel the next day.

"Where are we going?"

"Back to Galway."

The kids didn't question it. This time they took the train rather than a car. "Dad, look at all those cottages with the broken-down walls. Why are they left like that? What happened to them?"

"They're a reminder of the famine," an old man, with a peaked cap and a brown stained corduroy jacket over an Aran sweater and a pair of trousers tied up with string, interrupted. "The landlords used to come and knock down the house if the family missed their rent payments. That way they couldn't use it for shelter in the winter. If any other family helped them, the landlord pulled their house down too." The man muttered something that sounded like a curse word. "'Tis Yanks you are?"

"We're from North Carolina. Why does everyone call us Yanks?" Matt asked, his face lit up with curiosity.

"No idea, son. That's what we always called you lot. What are you doing in Ireland? Visiting the old home place? Me? I'd love to have a family to visit but sure isn't it just myself and Macarthur."

"Who?" Matt looked around the carriage.

"Lookee here." The man opened his tobacco-stained jacket. Carol and Eva shrank back as a rat-looking creature stuck his head up. "Mac is the best rabbit hunter that was ever born. Never be hungry with Mac around. Great company he is too. Keeps the thieves away. Many a one lost the tip of their finger trying to steal me wallet."

"You eat rabbits?" Matt looked green.

"Course I do. What else would I be eating, can I ask ya?"

Carol smiled at the old man's stories. They helped pass the time. He started to sing and the kids joined in with some of the songs.

And then the train pulled into Galway.

Kate's heart hammered as the train pulled into the station but she remained in the car. She didn't want Eva to feel ambushed. She'd warned the boys to go easy; hopefully they'd listen to her.

"Eva, look, there are boys over there on horses. Have you ever seen such fine animals?" Matt pointed out the boys. Carol assumed they were Kate's sons given they each led a spare horse. "Can I go talk to them?"

"Sure, Matt, Eva, go with him. We'll get the bags."

Eva nodded. Carol reached for Josh's hand, squeezing it tight. They got off the train and watched from a distance at their children chatting to Kate's sons.

Matt came running back. "Can we ride back to Bridget's? I know we don't have the right clothes but this is Ireland."

"Yes, son, just be careful." Josh ruffled his hair. They watched as both Eva and Matt swung up into the saddles, earning admiring glances from the locals.

"The Irish appreciate good horsemanship," a voice came from behind them.

"Alan, oh my goodness, my heart is in my mouth. Your boys mustn't have said anything."

"Kate told them not to but I can't promise that will last. They aren't feeling too charitable about their mammy being upset. The ride home will help them all, I think. Right, let's get your cases in the car. Kate's waiting over there."

They drove along the coast road, the powerful waves crashing against the shore making Carol wish she could walk on the beach, feel the sand between her toes. The trees and flowers were out in full bloom, the cherry blossoms decorating everything in a blanket of pink. The sun shining had to be a good omen, didn't it?

When they came to a turn into a long lane, surrounded on both sides by green fields filled with sheep, Kate asked Alan to stop the car.

"I want to go ahead on my own. Is that okay?"

Carol and Josh exchanged a glance before Josh answered, "Yes. We'll wait here until you call us. Good luck."

Alan gave Kate a hug before she got out of the car. Josh's grip on Carol's hand tightened; she fancied she could hear Kate's heart beating but maybe it was just her own.

Kate marched down the lane, determined to convince her daughter of her love. She moved quickly so she couldn't think about what she was doing. If she did, she might run in the opposite direction. What if Eva still hated her?

She kept moving, only stalling when instead of her sons and the horses she spotted Eva, a bag at her feet, sitting alone on the doorstep to the house, holding something in her hand. Kate's leg muscles tightened as she fought the urge to run. She kept walking at the same pace, her daughter now holding her gaze. Everything around them disappeared; it was just her and her baby.

"Eva, I..." Kate couldn't find the words. To her horror, tears spilled out of her eyes. She brushed them away with her sleeve but more just followed.

"I asked the boys to leave us alone for a little bit. I wanted to apologize. I didn't mean to hurt you with those things I said. I was so angry."

"That's all right."

"No, it isn't. None of this is. It wasn't right what happened to you, or what happened to Tony. Him dying in the stupid war. Mom and Dad not being able to adopt, having to come here to buy a baby. None of it is right. It's all crazy, so mixed up and I"—Eva stamped the ground—"I don't know how to deal with it. Any of it."

Kate took a step and then another when Eva didn't pull back. She put her arms around her, pulled her against her chest just as she had when she was a baby. "*Alannah*, baby, just cry. Let it out. It'll do you good, Eva, just cry. I love you so much. We all love you."

Eva sobbed as Kate's tears flowed too. She kept cuddling her child. "How I longed to hold you, I never thought I would. I love you, Eva. No matter where you are or what you do, I will always love you."

Eva hiccupped, pulling away slightly but only far enough to look Kate in the eyes. "I read your diaries. The ones you gave to my dad. It was like you were speaking to me."

"I was. I wrote you almost every day. Even if it was only a few scribbles. Being a student nurse just after the war was a baptism by fire. There were so many in need and I wanted to help. I worked all the hours I could so I would fall into bed too exhausted to think. But it never worked. You were always there, in my heart, my head. Eva, darling Eva, I never ever would have let you go. I promise."

"I know, Mammy. I love you."

Eva tightened her grip around Kate, or did she pull her daughter closer?

"Is there room for more or is this just for girls?" Niall's voice interrupted their moment.

Kate wanted to hit him and hug him, she wasn't sure which. But Eva answered for her. "I always wanted more brothers. Come over here, you too, Darren. And you, Matt." She put Kate's arm around Matt. "Matt and I share all our parents including you. That okay?"

"Yes, my darling girl, that's just perfect."

EPILOGUE

GALWAY, IRELAND

1970

Kate Hyland walked out the door of her childhood home, arm in arm with Alan, the smell of roses and petunias greeting her from her window boxes. "It's a perfect day, isn't it? Not a cloud in the sky, the racetrack won't be too dry given the recent rain but at least it won't be a muck pile either. Matt says Wild Irish Rose is better suited to dryer ground."

"How does he know that? With the Irish weather, does that horse ever get a chance to race on dry ground," Alan teased.

"Look at that sky, you English heathen. Those sun rays are breaking the rocks, they are."

He pulled her to him, kissing her soundly on the lips. "My wild Irish rose."

Niall interrupted to shout at them, "Mum, look at us."

The twins raced past in the pasture, on horseback as usual. "You would think they were born on a horse, never mind here in Ireland," Alan whispered. "They've even lost their English accents."

"They don't sound a bit like locals." Kate smiled, leaning her head on his shoulder. This man who'd loved and supported her through everything, including leaving England and moving to live in her own home in Ireland. Matt called Alan the gentleman farmer as he hired locals to do the actual farming. It made sense as he still practiced as a doctor.

A horn hooted the arrival of their guests.

Josh got out of the car, quickly followed by Carol and another woman.

"Mary!" Kate raced over to the car, enveloping her cousin in a hug. "You came."

"Try and keep me away. Ciaran is sorry but someone had to stay on the farm. The calves and all. For some reason I married the only man in Ireland not interested in horse racing. Where's Eva? Carol said she drove down ahead of us."

"She did but she didn't come here. She went straight to the stables. Wanted to check Wild Irish Rose again and she wanted to see Matt before the race. She'll be here shortly given how fast she drives. The girl thinks she's still in the US."

Mary laughed, her laugh just as infectious as it always had been. She'd formed a strong bond with Eva, sharing with her the memories she had of Tony, as well as the awful years trudging up and down to that convent trying to find out what had happened to Eva.

Alan and Josh walked to the pasture to round up the boys. They needed to think about heading into Galway shortly. This was one race they weren't about to miss.

Carol didn't stop to chat. "At my age, I need to use the bathroom before I can stand around chatting. Forgive me, I'll be out in a minute. Shall I put the kettle on?"

"Yes, go on. We'll have a quick cup before we set off. You know where it is seeing you're here so often you might as well move in."

Carol gave her a dig in the ribs. "Be careful, we might just do that. The builders have told us the renovations they are doing are going to take longer than they thought. I like living in the hotel, but the novelty is wearing off."

"Sure, I told you from the start you should move in while you wait. The place is big enough. I think Joe thought he was building his own hotel."

Carol hugged her but then picked up her skirts and moved faster than most people of her age usually did.

Mary smiled. "How is he getting on in your place over in London?"

"He loves it over there. You were right, he never felt he was back at home here in Ireland. Over there they know he's a war veteran and treat him accordingly. He's even walking out with an English lady, a widow with two small children. You'll never guess what else he did."

"With Joe, I think I would believe anything."

"He only went and found Shane. You know the orphan I told you about that lived with the Cumiskeys up the road. It seems he had a lucky escape. He was only in the industrial school a couple of months before he was fostered by a judge up in Dublin. Him and the wife wanted a boy and took Shane. They sent him to the best schools and he studied law at UCD. He's working over in London now and sees Joe regularly."

"Isn't that great? You used to worry about him. I'm glad he got out of that place; it has almost a worse name than our convent." Mary surveyed the kitchen. "Where's JB?"

"Sister John Bosco is where she was born to be. She's at the races already. Up in the VIP area chatting to the crowd. Matt drove her down but only after he made her promise not to bet all her money on Wild Irish Rose."

"I hope she keeps her interrogations to a minimum. Some people are making noises about her. She's upset the Bishop of Galway again."

"Sure that's easily done. I reckon he must have a bad case of piles."

"Kate Ryan, you're incorrigible. But then you always were."

"What are you two laughing about?" Carol asked as she made her way back into the kitchen. "Kate, you've been busy. The house looks amazing. I love how you've painted every room cream with one wall a striking color. The blues of the sea, the green grass, purple heather. You have it all looking great."

"I've a surprise for Eva. Here she comes now." Kate couldn't help it. Her smile widened every time Eva walked into the house, her long blonde hair tied up in French braids to keep them away from the horses.

"Mom, you look fabulous. Like a real Irish horsewoman," Eva teased as she kissed Carol and gave her a hug. "Mary, you look like you walked out of the pages of a magazine. You know it's not lady's day at the races."

"Come here, you cheeky mare. Give us a kiss." Mary planted a sloppy kiss on Eva's cheek.

"Mammy, you look radiant." Eva hugged Kate, whispering into her ear, "I collected the package but left it in the hall."

"Bring it in, darling. I want you to open it."

Eva looked confused. "I thought it was a present for Mom."

"No, sweetheart. It's for you."

"Me?"

Kate linked arms with Carol. "We wanted to give you something special. Wait for your dad and Alan to come in."

Eva opened the back door and roared for Alan and Josh to join them. Mary put her hands over her ears. "You're supposed to be a lady."

Eva wiped her hands on her dirty jodhpurs. "Not today, Mary."

Alan and Josh walked in, with Niall and Darren following behind. "Where's the fire?" Josh asked as he hugged his daughter.

"Mammy gave me a present and I can't wait to open it. She said it's from Mom too."

"Go on, open it. It's so flat. Is it cash?"

"Niall Hyland, wash your mouth out with soap," Kate berated her son, but nobody listened. All eyes were on Eva, who stared at the contents of the envelope. Just as the silence became a little uncomfortable, Eva whispered, "It's Tony and his parents—my grandparents. He was very handsome, wasn't he?" She held up the framed photograph. Her eyes glistening, she asked, "Where did you find it?"

"When your grandparents died, they left their house to a distant relative. She was clearing out some boxes and found an old film. When I wrote asking for information about your grandmother, she told me about them and offered to let us have them."

Kate blew her nose, trying to disguise her tears. She cried too easily these days. "I sent the film to a shop in Dublin where they could salvage that picture."

Eva walked over to the dresser and placed the picture front and center of the other family pictures.

"I have his eyes, don't I?"

"You have much more than that, darling." Kate blew her a kiss. "You have his kind heart and... his loud voice."

The room erupted in laughter. Then Eva put her arms around both Carol and Kate. "I have the best mothers in the world. Now, let's get moving. Matt's racing in an hour, and I don't want to be late. I'm driving. Who's coming with me?"

A LETTER FROM RACHEL

Dear reader,

I want to say a huge thank you for choosing to read *Stolen from Her Mother*. If you did enjoy it, and want to keep up to date with all my latest releases, just sign up at the following link. Your email address will never be shared and you can unsubscribe at any time.

www.bookouture.com/rachel-wesson

Thank you so much for reading *Stolen from Her Mother*. When my editor, Christina, first showed me the cover, I cried. It totally pictured the little girl from my dreams inspired by the horrible stories I had heard and read about. Irish papers have been full of articles lately about the mother and baby homes, in particular the number of unmarked graves being discovered on the old sites.

This book is fiction and for story purposes I had to move some dates. Nobody knows how many babies traveled to the USA but the majority are believed to have left Ireland in the 50s and not in the late 40s as outlined in this book.

The story of the mother and baby homes and the Magdalene laundries struck close to my home. Like most Irish people, my family tree has members from the clergy going back hundreds of years. I have both Catholic and Protestant relations, coming from a mixed rather than pure Catholic background. My grandfather was English, having been born when his parents were living over there. I have several relatives who were nuns during this time period and some who belonged to the orders now named and shamed. The nuns I was closest to growing up were ashamed of the legacy of their orders, which is sad. Some of these women were wonderful human beings and did a lot of good in their communities. Their good deeds are forgotten, overshadowed by the evil some in those congregations indulged in. It saddens me to hear all Catholic and other religious clergy being tarred with the same brush. As I tried to illustrate in this novel, you will find more good people than bad in any congregation. For reasons I can never hope to explain, the evils committed are remembered long after the good is forgotten. Only one nun is named after someone who meant a lot to me. Sister John Bosco was the principal of my primary school and a wonderful human being. The only thing she shares with the fictional JB is her big heart. She was quite old when I first met her or at least so she seemed to a five-year-old. The other nuns are purely fictional and bear no resemblance to anyone living or dead.

I've had friends affected by sexual abuse committed by those who should have protected children. Mam knew people institutionalized by convents just like the fictionalized convent in this novel. I didn't use a real place out of respect for the victims of these systems. Although this story is fiction, every act I described happened. Girls died in labor just like the character Ger, due to a refusal to bring in doctors, although whether the doctor would have treated the penitents with any more charity is debatable. Pain relief and stitches were not administered despite the injuries some women endured during labor. Such practices and worse continued into the 1980s in places in Ireland. Babies died too, some natural, more because of neglect, and are buried in unmarked graves. There were some acts so evil, so horrific, I couldn't bring myself to write about them. You can find out more by listening to the real victims of these places. Many have recorded their stories on YouTube.

Janet (not her real name) was pregnant at the same time my mam was pregnant with me. Mam had her baby surrounded by her husband and family. Janet was sent to a mother and baby home where she was forced to give up her son. The year was 1970.

The last mother and baby home was closed in the 1980s but it took till the 1990s for the last laundry to be closed. There are women in asylums in Ireland—not that we call them asylums these days—whose only crime was to have a baby outside of wedlock. Those women have been locked up for fifty years or more with no chance of escape. They cannot be released now as they have been institutionalized so they will remain living in care homes. Some have never been compensated fairly for missing out, not just on life and liberty, but on an education and a chance to have a family.

Several hundred women and several thousand children died in these homes since they were first introduced when Ireland won its freedom from the United Kingdom. Ironic really. At a time when we fought for the right to be free, we locked up innocent women and children and sentenced them to what in some cases was life imprisonment.

There is no way of knowing just how many Irish babies were sold to those looking to adopt white children. The numbers sent to America are a guess at best; the true number is believed to be much higher. There are people growing old in America expecting to collect social security who may yet find out that they are not American citizens. There are those who found out they had been adopted from Ireland when they tried to enlist for Vietnam or other conflicts. They were informed there was no record of them on the system as their adoptive parents wrongly believed that because they were American citizens their children would be too. Some adoptive parents knew the rules and ensured the children they brought to the States were documented. Some adopted children to give them a loving home and there is no doubt that they didn't realize the babies' birth mothers hadn't agreed to the adoption. But some of these Irish children went to homes not suitable to raise a rat, never mind a child. They were subjected to horrific physical and/or sexual abuse. There were reasons their adoptive families had been turned down by the American authorities. But so long as they had deep pockets and were "good" Catholics, some nuns and other clergy back in Ireland didn't care.

This is not an isolated case in that it didn't only happen in Ireland. It happened all over the world and, in some parts, it continues to happen. This is not a "Catholic" problem as the systemic abuse of children and vulnerable individuals happens across the world in various religions. We stand back and let it happen thus we are guilty too, just like Irish society bears guilt for what the women and children subjected to the industrial schools and laundries went through. Their parents, their communities condemned these girls.

In 2009 the United Nations Against Torture requested the Irish Government compensate, apologize and prosecute individuals for the suffering of the Magdalene women in Ireland. The leader of the government apologized, as did President Michael Higgins. But there are still some victims of the system yet to be recognized. Some are still too ashamed to come forward and tell their story. Some cannot prove they were victims and others lack the mental or physical capability to claim.

There are Facebook groups dedicated to finding the missing children. Families looking for sons, daughters, brothers or sisters, mothers, or fathers. You can find more information by checking on Mother/Baby Home Research: Catherine Corless.

If you or anyone you know has been affected by the contents of this book, you can find relatives by using the DNA checks offered by the various family sites. In addition, the Irish government actively encourages those with Irish roots to find out more about their family and ancestors. For more information check out https://irelandxo.com

There is currently a Bill passing through the legal channels to give adopted children the right to information. But many believe that this will not fix the problem as so many women used false names. The births were registered using false information; often the date of birth isn't correct never mind the details of parents.

There are many organizations working on this issue. We can only hope it will happen in time.

I hope you loved *Stolen from Her Mother* and if you did I would be very grateful if you could write a review. I'd love to hear what you think, and it makes such a difference helping new readers to discover one of my books for the first time.

I love hearing from my readers—you can get in touch on my Facebook page, through Twitter, Goodreads or my website.

Thanks,

Rachel

www.rachelwesson.com

facebook.com/authorrachelwesson
twitter.com/wessonwrites

ACKNOWLEDGMENTS

Writing a book takes a whole team and I struck gold when I landed at Bookouture and secured Christina Demosthenous as my editor. Christina has a knack of turning my scribblings into a well-paced, interesting story. Her careful and insightful editing always improves each draft and I love her for it. She also gets directly involved in the cover design, matching the story perfectly. The copyeditor and the proofreaders add further polish to the manuscript.

The marketing team under the direction of the lovely Kim Nash are responsible for spreading the word about my books and they do an amazing job. Thank you so much.

I'd also like to thank my readers as without you, I wouldn't do the job I love. Thank you not just for reading, but for the lovely comments you share on Facebook and other social media sites. Your reviews on Amazon and Goodreads help to sell more copies. I'm so grateful to you for taking the time to do that.

And last, but not least, my amazing family who understand Mom has to write and that means time at her computer. Thank you for your encouragement and your love.